SO-BJJ-835

TO LIVE
AND DIE IN
HARLEM

RELENTLESS AARON

St. Martin's Paperbacks

This is a work of fiction. All of the characters, organizations, and events portrayed in this novel are either products of the author's imagination or are used fictitiously.

Relentless Aaron, Relentless Content, and Relentless are trademarks of Relentless Content, Inc. Reginald "Push" Jackson and all related characters are elements of trademarks of Relentless Inc.

TO LIVE AND DIE IN HARLEM

Copyright © 2005 by Relentless Aaron.
Excerpt from *Lady First* copyright © 2007 by Relentless Aaron.

Cover photo © Herman Estevez

ISBN: 0-312-94962-6
EAN: 978-0-312-94962-4

Printed in the United States of America

Relentless Content, Inc. edition published 2005
St. Martin's Paperbacks edition / October 2007

St. Martin's Paperbacks are published by St. Martin's Press, 175 Fifth Avenue, New York, NY 10010.

10 9 8 7 6 5 4 3 2 1

SPECIAL DEDICATIONS

This book is inspired by all the true men who are about their business, and who take no shorts in this short lifetime. To the many radio personalities throughout the country who have supported Relentless: *Thank you for giving my words a voice. Bugsy, Champaign, Lenny Green, Chaila, Raqiyah, Talent & Bob Slade (Kiss FM/NY)* . . . Thank you, Ajuba.

Thank you Wendy Williams, Michael Baisden, The Power 99 crew/Philly, Champaign, for recognizing true talent.

Super Thanks to:
G-Unit Clothing and Violator Management
Sponsors of the Relentless brand

As always: To my friend & mentor: Johnny *"Jay Dub"* Williams: Thank you. To *Tiny Wood:* (My close friend & confidant). To my friends at Allenwood FCI, Otisville FCI, Fort Dix FCI and other prisons throughout the country: Thank You for your support in my personal struggle to be me, to be free, and to be progressive. I hope I represent all you can be.
KEEP YOUR HEADS UP & HOLD ME DOWN!

To Julie & Family:
(I KNOW I CAN . . . BE WHAT I WANNA BE . . . IF I WORK HARD AT IT . . . I'LL BE WHERE I WANNA BE!)

To Emory & Tekia Jones:
Still ticking, Big Dog. Hang in there!
(D.B.D.) Thank you for your support.

To all of you who helped me from my humble beginnings; thank you for sticking by me, helping me to make it through my rocky days. To my inner circle: Curt Southerland, Darryl, Tiny, DTG, Johnny, Danica, Lou, Rick, Demetrius, Angel, Renee Mc Rae, Shetalia, and of course you Lisa & T! Thank You all so much. To Ashleigh (wherever you are) I miss you. You need to know that, no matter how or when you find out. I want to be a big part of your life.

To Makeda Smith at *Jazzmyne Public Relations,* my publicist, banker, Diva & therapist . . . thank you ever so much. And stay away from the matches! Special Thanks to *Stephanie Renee*, the mogul from philly . . . Lorna/*Avid Readers,* Naiim, Mr. Perkins, Carol & Brenda, Petee (your world is definitely bond), *Courtney Carreras,* YRB has no clue! Welcome to my world! I hope to be a big part of yours, as well. And Earl Cox: thank you for all your guidence.

Thank you all.

To the many bookstores and websites and others around the world who carry Relentless Content: Thank you for affording me space on your shelves. I intend to cause a major increase to your bottom line.

Special shout to Vinny, Shetalia, A.J. & Mechel:
you're in the house now, girls. *Represent!*

To A.J. I want to say thank you for letting me stalk you!

And, last but not least,
to my earth, moon and star:
Paulette, DeWitt & Fortune
Love you guys to death.

A WORD FROM MY FAVORITE AUTHOR

Always pursue your greatness,
because there's no
other way you'll achieve it!

Michelle Scott was leaving the *Times* building for a dinner date with the mayor's press secretary. But she wouldn't make it, not this evening. The moment she stepped into the waiting taxi, a bag was pulled over her head and a hard object knocked her unconscious. She never knew it was coming.

CHAPTER ONE

UNCLE SAM'S FIRST big mistake was to trust someone outside of his circle. Especially a reporter. What was he thinking? What—because she worked for a distinguished newspaper, that was supposed to imply good faith? Did that mean her word was her bond and that her trust was guaranteed? Did it mean she would uphold her promise to keep certain facts and details out of her story?

And what of the *Times*, that so-called distinguished newspaper? Says who? Who was the authority in these situations? Who made up the rules and ethics, and who enforced them when they were broken?

Breaking the rules. Poor girl, that Michelle, thinking she was doing the right thing when in fact all she did was kill herself. Suicide. What was *she* thinking . . . that L.T.K. wouldn't come to get her?

Had she lost her mind?

"**MICHELLE WAS A** good friend, Evelyn. Unfortunately she got involved in something that was too heavy for her—but had I known just *how* deep, I would've told her to stay away."

"From who, Charles?"

"L.T.K. She got in—literally. She was right there with the major players. How else would she be able to videotape them?"

"You mean there's a tape?"

Judge Charles Pullman looked up from his drink, a Brazilian daiquiri: one part Bacardi light rum, two parts dark, one tablespoon of brown sugar, half as much vanilla extract, and two slices of pineapple.

The Judge had to sweep such unimportant things aside, how his mind had suddenly assessed the ingredients of his drink at a time like this. He was deep into Evelyn's eyes now, the daiquiri fucking with his head, making him fight to even think.

It always came down to this: *the matter of trust.* Somewhere along the line, there had to be someone you needed to trust . . . something or somebody who you had to confide in.

Can I trust you, Evelyn? Or will I be the next to die?

Charles shut his eyes—one of those slow-motion gestures—opened them again, then turned his gaze far and away from the moment . . . past the waitresses, the dining activities of this or that couple, the large dinner party over in the corner—

"For he's a jolly good fe-e-lloooow . . . which nobody caaaan de-nyyyy!"

—beyond the mirrors decorating the far wall of the restaurant, which made Copeland's seem so much larger an establishment.

The way the Judge's mind wandered like this was his way of foretelling the future, whether he would live or die. Hell, he did it for most everyone else or at least those defendants who stood before him day in, day out for ultimate judgment. Ten years here, twenty-five there, life without parole. Sure, in the courtroom he was immortal, he could play God. Make or break a man.

So then, why wasn't it just as easy for him to determine his own fate?

"Can I reserve my answers to that question?" replied Pullman, knowing that talking about the tape would lead to her wanting to see it. He didn't want to endanger her or anyone else.

"What the *hell* is that supposed to mean? Reserve your answer? This is not your courtroom, Charles . . ."

The way Evelyn put him in check made Charles take a long, deep breath—trying to maintain some sense of calm before his heart jumped out of his chest. It would be time for that next hypertension pill soon.

"Charles," said Evelyn, with that chuckle in her throat, "you might be the reigning senior court judge 'n all, but to me, we're like *this*." She twisted her middle and pointer fingers together—a python wrapping itself around a pole. "Since when do you know me to jeopardize our relationship?"

"Evelyn, this . . ." The Judge stopped himself. He was not in his courtroom. This was not his house. *Calm down, mister. Lower your voice*, he told himself. And to his future daughter-in-law he said, "This is about my *life*. I may be required to uphold the law at my day job . . . I even bend it— we *all* do—so our lawmen and -women [he remembered to add] can enjoy an *edge*. But darling, as a *human being*, I must save lives." The Judge took a moment to think, then went on. "If not me, then who? And if not by the book, then who else should have the authority to take the law into their own hands?"

"Charles, I'm trying to hook onto what you're saying, but I'm afraid you're not clear. Could you make your point?"

"Evelyn, we've got dirty cops committing crimes—and I know that's no secret—but lately, the dirty cops are killing cops. And they're not just killing the cops, Evelyn, they're killing anyone who gets in their way. As long as these . . . these imbeciles get what they want."

"I've never seen you like this, Charles. And I've never ever seen you take underworld activity so personally." Evelyn Watson, U.S. Probation Officer, put her young hand across the table, consoling the older man.

"It's never been this bad. And it's never touched me this close. Michelle was . . . was—" His voice broke off and he put his hand over his face.

He was losing it. And seeing him like this made her

tremble. It was as if the world was coming to an end, and he was the only one who knew how or why.

"Evelyn, we must proceed now. There are lives at stake."

"Okay, wait, let's back it up a bit. First of all, I need you to calm yourself and look me in the eyes, Judge." He did. "Don't think of me as strange when I say that I would give up my right arm to protect you. Do you believe that?" She squeezed Pullman's hand, hoping to drive her statement home.

Pullman was hypnotized by Evelyn's control, how she was able to be so direct with men, reading them with such depth and clairvoyance. He'd always admired this about her, that certain something that he had never experienced with women in his own life. No such personal encounters. Evelyn always kept her word in the courtroom. And it was amazing how she managed, mothered and sometimes manhandled the riffraff and gangsters on her caseload.

Pullman suddenly wondered how Evelyn handled men in other ways. What was she doing to or with Peter, his son, that had him so hooked? That thought jolted him. *Jesus!* What would make him think of such things? What was *wrong* with him? Evelyn was young enough to be his daughter—Peter's age, for God's sake—and here he was with his mind wandering in the gutter.

Still, despite all of that, he couldn't help but feel overwhelmed.

"Charles?" Evelyn's voice shook him from his spell.

"Y-yes . . . I'm sorry. I—I *do* trust you, Evelyn. No doubt about it. Yes, I'd trust you with my life." Evelyn sighed loud enough to be heard, glad to get past that stage.

"Was. She *was* with the *Times*."

"How do you know this L.T.K. group killed her?"

"I just know. She's been missing for three weeks, Evelyn. And that's just not like her. At the least, she'd have called."

"Maybe she's like you say: underground."

Charles wagged his head of wavy gray hair, an effect that Evelyn cherished about the older man, how he looked so wise and gentle . . . how he was set in his ways with the things he said and with his conclusions. It was hard to believe that anyone would want him hurt.

"Afraid not, Evelyn. We have scheduled calls and meetings. She's missed the last two. I'm telling you, these guys are ruthless."

"Of course," said Evelyn, already feeling a trace of sympathy for the woman, sight unseen. "But if you have all of this information, plus a tape from her, I don't see why we don't just inform the proper authorities—send in the boys—you have the power of the federal government to back you."

"I thought about that long and hard. The thing is, their network is too wide. Based on what I've been told, they've got members in local, state *and* federal agencies," the Judge explained, his skeptical eyes surfing the restaurant. "They'd find out in a heartbeat."

"Oh."

"And besides, a part of me is still hoping that she's alive."

"Michelle?"

"Yes, but I doubt it. Do you remember Amelia Cohen?"

"Of course. The former U.S. attorney who killed herself while she was parked down in Chinatown."

"It *wasn't* a suicide, Evelyn."

Evelyn's expression turned from curious to stunned.

"Now, think back to last Christmas Eve and Dudley Schmidt."

"Doesn't ring a bell," said Evelyn, wagging her head.

"No matter. Just another robbery/homicide. Just the brother of Mark Schmidt, one of NYPD's finest detectives, Evelyn," Pullman's eyes projected severity. "The man was strangled as he left Toys 'R' Us with a last-minute gift for his little boy."

"And Dudley Schmidt's killing is tied in with Amelia's?"

"Is it? Schmidt had more than a thousand dollars in his pocket when he was found. It was a hit, cut 'n dried. If I were to sit here and detail all of the complexities, cover-ups and conspiracies behind these murders—almost three dozen others—you'd lose sleep for the next month."

Evelyn was speechless in light of these revelations. It felt like someone had just revealed some truth about her: that she wasn't really a woman, but a cow. Hard to believe.

"Evelyn, you sitting here with me right now is even dangerous. I could very well be the next one to go . . ."

She made a face, somewhat doubtful. As though to confirm his theory, the Judge said, "Of the four hundred homicides in the last twelve months, thirty-two victims were law enforcement. And I'm not talking suicides. I mean unsolved murders."

"Slow down, Judge. What are you saying? What do those unsolved murders have to do with you, and why does my sitting here now have any relevance to that?"

For the first time this afternoon, Evelyn was uncomfortable. Afraid. And now she was glancing around the restaurant looking for possible threats.

"Because Michelle tried to get certain people to acknowledge this video. Anybody she spoke with . . . anybody that they *think* she spoke with is now dead."

"And she spoke with you?"

"A number of times. I was sort of receiving updates from her. We had our . . . well, secret meetings."

Evelyn noticed the hesitation in that statement and she read between the lines.

"But we never spoke out in the open. Not like this. I thought being amongst a daytime crowd might serve as a distraction in the event—well, you never know."

"Secret meetings, Charles? Would that be in your chambers? Or at home?"

"Uh . . . err . . . just business."

"I bet," said Evelyn, wanting Charles to know that she understood more than he was telling her. "So now, I guess I wanna know who 'they' are. Do we have specifics? Names? Can I see the tape?" Again Pullman was staring. He knew it would come down to this. "Who and what is L.T.K.?"

CHAPTER TWO

THE BASEMENT OF 442 West 128th Street was dark, damp and awaiting renovations. However, it was just right for Push. This was his little cave in the world where he could count on solitude, where he could get some stress off and where he meditated, even while he was beating the life out of a heavy bag.

A single bulb was wired up, reaching all the way from next door, because this address hadn't yet been rewired. There was plenty of work to do, even before that task. Holes in the walls, floors and ceilings had to be repaired. The roof had to be resurfaced. Pesticides and exterminators were necessary. And the building inspectors would need to issue his company a permit before he could lift a finger.

Today was May 1. The last rainfall had left wet spots on the furthest corners of the basement floor, indicating that there was work to be done. Along with electrical problems and the leaks, this virtual dungeon needed insulation. It was cold down here, despite the good weather outdoors.

Isolated from the rest of the world, this was where Push could get into his essence. He could be the pit bull. Only a few others knew the predator's heart that pounded inside of this man, such as his sister, Crystal, or his girlfriend, Yvette.

Here in the unfinished basement it was miserable enough to accommodate the dangerous thug that life had sculpted

Push. Much larger than a prison cell, it had the atmosphere necessary for his rage and aggression.

Each time Push's fist smacked the heavy bag, it gave, like some poor man's flesh and muscle, except it always came swinging back at him like some faceless enemy. A relentless one. But Push could easily imagine the faces. Sometimes it was an unscrupulous businessman who thought he was slick. Or it could be one of his rent-to-own tenants, who because of their own past experiences with landlords thought they could act or speak in a salty way. And even though most of those problems were behind him and the garden of his life had been stripped of its weeds, his past still tended to harden his heart and spirit.

But on the other hand, Push had common sense—enough to know that in the world of business it was best to leave the thug mentality aside. Thugs were vicious, and could snap at any given moment. However cordial the business climate was, it wasn't advisable to try and get the best of someone as potentially violent as Reginald "Push" Jackson.

Push had the street smarts and was the last person you'd want to have mad at you. Those characteristics were not necessarily money-making attributes—at least not when it came to real estate development and property management, his latest profession. This business that he created during the past two years required a mature attitude and wise decision-making skills, and not a thug mentality.

But what would certain folks think if they knew about the other man inside of Reginald Jackson—Push, the killer?

"Oh, Mr. Jackson, this is a lovely three-bedroom residence. And it's newly remodeled and so inexpensive too! I'd be glad to be one of your . . . oh, I'm sorry, did you say you pushed a man off a building when you were a teenager? Oh . . . well, I'm sure you've grown a lot since then. What? You did fourteen years in a federal penitentiary? Oh my! You what? You've killed three others since you were released? Um . . . say . . . I'd really like to think about this some more. This location might not be exactly what we were looking for—oops! Time sure does fly . . . gotta hurry and catch a cab—I mean, a train—I mean . . . Oh, never mind. I gotta go!"

Such fears never haunted Push, however. He adapted real well to the world of business. He had been well prepared, thanks to his prison education. He was speaking much more intelligibly these days, enjoying a larger vocabulary, a greater awareness and use of the English language. He was more outspoken, used diplomacy when necessary and kept his manners without losing his cool. He tolerated much more, but never compromised. After all, Push had grown up. He had a life—so what if his past wasn't all peaches and cream, wasn't one that had groomed him for success? He made do with the cards that he was dealt. Street life, orphan life, whatever— things would be as good as you made them: an incubator or an incinerator. And when it came down to it, the things that Push had been most experienced and successful at weren't really promising professions. He didn't work for the mob or the cartel, so the work wasn't consistent. And the one hit that Push did perform—for which he was paid $50,000 two years earlier—was a one-time-only affair. Even in a perfect world, how long would that kind of money last before he'd need to act again? Contracts in his new profession weren't exactly falling out of the sky.

Redirecting his energy, Push the real-estate entrepreneur planned on owning and renovating every abandoned brownstone within a two-block stretch along West 128th Street. It was an effort big enough that he could have his own community within a community. But, as with most things, he'd have to crawl before he walked, one step at a time. The commitment from Congressman Percy Chambers and his Harlem Empowerment Fund made things a little easier. There was a guarantee that supported the renovation of those first two brownstones, but no cash. Push decided against wanting to owe anyone. He felt that with his seed capital and his own labor, he could create equity.

Indeed, the effort was an uphill climb, especially for a

first-time developer. The first two brownstones, 440 and 442 West 128th Street, were all-too-consuming projects until Push got the swing of it, eventually completing the projects within a matter of months.

Push did most of the labor himself, while Yvette handled the business in the office. Reggie, Push's nephew, helped out some too. But how much could a nineteen-year-old devote himself to before it was time to get his party on?

"One day you'll understand the value of dedication, Reggie. Once the work is done, you'll always have time to play," Push told him time and time again. But as with most things, he'd have to crawl before he walked too.

Push decided to name his business Melrah, which was Harlem spelled backwards. And Yvette, his girlfriend from the time he left prison, had assumed the role of vice-president, while Crystal was on the board of directors as a silent partner.

Every unit was occupied. Melrah's office was on the ground floor of 440, complete with its own entrance, just below the front staircase. And just above the office, on the second level, lived Horace Silvers, the proprietor of Silver Wear, a large clothing store on 125th Street. Above Mr. Silvers, on the top floor, lived Denise Cosby and Sheryl Roberts.

Push originally had a problem with renting to the two lovers, figuring that their "way of life" didn't follow nature's own laws (that boy-meets-girl activity) and so they probably had some cards missing from their decks. And if that was the case, how responsible could they be when it came to maintaining a household . . . or paying the rent? But there were complications that helped to widen Push's one-way perspective. For one thing, there was The Fair Housing Act, which prohibited such discrimination. Just because Push assumed that Denise and Sheryl might not be perfect tenants didn't justify a rejection of their application for the residence.

Naturally, Push didn't want to commit any "prohibited" acts. Furthermore, Yvette was right there to witness the women coming to the office, their admission about being lesbians and how they were otherwise fine prospects for tenants.

"I think we should let them have it, Push. One is a doctor

and the other is the manager over at the Magic Johnson Theaters."

"I just wondered if they will be drama, you know, cat fights 'n what-not. I mean . . . okay, so what if I have my own issues about them. In time, maybe I'll understand how or why they are the way they are. But in the meantime I just want good tenants who pay on time and take care of what I put sweat and tears into renovating."

"I agree, Push; we've had our fill of the nonsense. So, what if I kept an eye on things? I mean, isn't that my job anyhow?"

"I guess."

"Okay then, let me do my job," said Yvette. She kissed Push on the forehead and that was the last of it. The girl-girl activity was a firm go. Next door, at 442 West 128th, Francine Oliver, who stood out in the short line of black record company executives, lived on the first floor. Above Francine was empty, except Francine leased the second floor on behalf of OCG, her employer. They took out a five-year lease, and she had it all decked out like it was Elvis Presley's second home, appropriate for an out-of-town guest that the record company ushered in. Lastly, there was the Wallace family—one of the latest headaches: the rent was late again.

With all of the rentals filled, Push was able to cover the monthly mortgage payments without delay or pressure. His tenants paid him, and he paid George Murphy. It was a simple and routine arrangement. Furthermore, as agreed, 50 percent of Melrah's payments were to be applied toward the total purchase after two years. But here was the headache. Time had run out on the two-year agreement. It was time for Melrah to fulfill its end of the lease option. Furthermore, there was a larger deal waiting in the wings. Murphy had agreed to sweeten things for Melrah, seeing how well the business arrangement was going. Since there were thirty-four properties in all—mostly abandoned brownstones—that Murphy owned, he offered the whole block of properties for a paltry thousand dollars each, a total of $34,000 per month, so long as Melrah could close on half of the properties within two years.

Push took the time to discuss the deal with Yvette, figuring all the labor they'd have to employ, the supplies required and other expenses that were necessary for such a large venture.

"Baby, we could do this," Yvette said in a most encouraging tone. "Except this time you won't have to break your back to get the work done. We'll hire contractors, and get it finished in half the time."

"It's a lot of work, Yvette. Do you realize that we'd be overseeing thirty-four properties? And if we're purchasing them at a hundred thousand each, the whole deal is worth more than three million dollars." Yvette shook her head, unwavering from her position—*the motivator*. Push continued, "Not only that, Murphy wants us to close the deal on half—*half*—of the properties, Yvette. What's that? More than seventeen million dollars? These calculations are off. Have you forgotten the color of our skin? We ain't *supposed* to have money like that. I'd feel more comfortable with doing, like, four or five properties at a time. Build my way up to that many houses. What you're talking about is a lot of work to be done in a *very* short time. Think about it. I don't think I wanna carry that much pressure on my back if it's not necessary."

Yvette approached Push, hands on hips, and took a stance, like she couldn't believe her eyes. "Is *this* the man I've devoted my all to? A *wuss*?" And there it was. She had to go and say a damned thing like that.

A wuss? Has she lost her fuckin' mind?

"Now just a *minute*, woman."

Yvette stuck her hand in the air, as if to officially tell her man to talk to the hand. "No, *you* wait a minute, Push. Didn't you once tell me that you wouldn't be the one to *always* make the decisions? That you would—what was the words you used?—*surrender* things for me to handle? Because, *why*? Because, as you said, you have faith in me. Well, where's the faith, Push? Huh? Where is it?"

Push still had his foot stuck in the quicksand of being called a wuss, but he couldn't deny Yvette's personal power. Her convictions. The woman was sharp. She had it goin' on upstairs, outside, inside and down there. And this latest confrontation only showed him that, yes, he chose a helluva woman to stand by his side. The old heads used to say it in prison: "You need a woman who's a lady by day, who cooks and cleans for you, and turns into a slut in the bedroom." Push always saw that as an outrageous thing to say, especially in this day and age, and especially since he had a grown-assed sister who had her hard times with this mack and that mack. His personal choice was to have all of Yvette—whatever that was worth—and if he was lucky enough, she'd compliment him with her right hand held high.

For now, with how she was speaking to him so sassy, in that spicy "I'm 'bout it" way of addressing him, with the sex appeal going in her favor, how could he ever disregard her? This was Yvette, in all of her ghetto fabulousness, and she had every bit of his attention, however she had to get it.

"All I need from you, sir, is your blessing. Because *we are* going to make this happen. And yes, there's work to be done, but no more than we've been doing. The biggest change as far as I can see is with the paperwork. And that's my department. And besides, we can always turn to the Empowerment Fund, Push. So we might as well make the most of this. Think *bigger*, because baby, we've already been thinking big."

Eventually, Push kept his own promise. He surrendered to his woman. Maybe not a wuss after all, he told himself. "I'll go with whatever you say, babe. You ain't let me down yet, Miss Donald Trump." Caught in the sparkle of her eyes, Push went on to say, "Just keep me informed. Any complications, I wanna know."

Yvette brushed up against Push like the prize catch she was. "Can I show you some of that appreciation I'm so good at?"

"Mixing business with pleasure again, Yvette?" Push's

accusation fell on deaf ears; Yvette already had her blouse halfway over her head. She enjoyed doing this for him— unwrapping herself for his eyes only. In a matter of seconds she'd be tasting his flesh, another peak moment in her life.

THE PROBLEM PUSH had now, a few weeks after that discussion, was that Yvette stopped filling him in about the closing—the purchase of those first two properties. She was either away from the office, busy on the phone with contractors entertaining bids or out shopping. The idea of Yvette, his other half, being away for hours and hours, being so busy with Melrah, was foreign to him. First off, taking on a partner was something like a born-again experience. But then, to miss her like this . . . to be so uninformed, felt too much like lonely. And Push was all too familiar with that way of life.

YVETTE WAS GOING through her own first-time challenges. Here she had taken this grown man, with his grown man's issues, to be her soul mate. It was at first one of the most wonderful joys, to be attached to a man so worthy of her attention, her time and her body. But now, she wondered if she hadn't bitten off more than she could chew. To have a good man felt like being a home-run hitter. Having that plus a profitable business was like winning a World Series every day of the year. The two could do no wrong. The only obstacles would be ones they might impose on themselves: maybe a dumb argument or some miscommunication that grew from either of them jumping to conclusions. But somehow, Push and Yvette avoided much of that. In her book, he was due a world of respect and honor. In his, Yvette was to be treated like a queen. Perhaps this was all too good to be true, a fairy tale maybe, since there was that old truth known as Murphy's Law. And of course, there was also Mr. George Murphy.

The man had changed his tune. Two years earlier there was the understanding that the first two properties would sell for $100,000 each. But now, after all the hard work the couple put forth, Murphy had the nerve to say, "I never agreed to that in writing."

Yvette was shocked, but she didn't show it. She merely responded, not interested in debating with the man. "Well, what *will* you agree to?"

And Murphy said, "Oh . . . I believe that, with Harlem developing as fast as it is, I could probably get somewhere around two hundred thousand."

No, he didn't just double the price! Yvette had to challenge it. He was being unreasonable. She said, "But that is unfair to us." And that might have been so, but the bottom line was the bottom line, and Harlem was indeed emerging as a hot property, from the Cross Bronx Expressway to Central Park; from the Hudson River Parkway it was a "seller's market." The fact that a couple of young, aspiring real estate developers entered into an oral agreement two years earlier was of little consequence.

Murphy's only response was a cold one. But one he felt comfortable with expressing to Yvette. He said, "Well, life is unfair, young lady."

"What about the deposit we just paid you for the seventeen new leases?"

"What about it?"

"You agreed to duplicate our former agreement. We figured that the price you agreed to—"

"I agreed to no such thing, ma'am. All I know is that you are set to buy those two brownstones, and I'm selling them for two hundred thousand each. If you don't buy now, then you forfeit your equity. All forty-eight thousand dollars of it."

Yvette was bubbling with rage. "We'll take you to *court*!"

"Good luck. And make sure you bring a tape recording of our oral contract from two years ago. I'm sure the judge would like to hear it."

"There's no—*you bastard*."

"Okay. I'm afraid you'll need to leave my office with your foul mouth," Murphy said.

Yvette suppressed a scream, wanting to kill the son of a

bitch. "Wait a minute, Mr. Murphy, I apologize for my language, but how you gonna be so cold at a time like this? We had a *deal*."

"Things change. That's all I can tell you."

IT WAS ONLY when Yvette got into her brand-new Toyota Camry; only after she took it for a long drive and parked along an emergency stop on the FDR Drive; only then did she break down and cry her heart out. Enough tears to fill a bathtub.

She and her man had so been looking forward to this purchase. They counted on the $48,000 in equity, plus the backing that was offered to them by Congressman Chambers and his Harlem Empowerment Fund. But Yvette knew good and well that this new revelation—*two hundred thousand!!??*—threw things way off. *Way off*. She knew that Push would be furious when he found out, to say nothing of her hopes and dreams, or the announcement she planned on making:

Push . . . I'm pregnant.

AND THEN PUSH felt it . . . something funny was going on. All he could do was squint and look into the depths of Yvette's eyes. "What do you mean, *Murphy canceled at the last minute*? We've been waiting for this event for two years. Plus, this is going on three weeks past our agreed date. We can't just keep rescheduling the lawyer like this. What's that man's problem?"

"He didn't say," Yvette lied. *Damn, I don't want to be this evasive with you, baby, but it's for your own good. God forbid—*

"Well, that makes a lot of sense," said Push. "Did he at least tell you when he'd get back to you?"

"I tried, but . . . no. I couldn't get him directly, not this morning. His secretary, I spoke with her."

Push noticed Yvette avoiding eye contact. He tried to read between the lines. "Well, I'm sure you're on top of it," he said. "Just lemme know when you want me to suit up."

And Push went back to work, mixing some cement he was making for laying brick for the backyard barbecue he was building behind 440 West 128th, Melrah's backyard.

THE LAST TIME Push spoke to Yvette was three days ago. And all of these things were on his mind—the business as well as the personal—taxing him heavily during his waking hours. When he slept, he slept like a bear. But when he was conscious, he was either working or he was alone, down in the basement of 442, one of the thirty-two abandoned properties that Melrah signed leases for. As soon as he received keys to all of the properties, he chained up a heavy bag, the type boxers use. Since there was so much work to be done, so many contractors to be called, a secluded spot like this served as Push's exclusive dark dungeon, haven to do his daily workouts. To relieve the stress. And maybe Yvette had been looking for him these past few days, but if he spent a good amount of time down here, how would he know that? It was only now that stuff began to fuck with his mind: the pressures of a freshman real estate entrepreneur.

The Wallaces' late rent.

The canceled contract date.

Left jab. Again. Harder! Right hook, bang!

This was how it went when Push was alone hitting the heavy bag. He was his own trainer, chanting commands and simultaneously performing the act. There were still those mental pains:

There was the desire to make up for lost time . . . fourteen years' worth.

There was all of the violence of his past . . . the blood.

There was the struggle to make the transition from street thug to upstanding businessman.

There was Yvette. For God's sake, he actually had a long-term relationship going. And now Yvette had popped this latest surprise on him. Pregnant? As in, "I'm gonna have a baby"? "*We're* gonna have a baby"?? Push didn't know whether to jump for joy or to fall to his knees in defeat.

A baby wouldn't be a financial issue, of that Push was

certain. Things were going well for him. Money in the bank. The new deal for half of the thirty-two properties.

He could just about taste the big money. It was only a matter of commitment.

Left hook off the jab. Right cross. Another! Jab, jab, body shot . . . again! Uppercut! BANG!

Why was there doubt in Yvette's eyes? What is she not telling me? Is she worried about having her first child? Is she concerned about not being married? Is there something going on with Murphy? What?

Jab. Jab. Hook, hook, hook. Right cross. Duck, pivot . . . bang-bang-bang!

Shit. Again with this fourth Friday crap. These goddamned probation visits. I swore I'd have a lawyer to get that ten-year probation reduced . . . I swore that life would be different for Reggie—that I'd be the father figure in his life.

I swore! I swore! I swore!

Left hook, right hook, jab-jab-jab!

It had gotten to the point that Push thought he was seeing things; for instance, the little girl standing in the distance. She had on a dingy skirt—one he recognized from the other day. But of course, Push was dizzy with adrenaline, the sweat dripping off of his brow, fogging his vision. The violence of the moment and the turbulence of his life cluttered his senses, but he continued the fight with the heavy bag, one punch after another. Push had this monstrous sea creature inside of him, roaming the deep waters of his soul, surfacing at will.

Bang-bang! Pop-pop-pop! Those sounds made only by his leather gloves. Then his barked commands. "Jab-jab-jab! Upper cut! Left hook! Again!" Push cut his machine-gun punches, holding the bag, momentarily stopping it from its own aggressive swings. He turned to look toward the doorway. It wasn't a mirage over there after all. That was indeed a little girl. One of the Wallace girls.

"Sharissa? Is that you, baby girl?"

Sharissa turned to leave the basement, guilty as charged.

"Sharissa! Now you be a good girl and come back here."

The five-year-old peeked around the doorjamb while Push curled his forefinger. *Come here, you naughty little girl.* But the way Push looked at her wasn't meant to frighten her. It was more of a kind admonishment.

"I'm sorry, Mista Jackson. I was just . . . I thought Stacy was down here. Maybe I'll check outside," she explained in her cute little voice.

"Sharissa? Come back here." Push took the towel off of a nail and wiped himself off. Then he crouched down into a squat so that he'd be eye-to-eye with the little girl. "Now, I want you to tell me the truth . . . what are you doing down here? And how did you get in?"

"I . . . I saw you. And I came through the back."

Push visualized the back: piles of sheetrock, fixtures, rubble, trash—mountains of debris that would detail the history of these properties. There were holes in the building that were big enough for stray dogs and cats to pass through, but nothing larger. Push noticed Sharissa's soiled dress, figuring that she crawled through.

"Oh, Sharissa . . . through the back? Look at what you did to your dress. And why aren't you in school? Where's your mom?"

"Um . . . in the house with Stacy."

"Oh," Push said, but he remembered the young girl saying she was looking for Stacy. Obviously, she was lying. But why?

"Well, I need to talk to your mom, actually." Push had finished toweling himself dry. He pulled on the wife-beater top he had hanging on a nonfunctional light fixture and took Sharissa into his arms. She suddenly had a comfortable seat that put her head just about level with his own.

"Oh, Momma's sick, Mista Jackson. She can't see nobody right now. It might be countarigeous."

"*Countriageous*, huh? Well, if that's anything like *contagious* then I think I should check on her. She might need a doctor." Push carried Sharissa up the darkened staircase, then to the front entrance of the building—the way he had come in.

Opening the door to the intense daylight weighed heavy on his senses, making him feel like a coal miner emerging from a cave following a desperate rescue. And for some reason, he thought about those few drivers who used 128th Street as a shortcut to the next block over. There wasn't much traffic, but Push couldn't help thinking what this might look like to others—how the two of them, Push and Sharissa, came out of the abandoned building all crusty-looking. Push hurried next door, knowing how people always jumped to conclusions. And, he supposed, they might be correct in doing so.

"Momma mighta went out for medicine," said Sharissa, still perched there in Push's arm. "You don't hafta take me all the way up. I can go myself." Another attempt to change Push's mind.

"It's okay, baby. I'm a strong man. I can handle the trip. I'm carryin' you, ain't I?"

Through a cute pout, Sharissa nodded. At the second landing, before Push went a step further, he asked, "Is there something you wanna tell me, Sharissa?" He was giving the young girl every opportunity to spill the beans. Something was going on, though he couldn't determine what.

But Sharissa wagged her head, still unable to break down the truth.

Halfway up the final staircase, Sharissa put her arms around Push's neck and buried her face in the nape of his neck as if to hide her fears. Push could feel her trembling and he braced himself as he approached the Wallaces' third-floor residence. There was no telling what was going on behind the family's closed door, considering that the youngest child was 1) not in preschool where she belonged; 2) wearing one of her same old dirty dresses; and 3) wandering in the abandoned building next door.

"*You* knock," said Push. "I wanna surprise your mom." Carrying Sharissa felt so normal, like she was his own daughter. And she did knock, except it was so hesitant, with so little pressure to it, that Push hardly heard it himself. When he tried to look Sharissa face-to-face he realized that her eyes were watering.

"Riss?" Stacy's voice chirped from inside, and the eight-year-old cracked the door to take a peek. When she saw who it was, she sucked her teeth, said, "*Hold on*," with an attitude and pushed the door closed so that the chain could be removed. Again the door was opened, enough for Stacy to slip out.

Okay. Now Push's curiosity was sky-high.

"What's going on here, Stacy? Where's your momma?"

"Oh, ahh . . . she's down the block to get milk."

"Good," he said. And he eased the door open despite Stacy playing gatekeeper. "Then she shouldn't be long. If you don't mind I'll wait with you guys. Don't mind me. You comin' in, Stacy?"

Push was at once alerted by the smell and look of things.

Stacy said, "Sorry about the mess. 'Riss always be leavin' her toys around." And Stacy deviled her eyes at her younger sister; for more than one reason, it seemed. Sharissa immediately got to picking up the few toys there on the living room floor. In the meantime, Push tried to make sense of the odors in the residence.

The Wallaces didn't have pets, and it had been a while since diapers were a part of their daily life. Then Push noticed that Stacy was wearing the same clothes she had on the other day. Hadn't her pants been pink once upon a time? *Doesn't Misty wash these kids' clothes?*

"What about television? I thought kids your age lived inside of that box."

Push was about to go and turn it on, but Stacy said, "Ain't nothin' on for us in the daytime, Mista Jackson."

"Oh. Well . . . how about the radio? It sure is quiet around here."

There was a pause, and then Stacy said, "We like it quiet, Mista Jackson. That way we can do our studying."

"Uh-hunh . . . is that so. And do you always study with the lights off?"

"It's daytime, whadda we need lights for?" Stacy had an

answer for everything, and that just made Push more curious, more skeptical.

Sharissa flashed a guilt-ridden expression toward Stacy;
more of an accusation than anything else.

Why are these two lying to me?

Push reached to turn on the table lamp, wanting to
change this dull and miserable atmosphere.

"The lamp ain't workin'," Stacy snapped.

"Oh," Push responded, wondering why, and he went on
trouble-shooting. Eventually he made his way over to the
wall switch, unaware of the latest funny look Stacy and
Sharissa shared.

"O-kay. Conference time," said Push, and he picked up
Sharissa from the floor to set her on the couch. He also gestured to Stacy, and now she was sitting too, whispering in
her sister's ear.

"Look . . . I need your help here, young ladies. You both
are home when you're supposed to be in school. You're lying
about your mom, just in case you think I'm stupid. Your
clothes are dirty, and I saw *you* in those same pink pants just
two days ago. They don't look like they've been changed.
Come to think of it . . ." Push leaned in and sniffed. "When's
the last time y'all had a bath?"

"Tell 'im, Stace."

Stacy turned to Sharissa with such anger that it appeared
as though she might smack the daylights out of her.

"Tell me *what*, Stace?" Push used the nickname like he
was a Wallace sibling. He had to take hold of Stacy's arm so
that she'd know he meant business. *"Tell me what, Stacy?"*

Stacy lowered her head and a tear fell past her cheek to
her lap. And now Sharissa joined in, sniffing and working up
her own sorrow.

"You did it now, *stupid*," Stacy told her sister. The blame
only made Sharissa squeeze her eyes closed, and she began
to cry.

"Don't be that way to your sister, Stacy." Push took the
girl into his arms, rocking her and patting her back like a
newborn baby. "Now tell me what's going on here. Please."

"Mommy and Daddy ain't come home in twenty-three days, Mista Jackson . . ."

And in the same breath Stacy said, "Please don't let the lady come get us."

"Who's comin' to get you? What lady??"

"The DCW lady," said Sharissa. "She be comin' to knock on the door all the time."

Now Push began to fit the pieces together. It was just his guess, but an educated one. He had experience to go on. The Department of Child Welfare—DCW—could only mean one thing. The children's parents were either hurt or in jail. That was likely the only way the city agency would know about abandoned children. And that a social worker was already knocking could only mean that Stacy and Sharissa were on a "pickup list" of some kind. The city was trying to take possession of the kids.

Push and Crystal had been in the same situation some seventeen or so years earlier. They were only thirteen and eleven years of age at the time, but, by the skin of their teeth, they were able to escape "the DCW lady," sneaking away while police were busy trying to make sense of the double homicide of their parents.

Three local thugs had forced their way into the Jacksons' apartment. Mrs. Jackson was home alone when the three beat and raped her. It was a cowardly, merciless act. But to make things worse, when Mr. Jackson arrived home, surprising the attackers, they murdered them both. And life was never the same again for Push and Crystal.

"Don't you worry, baby girl. Ain't nobody comin' to take you nowhere. Not the DCW lady . . . not nobody," said Push, now determined more than ever to get to the bottom of this. "Now how about a nice hot meal?" And as he pulled both girls into his embrace, he easily recalled those days—the getaway, missing his parents' funeral, renting a room for himself and Crystal and having no choice but to deal drugs on 125th Street, then prison.

Push wondered if things might've been different if he

only had someone to hug and care about him back then. Someone to help him with the pain and trauma of it all.

The little girls cried there in his arms, and Push was crying down deep in his soul, underneath his stone exterior and bold presence.

This was the first time Push felt such a chill in years—the realization that life and its tragedies were repeating itself right before his very eyes.

And before he could dwell on things anymore, there was the knock at the door.

CHAPTER THREE

ALL OF THEM were so accustomed to assuming nicknames. It went with the territory: law enforcement.

It was crucial for secrecy and hiding behind a sort of shield. Like going "undercover." In the event a name was overheard during a sting, or—God forbid—if somebody, a colleague maybe, was trying to set someone up, then there was a buffer—a level of protection, where "real" names wouldn't be revealed.

That meant one less problem to deal with, or at least it would be more difficult to identify a person since the name was fictitious, and its owner—a virtual ghost.

Ghosts. That was how these men and women saw themselves. At one time they were advocates for the good of all people—but no more. These phantoms with their nicknames had defected, one way or another, from their duties of law and order.

Now they were part of Uncle Sam's dream team that had come to life.

"We're the ultimate crime machine: L.T.K. . . . better known as Licensed to Kill. This is not to say that what we do is kill. No. But kill we will, if it ever becomes necessary. If it will preserve our mission." And the leader made it clear how L.T.K. was an elite, special breed of soldiers. Soldiers of a different kind, who went after criminal enterprises. Perhaps their individual agendas were simple. Greed. Revenge. Or maybe they just agreed with the concept, the culture of the high-risk, take-no-shit, badass cop-gone-bad.

Upon first sight, you'd think of Sam as wise, calculating, with the cigar added to his robust character. His morning ritual had been the same for more than twenty-five years: the protein drink—six raw eggs mixed with celery, carrot and grapefruit juices—was always ready and waiting for him by 4:30 A.M.

He'd wolf that down, do a series of stretches, let off a husky belch that was as loud as an outboard motor and off he'd go for his ten-mile run until 6:30 A.M.

The best time he ever ran was ten miles by 6:10 A.M., and he never missed a morning workout in all those years. If the weather was inclement, Sam substituted with two hours of weightlifting and calisthenics.

There was something very serious about Sam's way of life, as if any interruption could result in some memorable consequences . . . as if you might not live to find out what those consequences were.

His intentions were simple from the day he left law enforcement.

He'd organize the baddest group of motherfuckers to walk the face of the earth. They'd have to be bad seeds, otherwise known as bad cops. He'd combine the resources of these "soldiers," from as many departments and divisions of law enforcement as possible, to build a more powerful, sinister force for the purpose of financial gain. His group would be an ultimate allegiance, untouchable by any means, yet a presence that was recognized as fearless, deadly and not to be fucked with.

Finally, L.T.K. would be funded by the proceeds earned from its own organized criminal activities. Not just any crimes, but crimes against criminals themselves. A brilliant idea!

It was Sam's theory that this was a righteous effort. Criminals were taking in billions upon billions of dollars a year, and a big chunk of that dirty money flowed through New York City's five boroughs. If executed according to plan,

L.T.K. would take in a healthy percentage of that money. It wasn't a matter of *could* this be accomplished, but *when*.

No one was more qualified to take down scores from criminals than Sam was, because Sam was already a dirty cop. He took part in shakedowns when he was a New York City flatfoot. He easily graduated to homicide detective, stayed with that for a while, then made lieutenant. An opportunity came up with the Feds, another easy walk, since the big scandal was exposed. So, Sam crossed over to the FBI with his big dreams for higher pay and greater authority.

Sam soon found that was a mistake. He quickly saw through the mirage, the so-called distinguished organization, wearing suits and bagging the big bosses of the underworld—finding that there were employees and agents with the Feds who were just as dirty, if not more so, than his co-workers on the force. This encouraged Sam to set out on his own, to build a network amongst those he worked with and knew to be grimy.

Whenever or wherever there were i's that weren't dotted, or t's that weren't crossed, anytime he recognized shortcuts taken or authority abused, or when lawlessness raised that red flag, Sam went after a new candidate, another L.T.K. member.

Today, the group was thirty-two strong. And Sam didn't see the need for any new members, unless of course, there was a person—maybe with the CIA, the ATF or the newly formed NHS—who could somehow prove to be a new resource that would serve the L.T.K. mission.

Corruption was all over the place, a reality that would always guarantee jobs in law enforcement. But who wanted to march around on some eight-to-four tour, just to receive average wages and insurance benefits and a half-assed retirement package?

Not a bad cop, that's for sure.

The better choice was to join L.T.K. They had the market cornered, much like FTD had the flower market, or Crest had the toothpaste market.

And furthermore, they had absolutely no competition.

The cash flow was constant. There were s.
known criminal enterprises, confiscations, raidh.
rooms, "liberating" unclaimed imports at the pic.
airport, and their biggest paydays: payoffs from dru........
ers, drug runners and users. Payoffs from this mob and that
mob and so many other newly formed criminal organizations.

This business was low on inventory and high on human
resources. At every opportunity, physical resources such as
automobiles, jewelry and drugs were liquidated. The focus,
though, was always cash. Paper. Something with value (at
least by its concept), which could be moved quickly and
with ease.

For each member's contribution to the L.T.K. mission,
Uncle Sam paid a hefty sum of $10,000 a month. And he gave
out bonuses like a zookeeper feeds peanuts to the elephants.
Now, with that kind of money, who needed benefits or award
ceremonies?

Naturally, Uncle Sam had his own circle of members who
he kept closest. Pistol was one such person. Milton "Pistol"
James was a know-it-all when it came to weaponry. But bigger
than his knowledge was his access. He was a squirt of a
man who took up guns and ammunition as a hobby to make
up for his lack of self-esteem; that Napoleon complex he
had. Short, insecure and bossy.

An obsessive gun collector, Pistol had numerous contacts
in a few weapons rooms in certain Brooklyn police stations.
Even now, with video surveillance cameras, there was always
someone to be bought off, a small thing to Pistol, a
seasoned professional at getting what he wanted

Pistol also had massive street ties. He could obtain a
firearm at the drop of a dime, be it a long-range automatic,
or a simple pistol. He found out soon enough about new-jack
gun dealers, independents who acquired permits to come to
New York to sell their cache of weapons in a Bronx back alley,
or on a Coney Island beach. These newcomers even had
the audacity to try and sell their shit in downtown Manhattan
garages.

Once a month, twice if need be, Pistol would ambush these scumbags. The new ex-dealer would usually burn rubber, taking with him a warning: "Don't ever come back. *Ever.*"

Meanwhile, the weapons would be exchanged for cash or else stockpiled with the rest of the L.T.K. arsenal.

L.T.K. also had its intelligence men. Mark "German" Trammel was an active agent with the Secret Service, giving L.T.K. access to federal law enforcement activities. Jeff "Vegas" Parise was a Secret Service agent as well. He served as a courier of top-secret documents, traveling back and forth between New York and Washington, D.C., at least two, sometimes three times a week. Uncle Sam counted on Vegas for spicy details regarding the president, the secretary of state, and other top-level dignitaries.

Even though Sam's focus was mostly local, with so many scores to take down at a whim, it was also healthy to have a broader, global perspective on things, options and opportunities for perhaps, future exploration. German and Vegas provided information that could be put to use if necessary.

There were other spies—women—who were firmly planted, with access to computer networks, police files and other records. Gabrielle "Pinkie" Lang and Millicent "Fonda" Scriven, the blonde and the brunette, respectively, both managed records in separate NYPD offices. At the same time, Chantel "Star" Palmer, a Jamerican with dreadlocks, pretty oval eyes and an exotic way about her, had worked as personal assistant to the past two police commissioners as well as the current one. By the efforts of one or all of these women, records could be accessed easily and data added or removed. And even they had subordinates who they paid off in one way or another for small deeds that assisted with much larger goals. Whether it was fingerprint cards to be switched in Valley Stream, Long Island, or surveillance tapes downtown that needed to be "lost," no record, electronic or otherwise, was out of L.T.K.'s reach.

When it wasn't weapons, records, or management of resources, most other L.T.K. activity involved inside information at various Internal Affairs departments, and the most important resource of all: the go-hard grunt work in the streets. Teams and squads were organized for these occasions. These hard-bodied individuals were usually a big and bad enough brawler or gunslinger to execute L.T.K.'s dirty work.

There were the take-no-shit types that had plenty of disciplinary problems in their pasts—Chester "Ape" Galante, Maurice "Hitler" Mills, Jose "Sanchez" Martinez and Leon "D.C." Wilkenson. Others who had various axes to grind and who harbored certain bitterness, anger or hostility in their current positions included Johnny "Mule" Montovalli, Armondo, Cali, Serratos, Cody, El, Snow, Ryan "Turk" Jones, and Jesse "Mims" Wallace. And while these men still performed duties as DEA, FBI or U.S. Customs agents, they remained devoted to the L.T.K. mission.

Uncle Sam also had his live wire, a cowboy named Darren "Primo" Washington, who banged his head against cement walls now and then, just to preserve his own special brand of sanity. Known best for his I-don't-give-a-fuck attitude and an itchy trigger finger, Primo was once "excused" from therapy because he had "psychological issues that could not be identified."

"Let me ask you a stupid question," Uncle Sam had said about eighteen months earlier, when Primo was just getting his feet wet with L.T.K. "Why'd they kick you out of the army?"

"I was an MP down at the McGuire base . . . the president was flying in and I got into it with one of his Secret Service agents . . ." Primo's expression could cut through metal as he said, "I had to shoot the fucker."

Uncle Sam sized Primo up, approaching him in a way a contender might.

The two were somewhat mismatched, with Primo the taller man, stretching the limits of his T-shirt; Sam a little shorter and not as bulky. If there were an advantage here, it was Sam's experience.

"So, ah . . . if you and I get into a disagreement, are you gonna shoot me too?"

Primo hadn't changed his steely gaze, staring into Sam's eyes, wondering where he was going with this. Then he suddenly smiled. The phony type.

Mims and Hitler were standing by, unsure how this would play out.

"Nah, of course not." And the ex–military policeman looked up with stars in his eyes, his hands gesturing in relation to an imaginary name in lights. "I mean, you're Uncle Sam. The leader of L.T.K.! I'd be out of my mind to do such a thing."

Uncle Sam and the others shared a strange, head-scratching look.

Maybe he *was* nuts.

Then they all laughed hard.

TODAY, L.T.K. CLAIMED the Abyssinian Presbyterian Church on Adam Clayton Powell Boulevard as their home. Called "The Abyss" for short, the church had been shut down years ago, its pastor imprisoned for buying and selling child pornography. The building was soon abandoned and the pastor's congregation scattered, hoping not to be tied to or affiliated with the tainted fellowship.

The Abyss was a monster of a building, built in the late 1800s, and made of steel and five or six varieties of stone, with a slate roof with copper-topped domes and cupolas. The entire exterior of the church was weathered and unattractive. But that was just perfect, how it sort of kept that laid-back appearance of a dead tree whose home happened to be in Harlem, New York.

While The Abyss still had its historical landmark status— meaning, the dwelling enjoyed tax breaks and could not be torn down—it also had a haunting reputation. Neighborhood residents thought of it as taboo to look at, even that the imprisoned pastor left ghosts there. Since the city couldn't sell the building or destroy it, it remained a dinosaur with a tarnished past, perhaps waiting for an energetic minister to come along and bring it back to life.

Thick chains and locks secured the three sets of the

fourteen-foot tall bronze doors, all of them with their fos-silized decor. Stretching out for half a city block, the property also had a gated, fifty-car parking lot in the rear, with the back entrance to the church farther in, more or less hidden from public view.

IT WAS 6 P.M., with nightfall descending over New York, as more than twenty vehicles crawled into the church parking lot, quietly, as though a funeral were about to begin.

Other vehicles were already parked in the lot, one of them being Sam's Super Cruiser, a twenty-three-foot-long behemoth of a truck with a 300-horsepower, six-cylinder diesel engine. The red truck was parked at an angle, occupying close to four spaces on its own. Sam's other toys included a navy blue Dodge Ram, a black Chevy Tahoe, and a cream-colored, wide body Mercedes sedan.

The other trucks, vans and midsize vehicles now shutting down belonged to some twenty other L.T.K. members who had come to throw Uncle Sam a surprise birthday party that would not be forgotten.

Word was that Sam was turning twenty-nine years old . . . again. And every time one of the members shared that information riotous laughter followed.

INSIDE THE ABYSS was a 3,000-seat main sanctuary, with impressive hand carvings along the top of numerous limestone columns, each with four different images—angels with trumpets. The carvings were so detailed they looked lifelike, and were consistent with the mosaic designs on the worn carpeted floor, as well as with the paintings on the walls. The wooden pews were broken and piled in heaps; however, the carved-stone pulpit and altar were still intact, standing up front on a raised platform. A man-sized cross still hung high over the pulpit.

There were four smaller chapels, six rooms for Bible class, a chair room, a gymnasium with a rotted floor and a string of church offices that occupied most of the space in the old building.

One of those church offices was a lot larger than the others, with contemporary furnishings and a bright, airy atmosphere; its stained-glass windows were still intact. This was where Uncle Sam spent most of his time playing general and dishing out instructions over the phone or in person.

In the corner was his weight-lifting equipment. In the adjoining room was the king-size bed that he shared with Reesy. Reesy was Sam's niece-slash-assistant. She was also his sex toy, when he wanted to play. She usually occupied the desk across from him or stayed busy with chores. Reesy also had a hard body that was strong enough to bench-press 300 pounds of iron, but a face that could win first place for ugly pet of the month. Her eyes were small and shifty. Her cheeks were pudgy and naturally red. Her lips were thick and blubbery and she had a wrestler's neck with a slight, protruding Adam's apple. She actually did make an attempt at wrestling but quit as an amateur when her hip bone was fractured. Nowadays Reesy had a funny walk to remind her of those trials and tribulations from her high school years.

She was mature now. She saw herself as a woman of the world.

"I'll tell you what, Felix. I'm not gonna pussyfoot with you. You agreed to take one ton, and one ton is what I got for you. The shit will be ready for pickup tomorrow . . . we'll secure the transaction, end of story. A deal's a deal. Bring cash." Uncle Sam laid the phone down and kicked his feet up on the ex-pastor's desk. And lit the Cuban cigar that was wedged between his teeth. Eventually, he let out a cloud of his rich tobacco smoke.

The cell phone he set down was positioned next to seven others, all of them marked for different priorities. These were Sam's only means of communication. All of them stolen numbers and access codes, which were changed every two weeks.

He was on another call now.

"Yeah, it's me, Raymond . . . that's right, forty-seven altogether . . . well, make me an offer I can't refuse. Yes, Raymond. Same as always, no VIN numbers, no titles and no mileage. No, I don't thinks so. Why don't *you* give *me* a price and before you do, I should tell you that I already have an offer of sixteen . . . yes, each. Whaddaya think I run here, a soup kitchen? I'm here to make money . . ."

Sam scrunched his face in response. And now his eyes followed Reesy's wide ass, as he thought about how it was all trapped in those tight jeans.

Today had been an average day for her: she basically followed Sam's instructions, tended to the cash-counting—and there was always the maintenance of his vehicles, including "Big Red." She felt like a mafia princess, doing what she could to satisfy the boss, always going the extra mile.

Reesy scribbled something on a pad at her desk, ripped the sheet off, turned it over and scribbled something else. She went back toward Sam, holding up the paper for him to read as he continued with business as usual. It read:

I AIN'T KNOW IT WAS YOUR BIRTHDAY!?

Her uncle's eyes widened briefly and he shrugged. No big deal. Whoop-de-do.

"That's right, Raymond. Six BMWs, eight Infinities, two Jags . . ." By the time Sam got to the Lincoln Town Cars, Reesy was on her knees pulling his trousers open. Then she began her usual warm-up—the soft humming sounds as she took more of him into her mouth . . . the pulling and pushing at his foreskin . . . the tricks with her tongue. Somewhere during the activity, between the mention of the Mercedes coup and the late-model Saabs, Reesy held up the other side to the note she scribbled. Sam took it with his free hand. It read:

HAPPY BIRTHDAY UNCLE SAM!! SLURP, SLURP.

Sam twisted his lips into a subtle grin and balled up the note in his fist.

"Oh that? It's nothin', Raymond. My dog is drinking from his bowl . . . whaddaya mean, you didn't know? There's a lotta things you don't know about me . . . it's—it's a mutt," Sam said.

And he and Reesy shared a smile, he sitting with his legs open, and she between his legs, flipping her blonde ponytail.

"Yeah . . . I know the mutt is noisy."

Another of Sam's cell phones rang.

"Hold on, Ray. Yeah . . . Hey, how goes it, Pinkie, could you hold a minute?" Then into the other phone, "Raymond, I gotta take this. Call back in ten." Sam hung up one phone and brought the other to his ear. The mutt kept herself busy, making a thorough effort of this birthday gift.

"Gimme that again, Pinkie." Sam's face went through a series of expressions between pleasure and surprise. "You don't say . . . oh, really."

A moment later, as though he'd been bitten, Sam clutched a handful of Reesy's ponytail, pulling her face away from his half-erect penis, shaking his head. *No. Gotta handle this call*.

"Jesus! Are you *absolutely* sure, Pinkie? Your info is solid?"

Reesy smoothed her hands along Sam's thighs, using them to support her as she pushed herself up onto her feet.

Disrupted again.

"All right. Later, doll," Uncle Sam hung up and asked his niece, "Have you seen Mims or Hitler?"

"I seen 'em both downstairs, Uncle. They sent me up to get you. That's how I know about your birthday. There's a s'prise downstairs, Uncle. Don't tell 'em I said so. I promised 'em."

"Don't *tell* 'em? Woman, you belong to me. You're supposed to be the eyes at the back of my head . . ."

Reesy squirmed, unsure if her uncle would go off on her like he sometimes did, behind closed doors.

"What's everybody smokin' 'round here? Is a friggin' birthday this important to you all that the world has to stop spinning?"

Sam already had his trousers fastened again and he came from around the desk. He gave Reesy a soft pinch on her cheek, his way of appreciating her. "Okay. Tidy up around here, Reesy. Lemme see what in the hell these guys are doin'. We'll pick up where we left off later."

As Uncle Sam stepped out of his office, Erskin "Skin"

Yates, a goon with a spotted egghead and a misdirected left eye, was approaching from down the hall, passing rooms cluttered with stolen goods, bales of marijuana and household appliances still in their original packaging.

"I was just coming to find you," said Skin. "We got a little somethin' goin' on downstairs."

"So I heard."

"Hunh?"

"A little bird told me," Sam lied, his hand patting Skin's shoulder as both men headed for the basement. "But we've got a bigger problem. Did you locate the girl yet?"

Skin brandished a contented smile before he said, "That's why we called for you. She's downstairs."

"Alive?" Sam asked

Skin had a doubtful expression now. "Boss, Chico was the one who kidnapped her . . . so, you already know how he—"

"Please tell me she's alive, Skin. We need her alive."

"Last I checked she was breathin'."

Uncle Sam took that to mean trouble, and his steps quickened past the smaller chapels and empty classrooms, until he reached the basement.

"SURPRISE!! For he's a jolly good fel-low, for he's a jolly good fel-low, for he's a jolly good fe-el-low . . . which nobody can deny!"

As the song struggled on, Uncle Sam put on his best face and went on to shake hands with the two dozen or so men and women in attendance to celebrate his birthday.

When he reached Mims, he told him, "I got a call a little while ago. Pinkie tells me her contact at the courthouse thinks the Judge has a copy of the tape."

"A copy? Oh, shit. Sam, we turned the woman's whole apartment upside down. We had no idea."

"Well, we'd better find out what else is out there on the loose. Where is she?"

"That was part of your present . . ."

The jolly good song was just ending.

". . . For he's a jolly good fe-el-low . . . which no-bo-dy can deny!"

Now the whole group was clapping and chanting.

"Speech! Speech! Speech!"

"Okay, listen up! You know I'm a man of few words, so I'll just say thanks. Thanks for thinkin' about me. And I see you all found a good excuse for a party, with all the food and the drinks, so . . . now that the ass-kissing is over with—"

There was an eruption of laughter.

"—eat, drink and be merry, knock yourselves out. Cali, Turk, Ape . . . my whole Uptown Squad, I need you to come with me."

Close to ten men went with Sam, most of them hulks and hard bodies, as he crossed the long basement, with its gymnasium, kitchen, and choir room with an inoperable piano and closets stockpiled with dusty, mildewed Bibles and choir robes.

The area beyond the doors, where Sam and his L.T.K. members were headed, had been converted from a banquet hall—hard to tell that the room once accommodated many church functions—into a private shooting range.

"Goddamn, Chico, is she even alive?" asked Sam.

Chico and Hitler were already inside. "Sure she is," said Chico. And gave a little nod to Hitler. "Wake her up."

The group stood watching as Hitler moseyed past the counter, the area where L.T.K. members generally stood and fired their weapons at inanimate moving targets.

Hitler gave the woman two short smacks against the cheek, but she didn't budge. She just hung there, with her wrists bound in thick twine, suspended from a support beam above.

This was Michelle, the *Times* reporter. A friend and confidante to Judge Charles Pullman. Also, his lover. Only now, she seemed more like a helpless waif, naked from head to toe, her wrists blue, her feet barely touching the floor. The woman's face was bruised, her lips swollen. Dried blood caked under her nose and wherever else there were lacerations. Her head was slumped down close to her chest.

If she wasn't dead, she definitely looked it.

Uncle Sam asked Chico, "What the hell did you do to her? Are those safety pins in her nipples?"

"Just some of my special interrogation, but I guess things got a little out of hand."

Uncle Sam squeezed his eyes closed for a brief instant, imagining just how much *out of hand*, considering Chico's track record with women.

Hitler waved a smelling salts capsule under the woman's nose, causing her body to spasm into consciousness.

"Whew. I thought you killed her, Chico," said Sam.

"I thought you said you *wanted* her dead."

"Yeah, I know, I know. But things change. We can't kill her *now*. Not with this problem we have with the Judge. And the videotape."

"Judge?"

"Tell ya later."

Just then, Primo stumbled onto the range. "Hey! Don't leave *me* out of the fun!" he shouted. Primo had his weapon drawn, pointing in the direction of the reporter, who seemed unfazed by any of this activity.

Uncle Sam moved quickly. He swept past two others, grabbed Primo's wrist and twisted the gun so that it was redirected upward.

There was a little dance, while Sam and Primo moved and twirled, and seven shots rang out. Empty shells bounced against the cement floor.

Sam released Primo's arm and now had full possession of the firearm. With one hand, he hit the release so that the magazine fell out and rattled against the floor. He then returned the gun to Primo.

"What the fuck!" Primo barked, his speech slurred from having already had too much to drink.

Sam brushed his palms together, a job well done. "Nothing personal, Primo, but you really should think about getting a better weapon. You didn't even hit the girl once." Uncle Sam met Primo's angry expression with a broad, tight-lipped smile. "Somebody take this man out of here before somebody *really* gets hurt, namely him."

As two others did as Sam instructed, he turned to stroll over to where the reporter was suspended and awaiting her fate.

In slow, measured movements, he took out a fresh cigar and wedged it between his teeth. He pulled a set of keys from his pocket, extracted a silver cutter and snipped the end off of the cigar. When that was done, he found his lighter and ignited the log. All the while Uncle Sam's eyes evaluated the woman from head to toe.

"Funny thing about these Cuban cigars—" Sam was busy puffing, getting his cigar off to a good start. When his lungs were full of smoke, he took his time, letting a thick fog ooze from his lips. "They can become quite an expensive habit, but it's a lifestyle, ya know?" He was less than two feet away now, face-to-face with Michelle, though her eyes—what was showing of them—were focused on the floor.

"You deceived us, young lady. We did you a favor . . . granted you the interview. You gave me your word—*your word!*—that you would respect our secrecy. But what'd you do? Hunh? *Hunh?* You had the *audacity* to bring some hidden camera in here? What—did you think we'd just let it go? Forget that you jeopardized all of our hard work?"

Sam cut an eye at her now.

"I thought you were a professional. I swore that if anyone would uphold the ethics of a neutral party, it would be you. I *respected* you, bitch. And you went and played detective."

Michelle finally lifted her defeated gaze, locking eyes with the L.T.K. leader. Such sad eyes she had. Such a damaged expression. So many unspoken words. But Sam was still doing the talking, maybe performing for his inner circle of thug cops.

"Why couldn't you just keep with the plan? We gave you a hot story. Front page shit, Metro section. You coulda been a literary star—but no. You had to go and . . . Tell me something—were you even telling the truth about doing a story? Or was this the plan all along? Who put you up to this? Was it *him*? Was it Pullman? You know we're gonna find out. After all, we *are* the police—don't you get it? We don't just enforce the law. We *are* the law."

Sam studied Michelle a bit, more of a voyeur this time . . . getting his eyeful. She didn't have the pen and pad or the neat business suit to dress her curves. No disguise. This was a dif-

ferent person here. Unrecognizable, even. Withdrawn. Pow-
erless. Battered and bruised. Pale, freckled. A mole there by
her navel. At least a month's worth of hair growth under her
arms—*negligence*?—and damn, she smelled like roadkill already.

"Fuck you and your law," Michelle finally said, sputtering
her words through swollen lips. "You never *were* the law."

Sam turned to the others. "See that? Now *that's* not the
objective view you reporters are supposed to have—"

Hitler had stepped forward, ready to teach the prisoner
some respect, but Sam put a hand up.

Not yet.

"Sounds more like you're trying to be a hero . . ." Sam
looked back over his shoulders at those near the firing line.
"Or a heroine, if you wanna get all specific." Now Sam took
a step closer, practically nose to nose with her. He twisted
his face from the foul odor.

"I'll let you go if you tell me what I wanna know. We can
get you all fixed again and forget any of this happened. So
tell me . . . is there anyone else with a copy of the tape?" Uncle Sam put his palm to Michelle's face, a caress of sorts—
as if they were intimate.

"Come on, Michelle. Don't be this way. It's not your
fight. Let it go."

"Fuck you and the bitch who made you!" she managed to
bark. And she spat at him.

Sam wiped his face, again raising his hand to Hitler.

Not yet.

"See? I try to be nice to her, and that's what I get," Sam
said to his bystanders. Then, back to Michelle, he said, "When
I was a child, the elders had a nice little lesson for me if I got
the yuck mouth—even if they heard that I spoke foul—you
know how I was punished? This here . . ."

Uncle Sam loosened his belt and pulled it from his pant
loops with one long, dramatic stretch of his arm.

"Pop had a leather belt to whip my little ass. And you
know what? Sorry to say that I never really learned my
lesson . . ."

It seemed as though Sam might suddenly whip Michelle with the belt.

"So it wouldn't make sense for me to do the same to you. I mean, what would I get out of it? On the other hand—"

Sam handed the belt to Chico, who smiled shamelessly at the opportunity as he wrapped the buckled end around his hand.

"—have you met Chico?"

He nodded at Chico. On cue, Chico whipped the woman's body, provoking screams with each strike. The noise motivated a few spectators to put on the available soundproof headsets that hung nearby. Some of the others conversed amongst one another, feeding the atmosphere with a certain manic excitement.

The shrieks continued while Chico scarred the reporter's skin with blistering red marks, branding her ass, thighs and midsection with a zebra design.

"Hold on, Chico. Let's see if the woman has something to tell us," said Sam, approaching the wailing woman once again.

Her body was slick with sweat, and the red gashes appeared to be on the verge of bleeding, as fresh as they were.

"How about it, Michelle? Or are we gonna let Chico here beat you to a bloody pulp?" Sam was even closer now, his lips near enough to tickle her inner ear with his breathing. "Did they find out our address? Should we expect visitors? Come on, baby, help me out and I'll help you out."

Michelle appeared to murmur something.

"What's that? I didn't hear you."

"I . . . said . . . it's only a . . . matter of . . . of time."

"Okay now. We're getting somewhere here. A matter of time before *what*?"

"Before somebody sticks a . . . two . . . two by four . . . up . . . your . . . your . . . ass," Michelle purred with great difficulty.

"Humph. You've got a lotta nerve, missy. You really

do . . ." Sam seemed to admire the woman and let his expression tell it. "But I'm gonna disregard your belligerence."

Then, to Hitler and the others, he said, "Well? I guess that target practice is back on. Chico, what are you waiting for? Reload!"

Uncle Sam swaggered back behind the firing line and joined five or six others pulling out their weapons from holsters and waistbands, readying them for business.

"Alrighty then," said Sam, as if to confirm his decision. "You know the drill, fellas. We shoot until the body can no longer be identified. Aim!"

"W-wait—" Michelle could barely utter the word.

"Hold your fire. I think our friend has had a change of heart. Hitler? Go see what she wants."

Uncle Sam pulled on his cigar, letting the smoke sit in his lungs as he watched, wondering what she had to say.

"Easy, guys. Let's just see what we get here."

Hitler returned to the group. "She says there's one other copy, but she can't tell us who has it. She says it's not who you think it is."

Uncle Sam had the cigar wedged between his lips, working up an understanding nod. He released a puff of smoke from his lungs and simply picked up his .44 Magnum Ruger and slipped his other pistol, the .38 Smith & Wesson, from his waistband.

"You must love that man somethin' major, protectin' him like this!" he hollered.

Michelle realized where this was going. And before anyone on the firing range could think, she spat on the floor in front of her.

It was so small an act, but so large a statement.

"Fuck you and die," she repeated.

Within the next twenty seconds, Uncle Sam and his accomplices emptied their weapons, their bullets ripping through the reporter's body. Shell casings fell repeatedly to the floor, creating the illusion of a casino with many of its coin-operated slot machines paying out winnings all at once.

Blood and flesh oozed and flew from the woman until she was indeed unrecognizable.

Sam digested one last look at the lifeless, blood-dripping corpse. It didn't seem that one bullet missed.

"Men, hunting season has officially begun."

And now, just as in the past, Uncle Sam's L.T.K. soldiers would put their lives on the line to complete another mission.

The party was now over. It was time to pay a visit to Judge Charles Pullman.

Information such as his home address, his schedule and the security personnel who protected him would need to be acquired. No big deal considering the wealth of L.T.K. resources.

CHAPTER FOUR

IT WAS A late Thursday evening at Perk's Fine Cuisine. Yvette, who had come to see Crystal on the job, sat at the bar in a saucy wine-colored dress, legs crossed and mostly exposed, while her friend did her share of the cleanup.

Yvette considered how often she'd done this. So frequently that she knew the routine by heart. At a certain point the front door would be locked and someone armed would stand by, alert as a fox. Mr. Perkins, the proprietor and one of Harlem's mavericks, would check the register tape and compare it to the cash collected during the night. When he was satisfied, he'd either tell Crystal good night, or he'd invite both her and Yvette to breakfast, likely enjoying the attention he'd attract, sandwiched between two luscious-looking young women.

Once the clock struck 2 A.M., it was clear that Perk was going home alone tonight, and that Yvette would be joining only Crystal for a bite to eat at M&G's.

Yvette was starving, which was part hunger and part, well, nervousness. For Crystal, something light would be fine. She did, after all, have the menu at Perks to select from on any work night. But quality time with Yvette was important. Plus, there was no big rush these days. Not since Reggie grew up. Since he wasn't coming home like he used to, Crystal didn't have to be concerned about dinner being ready, that his clothes were laid out for the following day or that he was safe and warm in bed at night.

Sure as day, Crystal cared and loved Reggie, but she couldn't go on worrying all her life. She had to live as well. So those days were over. Crystal was no longer a working mom, but in the next phase of her life. Now, she felt alone.

She had survived all of the various labels:

Orphan.

Unwed mother.

Provider.

A statistic.

At one point she was "Mama," then "Mommy," then "Ma." Nowadays, Reg called her "Ma-duke," whatever the hell that implied. And Crystal couldn't help wondering what her next title would be. She wondered if she might be too old, at thirty-two, with so much pain, so many challenges and experiences . . . too much luggage, perhaps, to be marketable.

And with those questions in mind, making her somewhat insecure about her place in life. Crystal didn't mind spending time with her best friend. Except there was this question nagging her.

"Now you got me curious, Yvette. There was a time that I was too busy to hang out late . . . y'know, with a child to raise and whatnot. I just couldn't pal around like I wanted to. Like we used to . . ."

Crystal took a moment to suck at her cigarette—a habit that left that I-don't-give-a-fuck attitude hanging in the air along with the killer smoke.

"Okay," she continued. "Then it was *me* who had the free time, since my brat doesn't seem to know where his home is anymore, and it was *you* who didn't have time for *me*. Especially since you got a man 'n all." There was a funny edge to her words, considering that it was *she* who had played Cupid, virtually plugging Yvette in to make the love connection with her brother.

"Well . . . ain't that the pot calling the kettle black," joked Yvette, repeating a line from a book she'd just read.

"Very funny. But I'm serious, girl. Why all of a sudden the late-night powwow? It isn't like you been comin' around like you once did. Somethin' goin' on I should know about? You two ain't havin' problems, are you?"

"Problems? Us? Crystal, if I told you what your brother does to me, how he makes love to me, we could write a best-seller that every black woman would wanna buy. He makes my earth shake."

"Whoa," said Crystal.

But Yvette wasn't stalled. She just kept going. "I mean, it got so crazy the other day, he came over my place after work, he was all funky and, well, I didn't even wait for him to wash, I just . . ."

"*Yvette.*" Crystal had her hand raised now, a traffic cop in charge of the girl-girl talk. "This is my *blood brother* we're talking about here. What makes you think I need to hear how you two get down?"

"Sorry, boo." Yvette seemed to deflate. "Guess I got carried away."

"You guess you did?! But as long as you're getting along over there, that's all I care about. Remember our deal."

And Yvette *did* remember the deal—

"*Don't you do my brother wrong.*"

Which was *precisely* her problem right now.

"Yeah. I'm treating him like a king, Crystal. Anything he wants, girl. And I mean any-thing."

"Livin' the big fairy tale, hunh?"

"We have our messy moments, don't get me wrong."

"Sure. I know."

"But with Push? I . . . I just can't explain it, girl. I wanna share him with every woman on earth, just to fix everything. I mean, the world would be such a perfect place if every woman had a man like mine . . ."

Crystal rolled her eyes in that *oh brother* kind of way.

"No, I mean it, Crystal. I have had a few men in my life. So I definitely know what I'm talkin' about. Like you need to cut that smokin' out."

"What'd I tell you 'bout gettin' in grown folks' business?" Crystal said with a serious expression.

Yvette sucked her teeth. Then she said, "Anyway, even as

far as Push keepin' his word, there's no leak in his boat, girl.
He's every man like Chaka sings I'm every woman. Kenny,
Luther or Joe should sing a song like I'm every man, so my
Push can have something to play while we're doing the wild
thing."

Crystal blew smoke in Yvette's direction and Yvette
waved it away. It didn't stop her, however.

"Your brother and I have this thing we started, where if
we do disagree, first of all, we must respect each other. No
cussing. No calling each other out of our names. So, it's
okay if we disagree on something, but we always have that
respect. We never argue ad infinitum where it's like, Well
then, fuck you. I'm not putting up with this anymore. No.
It's not like that. We're on a whole other level. Like, Your
opinion is real twisted, but so what. You're in my life now
and I love you how you are. Maybe you'll see things my way
one day."

Crystal harrumphed. She said, "That's different."

"Think it ain't? In the hood? Shit, and boyfriends in *my*
past, I dunno about you—"

But she sure did know.

"—woulda called me all kinds of bitches, plus he woulda
slammed the door on his way out, leavin' me cryin' the
blues. With Push, the least I can expect is a hug and the most
I can expect, well, we like to call it angry sex. That's our
agreement." Yvette went on, "Yeah, girl. The deal is, whenever there's an argument, no matter how hot it gets, we must
have sex afterward."

"Is that so? What, you have is some kinda contract for
that?"

"An oral contract." Yvette couldn't help her smile.

"I *bet* it's oral." Crystal couldn't help saying.

The food was finished and there was just about nothing
left to say. Just about.

"He's treating me like a queen, Crystal. Always. And
sometimes, go on and call me crazy, but I wanna cry because
of how good I have it." And Yvette showed signs of tears.
"Sometimes I don't feel I deserve this and that one day, it's

all gonna disappear and I'm gonna wake up from my big dream."

Crystal was compassionate, finally seeing the truth in her friend's eyes—her eyes, those windows to her heart.

"Oh, Yvette . . ." Crystal took Yvette's hand in hers. "You should be happy. You *do* deserve him. Really."

"Yeah?" Yvette asked, pushing the tears away, unconcerned with who might be looking.

"Of course, girl. This is a blessing. Nothing to cry about."

Yvette sniffed and said, "These are happy tears . . . can't you tell?" There was a smile in her eyes and her voice made the transition from despair to joy.

"No," Crystal replied, with the matter-of-fact attitude showing in her pursed lips. The thirty-somethings both broke out in a sweet and sour laughter.

"Yvette, I'm happy for you. Really, life is short, y'know? So eat as much of it as you can—I don't mean *literally* either."

"Thanks, Crystal. You really know how to cheer a sista up."

"So why are you still crying?"

There was a silence between them, except for Yvette's sobs.

"It's something else, isn't it?"

"Sort of."

"Well, spit it out, girlfriend,"

"Do you guys talk? Like, brother-sister stuff?"

Crystal shrugged. "Depends, about what? And would you stop beating around the bush, Yvette? You're makin' me nervous."

"Has he said anything about marriage to you?"

Immediately, Crystal replied with, "Whoa-hooo—the M-word. Baby girl, you done took it there—"

Now it was Yvette with the shrugging.

"What's the rush?" asked Crystal. "You know he's been through a lot."

"Yes. I know he's been through a lot. But, well, I figure I'm not getting any younger."

"Girrrl, you're opening up a can of worms. For both of

us, seriously. Yvette, from my point of view, based on what you're sayin', y'all are fuckin' like rabbits. You're business partners with the real estate, and I haven't heard Push so much as whisper another woman's name. Is there something I'm missing here?"

"I guess you're right. Maybe I just needed a second opinion. Some assurance."

"Why? When all you need to do is follow your heart?"

Crystal had this compassionate expression that made Yvette want to open up. Yvette lowered her face in a shameful way. When she raised her head again, it was with one of those dead-serious gazes, one that prayed for you to read between the lines. And now Yvette swallowed, ready to spill the beans. No more beating around the bush.

"Crystal . . . you're going to be an auntie."

PUSH'S RESPONSE WAS everything she wanted, but never expected.

"What!? Oh shit! I mean, wow! God, I can't believe it! Are you all right? Sit down! I mean . . ." And Push had grabbed Yvette. He almost threw her up in the air, but he stopped himself, realizing that he must be gentle.

But he wanted to express his joy.

He hugged her, but then he stopped that too.

Shit. He didn't know how to act.

"A girl? A boy? A baby!"

Yvette later explained how it all went down. How Push took the news. But she didn't tell Crystal everything . . . how Mr. Murphy was more or less extorting their dream. How he was using the gray area of verbal agreements to get the better of Melrah.

She didn't tell Crystal, because she knew Push would then find out what was *really* going on.

And if Push found *that* out, *oh God.* They might lose everything. There was no telling how he'd react. Yvette wasn't naive, though she acted as much when it was necessary.

She knew damned well her man was a killer.

She'd put everything she owned and loved on the hunch that Push killed Raphael two years earlier, out on the dark-as-coal night on 122nd Street.

Hell, Raphael beat Crystal. So good for his ass.

What comes around goes around.

Yvette figured the guy got just what he deserved. But things were different these days. Push had conceived this business, Yvette had the man of her dreams and there was a baby on the way. There was no way she'd do anything to jeopardize this. In fact, she'd do everything to see that this played out until it matched her dream. Her "happily ever after."

When Yvette left Crystal that night, it was only the idea of being an unwed mother that hung in the air. Unwed meant nothing was secure or set in stone; although marriage didn't even necessarily guarantee that, at least it was something.

Yvette didn't say how she'd fulfill slumlord Murphy's request. What she was about to do was her business and her business alone.

"THAT'S ALL THAT these marshals are using t'day: black or dark blue Tahoes. Every now 'n then you'll see a Chevy Suburban. But chances are, those would be boys from Washington or maybe a New York director. Y'know . . . executive-type shit." Cali was explaining things to El, Mims and Mule, as if he was assigned to their three-man team as the professional regarding all things Fed.

"But these guys are minutemen. Like we all started out. Even you all in the NYPD, Mims, sedans, Tahoes, Suburbans . . ."

Mule was at the point of losing it. His tolerance had worn thin, and everybody knew what happened when Mule got annoyed about something.

"Sedans, Tahoes, Suburbans, what's the big deal already," he exclaimed. "We seen the truck in front of the house, end of story. Da fuck you gonna do? Give us the rundown on every kind of vehicle until we have it spillin' out our ears? Damn."

"What Mule is so eloquently trying to say, Cali, is shut it up. Too much jibber-jabber is givin' us all a headache when we're supposed to be focused. Let's relax and let our experience work its magic," said Mims. Then he got on the walkie. "Mims to Chester—I mean, shit." Mims pulled the walkie away from his mouth, realizing that he hadn't used the right name.

"You slippin', Mims," said Cali, quick to point out his comrade's error.

"Yeah, yeah . . . Mims to Ape, come in."

The speaker crackled below the dashboard. Then the voice. "Ape here. I coulda sworn I just heard you."

"Scratch that, homey. Anything yet?"

"Quiet as a mouse," was the reply over the squawk box.

"Sit tight. Should be any minute now, over."

Mims laid his head back against the headrest as the four of them—Sam called them the Uptown Team—sat waiting in a dark green Honda Civic.

This was the way for Mims to get past the unimportant conversation that was corrupting their clear thinking, while they prepared to kidnap Judge Pullman.

He prayed that Cali wouldn't say another word, knowing what he knew about Johnny "Mule" Motovalli's past.

Johnny had been excused from duty as one of NYPD's street-team members on account of his physical disability. He had been a part of the street team's notorious Night Squad, who were known to roll up fearlessly into the most dangerous areas of the city. Whether it was drugs, weapons or violent gangs, the Night Squad was the task force to close in and take out the racket. "Dead or alive" was their motto.

As things happen, luck sometimes was not on their side. One night a bust went foul. The target organization, known as the Triads, had sentries up on the rooftops; they fired first on the approaching squad cars. Mule was shot in the side of the face even before he made it out of the cruiser. Later, he would find out that what struck him was far from a stray bullet. He was a target.

He spent eight weeks in Bellevue Hospital's Shock Trauma Center before he was allowed to return home to recuperate. The bullet was never removed.

There were a series of reconstructive surgeries, but he had to accept the reality that his face would never be the same again. To look at his past photos, you couldn't even recognize Johnny these days. He was as ugly as a gargoyle; a mule for life.

Soon after the shooting, Johnny was given an "indefinite leave," and eventually he was called in and offered disability. He didn't even need to follow the normal procedure of requesting it, it was *offered* to him.

Constant headaches and incredible bitterness toward life followed Mule through his days and nights until he finally met Uncle Sam. He was like one of those lawyers who chased ambulances, coming to Mule's hospital bed, selling him all kinds of pipe dreams.

"How would you like the freedom to get back at every criminal who ever touched a gun?" Sam asked the wounded cop.

Johnny didn't understand at first; however, Mims explained how he would be paid for his part in L.T.K., a group of others—the bitter and the hateful who had an axe to grind—just like him.

Uncle Sam was the one to give Johnny his nickname. And now here he was in the backseat of the Civic, cradling a noise-suppressed Maunz 30.8-caliber assault rifle. Snipers generally used a weapon like this, but Mule didn't anticipate any more than ten feet to come between him and his target.

El was by Mule's side, while Cali and Mims were up in the front seat. Behind this Civic were two other vehicles, a plum-colored Maxima and a Toyota Celica, and all three vehicles were parked roadside on Riverdale Avenue in Yonkers, the city where Judge Charles Pullman lived.

They were all waiting for word on the relief, likely another SUV with two U.S. marshals, to come and replace the two marshals who had been sitting parked outside of Judge Pullman's home on Bayer Avenue, just a few blocks away.

THE JUDGE HAD been paranoid ever since Michelle's disappearance, especially when coupled with the untimely death of Amelia Cohen, the U.S. attorney, and the fact that Mark Schmidt had gone missing not long after his brother, Dudley, was slain outside of a toy store with $1,000 in his pocket.

The Judge didn't have to do too much speculating to conclude that Dudley's murder was directly related to Mark's awareness of certain things and that he'd found out about or viewed the videotape.

I'd have left town too.

And now, almost every fifteen minutes, Pullman was peeking out from behind shades and curtains. Watching the marshals' truck. Watching the hedges surrounding his home—wishing that he had cut them down for more visibility. Checking the motion detector and his home security system to be sure that, God forbid, the electric current hadn't been cut, and that the batteries were ready for auxiliary power.

This was crazy, Pullman had to admit to himself, as he checked doors, windows and the telephone line. Securing himself in his home. But how in tune could the marshals be, always sitting out there in front? *Why don't they circle the house?? Shouldn't they check the neighbors . . . see if these madmen have taken some hostages?*

And now Pullman needed a shower. All of this surveillance stuff was making him crazy!

THE BLACK TAHOE was a standout, moving at high speeds along the Saw Mill River Parkway, then taking the Riverdale Avenue exit. The truck was like a box-shaped beetle, a big shiny one, gliding through the night with nothing to deter its movement or intention.

Frank was driving, Ted on the passenger's side; and the both of them were anticipating just one thing during the next eight hours: another boring "sit" outside of the Judge's house.

Ted said, "I sometimes think these robes are cowards, how they pontificate before their courtroom audiences all day and hand down sentences, making smart remarks and quoting all kinds of philosophers—a real arrogant position, that is—but then they can't even take a walk in their own neighborhood without worrying about who they ticked off."

And Frank said, "Are you hatin' on the Judge, Ted?"

"Hardly. I'm just tellin' it like it is. Maybe if they didn't act like smart-asses up on the bench and just did their job. I mean, yesterday I was in the district court when Judge Tyler dropped a fifteen-year sentence on a sixty-nine-year-old women. Some family member spoke out and said, 'She can't do fifteen years!' But Tyler had the nerve to go and say, 'Well, let her do as much of it as she can.' And I'm thinking, this asshole just told the old woman to die in prison."

"No shit."

"What the fuck, man. You'd think that Tyler would have a little compassion. Maybe he'd say, 'I'm sorry, Mr. Whatever. You may appeal my decision if you like.' And then he could just step down, and end of story. But he had to go and be a jerk. Now, Morales is sitting with a team outside of Tyler's house in Larchmont."

"You know me, Ted, I don't get into the politics of it all. It's just a job. At the end of the day, we're the good guys, they're the bad guys. Bottom line. Now, put on your vest."

"Yeah. Yeah. But tomorrow, we'll probably be replacing Morales to sit for Tyler, because now he's got threats too."

"If he's alive," said Frank. And the two U.S. marshals laughed as they veered off of the Saw Mill Parkway.

"I brought the new *Maxim* and the *G.Q.*," Ted announced.

"Good. I hope they're showing some skin. I could stand some good ole fashion smut tonight." Frank stole the red light with that comment. There were no cars in the way, other than the beat-up Dodge observing the law. Frank easily shot around the other Joes driving along their path and pressed toward Bayer Avenue.

Less than ten seconds passed before there were sirens and emergency lights chasing the Tahoe.

"What the . . . who's this? A local?"

Now Ted looked out of the side-view mirror to see the vehicles behind them. "Looks like some detective. Must be, 'cause the car is unmarked. Better pull over. Just make nice with 'em. You never know when we might need a favor," he said.

Frank said, "Sometimes I think you're turning soft, Ted. If it was Morales behind the wheel, he'd have said, 'Let 'em eat rubber!' "

"Yeah, but Morales and I are nowhere *near* thinking the same. All he wants out of life is a good heavy metal CD and a blonde who can take it up the ass. Come on, pull over, champ . . . there, by the hydrant," Ted directed.

Frank put his own emergency light up on the dashboard, something he could've done earlier—sure, he'd have avoided this stupid traffic stop but there was something so daredevilish about doing 80 and 90 miles per hour on the parkway without a safety net, without forewarning, without concerns of highway patrol. The idea of passing so many other cars that did observe the speed limit was a thrill like no other. By the time any civilian motorists realized what was happening, the Tahoe would be just another black spot in the night. Here one minute, gone the next.

Once the SUV came to a stop, Frank let down his window and rested his left arm so that the cop, or whoever he was, would see the badge in his hand. U.S. Marshal, embossed on the tin.

"Hey there, buddy," announced Frank.

"Good evening. Can I see your license and registration? You were doing close to eighty-five and endangering law-abiding citizens."

Frank wondered if the cop hadn't seen the badge, and he turned it more so that there'd be no question. And for the record, that license and registration request was *not* gonna happen. Not in this lifetime. *Doesn't this dweeb see our license plates?*

But just as Frank considered that, the cop said, "Oh . . . hey, Charlie, take a look at this. These guys are Feds," said cop #1, reviewing the badge.

Frank made a face, noticing how the plainclothes cop had only a badge hanging from his neck like a medallion; plus, the handle of his weapon was in clear view, stuck in his holster.

Probably a peashooter, thought Frank.

"You two on business?" asked the cop.

"Sure, we're relieving a shift a couple blocks away. Top secret stuff," he added with a snide attitude.

Cop #2 was inspecting things through the lowered window as he said, "They're legit, Bobby."

"Looks all good to me, champ. You all have a good one."

Frank said, "Thank you," and reached to place his badge on the dashboard.

"Hey, y'know, my buddy here, Bobby, always wanted to be a marshal."

"Sure do," said the second cop. "How's the pay?"

"I thought you said his name was Charlie? And that *you* were Bobby?" Frank said suspiciously.

But before another word was exchanged, a series of shots blasted into the front seat of the Tahoe. Neither Frank nor Ted were ready for the attack.

Now a second vehicle rolled up, also with emergency lights flickering on the dark deserted road. There were homes within eyesight, so this would have to be quick.

Primo reached into the Tahoe, tugged at the door handle and pushed the dead driver so that the body fell into the back of the truck. He then reached past the second dead marshal to pull the latch so that Ape could get in. In the same swift movement, Primo snatched the other lifeless body, his hands wet with blood and guts, and pushed it back there with the other.

"Shit," Primo exclaimed. And he tugged at one of the marshals' T-shirts until it ripped from the torso. With the bloodless piece of material, Primo wiped his hands off.

"Go," said Ape, already grabbing firearms and the embroidered U.S. marshal cap from the would-be relief. "Hey!" He laughed. "They had vests on."

"Yeah, but against the Magnum, at close range, they didn't have a prayer," said Primo.

As heartless as this seemed, it was routine for Primo and Ape. Not more than two hours earlier, eight of Uncle Sam's riffraff took down a drug dealer in his Queens home. It was a surprise hit. L.T.K. had the inside information to help the hit go smoothly, and now there was a dead drug dealer and his whore, both lying in a pool of blood. The stash of drugs and money amounted to more than $180,000. This good day's work was still in a duffel bag, snug in the trunk of the Corsica.

That dead couple in Queens was just a warm-up for the kidnapping now in progress. An exercise to get their adrenaline going. And now, the very Tahoe that Primo and Ape had commandeered glided along Riverdale Avenue, heading straight for part two of the mission to grab the Judge.

Cali and El broke off from the four-man team, and were now in the other vehicles; Cali paired off with D.C. in the Civic, while El was in the Toyota with Hitler. The vehicles also split up so that they'd post at the far end of Bayer Avenue. Meanwhile, the Tahoe slowed some, so that it wouldn't pose a threat.

D.C. had watched the marshals' procedure through binoculars during the previous day, becoming familiar with how they executed the changing shifts.

It was a fairly simple procedure. The relief would show up and park in front of the first truck. The two marshals who were finished with their shift would hop out and go have a chat with their relief, after which they'd head home, probably leaving word with a central intelligence office—a fancy description for an operator.

But somehow, even though Mims and the others had discussed this at length, things went foul.

The Tahoe—the one that had been hijacked—pulled up in front of its twin, close enough so that the license plate, M-3, could be recognized. The L.T.K. members who were in on this ambush were counting on the Tahoe and the official U.S. Marshal license plates to serve as a free ticket toward their "mission accomplished." Close to a minute passed, and still, the two marshals who were scheduled to go home had not left their truck for the brief changing of the guards.

• • •

"**HIT THE HORN** one time real quick," instructed Ape. Primo did so quickly, so as not to wake the neighbors. It was nearing midnight now, and this suburban showcase of Colonial, Ranch-style and Tudor homes was fast asleep. Each property had a sizeable lawn and oval driveway with detailed landscapes, all illuminated by accent lighting. All indoor lights were off.

"Shit. This isn't right. They're supposed to be out of the truck by now," exclaimed Primo.

And now Ape prepared his 9mm Luger. The silencer fit onto the nose of the weapon with a quick snap.

"Ape to Mims . . . Nothin's goin' on. The truck's just sittin' here."

"Tell Primo to tap the horn. Maybe they're asleep. Over."

"We did that. Over."

Mims and Mule shared a look. Mims steadily hammered his fists together, the two-way radio receiver still clutched in one hand. He brought the radio to his lips again. "We're movin' in, Ape."

"But—"

"My call. I say we move in *now*. We'll roll in Pullman's driveway . . . force them to make a move." Mims spoke with conviction, but he honestly had no idea how they'd pull this off. More important, if they waited any longer, reinforcements might be called. It was even possible that a call had *already* been made to that effect. Maybe these marshals weren't so stupid after all.

On the other hand, if L.T.K. waged an outright attack the whole neighborhood would wake up. Showtime. No chance for a surprise, which had been the whole point here.

Mims radioed Hitler and D.C.

"Go *hard*. Fuck it."

"**THIS ISN'T RIGHT**," said Greg Hemingway.

Bernard Weeks, the darker of the two white marshals, was behind the steering wheel. Listening. Watching the Tahoe parked out in front of them. He replied, "How so?"

"They were supposed to ID themselves when they pulled up," said Hemingway. It was a part of the procedure that might be missed by someone in the distance, someone too far away to hear.

"Maybe they forgot," said Weeks.

"Forgot the procedure?" exclaimed Hemingway. "I don't think so. No way."

Weeks made a face, somewhat annoyed by his comrade's petty tirade.

"Why don't you just call 'em?"

"Why don't *they* call *us*? They have a radio too."

"Mmm . . ." Maybe Hemingway had a point there.

"It's not right, I'm tellin' ya. Pull into the driveway. I'm informing the Judge."

Weeks swallowed hard and guided the Tahoe cautiously around its twin. It made its way into the oval driveway of Judge Pullman's home. Hemingway was already on the phone with Pullman.

"Judge? Sorry to wake you . . . but, well . . . this might be a false alarm—but maybe it's not . . ."

THE MOMENT THAT the Tahoe pulled away from the curb and into the driveway, they all knew for certain that this shit was ass-backward.

"Fuck it," Mims repeated. "We're too deep to back out now. If we call it off they'll move Pullman, the tape will be exposed and it could mean the end of L.T.K. and you and me—"

Now he shouted into the radio, *"We gotta make the move now! Now! Now! Now!"*

As Mims barked, Mule mashed his foot down on the accelerator as far as it would go. Cali and D.C. were fast behind them in the Civic, with Hitler and El racing in from the opposite end of the block in the Celica.

"Ram that fucker!" growled Ape. Primo whipped the Tahoe into the driveway, the deadly weight of the truck charging head-on toward the marshals.

Then the unexpected happened.

The brake lights on the vehicle ahead turned into blinding strobes, as if spurts of nuclear lights were shooting Primo in the eyes.

"Shit! I can't fuckin' see!"

Neither could Ape. And now there was the big bang. The Tahoe truck ahead of them had gone into reverse, ramming the attackers. The impact was as explosive as two linebackers colliding at top speed.

The marshals had no doubt braced themselves for the impact. But Primo and Ape were caught off guard. Their brains were rattled, everything in sight was spinning and heavy, pounding pain added to their sudden distress. Giving in to unconsciousness seemed like the only relief.

"Shit!" shouted El. "Someone's leavin' the house."

"That's the Judge!" shouted Hitler. "Mims! Where are you? They got the Judge comin' out of the house! He's gettin' away!" Hitler threw his two-way radio down and braced himself.

"Not if I can help it," snarled El. And he pushed the Celica so it jumped the sidewalk that outlined the suburban home.

"Oh . . . shit!"

By the time Mims and Mule showed up with Cali and D.C. behind them, El had fishtailed the Celica so that it sandwiched the mashals in. But the marshals disembarked from the truck, both of them in different firing positions, emptying their weapons into the front windshield of the Celica and at the Tahoe that had attacked from the rear.

"Jesus Christ!"

It was already a big mess.

Mims and Mule had jumped the sidewalk, just like El, only they stopped short of the Judge's lawn. When they considered the circumstances, how their deaths might be imminent, they threw their vehicle in reverse and bailed out. The marshals were bigger than life, doing everything in their power to protect Judge Pullman, firing continuously at the two vehicles.

El and Hitler had to be dead. *They had to be.*

On the other hand, no matter how much those marshals reloaded and fired at their attackers, they couldn't harm the second Tahoe. It was an armored vehicle just like theirs, designed to survive such intense conditions. Primo and Ape had to be alive.

"Pull out, Cali! Pull out!" Mims commanded. "Ape! Primo! Come in! Can you hear me?" He was winded, though he hadn't exercised more than the slightest gestures. "Everybody, PULL THE FUCK OUT!!!"

"What about Primo and Ape?" Mule inquired.

"Listen, man. This operation is *fucked*. Can't you see what they did to Hitler and El? Look." Mims' voice went up another level. "Lights are poppin' on all over the place. Now let's get out!" Mims, with the common sense.

"Shit, man. We can't just *leave 'em* like this!" As Mule said this, bullets began to pelt their vehicle.

There was nothing left to talk about.

"God*dammit*!" Mims reached over in front of Mule, and even though he couldn't very well drive from where he sat in the passenger's seat, he threw the Civic into reverse.

"Move this motherfucka! Now!!"

The two surviving pairs—Mims and Mule, Cali and D.C.—backed away from the property, managing to swing their vehicles out of harm's way. They sped away from the neighborhood, its atmosphere now illuminated like a movie set, with just about everyone's front lawn coming to life with homeowners in their robes and slippers. *Who was filming a movie? And why weren't we informed?*

CHAPTER FIVE

ROBERT TURNER AND Hal Benson were rookie marshals, but if you asked Judge Pullman, these guys were better than that. And at the moment he didn't have a choice; they were the only ones he could trust.

When Pullman uncurled himself from the fetal position in the backseat of the Tahoe, the one occupied by real-life marshals, he realized some, if not all, of what just took place. There was a Honda Civic there in his driveway with most of its windows blown out. Two men, whoever they were, had been blown to bloody hell, with parts of their faces now just dark pits, still leaking.

One of the marshals—Pullman didn't even know their names yet—had his Glock .45 leveled at the bodies, just in case, as he approached, wanting to make extra certain that there was no further threat. The second was already on a mobile phone, calling for help, his expression still a confused one as he focused on the other Tahoe, the one that had . . . *attacked us?*

The sight of the truck behind them was haunting Pullman as he peeped back there. *Aren't those marshals too? Why aren't they helping?* he wondered. But that thought was disrupted by Robert Turner announcing, probably to some switchboard operator—"an attempted ambush."

"A switch," he had said, specifically. "Something happened

with our relief. They didn't follow procedure when they arrived, so . . ."

Pullman was ear-hustling, trying to piece things together, even if he was still rattled, still with fresh grass and soil stains on his pajamas from having dived for cover. It was the closest he'd come to his shrubbery since the new gardener took him for a stroll so many months ago—explaining his monthly fee and the need for the work to be done.

But *damn that*. An attempt had just been made on his life. *Were there two? Three? Or four cars? Two men each?? Jesus, this L.T.K. is already out to get me!*

For the first time since this all started, Pullman considered leaving town. He was a target. And according to Michelle, these were all law enforcement officers trying to kill him: "I'm not one hundred percent sure, Charles, but I'd bet everything that these are *all* cops. Maybe you could tell by the video . . ."

And that's where this all got serious, when Ms. Scott pulled out a copy of the videotape a few weeks earlier.

Pullman's mind wandered backward, wondering how anyone could have seen this liaison. *How could they? She was alone with me . . . in my house.*

But now, even that wasn't so much a mystery anymore. He didn't have the marshals' round-the-clock protection back then. So maybe someone had been creeping around. Pullman couldn't bear those thoughts any longer: Peeping Toms at his windows.

Instead, he considered the danger he was in, his memory revisiting those images on the video while Michelle described things. He observed the hard-bodied, tough-talking men. There was a side profile here and there, but nobody who Pullman could say he recognized.

How many cops had traveled through his courtroom? How many indeed.

"My camera," Michelle was saying, "is imbedded in my pen, Charlie. So you can imagine the time I had trying to direct anyone. I flat-out pointed in each man's face . . . *hey you . . . okay, now you*. Can you imagine? It's the only copy.

That is, you have the only copy; the original is still on my bookshelf."

Pullman wondered about that.

"First Corinthians," she said. And she chuckled some. "My Bible is phony. The tape is stored inside."

"I see. And your pen did all this?" he asked, his eyes still on his bedroom television set. Michelle showed the Judge her pen and he looked at it from every angle.

"This thing holds videotape?"

"Not actually. It's really just an eye"—Michelle pointed to the top of the pen—"here's the side I have to point, and it sends the signal of the images or whatever to a special video recorder I keep in my purse."

And now she hopped off of his bed to retrieve it. The device she produced was no bigger that an iPod.

"The things they come up with nowadays," said the Judge.

"I originally videotaped so that I could refer to the images later for my exclusive. But the idea of this underground hit squad was so . . . so un*believable*," explained Michelle, her bosoms jiggling there under the silk teddy, capturing his attention. "In this crazy time of political tension and uncertainty as to whom to trust, I knew I had something so hot that the world had to see it. The world had to know what they were up against."

"You speak about 'the world' as if you're from another world, sweetheart."

"I am, Charlie. Remember? I'm a reporter."

"Oh. Right. And you came down to our humble planet to do this interview. How'd you manage that?"

"I didn't. They called me. Out of the blue. Said they had a story that could make me a Pulitzer prize winner and that I should trust them. I stood near the island at 73rd Street, where Amsterdam and Broadway cross . . . they showed up with a van, I jumped in the back and they blindfolded me. That was the deal."

"No!" the Judge said in disbelief as he made a face.

"It was fine by me, really. Sometimes you've gotta take

risks to get a story. Believe me, my job at the paper is no cakewalk. There are tons of us—writers with this and that degree, a resume that stretches for two blocks. But ultimately, it's the ones with the big stories folks remember. The *exclusives*. The saying goes that there are good writers with no story, and there are those with a good story who can't write a lick. All I want is six of one, and a half dozen of the other. I want a John Wilkes Booth interview. Or Lee Harvey Oswald."

"They're dead, sweetheart. You're better off hunting for a terrorist. They'll be surfacing every few years or so, as fast as they're being born."

"That's fine by me. As long as I tell the story to the world."

"Well," Pullman sighed. "I guess you know what you're doing, Michelle. I just hope you're careful."

And the Judge pulled her closer to him on the bed as they went on to watch the video together. It was the last time they'd be intimate.

LITTLE DID MOST people know that Michelle Scott was now as dead as a doornail. And now, her killers wanted the same for Pullman. The Judge had to do some critical thinking while he still could. And it suddenly occurred to him: *If law enforcement is involved . . . if they can't be trusted, then who can?*

That conclusion woke Pullman from being so spellbound. That and the sudden *screech!* Pullman swung his head around. Neighbors stood dumbfounded on their lawns and porches. Others were bold enough to cross the street, into business that had nothing to do with them—an encounter that they could do nothing about.

The other marshal, having confirmed the dead, was now asking neighbors to get back.

The other Tahoe burned rubber backing out of the driveway, spinning out in a fog of smoke into the night air.

"Shit," exclaimed Turner. And now he was reporting the plates on the Tahoe, requesting a roadblock anywhere south of Bayer Avenue.

"Marshal . . . excuse me, marshal?"

"Yes, Judge," answered Benson.

"I need you to take me away from here."

"Sure, Judge. Just as soon as—"

"No. I need you to take me away from here now. Right now."

Marshals Turner and Benson looked at each other, and Turner was left stuttering into the mobile phone.

"No," Turner said. "Benson and I are okay—a few scratches, maybe a bit of trauma, but we'll shake it off. Just get us some backup down here quick." Turner hung up.

Benson asked, "I'm sorry, Judge Pullman, did you say you wanted us to take you away? You know we have plenty of manpower headed this way. All the protection you'll ever need, so this place is probably the safest place you could be right now."

The Judge looked out of the Tahoe's tinted windows at the neighbors in slippers and robes—probably waiting for the news reporters so they could be next in line for their fifteen minutes of fame.

"I'm afraid you're wrong," said Pullman. "To be around more police is *not* what I want right now. It's the furthest thing from my desires, do you understand me?"

"You call the shots, Judge."

"Thank you. We need to make it to the Cross County Parkway, headed for Mount Vernon. Pass me that mobile phone please."

After a brief how-to, Pullman dialed Evelyn. It was one o'clock in the morning.

"Sorry to wake you. I have a little problem . . ."

A little problem?

Within twenty minutes, Judge Pullman was at Evelyn Watson's front stoop, videotape in hand.

REGGIE JACKSON WAS more afraid than he looked. The tough-guy face was an act, a front so that nobody would fuck with him. But that's not how Reggie would put it. Reggie would substitute it with just an F. "Yo, F that dude, man . . . yeah, and F you too!" It was just one of those fads he'd grown into—heard it at the movies.

And now, he was the one who was F'd, handcuffed to a bench down at the 28th Precinct.

A fight had broken out on the sidewalk in front of P.J.'s Lounge on 132nd at Adam Clayton Powell Boulevard. It started out with one person calling another person a fake nigga on account of some knock-off Rolex he had on. From the nasty comment, things escalated to a push and a few shoves. Then, before anyone could blink, shots were fired. But that wasn't the worst of it.

So many loiterers scattered into the street that an oncoming motorcycle and a few cars swerved to avoid hitting anyone. And in doing so, two vehicles veered out of control. One plowed into a light pole. Another skated into the sides of numerous other parked cars. The motorcyclist was forced into a slide, his bike propelling through the street in a heated race with the cyclist himself. The cyclist had been separated from his bike, left to skate headfirst along A.C.P.

Police were nearby, and, as a posse, they rounded up anyone they could get their hands on.

Ma-duke is gonna kill me was all Reggie could think. But he also wanted to kick himself in the ass, partly blaming himself for not joining the army as he had planned . . . partly blaming Uncle Push, who he felt sold him the dream about the dozens of properties he'd fix up and manage on West 128th Street.

Some dream.

Reggie was aware of just two properties that Push owned, and he didn't even own those; well, not all the way, as far as Reggie knew. It was some kind of lease-option agreement, was all he heard, *Blah, blah, blah*. What*ever*.

All Reggie cared was that the whole helium-filled dream about him in a new ride, showin' off some $500 rims, with chickenheads in thongs spilling out of his car, was not a reality. The balloon had popped long ago.

Gimme a year, his uncle Push had said. But it was past

two years now. There was some talk he heard about more properties, and about closing a deal, but Reggie had already fallen for the false images once.

And now look at him, hangin' out with that meathead, Ronnie, and Logic. Ronnie's biggest hotshot claim was that he once went to school with Cam, the rapper, while Logic was steady selling cell phone numbers and access codes that were snatched out of the air by a friend, some other brilliant criminal mind.

Reggie was more the passive member of the trio, except that *he* was the one with the magnetism, the "good home training" and the promising future. That is, maybe, until now. It was something of a sudden consideration, how this involvement with the police could prove to be a pivotal point in his life. And yet, despite the current dilemma, Ronnie and Logic were the ones to look at Reggie for life's clues. It was Reggie's company they enjoyed, a sort of confirmation of their existence; his presence certified that this was the thing to do, and that this was where to do it. At least, until now.

Reggie wasn't one to ride this wave of respect and devotion he received, it's just the way things were.

It was what it was.

Working beside his uncle for all these months was somehow growing on him. The sincerity, the conviction and even the facial expressions were having an effect on Reggie. That's why his punctured dream was hard to accept. It was unusual for his uncle not to keep his word, and so Reggie would find himself rationalizing the situation: *My dream is a work in progress. It's coming . . . one day. The car, the girls . . . one day.* Push was a man who meant what he said and who held stable opinions. There was that face he made when something didn't seem right, as if tapped from some higher power.

The things that Reggie was having a hard time keeping up with (and in some instances, things he flat-out rejected, if only in his mind) were Push's discipline, his hard-work ethic and his willingness to endure tough challenges. Reggie always found himself saying, *There must be an easier way.*

Perhaps it was Reggie's youth that caused him such confusion; but then, he was only nineteen, who was he to come to such conclusions about the complexities in life? For now, there were his own challenges to figure out. These "damned influences of his," as Ma-duke would call them—the two Reggie called his friends.

"Who you gonna call?" asked Logic, sitting right next to Reggie, cuffed to the same wooden bench.

Reggie was feeling the pressure, and caught himself turning a bit sarcastic. "You're the one who's supposed to be the brains in the crew. What seems *logical* to you?"

"Oh. You got jokes now."

Reggie sucked his teeth. "It ain't you. It's this F'd-up situation . . . all because of a fake-ass Rolex? *Damn*. How'm I gonna explain this BS to Ma-duke?"

Logic made a face, his most sincere in a while—like: *Don't look at me with that problem*. "Good luck," he said under his breath.

"Shit," said Ronnie from the next bench over. "They ain't gonna hold us in here. They bluffin'. Money says they let us go in less than a hour."

These were the words from an eighteen-year-old, handcuffed to a bench inside of the notorious 28th Precinct police station.

"First of all," explained Reggie, so in the mood to put things in proper perspective. "You ain't *got* no money. And secondly, we already been in here for a hour. It's almost two in the morning."

"Wake me up when the man brings the key," said Ronnie with a yawn, slumping down on the bench, the only comfort he could manage under the circumstances. "I still say they're bluffin'."

"F that," said Reggie. "I ain't sleepin', I heard about this jailhouse. They beat dudes up at will."

TWENTY MINUTES LATER, an officer showed up with a clipboard. "Okay, who needs to call Mommy and Daddy?"

Reggie made a face, not at all appreciating the way the pig was talking. "I need to call my uncle. When he finds out y'all got me down here on some bogus charges, he'll wup all your asses."

"Is that a threat, young man?"

"No. It's a promise."

"Well, ex-cuse me, because I'm *so* scared of your uncle. Who is he? Captain Marvel or Spidey? 'Cuz right now, you sure need a superhero to come out of the sky and rescue you malcontents."

"What'd you call us?" argued Ronnie, slow as usual. "Mal—what?"

"Listen. You want your phone call or not?"

Reggie gave the officer his uncle's number, already fretting the explanations he'd have to give about not showing up for work today. That had him shaking even more than the sudden lockup.

"DAMN!" PUSH BARKED after slamming the receiver in its cradle. Then he closed his eyes and squeezed his fists as tight as he could, feeling the tension throughout his body. In that fleeting instant Push recalled his own visit to the 28th Precinct police station. Even though it was two years back, the happenings were still very fresh in his mind.

The group of cops that took turns hitting him. Fists. Night sticks. Verbal jabs.

It was these memories that kept Push from rolling back onto his bed and perhaps saying to himself, "Good for him. He deserves exactly what he gets. Let him roast there for the night—that oughtta straighten him out."

But that would be too cold. This was his sister's son, for God sakes!

Push couldn't help the grunt that came up from his bowels.

He knew all too well the devils that police officers could be. Deadly choke holds. Plunger sticks up the ass. And that old "self-defense" excuse that served as the all-powerful, all-purpose excuse used so often through the decades. Police brutality was no joke in New York (and certainly not any-where else). There would always be the individuals who made it on the force with their malicious intentions.

But all of the ills within the world of law enforcement were irrelevant to Push until now. They had his nephew down there. *His nephew!?*

The mere idea of it was no better than the taste of fresh dog shit on his tongue, an idea he couldn't stand to think about.

He had an urge to strap up and roll on that police station like a juggernaut . . . guns blazin'. He'd show his indiffer-ence toward their lives just as they had toward civilians time and again. But Push was civil-minded, or at least he was try-ing to be. This was a desperate situation, however. And it could very well call for desperate measures. There was only one person Push knew with the clout to prance in and out of precincts, and who was close enough to him and his ex-tended family to take on this challenge as aggressively as if Reggie were her own son.

AND WHO SAID that timing wasn't everything?

When Evelyn's telephone rang, she was up having coffee with Judge Pullman and Marshals Turner and Benson. Turner was the black one with the crew cut and thin mustache. Ben-son was white with no facial hair, and his head of brown hair was cut in a military fashion—high and tight, they called it.

At close to 3 A.M. the four of them were sitting, discussing the events of the previous evening.

There were peculiar looks between the marshals that, maybe, required some reading between the lines. However, considering the threat to her good friend, Evelyn focused her attention. That is, until the telephone rang and every one of them froze, with every eyeball glued and wondering.

"This *has* to be a wrong number," said Evelyn, hoping that one of these marshals hadn't given her number to one of their secret agent friends. But then she was embarrassed, re-alizing that there was no way for them to know her number. Unless—and Evelyn turned toward the Judge, a gesture which he shook his head at.

Finally she said, "Nobody calls this late . . . not since I was young and wild." She got to the phone and raised her finger for extended silence.

"Hello?"

A voice said, "Ms. Watson? I feel really bad about this, but—"

"Who is this?"

"It's Push, Ms. Watson."

"Mister, do you know what time it is?"

"Yes, ma'am, and I'm real sorry, but . . . I—"

"Mr. Jackson, unless you are calling me from a jail cell, or you're confessing about a crime, I suggest that you call me during the daytime. You know my office hours."

"But, Miss Watson—"

"Good night, Mr. Jackson." And Evelyn hung up, turning to make a face to the others.

"Some nerve," she said. "Can you believe that was one of my probationers?" She wagged her head, telling herself that Push would somehow pay for the indiscretion. But at that very instant, she caught herself slipping. *Push? Shit, I should've treated him a lot better.*

Evelyn's thoughts raced around; she never would've spoken that way, *especially* not to Push, if there wasn't her present company to consider. Jesus. Two U.S. marshals and Judge Pullman? She had half the federal government over her house!

Okay, so she was exaggerating. But *really*, she couldn't afford too much exposure with certain relationships. If Charles ever found out that—

Evelyn had to get right. She was set to apply herself, to jump back into the conversation, but the phone rang again.

This time she *did* recognize the number on the caller ID screen.

"Gentlemen, you must excuse me while I take this in another room." And Evelyn put on the act again, marching into the kitchen and snatching the phone off of the wall. Before she said a word she had to take a deep breath. She considered apologizing.

"Push—"

"Miss Watson. Sorry about the time, but it's my nephew, Reggie. He's in some mess down at the 28th Precinct." And Push explained as best as he could about the situation.

"Slow down, Push. Take your time."

"My nephew may not be perfect, Ms. W, but he's no criminal. He was just in the wrong place at the wrong time. But I'm afraid of what they'll do to him down there."

Evelyn remembered the 28th Precinct and the trauma that Push had experienced. He was a horrible sight on that cold morning two years earlier. She still felt a little uneasy about it; about not getting him out of there sooner. But people might've gotten suspicious had she sprung him so quickly.

Some things you had to live with.

But now, this mention of Reggie being down there, perhaps coping with those same inhumane conditions, maybe reliving his uncle's past, was a chilling thought. "Push, you know I have no jurisdiction over your nephew. He's not on my caseload. He's not even on probation. So how would I be able to help?"

"I know, Ms. W. But you know them folks down there. And, well . . . I was thinking since Reggie and I have the same first and last names . . ."

Jesus, no, he didn't go there. He wants me to lie—to say that his nephew is on my caseload, when he isn't. How naive . . .

In that instant, Evelyn's mind went for a wild ride. It was as if she'd closed her eyes and opened them a second later only to find herself on a roller coaster. She was in the first car, soaring down, down, down, and then coming up for a double loop. All the while, she was seeing the images: Push stepping out from beneath that brownstone to squeeze off two slugs into the body of the man who'd beaten his sister . . . Push making Swiss cheese out of one of the three who had killed his parents . . . and then Push fulfilling the hit on Sara Godfrey, the hit that Evelyn actually helped to set up.

No, he didn't know that she arranged it.

Evelyn still kept that authoritative demeanor when Push

showed up at her office for his monthly visits. However, she continued to harbor these secrets. Secrets she had to keep to herself about so many lives that were destroyed by one man, but for good reasons. These images came at Evelyn like a whirlwind, all of it suddenly opening her mind to an idea— a solution to her problem with Judge Pullman.

"Push?" Evelyn was back in the present. The now. There was a sudden energy in her tone. Energy that even *she* wasn't ready for.

"Yes, Ms. Watson?"

"Meet me at the 28th Precinct—that is, *outside* the 28th, in thirty minutes."

"Yes, ma'am," Push answered.

But Evelyn had already ended the call. After a deep breath, she whirled around with deep devotion, determined to go through with this.

HE WAS STANDING right there.

"Charles. *Jesus*, you scared the *shit* outta me—" Evelyn shivered, her head and lips shaking off the instant shock. "Don't *do* that."

"Always the disciplinarian, hunh, Evelyn?"

"With all the men I gotta deal with? There's no other way, Charles."

"In that case, I feel sorry for Peter. How's he holdin' up, anyway?"

"Your stepson is gonna be the death of me. I wish he'd hurry up and heal that leg of his, down the stairs, up the stairs, down. I need an elevator in this house."

A half chuckle as Pullman said, "I don't know what he was thinking going out there, mountain climbing."

"Wiser words were never said," replied Evelyn. "Maybe his job was getting to him . . . that, or he's got that Jack and the Beanstalk syndrome." She and Charles laughed aloud.

"You kept our promise, didn't you, Evelyn?"

"Don't worry, Charles. He's still on painkillers. The only two things he knows about now are food and sex. Oh, and sleep. I couldn't bear to get him worried about his stepfather, who happens to be ducking bullets and running from some outlaw police officers . . ."

One of the marshals came to the threshold of the kitchen. "I was wondering where the bathroom was."

Evelyn gave him the eye and the twisted lips. "About-face, and make a left. It's the room with the toilet."

There was that slight embarrassment, and the lawman disappeared.

"Do I have any privacy in my own house?"

Evelyn took the Judge's arm, escorting him to the kitchen table. "Sit down, Charles. I want to run something by you. It could help with your L.T.K. problem." Evelyn was sure to keep her voice low, in case there was a second fly on the wall.

Charles took a seat, asking, "Does this have anything to do with you being at the 28th Precinct in thirty minutes?"

"I see your hearing is working better than ever," said Evelyn, raising an eyebrow at Pullman. And now she too was settled at the kitchen table. "This is a small problem, Judge. I'm gonna need you to make a phone call. That's number one. Number two, you and I are gonna have to arrange for your escape from these two minutemen."

"Escape?"

"Shhh . . . Judge, you're not safe here."

"Evelyn, they saved my life. They're legit."

"So it seems. And how about me?"

"You too, Evelyn. Christ, you're practically my daughter."

"We're only engaged, Charles. I say that because if I have to run up and down those steps one more time for his whims, you're gonna have one dead stepson on your hands and a woman on death row who would've been your daughter."

Pullman rolled his eyes and shook his head. Thank God there were still a few things to be amused about.

"But let's be serious here . . ." Evelyn got up to check on Turner and Benson, still in the next room.

Pullman swept the kitchen with a quick glance, admiring the bright colors, the plants and the floral wallpaper. You could take a deep breath in here and feel nature's essence.

"I told 'em to kick their feet up. I hope they get the message," Evelyn said once she stepped back into the kitchen. "Now, where were we?"

"The escape."

"Oh, yes. You've got to trust me, Charles. And you've got to do exactly as I ask . . ."

Evelyn pulled up the wall phone from its cradle and dialed 411. "I need the number for the 28th Precinct police station, please."

"COME ON, PRIMO. We got everything," said Ape, looking back and forth nervously, wondering if anyone was witnessing this.

The two had driven just a mile away from Bayer Avenue, and were now parked on the shoulder of Mosholu Parkway, dumping the truck. There was nothing but trees and grass out here, a car passing by at 50 mph every so often. So he was probably being paranoid about things.

Ape was bouncing in place now, constantly eyeing the grassy embankment for the direction that they'd be running . . . *as soon as Primo finished wiping the fucking fingerprints from the truck. Shit!*

This was not a game. With two dead marshals lying in the back of the Tahoe, there was enough flesh, blood and badges to hang *and* electrocute Primo and Ape eight or nine times over. So, regardless of how uneasy Ape was getting, Primo was doing the right thing. And besides that, he'd sleep better knowing he did a thorough job. And to think that the doctors called him a bona fide mental case.

When he was sure all the fingerprints were gone, Primo threw the gearshift into neutral, sending the truck for an easy descent down the embankment. With each passing second, the truck picked up speed until it finally took its last hop into the Bronx River.

There was no explosion, no big crashing noise; the truck, once discovered, might even make it to auction someday, sold to some poor soul who'd never know its true history.

The other side of Mosholu Parkway led to a public park,

and beyond that was a city street. Despite it being three in the morning, Primo and Ape didn't have to wait long for a taxi to pass by, and then another, to take them to their respective homes, both of them deliberating on the explanation they'd give Uncle Sam come midday.

CHAPTER SIX

WHILE MIMS AND the others failed up in Yonkers, a bigger picture was being painted elsewhere in the city. Six other L.T.K. members were in Manhattan, Queens and Brooklyn, taking care of business as usual.

Ryan "Turk" Jones, the ex–D.E.A. agent who lost an eye in the line of duty, and Milton "Pistol" James, the L.T.K. munitions expert, both went uptown to the Bronx. On Gunhill Road, just outside of the subway station, the Roots Crew hustled dope each night as though they had a license to do so.

The ongoing agreement was that L.T.K. would ensure the group's nightly transactions, permitting the thugs to peddle their smack freely, without concerns about law enforcement intervention. Even if there was some hotshot squad that targeted the area, the Roots Crew would be forewarned and the $500,000-a-week operation would resume once things cooled down again.

The arrangement had been going very well for almost three months—until the pushers began coming up short on L.T.K.'s $50,000 weekly shakedown fee. Uncle Sam not only decided to impose a late penalty, but he also called for a "warning."

And so, with Pistol behind the wheel, Turk sat in the backseat with the window lowered and two 9mm Uzis pointing out. With no concern about incidentals—like local business owners or pedestrians—Turk sprayed the street with continuous gunfire, emptying two full clips and sending dozens of people diving for cover.

When the smoke cleared, there were no fatalities; however, a number of injured victims were rushed to Montefiore Hospital for bullet wounds, cuts and bruises. The blame would fall in the lap of the Roots Crew.

Further downtown, on Fordham Road, Jose "Sanchez" Martinez and Erskin "Skin" Yates, both of whom still maintained their day jobs as a U.S. Customs agent and NYC Transit cop, respectively, went for their monthly meet with the Jamericans, a group of hijackers who went after 18-wheelers trucking hi-tech equipment for a living, and high-priced SUVs as a pastime. The meeting ended as usual, with the two cops driving back to The Abyss with $100,000 in a duffel bag.

Don "Chico" Cortez and Tyrone "Duck" Flowers were on an entirely different mission. No short 'n sweet drive-bys or cash pickups for them. Armed with semiautomatics and wearing ski masks, the two were parked in a stolen evergreen Pathfinder jeep down in Chinatown. Parked just behind them were five more L.T.K. gunmen in a jet-black Lincoln Town Car. The minute the drug kingpins, Bobby Chin and Chang Lee, stepped out of the King Chow Fun restaurant surrounded by four of their bodyguards, Chico and Duck led their seven-man hit squad in a robbery that went down like clockwork. One of the kingpin's henchmen was carrying an attaché case handcuffed to his wrist. That was just fine by L.T.K., since they'd have one less hand to be concerned about.

The Triads were already outnumbered; the odds were in favor of L.T.K.

Turk immediately noticed one of the mobsters reaching under his blazer. "Freeze, muthafucka! You understand English? Hunh? Tell 'im to take his hand from his body, Chin! I'll splatter 'im! I swear to God!"

"Get your hands up, Chang! You too!!" shouted Duck.

The Triads were hesitant, but obedient. Soon they all had their hands raised or at least suspended some.

"Who are you to call me by name?" asked Bobby Chin as the masked men patted him and his comrades, pulling weapons out from under their blazers and from their waistbands.

"We're good friends. That's all you need to know. Just make sure to tell your boys to behave—we wouldn't wanna get your blood all over the sidewalk, not here in front of the King Chow."

"Shit, why not here," noted another L.T.K. goon. "The less food they'll have to buy for the restaurant . . . just a little clean up, some choppa-chop-chopping and there ya have your main course!"

Laughter followed the tasteless joke. "I bet he tastes better than the dogs and cats they serve!" More laughter.

Now the one with the attaché case swung it at the closest head. He connected, throwing the goon back to the pavement.

"Shit!" Chico retaliated with the butt of his AK-47, striking not the one with the attaché case, but Chang Lee, who instantly toppled over into the arms of Bobby Chin. Chico then cocked the assault weapon, about to fire at the Triad with the money.

"Chico, no!" shouted Turk.

The other Triads were looking straight into the barrels of this and that weapon. Heads were still but eyes were darting, everyone looking for an opportunity, or perhaps the next assault. Then Bobby Chin said something in Cantonese, a command that his soldiers obeyed and that the L.T.K. took to mean surrender. He was kneeling with his unconscious partner.

"Please!" Chin finally said to his masked assailants. "Do not shoot. I'm sure we can work this out."

"Yeah, we can work it out just fine. Take that suitcase off of his wrist. Unlock it now!"

"I'm afraid that you are—you call me by name, but I cannot see behind your mask." While Bobby spoke, the street began to change its face. Traffic had stopped partway up the block. Patrons inside of King Chow and nearby businesses were peeking from the various picture windows. He went on to say, "If you know my name, you know my reputation. And if that is the case, you are very mistaken."

"Is that so?"

"Go now, and we will disregard this incident. There has been no harm done here." The way Bobby Chin looked up at the L.T.K. with that condescending way was the expression of a wise young leader. Behind those eyes was a promise of violence and death if his requests were not met. "Go. While there's still time. Go," he repeated.

"Here's what I think of your reputation, asshole." And those words were followed by spit, the glob hitting Chang Lee in the face.

Bobby looked down at his partner and wiped the spit away. Then he looked back up with half-lidded eyes, eyes that were determined for revenge.

"Now, if you don't unlock the briefcase, I'll shoot you in the head myself."

The nose of the assault weapon pressed against Bobby's temple. There was silence all around. A calm could be sensed throughout the atmosphere.

Bobby said some gibberish again, and the Triad with the attaché put his hand out for the key.

Once the money was passed, each of Bobby Chin's gangsters was brought to their knees—kicks to the backs of their legs, gun butts to their spines—and plastic cuffs were produced, wrapped around their wrists as easily as a matador might restrain a bull.

A faint sound of sirens waged a sense of threat over the operation, and the L.T.K. backed away from the area, hopped into their waiting vehicles and sped away.

Some of those employed at King Chow rushed out to free the Triads from the plastic ties, and Chang Lee was carried inside to be nursed back to consciousness.

Bobby Chin was speechless before his disciples. This was the most embarrassing event of his life, and it would not go unanswered.

"Ki!" he barked. And when Ki was close enough, Bobby grabbed the man's lapels, more or less sharing his rage. In Cantonese, Bobby growled, "Chico! You find out about this Chico! I want him alive. I want him breathing!"

◆ ◆ ◆

THE GROUP THAT executed that successful hit on the Triads returned to Uncle Sam with the attaché case and indulged in a celebration. The case sat open on a table for all to see as they recalled the hit in detail. A quarter-million-dollar job.

"Did you see that prick's face when you spit on Chang?"

"Yeah. He looked like a nightstick got shoved up his ass!"

Laughter.

"And the shit you said about eatin' cats and dogs! I almost pissed myself, that shit was so funny!"

"You shoulda gone ahead and wet y'self, then; that way we coulda left 'em somethin' to drink!"

Big laughs.

"Any word from Mims yet?"

"Nothing yet," said Uncle Sam. "But then, we're not supposed to hear anything till noon tomorrow."

Duck nodded and said, "That looks like a hell of a birthday present," indicating the neatly stacked money.

"Yeah," said Sam. "A bit belated, but it'll do."

Chico approached the two now. It was clear that he'd had one too many.

"Hey, great party, but I gotta go."

"You're not going anywhere like that," said Sam. "Duck, take him home to the wife. He needs a little assistance."

"You got it, boss."

"Lemme go! I can at least *walk* myself," said Chico.

On the way to Brooklyn, Duck asked the red-eyed Chico, "I thought you two were getting divorced?"

Chico began laughing.

"What's so funny?"

And that question encouraged further laughter.

"Whatever," muttered Duck.

The next thing Duck knew, Chico had grabbed the cell phone, punched in a number and brought it to his ear. While waiting for an answer, Chico said, "Take the next exit off the Belt." Then into the phone he said, "Hey, it's me. Yeah, I know it's late, but I just won a whole lot of money out in Atlantic City . . . I thought I'd give you some. Are you alone?"

While Chico listened to the response, Duck shot him a perplexed look.

"Good. Anything to help you out," said Chico. "Just throw on a robe and come to the front door. I have enough money to help you with the next six months' worth of expenses . . . yes, that much." He told his wife to hurry up and ended the call. "Take a left turn at Linden."

"Okay. Curiosity is killing me, Chico. Atlantic City? Money? What's goin' on?"

Chico turned to Duck with a devilish smile, but he still left his L.T.K. associate in the dark, saying, "Take a right turn when you get to two-o-six."

Soon, the car was double-parked out in front of a wheat-brown-sided house on 206th Street, although it all appeared gray in the dark.

"Wait for me, this won't take long." And Chico hopped out and trekked up the walkway.

The light over the doorway flickered on. Chico's wife appeared just inside the screen door and opened it for him to enter. Duck caught her strained expression just before she shut the door behind her.

It was the last time anyone but Chico would see her alive.

"YOU HAVEN'T BEEN home in three days, Chico. And now you're callin' me at three in the morning, talking about bringing me money? What's this about?"

"I just had to say farewell."

Shock and fear overcame Mrs. Cortez when she found herself facing the .357 Magnum in her husband's hand. Before she could make a sound, Chico shot her in the head at close range.

Even as the woman lay dead, with part of her head torn away, Chico stood over her and fired a second shot into the corpse.

The body jerked.

Duck hopped out of the sedan at the sound of the shot.

Then he saw the flash inside the house to accompany the second shot fired. He was sure they weren't taking pictures in there. But he was even more concerned that there might be a dispute or a robbery in progress. Unconcerned with the lights popping on in the neighboring homes, Duck unholstered his pistol and raced toward the front door. At the same moment Chico emerged.

Chico said, "Come on. We gotta go."

"What the f—"

Chico spun Duck around so that they could both hurry back to the car. They hunched as they moved, hiding their faces, conscious of potential witnesses.

"What did you do? What the *hell* did you do?"

Just as they reached the car, Chico replied with a tight grin, "I finalized the divorce. Now let's move it before somebody calls the police."

PUSH DIDN'T HAVE to wait long. Evelyn came out of the 28th Precinct police station with Reggie and his two friends after just ten minutes inside.

Push was careful not to punish his nephew with a hard look, but at the same time he had some difficulty with being grateful.

He pulled it off, however, roughing his hand atop of Reggie's nappy hair as the group of them made their way back to Evelyn's new Volvo sedan.

"Reggie, after we drop your buddies you're gonna stay at my place. I already talked to your mother—don't worry, she doesn't know about tonight. I told her you were with me." Push looked back over the seat, fully understanding the relief Reggie exhibited. Then he looked at Ms. Watson, not so sure he wanted to be such a good liar in her presence.

This evening—although it was now the early morning—took their relationship, that probation officer/ex-con rapport, to another level indeed. The full weight of this favor Push asked for hadn't made its impact until now. Reggie and his friends were free from the jaws of the 28th Precinct.

Since Ms. Watson didn't have any special connection

with Push (that he was aware of) outside of the visits he had to make to her office every fourth Friday, he was probably just another name and number on her caseload. So there was a big question to be answered here.

Why had she gone out of her way to help?

A bigger question was, what would he owe her now that she had done such a favor? After all, Push had been willing to do nearly anything to get Reggie out of that bind. But it was a price he could not assess. These thoughts weighed heavily on his conscience as the night gradually came to an end.

"I'll be up shortly, Reggie. Yvette and, well, a couple of visitors are inside, so don't be loud and wake everybody."

"I won't, Uncle Push. And thank you, Ms. Watson."

"Don't mention it, Reggie. Just keep your nose clean for me, you hear?"

With utter relief, Reggie answered, "No *question*."

This night had asked so much of Push, so suddenly. Not only did he have to stoop so low, asking a favor from a woman whom he had no business calling at three in the morning, but he'd also had to call Yvette and ask her to come and watch Sharissa and Stacy.

It occurred to Push that the Wallace girls were fast asleep and probably would be until morning. He could shoot down to the police station and, hopefully, return with Reggie and everything would be fine. However, his conscience told him no. He couldn't leave these girls alone. They'd been left alone enough. And Push quickly recalled how dangerous life was as a child without parents.

"I'll explain later," Push told Yvette before he'd left. And Push was sure there'd be even more to explain, knowing that Reggie's arrest—could it even be *called* an arrest?—couldn't stay a secret for long.

But that was drama that he'd address later. Right now, here was Ms. Watson sitting across from him in the front seat of her car like some unpaid bill.

He wasn't receiving any such signals from her, but he

couldn't help telling himself, *I'll die if this is some kind of sexual thing she's gonna ask for*.

Not that Ms. Watson wasn't attractive, because in her own way she was. Push figured her to be in her late forties, a healthy full-figured woman with a glowing coffee complexion and large glistening eyes. Her silver-gray hair was at least deceiving, making her appear older and more sophisticated than Push imagined she actually was. He had clocked her alternate hairstyles over the past two years; a golden color once upon a time, absolute blonde at another, brown, black. Push guessed that these weren't themes she experienced, but phases she was going through. Or maybe she just liked to play games with her hair.

There was a time he wondered about her sexuality. Never did they discuss her personal life during their monthly meetings, although she was definitely all up in his. That was her job, however, to be all in his business. And she was thorough, he had to admit. But Evelyn Watson was one of those mysterious people who Push was forced to cope with in life. And if it were up to him, there'd be absolutely *none* of them.

"So, I feel like I owe you," Push finally said.

"Humph, a bit," Ms. Watson replied. "I hope you don't think I do this for everyone."

"I didn't think so. So . . . why did you do it?"

"Let's just say I need a favor from you."

Whoa! There it is, on the table. You asked for it.

Push turned his eyes away from her. 128th Street had changed a lot since he'd begun to renovate. You could say this area was officially under construction.

As far as he could see, all the way down to Fifth Avenue, was going to belong to him one day. But for now most of the properties were run-down and deserted, their front doors and windows sealed with cinder blocks.

Where Ms. Watson was double-parked in front of 440, there were other vehicles, all belonging to the tenants who occupied Push's residences. Looking ahead, all Push could see was the work, the challenges and the inevitable complications.

These were all responsibilities that he'd have to address, and he'd do so no differently than before, without compromise. Push couldn't help wondering just exactly what Ms. Watson wanted.

She asked, "Can I have an hour of your time?"

Oh, shit. It is *a sex thing.*

"When?" asked Push, thinking about his things-to-do list that Yvette set up for him.

"Right now," she replied with confidence. "I'm gonna need to take you up to Westchester, near my house."

Aww, shit. This woman does not beat around the bush.

Push revisited those thoughts he had while sitting in Ms. Watson's office. It was merely something to do during those boring moments; to imagine her naked, maybe seated on her desk with her legs spread apart. Ms. W would go on with her questions: *Any problems you need to tell me about? Any arrests? How's business?* Instead of yawning and making an already sour interaction worse, Push just let his imagination wander. It helped him cope with it. It kept a sincere smile on his face in light of irritating circumstances. Now, was she more or less proposing sex?

"Is that gonna be a problem?" she asked.

"Uh . . . I . . . No. No problem." It was the first time Push stuttered in . . . he couldn't recall. Then he remembered the first time he got with Yvette; those first intimate moments.

Oh damn! Yvette!

"Uh . . . Ms. Watson. I don't think this is the right thing to do. I mean, you know I'm with Yvette 'n all. Plus she's having a—"

"Push, what are you talking about?"

"I'm talking about . . . *sex.* I ain't never cheated on her. And if I can help it, I never will."

"Push, you gotta be kiddin' me. You thought . . ." Evelyn's words cut short and she let out some hell-raising laughter. "I can't believe you would think such a thing. Push! Is that what's been going through your mind when you come to my office? Is *that* how you see me??"

"I—you—but, your house . . . and, well, you said an hour of your time. What'd you expect me to think?"

"Oh-h-h-ho—that. I just want you to *meet* somebody, Push." Evelyn wagged her head and rolled her eyes upward in a search for some sanity. "Push, this is not about sex," she said with a soft chuckle. "I assure you."

"Okay. Then what *is* it about?"

Evelyn finally pulled the Volvo out of park and drove north. There were things to talk about. Things that were no laughing matter. "There's something you need to know. Call it my little secret I've been keeping to myself for the past two years . . ."

To lighten the mood, Push interjected, "What? You have a crush on me?"

Evelyn didn't mind the kindhearted joke and she flashed one of those phony smiles that lasted two seconds before it dropped down to a frown. Push apologized, and they both laughed it off.

"Let me not beat around the bush with you, Push. Two years ago I watched you kill a man—and before you say a word, I want you to hear me out. I did my research on you. My caseload is thirty-five strong these days. I have every *kind* of ex-con that you can imagine. From the weirdos to those that have been scared straight. Too many to mention . . ."

Evelyn spoke in an unthreatening tone, however threatening the subject. At some point in her dialogue, she wondered if Push was as nervous hearing this as she was saying it. And now, she couldn't stop talking, wanting to relay her testimonial; wanting Push to maintain his confidence despite these revelations.

"But you—you are the most fearless, most aggressive person I know. You actually symbolize things I sometimes feel in my heart, but that I'm too much of a pussy to act on . . ." Evelyn had to swallow here, realizing too late her vulgar choice of words. But a switch inside of her was flipped to "I don't care," and she didn't mind telling it all.

"No. I haven't done or gone through the things you have. I

believe that life needs people like you to keep it balanced; just like the lions and tigers rip the deer apart to feed their young, people like you help set things straight. I mean, you're not the malicious type who goes around stomping every insect you see. And none of the work you've done, for the lack of a better word, was . . . can I say, *unjustified*?"

Push felt his heart racing as he wondered where Ms. W (his probation officer, for God's sakes!) was going with this. The car seemed to be closing in on him. A trap. He almost wanted to jump out of the car while it was in motion.

"Of course, that's only my opinion, but . . . I just believe that in this day and age life needs someone like you . . . a . . . a thug. Someone who lives by the code of the streets."

Push was tuned in to every word and every gesture. She was sincere. He could see it in her eyes, even though she was looking straight ahead watching the road. Ms. Watson was speaking her heart—it was in the beads of perspiration about her brow and in her trembling voice.

"Maybe you don't feel this way, but there are many helpless people who need a man like you. Not just the elderly, but the children, the poor . . . the good people of the world sometimes need an avenger. A . . . a superhero."

Push uttered an exhausted sound before saying, "Ms. Watson . . ."

"I think you can call me Evelyn now, Push. I think we're on another level by now."

"Okay. Well . . . Evelyn . . . that don't even sound right comin' out of my mouth. But . . . I don't know, what'd you call it? Avenger? That ain't me. I ain't no superhero. For real. I'm just anotha nigga from around the way tryin' ta eat. Tryin' to get a life. Tryin' to plant seeds for my future."

"And that's good leadership, Push. You're a role model, and you don't even know it."

"How could I be a role model with my past?"

"Oh, trust me, Push. Growing up the way you did—no parents, left out on the cold streets to deal with life on your own, taking care of your sister—and then there's your big fall . . . fourteen years in prison? Push, just to survive all of that is a success story. And you've even gone a step further; you're not sitting around, using your past as an excuse. No, you've actually started your own business. Legitimately. I can name dozens of men whose footsteps you've followed, beginning with fictional characters like Robin Hood and working up to modern-day leaders like Colin Powell. Imagine that. And Colin Powell was from Harlem, like you. He went on to become a soldier, a general. A man who led in wars and whom even the president called on for guidance and leadership."

"Ms. W—ahh . . . Evelyn, I'm far from a leader. I'm just me. I work hard and live from day to day. I don't need no medals, and I definitely ain't fightin' no wars—"

"The streets don't have wars?" Evelyn argued.

"Okay, true. But not like no world wars. You talk like I'm Superman, when I ain't no better than the next nigga they spit on. How many of us are like that? A million? A billion? I'm not a hero. I'm a survivor. And that shouldn't be the case. Wild animals are the ones who need to fight to live— people ain't supposed to live that way."

"I'll give you that, Push. Living shouldn't require that you fight to stay alive. But that's the way it is, at least for now. And that being the case, you're one of those fighters on the front line. A real warrior. A modern-day Shaka Zulu."

"See, there you go again. That was a different time. Man wasn't doin' nothin' but shootin' and killin' back then."

"Maybe not shooting." Evelyn with the correction.

"Well, using spears—whatever."

"Push, if you really see what I'm talking about, you'd recognize that just as there was good and evil back then, there's good and evil today. There's only two ways to live, Push." Push made a face; no challenge there. "So . . . I think I stand for good last time I checked. What do *you* stand for?"

"You see that boy we just dropped off? I stand for him. His mother, my sister? I stand for her. Even my woman and our baby on the way. I stand for them."

"Oh, my God. Push? You're gonna be a father?" Evelyn was able to smile and it felt good.

"She just told me," Push said, not so enthused.

"And what? You're not happy?"

"Oh, I'm happy all right. Until now—now that you dropped the A-bomb on me. You say you seen stuff, stuff that can get me locked up for life."

Evelyn shook her head. Absolute denial. "No. It's not what you think."

"Then what is it?"

Evelyn breathed hard, searching for some way to get through to him. "What about your parents?"

Push could've cut her with the look he gave.

"Push, let me tell you a little more about what I know. And please don't take it as a threat. I just want you to know we're on the same page . . . there was a young man named Chris Block, also from Harlem, who happened to die in a freak accident in prison. A weight bar crushed his neck and he—"

"What's that gotta do with me?"

Evelyn had just peeled off of the Cross Country Parkway and came to a red light, the first at this Mt. Vernon exit. But she didn't merely stop at the light, she put the Volvo in park.

"What's it gotta do with *you*? Do I need to lay it out for you, Push? Do I need to talk about the strange coincidence of you, Reginald Jackson, being right there when it happened? Do I need to talk about the FBI investigation? The other two or three convicts who were there with you? Who also happened to be from Harlem?"

Push couldn't keep looking at her. It was as though she could see in his eyes, the radar screen to his every deed.

"Here's my guess, Push. You ready? I'm guessing that Chris Block did one of two things. He was either somehow involved with you being stabbed in prison, or he was one of those creeps who murdered your parents. And I hate to play detective, but Blocks' MO was small-time burglaries. So, if I had to choose, I'd say he was—"

"Please! Do I have to hear this?"

"No. No, you don't, Push—" Evelyn put her hand on his shoulder. The touch awakened a different feeling, another way to look at her. There was compassion. "—and you don't owe me any explanations for what you did. It was in your heart. And if I was in your shoes ... if I had ability, I would've done the same."

CHAPTER SEVEN

"SO YOU MEAN to tell me, we made all this mess last night, did all the planning, so that you could fuck up the show? I put you in charge, Mims. You were the responsible one. Every angle was supposed to be covered. And now what do we have on our hands? Two dead and a judge on the loose. Fuck!"

Uncle Sam paced back and forth, there in the large sanctuary of The Abyss, kicking the already broken pews and raising a lot of dust to accompany his shouting. The echoes carried throughout the domed chapel same as it would for a preacher, only there was no congregation, only Pistol, Mule, Primo and, of course, Mims.

"How can you morons leave things undone? How could you just sleep it off till the next day?? For all I know that videotape is probably on every news desk in town! Fuckin' idiots. As if the sun would rise and solve all our problems!" he hollered.

The way Uncle Sam carried on you'd think he was a lion, prowling back and forth until he was ready to strike with those lethal claws. Mims anticipated this. The last one to cross Sam was the reporter, as good an example as any. The range downstairs still had the odor of blood lingering in the air, a reminder that you couldn't cross Uncle Sam and live to tell about it.

But Mims hadn't intentionally fucked up. He did the best

he could last night. Circumstances had spun out of control. Only he realized that there was no room for excuses. He and all the others on that mission had been trained to expect the unexpected. That's how it was on the job, and that's how it should've been last night. Mims knew better, which was why he showed up today. He figured, fuck it. Sam would either accept what happened, or he wouldn't. And if he wouldn't then Mims was ready for that too.

He wasn't one to hide like a coward.

And for this reason, Mims was packing serious heat. In addition to his Kevlar vest, both ankles were strapped with 9 millimeters. At his waist—at the small of his back and in front—he had a Glock and a nickel-plated .45 automatic. His sidearm crisscross holsters had the big work—the .357 Magnum and the .44 Ruger. All were fully loaded, safeties off; and he had additional clips in the inside pockets of his leather jacket. The jacket was closed over the vest—Mims didn't want Sam to think he posed a challenge. And his attitude followed the same theme: calm and somewhat vulnerable.

But that was part of Mims' surprise.

And now Sam had his back turned to Mims as he rambled on about the fuckup.

Mims figured the man was a little hyped up, probably from one of those high-protein drinks that Reesy fixed for him. *Where is that chunky-necked Amazon, anyway?* Mims wondered.

Sam still had his back turned—

Bad idea, Sam. Real bad idea.

—and Mims could sense something was going on beyond his eyesight.

"How can the rest of us depend on a man who blows the ball game in the ninth inning? We have our lives to think about . . . our families and our homes! The freakin' L.T.K!"

Blah, blah, blah. Get to the point, mister. I'm ready.

Now Uncle Sam had his empty hands reaching up as if he were pleading to the great heavens above. "For God's sakes! Hitler! El! I'm so sorry! We have forsaken you!" Sam's voice reached its peak, even turning hoarse.

The fuckin' fool and his theatrics.

His arms came down and his upper body buckled over so that it seemed he hurt from a bellyache.

You still have your back to me, Sam. I'm not stupid.

Mims felt that time was running out. He calculated his chances of survival, his eyes shifting here and there, weighing it all carefully. The three others were standing behind and beside Mims like some kind of guards—a rival's goons. Already he assumed the worst: they were against him. Enemies. Even Mule, who rode with him. So much for friendship.

Uncle Sam made that long-awaited turn. It was quick, but Mims was more alert than anyone could've anticipated. He knew the man was an athlete and that he was handy with he 9mm Beretta, but . . . why was he empty-handed? It was a false alarm. Maybe one of the others, Mims mused.

He turned his head slightly to take that sidelong view. Primo was behind him, so far empty-handed. The thoughts came whipping at him, all the details he knew about the goons:

Mule had that head wound going on. The bullet-head fuck. *You're too slow for me, buddy. Don't even think about it.*

Pistol was too much of a twerp, him and his bookworm eyeglasses, plus Mims was too familiar with the small man's Uzi, how he used it for drive-bys and such.

Too much weapon . . . bullets would spray everywhere.

Gotta beat him to the punch.

As for Primo, Mims thought of him as his true threat, since he and Ape had been left behind, dizzied by the Tahoe ramming them rear-first. Left for dead, was how Uncle Sam put it. But Mims had to make a life-or-death decision. He and Mule might be dead now, if not in police custody, had they hung around any longer. There might be four coffins to fill instead of two.

Don't do it, Primo. Dumb, crippled or crazy, I will fuck your ass up.

"This is hard for me, Mims. But I've gotta answer to everybody else if I don't make the right decision here . . ."

This is it, thought Mims. Sam had his back turned again. His hands were out of sight. *No, buddy.*

Mims snatched open his jacket and swung around, ducking down as he did. The maneuver was unexpected, Mims pointing his guns now—the .357 Magnum and the Glock .45 automatic. Without thinking or blinking, Mims popped Primo in his knee. A yell immediately followed the gunshot. Pistol's inaction hurt him as well, since Mims took the opportunity to quickly sidestep, grabbing Pistol's cocked elbow before the Uzi could emerge. In the chaos, Mims was behind the twerp with his arm and neck in an all-in-one half nelson, the yet-to-be-fired .357 to the man's temple. His .45 was on Mule. Pistol could only whimper helplessly.

Uncle Sam had buckled to a duckwalk, his Beretta in hand, hiding behind a heap of broken pews. As far as Mims could see, he'd made the right decision, and none too soon. Primo was still hollering, only louder, holding his leg for dear life.

"Don't do it, Sam! I'm fuckin' tellin' you. I'll blow holes right through that shit until you bleed like a waterfall." Mims put some pressure to Pistol's temple. He growled in his ear, "Tell 'im to show himself, or your next thought is gonna be lead-plated!"

Pistol didn't say the words, instead he whined like a high-pitched bitch: "Sam . . . he's gonna kill me!"

Mims rolled his eyes, finally seeing the truth behind all these so-called soldiers. "Sorry, Mule. I didn't want it to go down this way, but you see the shit I'm dealin' with. What would you do?" He swung the Glock back and forth between Mule and where Uncle Sam was crouched. "Sam, I'm leavin' out of here, and I'm leaving alive. Sorry about that, Primo, but you's the craziest mothafucka I know."

Primo grunted in response, writhing on the floor in a partially fetal position.

"Put the guns away, Mims. Don't be insane," said Sam. "Do you really think you can make it out of here alive?"

"Oh, and by saying that you expect me to drop my guns? Have you lost your fuckin' mind?" Mims fired the .357 at the wood pile. Three shots in rapid succession cut into the pews. There was a shout that was overwhelmed by the gunfire.

Mims smirked and reached down to snatch the Uzi pistol from Primo's holster. Then he approached the pile of wood where only Sam's foot could be seen.

When Mims got close enough, Sam leaped out and fired two rounds, one hitting Mims in his chest and another grazing his hip. But Mims got a shot off as well. It struck Sam in the upper right side of his chest. Sam fell back to the floor, his weapon skittering out of reach.

Mims winced and ripped the vest partially from his chest to prevent the hot lead from burning through his skin. "Now do you think I'll get out of here alive?" Mims asked, pressing the sole of his foot on Sam's chest. "See, Sam, the thing about you, about all of us, is that we're getting that untouchable mentality . . . playing judge and jury with people's lives. But that's not the problem, Sam. The problem is, if we're above the law, then who's above us? I thought about that on the way over here: When it comes down to it, we're nothin' but a band of unruly mobsters. And if I'm already unruly, who are you to tell me what to do? Here I am putting my life on the line, and for what? For a little more money? To hear you talk shit to me?"

Uncle Sam grunted. The pain hammering at him.

"Aw, shit, Sam. That ain't shit but a shoulder wound. You'll be fine. I'll even call Doc for you and poor Primo over there." Mims was checking the other three periodically, taking nothing for granted. "And for your information, I am gettin' out of here. You just need to be grateful that I'm letting you live," said Mims. And he began backing out of the church.

"I'll take this as my severance pay," he said, picking up the duffel bag that had been brought in an hour or so earlier. "And don't think about sending anybody to get it back. Remember, I know how to shoot . . ." Mims hadn't reached the double doors when out of nowhere Reesy reached around and bear-hugged him.

"Uncle! I got 'im, Uncle!" she said with her husky voice.

Unwilling to give up now, Mims lifted his right leg up and slammed it down, the heel of his boot cutting into

Reesy's foot. She instantly released him, crying out with a yelp. Mims turned around and smacked her with the barrel of the Magnum. "Dumb bitch." Mims hopped in his Corsica, telling himself to hell with this L.T.K. bullshit. And he thought about returning home to make up with Tuesday. He missed his daughters like he missed oxygen. Only a responsible husband and father would take that first step, no matter how hard it was, toward reconciliation.

YVETTE MADE UP her mind to go for it. She figured she only had one life to live, knowing what a good man she had, with his baby on the way and the business opportunities she helped him manage. And besides, she knew enough about what she was doing to be safe . . . to not get caught. This, Yvette considered, was merely a matter of heart. Hers.

"Okay, Rooney. What's it gonna take to close this deal?" Yvette asked this while sitting there in front of his desk, her legs pressed together and her purse in her lap as if she had to pee, or more specifically, as if she was about to commit all the money she had to make this work.

"Well, now you're talkin', sweetie."

"Uh, Rooney, before we go on, you need to cut the sweetie stuff. My name is Yvette, or Ms. Gardner. I'm a businesswoman. And might I add that I'm engaged to a very . . . how should I put this . . . brutish man. In other words, he wouldn't appreciate it if you spoke to his woman like that. So lose the chauvinism, your womanizing eyes and the steamy tone in your voice."

Rooney cleared his throat and sat up in his seat. To make the medicine go down easy.

Yvette said, "I don't mean to be harsh, I just wanna get down to business."

"Sorry to be so rude, ahem, Ms. Gardner."

"No offense taken. Now let's have it."

"Here are the figures," Rooney said, swiveling around in his executive chair. Meanwhile, Yvette had her calculator out. "You say this Murphy guy wants two hundred thousand for each property?"

"That's right. Four hundred thousand altogether."

"Whoa . . . well, here's the deal. My company can give you the first mortgage on the property, but we're gonna need an inflated appraisal."

"Inflated?"

"Yes. There are certain licensed appraisers who, for a price, will give you what's known as an M.A.I. appraisal. Any bank will accept such a document at its face value. The loan officer won't go out and double-check after the appraiser. The house can be made of playing cards for all they care. The bottom line is they take the appraiser's word in good faith."

"Okay. So break it down for me. Layman's terms, please."

"Your slumlord wants a total of four hundred thousand, and you only have forty-eight thousand in equity. So there's a difference of three hundred fifty-two thousand. Trust me, any bank is gonna want you to have a little more equity. So basically, we're gonna need an appraisal to come in at a hundred, maybe a hundred and fifty thousand over the true value of the property."

"Wait. Are you saying the M.A.I. guy is gonna make the property seem like its value is almost double? How's he gonna do that?"

"It's kind of sticky, really. Let's say your property is really worth three hundred thousand. Well, what they do is make up phony appraisals for the properties to the left and to the right."

"Three appraisals?"

"Well, see, it's basically an illusion. Its not like they actually appraise those properties. They just fix up some documents, backdate them accordingly and do some other razzle-dazzle with the numbers. Bottom line is that they know what the bank looks for. They do this type of thing every day. It's their livelihood."

"Wow. You learn something every day."

"Now, you'll have some steep monthly payments, because the mortgage-debt will be about six hundred thousand."

"How much is steep?"

"Oh, I figure seven grand, give or take . . ."

Yvette's eyes widened at the thought. *God, we're already paying four.*

But Rooney went on to say, "Mind you, that can fluctuate depending on what interest rates are and how many years you want the loan to stretch."

As long as possible, thought Yvette. "Do they have loans that'll stretch for life?" she asked, not expecting an answer. She already realized that this would be a difficult decision, and harder still to carry out.

After Rooney made a face, he asked, "Now you're taking in close to seven thousand a month in rents, is that right?"

Yvette nodded.

"Then you should be okay. Only, you'll have to weigh in all of your other expenses . . .'cuz I'll tell ya now, there's a downside to this."

"What do you mean by that? Downside?"

"Well, let's say you raise the rents to cover your expenses. And everything goes well for one year—six years, even. Then, just when the property value has increased enough to reach your appraised value—I'm talking about the price that our M.A.I. man quotes today—let's say one of your renters dies, and maybe another loses a job; you never know, Ms. Gardner. But if, and that's only if this should happen, you'll be short with the mortgage payment. Things begin to go downhill—"

Yvette swallowed at the idea, like some nonexistent gumball.

"Maybe you'll grow some new bills, like another child. Well, the bad news is, if the bank ever decides to check back to the beginning—back when you purchased the property—and if some hotshot loan officer should find something funny about the deal, like the hyped-up appraisal, he could very well call in the loan."

"Call in the loan? You mean, I'd have to pay it all back?"

"Every cent."

"But I thought your mortgage company was making the loan?"

"Oh, sure. In the beginning I can make this fly easy. Cash on the table. But, Ms. Gardner, I'm in business to make money, not hold paper. The day the contract closes and I pay the money, I'm gonna sell that for an instant profit. And whoever I sell it to is probably gonna sell it to somebody else. Humph . . . in six months' time, the first mortgage I give to you could change hands six times, with your monthly payments going to whoever owns the mortgage note. Most likely, a bank that is federally insured will end up with the paper."

Yvette took a deep breath.

"It's complicated. I know. But the bottom line here is this: if an investor, a bank or even a group of doctors finds out that things have been hyped up and that they'll have a problem getting paid on time . . . They're gonna most likely contact the FBI."

"You're joking."

"Does it look like I'm joking? To be honest with you, if I was in their shoes, I'd call the Feds too. But, heck, I'm gonna pass that sucker off quick since I'd have nothing to lose. I'll make money up front."

"You'd have nothing to lose. What about me?"

"Would you like the oil paint or watercolor version?"

"Just give it to me straight. Are we talking about court? A fine?"

"Court? Fines? Lady, I'm talkin' about jail. One person I know who tried this couldn't make their payments the second month, and the FBI investigated . . . he's still workin' off a ten-year stretch in a Florida federal prison."

"Ten years?" Yvette repeated faintly.

"Fraud. Bank fraud. It's all the same. These days if you do a crime and somehow weasel your way around the rules with shortcuts, they'll create a law to put you away."

"But you say that only happens when payments can't be met."

"Naturally. If you're making your payments on time, nobody gives two hoots about the how or why . . . they're happy and you're happy."

Yvette told Rooney that she needed to think about it. She went home to her Riverside condo and hammered out some numbers, determined to see the positive side of things. She considered the best-case scenario, not the worst.

Jail? Huh. People like me don't go to jail. I'm a good woman with a good heart who's God-fearing. Yvette figured she could raise the rents by $100 for each of the five tenants, projecting that $500 extra might cover additional expenses, repairs, taxes or emergencies. When that didn't seem satisfactory, she added another $100. That meant an additional $1,000 per month. The burden of raising rents $200 was a bit much, and Yvette's conscience kicked in. She wondered how she might feel if all of a sudden the landlord came to her and said, "Sorry, ma'am, I have to raise your rent."

However that idea touched her, it didn't make a true impact. It had been a long time since Yvette saw the flipside of any coin.

She was living lovely. The condo. The car. A good man. And that was another thing to think about. Push.

He hadn't yet committed to marriage. There was a baby on the way. There was love in the air—at least, she assumed as much.

But still, Push hadn't said it: "Yes, baby . . . I want to marry you and give our child a happy, secure home to grow up in."

Oh, sure, Push performed the duties Yvette looked for, as if he were already her husband. He made her feel like a wife, not a "wifey." But there was this thing Yvette had about the license, the ceremony and the rings. She wanted to someday live that big dream, an event that would complete her.

There was so much to think about. So much. But in the end, she'd commit all of her life savings to make this work.

We'll never default on a payment. It will never come to that.

And after Yvette told herself these things, she cried. It was a painful, distressed, angry-at-the-world cry that wet her blouse and bra like a heavy sweat. In bed she hugged the pillow and soaked that too. She had just made the hardest decision of her life.

THIS WAS ASONDRA'S dream all along, to live a prosperous life; a glamorous life, as the wife of someone with money, power and respect. She never could've imagined herself in such an amazing life. She had her fill of the street life and its thug-celebrities. No more mack daddies or sugar daddies such as she had once upon a time.

Roy Washington, the loan shark.

Tonto, the dope pusher.

Rufus, the credit card thief and numbers runner.

Finally, no more risking her life or indulging in what others wanted. It was all about her, her son, Trevor, and her husband, Fred, now. The Allen family. It tickled her to think about it . . . to say it.

The Allen family. Asondra shivered with delight. It was the big picture, how her life had changed so dramatically from that woman with no choice to a woman of many means. Yesterday, she was a vamp and a vixen. Ass up and face down . . . in the pillows.

Today, she still had a little bit of slut in her, but at least it was her choice to go there. (And Fred's pleasure.)

Today, Asondra didn't have to settle for less. She had her own six-figure bank account. She had triple-A credit, with plenty of gold and platinum credit cards to shop with. There were so many other devices she could claim ownership of, like the cell phone that was also a two-way pager, that was also a BlackBerry, that was also a digital camera and a place where she could trust that all of her personal data could be stored. Her phone list: the housekeeper's pager number, her accountant's private number, the numbers to a half dozen boutiques, her doctor and dentist, all of Fred's contact information and, of course, the phone numbers, birth dates and even the dress sizes of her two business partners.

Asondra was co-owner of Heavenly Glam, a full-service salon that she and her best friends, Mya Powell and Lola Brown, operated on 125th Street, in the heart of Harlem.

The business stuck out like a glittering diamond with a waiting list just to get into the appointment book.

Heavenly Glam was a business that other women could look up to, with a constant presence in the various trade magazines and frequent representation at the area's beauty shows and expos. *Salon Magazine* had already featured Glam on its cover, including a six-page spread inside. Asondra, Mya and Lola had themselves a prize.

Aside from her responsibilities with the salon, Asondra was appointed as Fred's director of the Harlem Empowerment Fund.

Her job was simple. Keep your eyes and ears open, Fred told her. And that meant she'd serve as the sensitivity the fund was missing. Red tape and bureaucracy always tended to alienate folks, and Fred knew that. More important, Asondra's foot in the stream of Harlem commerce gave the Fund an edge in terms of what businesses and ideas were bankable ones and who were the personalities who spearheaded these ventures.

Asondra had her finger on that pulse.

Neither position, be it at the salon or with the CBH—Committee for a Better Harlem—required Asondra's full-time presence. So there was more than enough time to give to her son and husband. She wasn't quite the stay-home mom, not with all of the events she had to attend—the Chamber of Commerce, 100 Black Women, the NAACP—and with the more social functions—The Essence Festival, the Black Cotillion and, of course, Wendy's Dons & Divas gatherings. But then, wasn't this all part of the lifestyle? The dream?

Asondra was thirty-two years old now. So why shouldn't she have a life?

Everything was so enchanting. She loved the way she looked and what she represented in the way of womanhood. She couldn't see herself falling backward, no matter what.

After the fairy-tale marriage to Fred, who was still the right-hand man to Congressman Percy Chambers, life seemed to fall right into place, with the cards all in Asondra's favor. She had the most incredible wardrobe! From the chartreuse

Panne-Velvet gowns, to the mauve silk side-tie skirts, to the Dolce & Gabbana tops, to the Fortuna Valentino shoes, and enough Tiffany jewelry and Gucci handbags to suit the most imaginative ghetto princess.

She had it all.

For her last birthday, Fred not only pampered Asondra from head to toe, but he purchased the full spring and summer clothing lines from Baby Phat, Seven jeans, and Lady Enyce, with select pieces from Roberto Cavalli.

Whatever she didn't have use for, she donated to the Boys & Girls Choir of Harlem, which Trevor had once been a member of.

And here was Asondra's place to indulge in it all. Her little vanity with the bulbs surrounding the mirror, as if a Hollywood star were reflected in the glass.

She could look at this picture forever—not to be conceited, but to feel okay with loving herself. Fortunately she didn't have to have any operations or other enhancements. She was fine just as she was.

It was Asondra's conviction that she deserved this. That she'd paid her dues, and that blessings never ceased. All she could do was be thankful.

She was preparing herself for an evening dinner, another top-shelf crowd that she'd set out to dazzle in the name of Mrs. Fred Allen. This wasn't like the other $1,000-a-plate dinners that Fred attended, showing her off as men in high places did with their high-maintenance women. No, this was a benefit for the Riverside Adoption Program, the same organization that would soon make the Fred Allen family complete.

Fred and Asondra both agreed that she wouldn't bear any more children. But Asondra so wanted a daughter to call her own. A girl to have to call her Mommy, to teach and guide so that she could live a childhood and a teen life that Asondra didn't have. Maybe she'd be a model, an actress or a singer. Maybe she'd be a doctor, a dentist or a psychologist. Whatever she chose to be, so help Asondra, she'd have the upper hand. She'd have all the right cards, cards that were belated in Mommy's life.

Mommy. What a chilling thought.

"Sweetheart, you really look good enough. I wouldn't want to see you overdo it," said Fred, fixing his tie as he approached Asondra.

"Ya think? I mean, I want this to be perfect. I want to look elegant. Respectable." Asondra turned her face this way and that as she spoke. Her skin glowed, like bronze. Her teeth seemed brighter than brilliant, casting a gleam when she smiled. Her eyes were shaded and lined to perfection. Her lips were a glossy rose-red and her long, free-flowing hair had been cut earlier into layers and streaked with gold highlights—it looked as though her hair and skin had been kissed by the sun.

"Baby, if you looked any prettier or any more enchanting, they'd have to arrest me."

"Arrest you? For what?" Asondra had a mix of seriousness and playfulness in her eyes.

Fred came close enough to bump noses with her, then said, "For causing a riot, baby! 'Cause you's about to create a world of commotion!"

Asondra had that girlish smile as she rose up on her toes, circled her arms around his neck and planted a wet kiss right there on his lips. "You-are-so-corny," she said, kissing Fred between each word. "But that's exactly why I love you. Causing a riot. Huh. How about a little riot right now?" she suggested, and then went immediately into an open-mouth tongue kiss.

And this was how these two carried on; sickening to the people who lacked this kind of overwhelming affection in their lives.

"HON, I GOT a call from a woman, Yvette Gardner. Ring a bell? She's with a company called Melrah. We helped them with the guarantees on two brownstones over on 128th Street a couple of years ago . . ."

"Now, Asondra, you know I'm too busy to remember

every applicant. We've done so much since Chambers took office. What'd the woman want?"

"Their lease options have come due on the properties and, basically, they're ready to purchase. Plus they want to develop a number of other homes along the same street." Asondra helped Fred with his tie as they discussed this. "They want a loan from the Fund for a closing that's supposed to take place soon."

"How soon?" Fred asked.

"She didn't leave that kind of information. But from the sound of her voice, I'd say very soon. I called back to talk to her again, but there was no answer. I left a message explaining that things have changed some with the Fund—how there was a two-month processing time for—"

"Wait a minute. Melrah. Was that the company? A black couple owns that company?"

"See? You're not losing your marbles, baby. That was them. They came by the office once or twice, back when the congressman won the election."

Fred seemed to experience a clearing house of thought, memories and ideas. He quickly asked, "How much does the guy—I mean, the company need?"

"She mentioned a couple hundred thousand, but I did as you asked, mentioning the processing—"

"Shit."

"Did I do something wrong?"

"Oh no. Not at all. It's got nothing to do with you, I just need . . . er, I want to make that deal happen."

"That would be nice, 'cause she sure sounded upset, like she expected our help right away."

"Asondra, on Monday morning I want you to contact this woman and set up an appointment. Tell her we'd be glad to help her."

"That soon? I thought . . ."

"Asondra? My candy-apple delight . . . my chocolate cream pie . . ." In between compliments, Fred kissed her again and again—the cheek, the forehead, the nose. "Please just set the appointment, okay?"

Asondra held in a chuckle. "That sounds like one of those sugar-coated direct orders."

"No, baby. Only you give the orders around here." Fred Allen, the politician.

Asondra smiled that satisfied smile as she smoothed her hand along her husband's cheek, thinking of how clever he was to always let her feel like the winner. She was sure, if nothing else, that she married the smartest man in all of Harlem.

HEAVENLY GLAM WAS a duplex arrangement, with both the floors visible through the all-glass façade. It was as if every passing pedestrian and driver could witness this diamond in all of its glory. Every appointment was more or less a stage show.

Mya's end of the business was the entire first floor, where ten stations accommodated patrons while beauticians crafted hairstyles of one sort or another. No longer did she have to work out of her home on 122nd Street. No more dealing with loan sharks like Roy Washington. Right or wrong, Mya rejoiced when she heard that the creep was shot while trespassing. And then the irony of Asondra, one of her own clients, being there at the time. Do tell.

The icing on top of the cake was when Asondra called Mya some time later to have her plan the wedding with Lola, and then, the business arrangement between the three.

It was enough good news to make a city girl cry. And Mya did.

But this new environment gave Mya so much more room to breathe . . . to grow. Thank God for Asondra and the blessings she brought to Mya's life.

Lola's section of Glam was the upstairs half, a more intimate setting since the window curtains could be pulled from time to time. Some clients needed that kind of privacy. Vivica was a client. Eve and Foxy were clients. Halle was a client. Angela was a client. And so were a high percentage of fashion models, singers and video chicks who called Harlem home. The second floor had a half-dozen manicure stations, just as many pedicure stations and, further back, behind oriental-designed partitions, were comfortable chairs for facials. In the very rear were two rooms where massage therapy was offered nonstop, morning, noon and night.

There was always some type of ongoing activity at Glam, whether it was early morning, when supplies were delivered, or late at night, in the event a certain high-profile client needed confidential attention for something as petty as a pimple. A pimple might be petty to some, but not to a $10-million-per-film actress who was due on *The Tonight Show* in twenty-four hours. During regular business hours, however, soft jazz played over the salon's surround-sound system; that constant entertainment was interrupted only by the nonstop chirping of the telephone.

"Darlene, could you get that, boo?" said Lola, and yet her instructions blended seamlessly with her ongoing explanation of how the client before her should go about cleansing her face, while at the same time mashing a banana in a bowl.

". . . So, when you wash your face, Debbie, you're gonna want to use the nubby washcloth, and be sure that you rub in upward circular motions . . . you'll want to also make sure not to pull or tug at the finer, more delicate areas around the eyes . . ." Now Lola was adding a tablespoon of honey and a few drops of lemon juice, then went on mashing and mixing until the combination formed a pasty consistency. Next, she applied the banana-honey-lemon goo to her client's face.

"See, when you use that certain washcloth, it helps to provide a gentle exfoliating treatment."

"What's that? Exfoliating?" asked Debbie.

"That simply means the removal of the dead cells that build up naturally on everyone's skin."

"Mmm . . . that smells good. Almost . . . like . . . banana and lemon," said Debbie, unable to see since the cucumber slices were covering her eyes.

"That's because it is banana and lemon. See, the banana base calms the skin. And the acid in the lemon helps to remove the surface layer of flaky, dry skin."

"Wow. I feel like a fruit cocktail!"

Meanwhile, Mya was downstairs just about finished with

twisting a customer's hair onto rods so that once she spent some time under the hair dryer, her locks would be released, falling into loose curls about her head.

"But girrrl—I really feel sorry for those poor Wallace girls," said Mya's client.

"With their momma locked up they're left with no choice. Their father's gonna have to take care of 'em."

"I thought you said he left his wife," said another client who was about to go under the hair dryer.

"Yeah."

"So then, who's gonna take care of the girls?"

"I dunno, maybe a relative or something, how'm I s'pose to know?" replied the first woman, who seemed to have all the answers. "Anyway, that's not even the point. The man ain't no good. He ain't but one of those abusive cops. Poor Tuesday."

Mya interjected something positive, saying, "Tuesday's a nice person. I'm sure they'll give her bail. I mean, there is such a thing as being innocent until proven guilty."

"Ha! Where you been, girl? That woman got caught with a mess of them E-pills. Bail? She'll be lucky if she gets a cell with a view. You know how they do us black folk. Unless you got that dream-team money, you ain't got a chance in hell of getting justice."

Mya came to recall that age-old rule taught to her in beauty school: no discussions about politics or religion or other people's personal affairs. "I guess you're right, boo. But let's wish the best for her children, okay?"

Mya thought she had put out a potential fire, but the woman two chairs down joined in on the conversation.

"Not just the children, but all of us. Did you see the papers and the news? There was so much violence this weekend. The shootings up on Gun Hill, the stuff in Chinatown. Some other kind of kidnapping is still unsolved."

"That reporter chick?"

"Yeah. Plus, there was a story about two U.S. marshals killed up in Yonkers. Jesus."

"Maybe it was a full moon last night. Anyone know?"

"Now, Mya, I know you ain't gonna balance and blame all that stuff on the moon." The gossiper made a face, twisting her lips and cocking her head. "The moon didn't shoot that woman in Brooklyn at three in the morning."

Mya shrugged. There was no arguing with common sense, or lack of it.

"Well, anyway . . . I'm lookin' at possibly movin' down to the Carolinas," said another client. Two others answered simultaneously.

"Hunh??" As though their tongues tasted something notoriously sour.

"Shoot—what's wrong with that? I got a little boy to raise all by myself. The last thing I wanna hear is that my baby was hit by a stray bullet. Honeychile, I'd be the next madwoman on the six o'clock news."

"I think Patty done lost her mind."

"Why? 'Cuz I want my boy to live?"

"No, silly. Because you can't go runnin' every time you hear about violence. How many times this year did they say the country is under attack by terrorists? How many times in a month do we have to hear about a high alert? A hundred?"

"I don't care if it was a hundred or twelve. Me and my boy need a safer place to live."

"Okay. That's all fine and good. But don't you think they have problems in the Carolinas?"

"Maybe there is, but not like here. Not as much either."

Another customer added, "That may be so, but where you don't have the threats of violence, you have racism. If not racism, you have sexism, classism, maybe a swarm of wild bees will come at you. There's always gonna be problems, young lady. You just can't avoid that."

"Okay. So I'll take your advice. We'll just live and die right here in Harlem." Sarcasm in the air.

"Come on, girrrl . . . never that. Life is about living and surviving and contributing, until your very last breath. And nobody can predict when that is, regardless of how many def-con threats they sell us on TV. The truth at the end of the day is that a higher power is calling the shots. He or She is gonna decide when it's over, and not a moment sooner . . . not a moment later."

"You go on, Miss Darcy! Preach!"

Mya sighed, wishing for the good ole days when salon talk was strictly sex, men and kids. But in the meantime, she merely smiled. Better to have a full salon of wayward opinions than an empty one with absolute agreement.

CHAPTER EIGHT

PUSH WAS SLAMMING his fists into the heavy bag. The whole *bang-bang-bang, pop* routine again. It was early Monday morning, three days after his meeting with his probation officer—he couldn't lose that view of her telling him all that she knew, as quickly as she'd suggested. The revelations were gnawing at his last nerve like some annoying hornet he wished he could catch and kill.

Damn! How clumsy could I be? My P.O. She caught me cold. Shit! Of all people to follow me.

And Push cursed himself this way right through the workout, letting out one of those husky grunts here and there as he pounded the leather bag harder, trying like hell to knock out the ghost, the one thrusting the bag back at him over and over.

He had to put a face to the target to really get off, to really relieve the stress that so entrapped him. Right now, that face was his own—a fight with his own destiny.

But, by putting things into proper perspective, things didn't seem quite so bad. Since Ms. Watson—he couldn't stop calling her that either—witnessed these killings so long ago, two years to be exact, the things she said to Push had to be sincere. Otherwise, he just might be on some warden's death row, awaiting his fate.

This was so unusual, almost like he was the subject of a practical joke. Only, this was not one bit funny. And now there was this other thing—Evelyn's friend, the Judge.

Push had to admit, if Ms. Watson witnessing him take a life was scary, then her introducing Push to a judge (a senior court judge at that!) was worse than a thousand lifetimes with no oxygen. Instead of his secret profession, it seemed that everybody in the world knew what he was capable of.

If ever Push had the opportunity to exhale after such executions, then that idea was gone now—or it turned to a poisonous gas.

The conversation was still branded on his brain tissue. The late-night introduction. The proposition.

"This is Judge Charles Pullman," Evelyn said. And the Judge had that surprised expression working, maybe not expecting the specifics or that he himself unconsciously reached out for a handshake. "He's a very good friend of mine."

"How are you," said Pullman, wanting to get this off to a good start. Push didn't respond at first, still with that stone face, looking down at the man's hand as though it were a trick.

Evelyn intervened, saying, "Did I mention that he's the one who made the phone call . . . to help get your nephew out of jail?" Evelyn might've put her hands on her hips if she were standing. But the three of them were at an all-night diner fifteen minutes away from her home.

The Judge had had to give the marshals the slip, even sneaking through other folks' backyards (trespassing!) to do it.

And now Push saw the light. Pullman's hand didn't feel feeble and contagious after all, and the skepticism disappeared just as fast. "I didn't know. Uhh . . . I appreciate that. Thanks."

"It's no problem. I thought if there should be anyone to show that first sign of good faith, it should be me."

Push expressed his own brand of appreciation, no longer with the stone face.

"Evelyn has explained to me about the injustices at the 28th Precinct, as well as what you went through during your brief visit there. It was the least I could do. How's Reggie?"

"He's in his glory. Trust me, I know the feeling of being sprung."

Pullman glanced at Evelyn and nodded as though reading between the lines. He stirred his coffee, creating those *ting* sounds with the stainless spoon tapping the mug.

All of the sounds and smells in the diner kept Push grounded, despite how light-headed he felt, floating inside of such unbelievable circumstances. He also thought about that weekend, his "brief visit" there and the police beating him with nightsticks. The drama was fresh on his mind, like the scent of burning flesh. But then there was another shocking truth revealed: if Evelyn saw what he did to Raphael on 122nd Street . . . if she was the law enforcement officer who had come to spring him that following Monday . . . Push recalled that cold Monday morning when Ms. Watson came to see him, with only the cell bars between them. He had the bruises of a man who'd just fought and the eyes of a bitter soul.

"Okay. They say they picked you up, but they don't say why. Then there's a note here: Known criminal in the immediate vicinity of a homicide. Now you know how these things work, Push. If you're anywhere near some kind of serious crime, and they identify you as an ex-felon, with paper still left to your name? The rule is, ask questions later. Now, you wanna fill me in before I draw my own conclusions?"

"I was at the Lenox Lounge havin' a—uhhh—orange juice . . ." Push had smiled, and so had Evelyn, reading between the lines and past the little white lie. "And the cops just came in like gangstas, they shut the music down . . ." Push had explained these things down to the smallest detail, minus the bit about the Ruger.

"So, did they find anything on you?"

"Nope. I was clean. They was lockin' cats up who had nail clippers, Ms. W. I was free to go, they said. But then, when I got outside, another cop called me over to his car and asked for my ID. They asked me some other questions and then locked me up."

Push could've laughed now, thinking back to that jail-house conversation. There he was, thinking he had the talk game of all talk games . . . thinking he was finessing his way out of jail, and the bitch knew all along that it was him!

She should've won an Oscar, she was so good!

"And the bruises?" Evelyn had inquired.

"Ms. W, I ain't cryin' about no beat-down or no police brutality. What they did to me was child's play compared to where I've been." Push lifted his shirt some to show her his scar. "Remember reading about this in my records?"

She had closed her eyes at the sight, and now that Push knew more about Evelyn, he could tell that she hadn't been phony about that moment. Now that he knew better, he'd swear there was some guilt there too. Guilt for a lot of things.

After Push let his shirt down, he'd said, "I'm just tryin' to get up outta here. I need a shower."

"Not so fast, soldier. You were in the vicinity of a capital crime—"

"Hmmm . . . and I wasn't the only one."

"Didn't you and I discuss this? Zero tolerance?"

Push had put on a defeated expression. He said, "Of course, Ms. W, but how am I supposed to know what's goin' on outside on the streets if I'm in a club gettin' my groove on? Fourteen years, baby."

"What did you call me?"

Push then cleared his throat. "I lost my head, Ms. W. I'm just sayin', if I happen to be at a coffeeshop down near Wall Street and some hard-ons wanna fly a plane into the World Trade Center, I'm supposed to be responsible?"

"That's different."

"How? It's a crime to fly a plane into a skyscraper, isn't it?"

"Sometimes I think you're too smart for your own good, Push."

And now Push knew exactly what she meant. Exactly.

There was one other thing Evelyn had said: "Now I want you to look me in the eye and tell me you didn't have any-thing to do with the homicide near the Lenox Lounge."

Whoa. That was the mosquito in the soup, because if the woman witnessed what he did, then what did she go and say that for? Push wondered if it was some kind of test. And if so, for what reason? For this? For a proposition two years later? There had to be more. Push sat there at the table, his eyes gradually switching to and from Evelyn when she wasn't aware. There was so much more to this woman than one might imagine. She had power. She was intelligent, and she was mysterious like a communist spy.

I should've said "yes, baby." I should've told you the truth right to your face. How impressed would you be then?

Evelyn went on to say, "Push, this happens to be a meeting of people who need one another. Just like Judge Pullman helped you, he—or rather, we—need your help in return."

"You need my help? What could I possibly have to offer to a judge and a probation officer? Didn't anyone tell you that I'm the bad guy?"

"You'd be surprised, Push. There's a lot that a . . . talented person like you could do to help us."

"The federal government needs me? What? Now you want me to get on your side? You wanna blackmail me or somethin'?" Push got up from the table. "Well, I got news for you. I did almost fifteen years for your federal government. And I'm done bein' your slave."

Evelyn grabbed Push's wrist. "Sit!" she more or less barked.

Push was wide-eyed. So many contradictions flashing before him. But Evelyn quickly changed up.

"I'm sorry. I apologize—" And her grip softened, sliding down to gently grasp his hand. His eyes rested there as well. "I didn't mean to speak to you like that . . ." It didn't matter if the waitress overheard her. Egos weren't the issue here. "And Push, we are not here as representatives of the federal government. We're not," she repeated for emphasis.

Push tried to get comfortable in his seat again. Tried to hear these two out, despite the rejection steering his thoughts and actions.

"First and foremost," said Evelyn, "we're gonna need a temporary home for the Judge. Someplace where nobody would ever find him."

Push asked, "How could you need me for that? Why don't he just check into a hotel or something?"

"It's not that easy, Push. You see—"

The Judge jumped in. "They're after me."

"Who's after you?"

"It's a vicious, vicious organization known as L.T.K."

"Sounds like a company that makes videocassettes."

Pullman and Watson shared a look at Push's choice of words, acknowledging the irony.

"Much worse than that, my friend. L.T.K. stands for Licensed to Kill. And they have the badges *and* the guns."

Push raised an eyebrow and folded his arms. Indeed, this was highly unusual, but it might also be something right up Push's alley. "You say they're organized? With badges?"

"These are cops. Federal, state and local."

"Feds are after you? Who'd you piss off, Judge?" The idea amused Push some, how this might be the back end of the Judge spitting in the wind. *You made your bed, now you're afraid to lie in it, hunh?* But Push eventually got that deep breath in, considering all angles of this. Nothing, not even a scared judge, was more intriguing than a crew of bad cops.

"To tell you the truth, this doesn't have anything to do with any court decisions, or a defendant who doesn't appreciate the sentence I've given. It's not that . . . this is more personal. Someone, a friend of mine, came to me with some, shall we say, intimate details about this L.T.K. gang. It's not just any group, but an intelligent one—at least from what we know. But their modus operandi is to perform hits on the city's criminal organizations. This, we believe, is how they justify and finance their own existence."

"Gangsta cops? Goin' after gangstas?"

"Something like that," replied Pullman.

"Well, excuse me for asking, but what's the problem? I mean, these guys are taking the short cut, but isn't that your business? To put criminals out of business?"

"Sounds easy, but it's . . . it's diabolical, really. These are

loners, they're not any righteous group. Call them oppor-
tunists, if anything. But they're definitely not angels. There
are laws and rules that people must follow. It's called being
civil. L.T.K. is far from civil. And now that they've involved
me and friends of mine, it's become personal."

"One more stupid question, Judge. How can you uphold
the law and break the law at the same time?"

Pullman took a moment to answer. "They—"

"I'm talkin' about you, Judge. If I got this right, you want
a . . . an experienced man on your team."

You want a killer.

"I realize it's a double standard. You don't need to break
it down. I understand fully the ramifications here. But sometimes extreme circumstances require extreme measures. You
see . . . more than robbing criminals, L.T.K. has been involved in kidnapping and murder. We know for sure about
people they've killed already. A U.S. attorney. The brother
of a New York City policeman . . ."

And Evelyn added, "Not to mention what they did tonight, Push. From what I heard, there are two other marshals
missing from tonight . . ."

Push didn't take danger lightly, and was naturally alert,
periodically checking their surroundings in the diner. The
waitress. The cashier. The few customers. The parking lot
and whoever might pull in was visible from where they sat.

"Just a few hours ago," said Pullman. "That's why I'm
sneaking around. That's why it's not so simple as calling in
any others."

"Ain't that a trip. Can't even trust your own."

"I've been on round-the-clock protection for the last
week. Ever since I found out about Michelle."

"Michelle?"

"The reporter," said Evelyn.

"It's been a hell of a night, Mr. Push."

"Just call me Push, Please."

"Of course. Push, this is a different world for me. The
gunplay, the violence. I watched two people get shot to death
tonight. I'm not sure my heartbeat is back to normal yet."

"So you see how serious this is?" asked Evelyn.

"Yes. But if I were you, even if police were after me, I'd probably call the director of the FBI or somethin'. I'm sure *he* ain't bad. And the FBI is gonna take care of this better than a . . ." Push never advertised what he did. Bragging always had a sour taste to it. ". . . better than me."

"There's . . . more I—eh—I haven't told you . . . that I can't tell you." Pullman seemed embarrassed. Even guilty.

"Some kind of dark secret, hunh? So that's why you can't take it to the FBI."

Evelyn reached across the table to put her hand over Push's. "The bottom line is these guys are after Charles. Will you help us? Just put him up and look after him?"

Push shrugged. It didn't seem like a big deal. "Protection. That's all you want?"

But that wasn't all they wanted.

THE WEEKEND WAS still very much on Push's mind as he attacked the heavy bag with livelier punches. Wild left hooks and powerful jabs. Out loud he said, "Those two are trippin'."

In between combinations he was thinking, talking aloud, maybe he was going crazy himself.

"Shee-it. They got the wrong dude if they think I'm goin' for some suicide mission. Ain't no way."

Bang-bang . . . bang-bang-bang . . . pop!

UNCLE SAM WOULD be fine, said the private physician who was always on call for such emergencies.

It was only a flesh wound; the bullet ripped through the pectoral muscle, close to the armpit, and passed out of the body. Sam lost some blood, but he'd fully recover in a few weeks.

Right now Sam's upper chest was stitched and bandaged, but didn't prevent his routine. There was the throbbing pain when he ran in the morning, but he toughed it out, figuring that his mental strength would help him win any such challenges.

"So, we're clear on what needs to be done," said Sam. "This is our organization, my big dream. It puts extra dollars in your pockets and good food on your dinner tables. L.T.K. is forever; as long as we do what's necessary to preserve it. If there is a threat, it must be identified and addressed, no differently than any of us do, or did, on the job."

Most of L.T.K. was present, called to this emergency meeting, and responded with a wave of agreeing murmurs. German was still en route from the Secret Service Agency in Washington; and Star, the pretty dreadlocked Jamerican who was assistant to the city's police commissioner, had been delayed in picking up Pinkie, the NYPD records girl.

However, everyone else was congregated in the large chapel, including (fresh off of the failed kidnapping) Ape, Cali, Mule, D.C. and Primo. Of course, Hitler and El were dead now.

Turk wore dark shades, hiding that gaping hole where an eye once was. Next to him was Pistol; then Sanchez, the black Cuban with U.S. Customs; Skin, the transit cop; Chico, former SWAT man who had just shot his wife at point-blank range; and Duck, with the fixed smile, sitting up on the marble altar with something of an aerial view of those and so many other faces that made up L.T.K.'s strong membership.

"We've got two big problems, and maybe a few small ones. Right now, we're here for the big stuff. Judge Pullman is our number-one problem. We had 'im the other night, but he slipped out of our hands. We need to relocate him—as in locate him again . . ." Uncle Sam took a break from pontificating to take a pull from his cigar.

"Second problem . . . There's a videotape out there that could get us in deep water. The reason L.T.K. is so successful is because our members are a mystery. You're nameless and faceless—if you know what I mean. I'd like to keep it that way. This has to be nipped in the bud . . . Cali, any word on where the marshals have Pullman?"

"Still workin' on it, sir. We should have an answer soon."

"Good. See if you can't make it sooner."

"Uncle, can't we just wait till he arrives at the courthouse early one morning?"

"Good idea, but too much exposure. Good guys all over the place. Plus, now that we've had our fumble, they're no doubt gonna have more men watching him. We have to do this like ghosts in the night—when they least expect it.

"Now, for the small stuff. Duck, make contact with your people down at the coroner's office—hopefully it's not too late. We need the dental records and other files rearranged for Hitler and El. We need them to remain unidentifiable. If not, we go to plan B."

"Plan B?"

"Exactly. As in confiscate the bodies and conduct our own private funeral."

There was stirring among the membership.

"Pipe down, folks. These guys at least deserve to keep whatever honor possible. They served justice, so we've gotta do the same for them, for any of youse. Can't let the press have their way, muckin' up their names as assassins or some other bullcrap."

"I'm on it, sir. I'll have some news within the hour."

"Fine. If we need to proceed with plan B, take a team with you tonight. Get those bodies."

"Ten-four."

"Finally, there's our former colleague, Mims. As you all probably know, Primo and I . . . came into contact with Mims earlier today. I won't go into the details, but I'm sure you also know by now that Mims turned on us. He strolled in here, made targets out of us and robbed us. We're lucky to be alive. He must be neutralized!"

Uncle Sam counted on his false information to cause a disturbance amongst the membership, and so far so good. He seemed to have their compassion and loyalty. Primo had an angry smile as he sat, perched against a stone column, his knee heavily bandaged and a pair of crutches on standby.

"For the record, the man's real name is Jesse Wallace. And for the man or woman who brings me his head in a box, I've got a fifty-thousand-dollar bonus, so let's not wait around any longer. The last thing we need is that video on the six o'clock news with all kinds of reporters swarming with their speculations and investigations as to who our members are. That could become the death of us."

JUDGE PULLMAN FELT so out of place here, as if he himself was a heart that had been transplanted into someone else's body, trying to adapt. But then, he felt some relief. If there was anyplace in the world where he wouldn't be found, it was here in one of the brownstones that Push had renovated. A good job too, if Pullman were to say so himself.

Pullman's relocation was so much easier than otherwise, since he had been a loner lately. His wife had long been deceased. His two children were no longer children, but now had their own families. If he was lucky, he'd get a holiday visit or a greeting card. Peter, his stepson, was at home with Evelyn, nursing his leg. It wasn't so much that the Judge was unpleasant company, or that there were family beefs. The job simply demanded his time. Late court sessions. Meetings. Politics. It seemed like the more passionate he became about his job of upholding the law, the more he was pulled from what he always knew was the foundation behind civility and law-abiding folks. Family.

The only other person in the past two years who would've missed Pullman's presence was Michelle. That was how he knew she was dead. He couldn't go a day without a phone call, a kiss or the fun they had in bed. Okay, so he was more than thirty years her senior and, sure, she probably lacked a father figure in her life. But the relationship worked for them, which was all that mattered. And now with Michelle gone, there was only Evelyn who would be concerned about him.

She wouldn't have left him here in this residence if she wasn't certain of his safety.

"He turned his life around one hundred eighty degrees, Charles."

Damn, she'd done a hell of a job convincing him that Push was so righteous an ex-con . . . how he'd developed housing here in the heart of Harlem, that he was always on time for his visits with her, that he had managed to maintain a relationship with a self-made woman despite the odds against him.

"He's got a baby on the way too," Evelyn told him.

"A baby doesn't necessarily mean he's grounded, just that he knows how to use his tool. I've locked up too many thugs who were fathers—nothin' but a bunch of Johnny Appleseeds. Planting them wherever they could lay down."

"Well, Push is different, Charles. He is."

"I hope so," he said with a tiny laugh. "For my sake."

And here he was, in that very brownstone residence. It had apparently belonged to a family at one time, a guess of his since everything was left so lived-in. He figured somebody had been evicted for nonpayment of rent, an equation that was familiar to him when he was a legal-aid attorney in his earlier years. There was a family photo. A black family. The husband with the subtle smile, the wife doing her best to measure up as partner and two beautiful little girls.

Charles missed those days at times. Family. It wasn't hard to feel at home here. Except the refrigerator was near-barren, as were the cupboards. Push and Evelyn were supposed to get things; Evelyn was paying for some grocery shopping.

"Where are they?" Pullman asked himself, resorting to the last slice of pizza and a can of Pepsi to wash it down.

Pullman picked through the shopping bags of clothes that Evelyn brought that day. It occurred to him to ask where she was getting all of this money. The clothes. The utility bills for the residence. The proposition for Push to take care of his problem.

Charles fell asleep with those thoughts.

When he woke, it was close to eight in the morning and someone had come in through the front door. Push? Evelyn? he wondered. But his mouth said, "I'm starved."

CHAPTER NINE

THERE WAS A war going on. It was all internal, all in Jesse's head, how he fought all of these thoughts related to reconciliation with Tuesday, his wife of ten years.

For twenty-four hours Jesse made excuses, rationalized and melted in and out of surrendering to the pressure of conscience.

He even practiced. "I'm sorry, Tuesday. Maybe we can start over again? I'll get some kind of help if you want . . . whatever you want. Just don't say it's over. This is our family. I love you. I love our daughters. They need a mother *and* a father. Will you ever forgive me for putting my hands on you?"

Alone in his hotel room, Jesse recited these words, something as foreign to him as deep-sea diving. "They say that love is better the second time around . . . could we try it together? Please?" These were necessary words, because their breakup had been so painful. So hostile.

But Jesse also had to be honest with himself. "These words don't even sound right coming out of my mouth."

Jesse and Tuesday had been growing apart with the passing years. Tuesday was consumed with raising the girls, keeping them well grounded, away from those damned music videos and looking pretty in dresses and hairstyles like little girls were supposed to look.

Sharissa had begun day school. Stacy, the older of the

two, was in the third grade, and already asking questions about sex and violence. It was a cinch for her to address both:

"Mommy? Why do Daddy hit you? Is that love?"

But while Tuesday dealt with the mothering and other household chores, Jesse didn't make things any easier. He was too desensitized to be the loving, passionate husband she so desperately needed, often coming home to argue with Tuesday, the only sounding board for his frustrations and anxieties. In a nutshell, he was taking the job home with him.

Recently another scandal was born down at the police station. In addition to that, there had been another of those shootings that the media (and thereafter, the public) called "senseless." And just as each incident before, every cop on the force of 50,000-plus had to carry some degree of the next man's burden. Some accountability. Whether it was as simple as addressing the concerns of the everyday pedestrian (an irritating task that required mountains of patience), or the dark cloud of risk that hung over the other officers, the many threats that followed those "bad cop" campaigns, and the idea of some maniacs who thought it was cute to use police cruisers for target practice. If that pressure wasn't enough, there was always Internal Affairs or the Civilian Review Board representatives snooping up a cop's ass. Jesse was just one officer of many to bring it all home.

And then this last argument of theirs turned into that whole back-and-forth volley with words, and eventually with household items like pots and pans. In the end, Jesse thought of himself as the victor, since smacking Tuesday's face went unanswered.

But Tuesday had the last word.

"I called your job, Jesse," she told him the following day when he tried to make up with her.

"What're you talkin' about? Called my job?" The idea turned his heartbeat to an irregular one, something like a pair of sneakers knocking around inside of a clothes dryer.

"Just what I said. I saw one of those talk shows and they

say it's common for a cop to come home to beat his wife. They say it's an epidemic, Jesse. And I'm sick and tired of being at the other end of your hand . . ." She trembled as she spoke. Before Jesse could react, Tuesday said more. "They had a help line for spousal abuse. I spoke to them . . . and they told me about the help available at your job."

And the sneakers in the dryer thumped more intensively, the volume increasing with every word from Tuesday's mouth. It was becoming more and more unbearable. He felt violated. And he went off.

Before he knew it he had Tuesday's back against a wall while he smacked her silly. Her face was still sore from the day before, but that didn't stop her from defending herself.

It was something else they taught on that same talk show, how the assailant generally wouldn't expect the victim to strike back. And per the expert's instruction, Tuesday used that information to her advantage, using a hard knee to spike Jesse right between the legs. Jesse buckled, giving Tuesday a chance to grab a frying pan and smack him in the head. By now, Sharissa and Stacy were both crying and screaming, the last sights and sounds that Jesse experienced before the sneaker-tumbling stopped and things went black. When Jesse woke from unconsciousness, Tuesday and his daughters had gone. A note was left that read: HAVE YOUR ASS OUT OF MY HOUSE BY MORNING.

At first, Jesse grabbed his gun and was ready to hunt his wife down like wild game, but common sense had somehow kicked in. So he packed a few things and checked into a downtown hotel.

Those events were now more than two months old. Jesse called home once or twice to speak with Tuesday, and if not, at least to tell his daughters he loved them. But Tuesday hung up at the sound of his voice.

The next time he called, the number had been disconnected.

Jesse thought about apologizing. He thought about working things out. But as the epidemic goes, those were afterthoughts, things he should've considered before he injured his wife, the woman he supposedly loved.

Jesse's desire to make good was too late. It was his actions that took things too far. Thoughts and dialogue were one thing. However, once things escalated to actions, very often things couldn't be reversed. The damage was already done. Final. And beyond a reasonable doubt, Jesse had caused some serious damage, more than he could ever know.

"Anybody home? Tuesday?" Jesse called out.

"Tuesday? It isn't even Monday yet," said a man's voice from another room.

A surge of rage stabbed at Jesse's heart. Oh God. She couldn't have found another man already!? From one extreme to the next, Jesse dropped his bags—one with clothes, the other with more than $100,000 in cash—and went for his Magnum.

I should've killed her when I had the chance.

A man appeared from Jesse's bedroom. He was a brown-skinned man, somewhat shorter than Jesse, with large eyes with slight bags under them. He had to be almost twice Jesse's age, with a frail body and a receding hairline. This man was familiar. It took a moment to register, since Jesse hadn't met him before now.

It was the photos that Uncle Sam showed the hit squad. Photos of Judge Pullman. The memory of this man, running from his house just a few days earlier, was still replaying in his mind . . . how the Judge crouched down behind some shrubbery while the marshals fired at different oncoming vehicles. And now, here he was, of all places!

"Make another move and I'll ventilate you!"

"Wha—oh God," the Judge gasped as though it was his last.

"Where's my wife and daughters! What are you—"

"What wife? I don't know anything about your . . ." Just then, the Judge froze as if he'd seen a ghost. But Jesse wasn't deterred, still with a firm grip on the Magnum's handle. "Be easy with that gun."

"I asked you a question, mister. Where's my wife and children!" Jesse could feel the veins swelling in his neck and temple. The next thing he felt was pain, with his arm and his weapon forced upward. Someone was behind him; someone stronger and perhaps larger than he was. All he knew was pain for now. And it caused him to pull the trigger on the Magnum. The ear-popping blast discharged into the ceiling, taking down a chunk of plaster and a fog of dust with it. The Judge was at it again, now diving behind the couch. Judge Pullman, the athlete.

Now, a knee forced Jesse's legs to buckle and his neck was hooked by a man's rock-hard bicep. The Magnum was stripped from him and he lost track of his breathing, collapsing to the floor. Again, in his own home, Jesse blacked out. Except things happened much too fast for the coincidence and irony to be realized.

"Wow. Evelyn was right. You are vicious," confirmed Pullman, feeling very much the cat with nine lives.

Push was neither proud nor flattered by the comment. "If you were in my shoes, stepping in to save a life, would you feel vicious? Like some animal? Or would you be just another human being who gave a damn?" Push's statement sounded less like a question and more like disapproval.

"No—no, I didn't mean that in a bad way. I'm just . . . amazed, is all. I've never seen a man act like you did—so quick and calculated. It was something off of the big screen."

"Well maybe I should take up a new profession, hunh, Judge? Thanks for the inspiration, maybe I'll drop an application at a Hollywood studio." In the same breath, Push added, "Are you okay?" Meanwhile, he was looking up at the damaged ceiling, feeling the wound as if to his own flesh.

"Yes, thanks to you. I think I heard keys, and then he just appeared. Said something about his wife and children. Any idea what he's talking about?"

Push drew conclusions "O-kay. I see we've found Mr. Wallace. I didn't recognize him from behind." Push went down on one knee to turn the unconscious man some. Shit. "Yup. That's Wallace."

"Mr. Wallace? You mean, you know this man?"

"He's actually a tenant of mine. This is his home, only he's been late with the rent for two months."

Pullman looked down at Wallace, still confused about things. "But why the gun?"

"For some reason this guy and his wife left two little girls alone in this apartment. I knew the husband was a cop, but Yvette usually does the rent collecting around here . . ."

"Yvette. Is that your lady?"

Push had to think, and not about Yvette. Then he said, "She called the police department too . . . tried to get hold of him. But, if I remember right, they said something about a leave of absence."

Push didn't know it, but Judge Pullman was steadily thinking about this cop before him. "You don't think he's one of them, do you?"

Push sighed with that doubtful expression in his eyes. "Hard to tell. I hope not, because if that's it, then you're not even safe here. You didn't contact anyone, did you?"

Pullman shook his head.

"Evelyn?"

"Wait. When he came in, he was calling out something about Tuesday. And I said—"

"Tuesday. That's his wife's name."

Pullman made a face. Figured.

Push added, "That still doesn't explain the gun. Or maybe . . . of course . . . he thought you were a thief or somethin'. Either that or you were bangin' Tuesday."

"Bangin' Tuesday?"

Push shook his head. "I mean, he probably thought his wife was cheating. Think about it. A strange man in pajamas, in his house . . . plus he's been havin' problems with his wife?" Push laughed internally. "I could've done the same thing myself, jumped to conclusions."

"Well, I'm so glad he didn't jump any further," the Judge said. "Where is the wife, anyway?"

"That's been the big question around here. It's crazy, because a mother never leaves her children alone like that. A dude'll pick up and leave in a heartbeat. But a woman? No way. She's glued to them kids for life. Or at least till they're grown."

Pullman reexamined the family portrait, that photo on top of the TV set. They seemed so happy on Kodak paper.

"Yvette called a few hospitals to see if maybe she was hurt or something. But nobody could find a Tuesday Wallace. So it's just me and Yvette taking care of them, taking them places, shopping and whatnot."

"My goodness. How long has this been going on?"

"We've only had Sharissa and Stacy for a week and change, but their parents have been gone for over a month. The girls were living here all alone for three weeks, ignoring the knocks at the door because of the DCW lady."

"Who's that?"

"That's our name for the social worker who comes asking, 'Are your parents home?'" Push was checking out the Magnum now. "For real, they're like slave traders working for the Department of Welfare."

Push stopped himself because he could've aired all of his grievances about the issue, even if it was just his own opinion. The Judge seemed to understand, and it dawned on Push that Evelyn had explained his history to the man.

Pullman was looking at Push with the Magnum then to Wallace slipping back into consciousness on the living room floor. "I think I've seen more gunplay in the past few days then I've seen all my life."

"Trust me, it's not all it's made out to be. It's natural to feel shock, but when all you know is guns and violence—"

"Sure. Sure, I understand," said Pullman. And again Push tried to read between the lines, wondering if Evelyn had shared every detail, a possibility that was growing stronger by the minute.

"What do we do now?" asked Pullman, more at a loss for words than usual.

"Help me get him to the couch, would you?"

Afterward, Pullman suggested, "I'll get a washcloth . . . some cold water."

The two went on to nurse Wallace back to consciousness.

◆ ◆ ◆

WITHIN THE HOUR, Push and Pullman learned about the Wallace relationship from Jesse's own lips. No, he didn't know where Tuesday was, but, hell no, she would never leave Sharissa and Stacy alone. To help solve the mystery, Push paged Yvette, hoping that she'd learned more about the woman's whereabouts.

While the three sat there waiting for Yvette to call back, running out of things to talk about, Jesse said, "There's something else I should tell you—" At the same time there was a knock at the door. Jesse started to get up to answer it.

"You all right?" asked Push when his tenant wobbled some.

"I'm good. I once had a prisoner, seven feet and three hundred pounds, who knocked me down. On the force they use to call me blockhead, because I was up and at 'em— back to work after just ten minutes."

Push and Pullman shared a look, both of them recognizing the man's ego at large.

Jesse didn't bother looking through the peephole. He just pulled the door open.

"Mr. Wallace?" said a woman in a denim dress, briefcase in hand.

"That's me. Can I help you?"

The woman seemed anxious, looking past Jesse on the left, then the right. Searching . . . "I'm, ahh, I'm a social worker with the Department of Child Welfare. Ahhh . . . may I come in and speak with you for a moment?"

Jesse had a hand on his hip to go with the aggravated look in his eyes. If it wasn't for the badge and identification card in her hand, he might've slammed the door shut already, a response to the balls this woman had—balls that would be outweighed by her monster breasts.

But before Jesse could answer, the DCW lady swept past him with unquestionable authority. She had to be a pro at this, the way she quickly appraised the other two men in the residence, just as quickly shifting her head this way and that. "Okay. Where are they, Mr. Wallace?"

"Where are who?" replied Jesse, trying to be evasive.

"Your children, that's who. Where are Sha—" The woman stopped to check the papers on her clipboard. "Sharissa and Stacy."

"Oh. My daughters? Well, thanks for asking, but don't you worry. They're in very good hands. Nothing to worry about, ma'am." Jesse avoided eye contact with Push, who at once realized how convenient it was that he had the girls next door under the watchful eye of Crystal.

"Well, I'll need to be the judge of that. Are they here?" Without warning the woman marched into the nearest bedroom.

Jesse pressed his lips together, tolerating this nonsense. "Excuse me, Miss—what'd you say your name was?"

"Shamm. Mrs. Shamm."

"Okay. Well, Mrs. Shamm . . ." Jesse paused to consider his words. He could see the burn in Push's eyes, a gaze that was ready to sever Shamm's head from her neck with one stroke of a butcher knife. "My daughters are away . . . in Texas . . . with my brother and his wife."

To put a price on Push's smile . . .

"Is that so."

"Yes. That is so."

Strapped with plenty of attitude, Mrs. Shamm said, "Then I'm afraid I'll need a name and address. A phone number as well."

You're afraid? What, I'm supposed to feel threatened by you? "Mrs. Shamm, why are you all of a sudden interested in my children? What's the deal?"

"Whenever a single parent is arrested, DCW is called in to see after the children."

"Arrested? Single parent? You must have the wrong family—"

"Aren't you the ex-husband of Tuesday Wallace?"

"*Ex*-husband?"

"That's the information the children's mother gave to the arresting officer," said Shamm.

Jesse looked up at the ceiling, then closed his eyes and

asked, "Mrs. Shamm, why did Tuesday get arrested?" Jesse was almost afraid to ask the question. With so much happening so quickly, he felt like all of the air had been sucked out of him. Call it exhausted.

"Something to do with drugs. I'm almost sure you know more about it than I would . . . which is all the more reason why I need to see those children."

Jesse realized now that she was finger-pointing, only not with specific allegations. At the same time, Push mumbled, "So you can stick 'em in a home." The comment made the social worker look again at the other two men in the room, finally seeing their faces and not just blurs of humanity.

"Excuse me, but what did you—" Shamm approached them while she spoke. "Well, well . . . aren't you Judge Pullman?"

Pullman managed a smile, however uncomfortable. He said, "Yes, I am." It was a hesitant response. After all, he was still on someone's hit list.

"Don't you remember me? Grace Shamm? We worked with the same client, ohhh, maybe eight years ago? Well, she was actually your client. I was in for the DCW."

There had been no reason for Pullman to get on his feet up until now. "Sorry. I didn't recognize you. It's been quite a while," recalled Pullman.

"It certainly has, Judge. And might I say I'm proud of your progress. We all are. You're a senior judge now, correct?"

Judge Pullman had a resolve about him, now more exposed than he expected under the circumstances. "Yes. On the federal bench."

"Right. Right. I keep track . . . well, a little, anyways. I may be stuck on this job, a bug in a rug, but I never forget a face."

The rapport between the Judge and the social worker was obvious, quickly changing the tense atmosphere in the room. The DCW lady went from being an enemy who came to snatch two children to a mutual acquaintance who could be reasoned with. Her attitude also changed from a predator to that of a Good Samaritan.

"Listen, Mrs. Shamm, may I speak with you? In private?" Pullman asked. Shamm seemed starstruck, more than happy for the opportunity, and she went with the Judge into the next room.

Government workers united.

Jesse and Push looked at one another, wondering what this powwow was about. As they sat apart, appraising each other now and then, the doorbell rang.

Push went to answer it this time. And this time, it was Yvette.

"Hi, baby," she said, stepping in and kissing him on the lips. "Oh . . ." The word came out somewhat swallowed as opposed to spoken. ". . . Mr. Wallace." Yvette had a blend of compassion and concern both lobbying for a place in her eyes. "Ahh . . . baby?" she uttered in a low-pitched sigh. "Can I see you alone?" And Yvette didn't wait for agreement. She simply spun around in her business attire—the cream-colored blazer and skirt above the black pumps—heading back through the front door of the Wallace home.

Push put on the humble grin, feeling a bit pussy-whipped, as he followed his now-pregnant girlfriend and business partner into the hall.

"What's up?" Push asked, sincere as could be.

"Did you know that man beats his wife?"

Push didn't quite measure up to her concern, but he acknowledged his awareness. "I can't be a real estate developer and a marriage counselor, Yvette. Besides, it's your job to deal with the tenants, isn't it?" Yvette lost some of that glow that was her charisma. Push took it hard. He said, "What?" as if she was blaming him. "You want me to go throw him against the wall? I should discipline him? Naw, baby . . . it's none of our business."

"You would take the man's side, wouldn't you."

"What's that supposed to mean? Man's side. Isn't that a strong statement to be makin'?"

"Well, at least be a little outraged or somethin'. You don't have to be all nonchalant about it."

"Yvette . . ." Push started to smirk. "I can't be a babysitter or a marriage counselor for every man I meet. I hardly know this cat. A cop at that."

"Push. Tuesday is locked up."

"Mmm, I know. That's why we called you over. I figured you could do some of the . . . networking that you're so good at, and come up with some answers."

"They say she was part of some kind of drug ring. Something to do with E."

Push was very much aware of the Ecstasy drug trade, something new on the scene since he'd come home from prison. Since he'd paid dearly for his own involvement in pushing drugs as a teenager, these frequent topics in the news about drugs and their impact on the community played a certain role in Push's life, even if it was something small in the back of his mind. It was a concern he considered addressing one day, maybe one he'd help to resolve, if even to satisfy his own conscience.

"Now you're telling me something that concerns us. Number one, we can't have drug dealers living in our homes. And number two, there's the issue about the little ones." Push being vague—the little ones—was a natural response; on account of the DCW lady being so close, even if behind closed doors. The presence of that woman, no matter how good she and the Judge got along, was a dark cloud lingering overhead, blocking the sun, interfering with the bright sky, promising rain.

"Don't get excited now, but the DCW lady is inside. She came to find them."

"DCW lady?"

"Remember how I told you me and my sister put the slip on a woman when we were young? When our parents were—"

Yvette was sharp enough to break in mid-sentence. "I know. I remember."

"Okay, well, the lady we ran to hide from was the DCW lady. Same title, different face."

Yvette erupted. "Push! We can't let her take them!"

"Shhh!" Push motioned for Yvette to keep her voice down.

"I know we can't let her take them. Don't worry. She don't even know where they are." Yvette was visibly relieved. "But we still need to figure something out. I can't raise two girls right now. We already got our hands full."

Yvette couldn't agree more. She said, "Push, I heard something else about Tuesday. The other side of the story is that she was set up. That she had nothing to do with any drugs or drug dealers."

"Oh brother. Now who's takin' sides? I guess the next thing you're gonna tell me is that she's innocent until proven guilty. Do you know how many times I heard people say they didn't do it, when they know damn well they did?"

"You of all people can't be cynical, Push. You gotta give her the benefit of the doubt."

"You're right. I'm trippin'. I guess I've been burned, so it's easy for me to tell when flames are comin'."

"It might help you to know that this is a different situation."

"How?"

"Some kind of police mess. I was by the salon. Everybody's talkin' about her taking the blame. She was at some club up in the Bronx. There was a raid in the parking lot or somethin' . . ."

"Mmm. You already said a mouthful there. How's the woman gonna be at a club and leave her kids home alone?"

"That got to me to me too, Push. But people do that all the time, when the kids are asleep."

"And those ain't people. Those are pathetic mothafuckas that should be shot, hung and burned."

"Crystal used to do it, Push. Back when you were away. When she couldn't find a babysitter."

"Bullshit! Crystal loves Reggie more than life itself. I don't ever wanna hear that . . . that lie come out of your mouth again."

Yvette was close enough to Push so that she could smooth her hand along his cheek, partially covering his mouth. "Push, there's so much you don't know about people . . . sometimes we're not too bright. We do things without thinking and get our priorities all twisted. Your sister had to survive. She had to do what she had to do to make it on her own. You were gone, and . . ." Yvette's words faded. She pulled his face to hers, cuddling his head with her arms and hands so that they had this very quiet, very intimate moment from the rest of the entire world.

Just then, the front door of the Wallace home opened. Jesse would've let the woman go on her way, only the two of them stood there in the doorway, eyes wide like they'd stumbled on something so fascinating. Push and Yvette were interrupted, their red, teary eyes still trapped in the emotion as they awkwardly stepped aside. Jesse thanked the woman, her pink skin reddening, and she offered a subtle smile as she slid past the lovers toward the staircase and down through the brownstone's entrance.

Yvette didn't recognize the third person standing behind Jesse before the door closed. "Who was that?" she asked.

"Just a friend," said Push. "So, did you find out where Tuesday is? Is there a bail?"

"I did better than that. I went to see her."

"You what?"

"You heard me. And if you didn't want me to get involved, you shouldn't have decided to play surrogate father to those pretty little girls."

"Now, that's silly. You know I wasn't gonna leave them girls alone."

"Okay, then. We owe it to them to see about their parents. Now, to answer your question, Tuesday needs a hundred thousand dollars for bail. As far as the lawyer . . ."

"Oh, ho-ho-hold *up*! That's what we're about to discuss? You want *us* to pay the money for bail? And a *lawyer*? Woman, you done gone off the deep end and lost all your marbles."

"But her husband is here now. So—"

"You ain't gotta say another word, boo. Like I told you, this is *not* our problem." Push took Yvette's hand and led her into the Wallace residence. "Let me do the talking," he said, with that uncompromising way about him.

Judge Pullman was obvious, turning his head down, stepping toward the couch for a seat. *No. This isn't just another visitor*, Push said, if only by telepathy. And then he added things up.

The Judge had to feel pretty vulnerable about now. This place was supposed to be his hideaway, and yet it turned into a popular spot in less than an hour. First, a man—*a cop!*—pulls a gun on Pullman, demanding to know where his wife and kids are, blasting his gun while he's at it; then the DCW lady—an old friend, no less—stumbles in. And now Yvette.

"Jesse, you already know Yvette," said Push, leaving no room for her to play abused wife advocate. He simply shifted her attention toward Pullman. "Yvette, this is a friend of mine . . ." Yes, it was a lie, but also great irony: the Judge and the ex-con, *friends*. "Judge Pullman? Meet Yvette Gardner. She's my better half, Judge. She thinks, eats and breathes like me. So you don't have to worry about our secret getting out of the bag."

Yvette had to quickly change expressions from the way she squinted and pursed her lips at Jesse Wallace, to the gracious smile that greeted Judge Pullman. *What secret?*

"How are you, sir?"

"Nice to meet you," replied Pullman with the gentle handshake and gentleman's smile. He seemed helpless in a way, like he didn't know what he was doing here, or rather wished he was somewhere else.

Jesse was too interested in his wife and her dilemma to stand by for the how-do-ya-do's and please-to-meet-you's. If this woman (Yvette) had details about Tuesday, she needed to sound off with it now. "Ms. Gardner, this arrest-business with my wife doesn't even fit."

Yvette turned toward the wife-beater as if looking forward to it. He wasn't a good cop anymore, not in her eyes. "I don't think it fits either, Mr. Wallace. Your wife is a very nice woman, and a fine mother . . ." Yvette wanted to say more, but didn't. It was another awkward moment.

"So," Push intervened, "it's good that we all agree she

don't belong in jail." Push, the mediator. "The question is, what are you gonna do about it? Aren't you still a cop?"

"Almost ten years on the job."

Push noticed how Judge Pullman was suddenly restless over on the couch and cast an expression his way that suggested that he relax.

Yvette said, "I understand her bail is one hundred thousand. And she needs a lawyer."

Push could've pinched Yvette on the ass for not going along with the plan for him to do the talking.

Jesse said, "I'll find out about this," and went to pick up the phone near the couch.

Push shared a knowing expression with the Judge. At the same time, Jesse tapped the cradle of the phone trying to get a dial tone. "Damn, no dial tone," he said.

Push came to wonder so many things at once: the rent, the electric bill. If the minor things couldn't be handled, how would this guy handle bail and a lawyer?

Jesse put down the phone, leaving the others to guess about the wheels turning in his head as he tapped his foot on the floor. "Listen, there's family concerns I need to take care of, if you all will excuse me. Oh, and Judge, thank you for all your help. From the bottom of my heart." Jesse wanted to say more: about L.T.K. wanting him dead, and maybe about his pulling out of that involvement (however late). But the Judge's life wasn't the priority just now. He had to get Tuesday out of lockup before God knows what happened.

He hurried around, gathering up his bags, disappearing and then emerging in another jacket, with some folded money in his hand. "I think I owe you something," Jesse said, passing Yvette the money. With the attention a circus act might attract, Jesse turned to Push. "Can I talk to you a sec?" And the two men went out into the hallway, that makeshift conference area.

"This is getting complicated, but I'll keep it simple. I think you should move the Judge to a safer place. I can't go into too much detail, but his life may be in great danger," Jesse said bluntly.

"That's why I had him here at your place. I figured—what kind of danger?"

Jesse put a hand on Push's shoulder. The touch was foreign, sparking a certain static electricity. "I'd like to tell you more, but I can't. You need to move him right away. For his own good."

Push pretended not to know as much as he did, but he instinctively knew that Jesse Wallace was familiar with—or worse, involved with—L.T.K. "I think I can arrange something," Push said in a mellow manner.

"Good. I need to get down to the Tombs to see about Tuesday. This shit is wrong. *Dead* wrong."

"She's not at the Tombs. They already have her at Rikers."

"Thanks," said Jesse. His intensity was convincing, like he had all the answers, like he was somehow above the law.

Before Push could contemplate another thing, Jesse was off and running. A small stack of money fell on his way downstairs. "You dropped something!" Push hollered.

Jesse backtracked to pick up the cash. He also took the time to thank Push. "Hey, it was nice what you did for my girls. Thanks. I owe you big-time. Just give me a little time to straighten things out. I need to get my house back in order."

If you say so, Push told himself as Jesse made his way out of the building.

When he returned inside, Push announced, "Okay, Judge. We need to get your things together. I gotta move you."

"Oh. So you're a mind reader too," said Pullman.

CHAPTER TEN

DRUG CONFISCATIONS AND shakedowns were among the biggest sources of cash flow for Licensed to Kill. There was big profit from the drugs, since they could simply be distributed to small-time street thugs who otherwise wouldn't be privileged to handle sizable consignments. Whatever cash the pushers returned to L.T.K. was clear profit anyhow, so there was zero risk.

These shakedowns were where the consistent cash flowed. Yes, they were small payments: $10,000 from this white-collar maverick, $25,000 from another small-time jacker. Of course, the Gold Club and The Sports Bar, two large strip joints in the city, chipped in with their weekly payoffs, along with dozens of other underground sex and gambling outfits. But every dollar added up. And even as those routines set the foundation, there was nothing so exciting, no better thrill ride, than a good old-fashioned robbery.

It was already a routine practice for this or that police agency, be it the NYPD, DEA or ATF, to bust into a situation, neutralize certain threats and then decide the immediate outcome: who would be arrested, what resources would be grabbed up? The activity was constant, and it did nothing less than make gung-ho commandos out of the men and women who executed them.

Sure, they were supposed to be protectors of the peace. But when it got down to it, they hungered for these raids, where guns, drugs and money were discovered. Where assault weapons and paramilitary armor was the norm, and where the element of surprise was a greater resource than oxygen or water.

"And you thought this was only in the movies," said Chico, who at the moment was too hyper to be still . . . to keep his mouth shut.

Skin was there by his side, aggravated, in the passenger's seat of the mud-colored Grand Am. In the backseat were Mule and Primo, whose knee was still in a bad way from the gunshot wound. But he didn't want to miss this for the world.

It was 11 P.M. And this was one of those special occasions where an armed robbery was about to go down.

Four L.T.K. members were out in the car, positioned at the rear of the Pelham-Bay Bronx mini-mall. The post office, the Baskin & Robbins ice cream shop, the American Savings Bank and Bronx Korder Supply Hardware were already closed for the day. However, the Shoprite supermarket was open twenty-four hours. Most of the young female cashiers were letting out through the store's front entrance, probably heading home to do their homework assignments, their toenails or to tongue-toss with a boyfriend.

Meanwhile, inside the store, the manager was left with just four employees: two cashiers, an assistant manager and a stock boy. There was also a rent-a-cop on duty, standing impartial to the majority of in-store politics and focused mainly on petty larcenies and possible robberies.

Shoprite used an outside security firm that was bonded and insured, and that rotated its manpower so that no cop would settle in at any particular job, perhaps surrendering to the usual temptations.

When big Tyrone "Duck" Flowers got the tip that he'd be working at the Pelham Bay Shoprite, he immediately got with Uncle Sam on it. They'd been chasing Shoprite for months now, and it was only a matter of time before Duck would be called to the location. "This will be the sweetest job we ever pulled," promised Duck, as he and others sat and planned the score the day before.

And now, here he stood wearing his weapon, the authentic blue uniform and a badge, feeling as phony as he looked.

As scheduled, Duck went to the window where the store manager was making his end of the day preparations. When he was satisfied that it was time, he turned and went to stand next to the bubblegum machines. It was a spot that could be seen clearly by anyone out in the parking area. He took off his hat, wiped his brow with a tissue, replaced his hat. Though it wasn't necessary, Duck also nodded, just in case the others didn't get the point.

It was extra still and quiet out in back of the mini-mall, except for the rats that scrambled, scurried and climbed around, underneath and inside of the Dumpsters. There was also the wafting odor, however faint, along with the annoying motor buzzing on the rooftop of the building.

"RELAX, CHICO. WE gotta be on point here."

"You sure this is goin' down, Skin?"

"I'm sure. Should be anytime now. Look," Primo said, "that's the signal. Let's move." And the car was wheeled further along, to where they could park.

"That smell is re-fuckin'-diculous," argued Chico.

"It ain't that bad," said Primo. "I changed the bandages a couple hours ago." Primo had an AK-47 laying across his lap; his wounded leg was extended, exposing an abundance of blood-soaked gauze wrapped mostly at the knee.

Skin had his window down, his head part in and part out, playing lookout as much as he was vying for fresh air, what there was of it. "I just hope you'll be useful if the shit has to hit the fan. You and your knee."

"Chill, Skin. You know I'm a freak for pain."

Skin rolled his eyes.

The hooded loading dock stretched for the entire length of the strip mall. There were lights over the rear doors of the various stores, casting varying levels of light on the six-foot-high concrete loading dock. Chico and Mule got out of the car and assumed their positions.

Chico posted up on the walkway, to the left of the steel

doors, while Mule crouched below the loading dock, right there where truck drivers would back up to unload their day-time deliveries.

If this had been a big job, the goons might utilize two-way radios. But this was such an isolated robbery, with an at-mosphere so calm and unthreatening, that the electronics were unnecessary. No heavy armor, or night-vision equip-ment, or red-dot lasers for the automatic weapons.

Duck's promise was stuck in their heads: "This'll be the sweetest job we ever pulled."

"You ready, Mr. Flowers?"

"Certainly," replied Ray Levy, Shoprite's night manager.

And Duck escorted him from the front office of the store, down the frozen food aisle and straight toward the back, where a pair of swinging doors separated the customers from behind-the-scenes activities that ordinarily kept such a large supermarket clean and well stocked. A sign on the doors stated DO NOT ENTER.

Mr. Levy seemed like an easy target. He had a bushy mustache, but nowhere near a full head of hair. He was a tall, lanky white man who loped about, but who might've been involved in some sort of sport when he was younger—maybe running. He also had a chipper attitude and dancing green eyes, even now, at the day's end.

Duck had watched earlier as Levy filled a brown shop-ping bag with cash (Duck guessed it amounted to between $50,000 and $75,000, money that he'd personally drop in the Citibank night deposit box over in Co-op city. The night deposit there was a drive-through type, and wouldn't require Levy to leave his vehicle, a gold Toyota 4Runner parked be-hind the mall. It was a procedure that allowed the Shoprite proprietor to forgo the expense of an armored car service. If only he made it to the 4Runner safely.

GELAINE WAS ONE of Levy's employees who'd just gotten off from work, and was just about the hottest girl Kevin had ever met. But, of course, that was how Kevin felt about every girl he met, whether this month or last. Kevin's pickup line was a sure thing for this babe, whom he'd noticed parading down the walkway in front of the mall just weeks ago. He already had a supply of those business cards, the ones that you could purchase from the Create-A-Card kiosk there at the post office. For $5, Kevin could call himself the President of the United States, official seal and all, if he so desired. Like a vulture, Kevin swooped down on Gelaine to compliment her on her looks and gave her his instant *Vogue* business card.

Kevin was brief and cowardly at first, tossing his practiced one-liner and telling Gelaine how he was "blown away" by her pretty eyes and picture-perfect smile. But underneath the surface of his introduction he was more interested in the girl's obvious innocence. He was even counting on it as his advantage.

It took only one after-work dinner at Sizzler and a second date at the movies, plus a week's worth of carefully crafted phone calls, to get Gelaine here in the backseat of his dad's Lincoln Town Car, another huckster-move of his since he was supposedly heading to the supermarket for a few things.

It was just Kevin and his father these days, so somebody had to do the shopping. And, like magic, the Lincoln was parked here in the Shoprite parking lot, far enough away so that the storefront glow wouldn't intrude on their intimate encounter. Intimate indeed.

Kevin worked his way past the first-kiss jitters on the last engagement, at the movies. But here, he had graduated to that next level, with his girl-hungry lips eating further down into Gelaine's cleavage. He'd have eaten that bubble-gum-pink blouse she wore, as sweet as it all smelled, but he wasn't an animal. Not yet, anyway.

Whispering into Gelaine's ear, Kevin said, "Would you mind if I did something to you that doesn't involve sex, but something that could drive you crazy?" It wasn't the easiest line to remember, but Kevin figured he had it correct, words from one of his favorite male chauvinist fiction writers. And why not, since it worked in the book.

Gelaine giggled, not only because Kevin's hot breath was

tickling her inner ear, but because she really didn't know how to respond. She was giggling too, because that's what many sixteen-year-olds do; they giggle when they're unsure, when they're propositioned, even when they're saying no.

And Gelaine did say no. But Kevin kept at her. He kept seducing her and exciting her. These were sensations that she couldn't deny . . . that she had to enjoy, no matter how much she trembled. No matter how unfamiliar the touch.

Kevin knew from past experiences that the more pleasure he showed Gelaine, the closer he'd come to what he was after.

"Okay. Then could I . . . could I sniff it?"

"Sniff it? You nasty!" Gelaine answered, naturally with more giggles.

"But you know you like them nasty boys," he said, trying to keep the bass in his twenty-eight-year-old voice and the bulge in his pants from being discovered.

"Do not."

"Do too."

"Uh-uh," Gelaine replied. But it wasn't enough to convince Kevin, who steadily ate his way down her blouse.

Damn, her fragrance and perspiration smelled good together. And he couldn't keep his hands from the petting, his hand sliding further and further, up and down her thigh, smooth against the thin fabric skirt she wore. That was another Kevin-the-huckster exclusive: "You should always wear short skirts to impress the important magazine people. You never know . . . before long they'll have you in those VH1 fashion shows with all the celebrities. Maybe even on the cover of *Vogue*!" And Gelaine had said, "Really??" After which the two had discussed her wardrobe at length. She had one of those short skirts on now. It was also pink, and fit like a glove so that her innocent curves would show. At least they had been innocent.

Kevin got further along, with his head down there, wedged between her legs and his mouth eating through the white panties she wore. The hot air of his breath made Gelaine spasm, frightening her with more never-before sensations.

Gelaine became afraid. She muttered, "St-op," in that soft purr that was but a plea for more of the same.

Kevin thought about smacking the doo-doo out of her, a tactic he also read about but was too cowardly to execute.

A car door closed nearby.

Kevin was startled, thinking only of police and how men his age went to jail for occasions such as this. He raised his head to see what seemed like a small army of women wearing aprons from the supermarket headed his way. That's when Kevin realized he'd parked in the employee section of the lot. Some girls went to their own vehicles, while others hopped into double-parked cars near the entrance of the supermarket. The clock on the dashboard read 11:05. That meant he'd been struggling with Gelaine for an hour and change.

Shit.

"Where you takin' me?" Gelaine asked, tugging her skirt back down over her hips.

"A quieter spot."

"I wanna go home."

"Relax, boo. I wanna show you somethin' real nice."

Gelaine sucked her teeth and made the icky face, the corner of her upper lip curled some. "Nice, like what?"

"It's a surprise," said Kevin with the devil's tone in his voice. And he steered the black Lincoln around back of the mall where it was darker and secluded. The Lincoln's headlights were off so that no one would see the car.

"I wanna go home," Gelaine repeated, now with her brows in a V and her lips pouting.

"Just hold on, babe, I wanna talk with you for a minute. I'm telling you, you won't regret—hey, look over there."

Gelaine did, adding to all of the sets of eyes looking up at the loading dock, all from their various perspectives.

From Kevin's perspective, there was a robbery in progress, and thank God the Lincoln's motor was quiet.

Two men had exited through one of the rear doors of Shoprite. One was the rent-a-cop. "That's one of my bosses," said Gelaine. "You better not let him see us. He knows my daddy."

Now, Kevin noticed a third man hiding in a doorway, not far from the rent-a-cop and Gelaine's boss and his brown bag. "Oh shit! There. Down below. And . . . he's got a gun! It's a robbery!" Kevin concluded. He mashed the accelerator, and hyper energy pumped through his body.

Gelaine screamed and held on to the door.

When Skin shouted, "Car!" Primo pushed the AK-47 aside and shifted his body over to the driver's side. He threw the Grand Am into drive, floored the pedal and yelled at the top of his lungs. The pain.

"Aw, FUCK! I knew it! I fuckin' knew it!" growled Skin. He grabbed the AK, pointing it out of his passenger side window, and aimed for the speeding Lincoln.

Mule had been crouched down long enough for his legs to cramp up—like he'd done a hundred deep knee bends all at once—and now the pain and fatigue of it was catching up with him.

He knew it was okay to show himself since Duck and the store manager had slammed the rear door shut and proceeded along the landing, discussing the New York Knicks. Those were the cues. It was during the bullshit basketball talk that Mule heard car tires screeching, and then shots being fired. From a quiet night to the chaos of loud blasts, things went haywire so fast. The gunfire sounded like so many hammers repeatedly banging at empty garbage cans.

Mule turned to see if he was being attacked. No bullets had hit him yet, but he could feel the vibrations—or maybe that was his heart. A luxury car was coming at him now, and he was impulsive with his reflexes, directing his twin-barrel twelve-gauge at the vehicle. He cocked it.

Blinding headlights were cut on. Like a frozen deer, Mule was stapled with fear.

Duck swore he was losing his mind.

He had no idea where the gunshots were coming from, but what he did know was that this had nothing at all to do with his master plan. Somebody was sabotaging his robbery, he just had no idea who.

Gunshots. A Lincoln speeding semi-parallel near the dock.

Mule standing down there looking up at Duck, then back at the Lincoln . . . a stupid expression on his face. And now Mule was also shooting at the Lincoln. One shot took off the vehicle's front grill, and the car swerved in a zigzag before it picked up speed.

Duck's eyes were spinning in his head. He wasn't sure who was in the car, or if Primo and Skin had switched vehicles. Nothing was right. A million questions, and no time to contemplate. Everything was so spontaneous, with complex decisions a trained officer couldn't even make correctly.

While bullets were flying, ricocheting off of the Town Car, the mini-mall walls and the Dumpsters, Duck's greatest concern was for his life. The echoes from the blasts were delayed in relation to the flash-fire from that distant weapon. But if Duck wasn't mistaken, that second vehicle was the Grand Am, and it didn't make a bit of sense that they were firing at him. There was a toss-up happening in his mind—a choice. The money or his life, his duty as a rent-a-cop was the furthest thing from the agenda.

Piece of cake, my ass!

Mr. Levy was on the move. He tossed the bag of money into a stack of empty milk crates, and then he bent down on one knee. A pistol was drawn. "Duck for cover! Don't just stand there! Get down!" he shouted.

Duck shook the rigor mortis and hid by the milk crates.

A crash upset the atmosphere and there was a desperate cry that followed. The Lincoln had sideswiped the wall of the dock with every bit of its muscle and, Duck guessed, plowed into Mule as well.

Mule's cry. Mule's body crunching behind the impact of the Town Car.

Shit!

There were sparks shooting up along the underside of the dock; there were gun bursts in the distance as well.

Skin and Primo? How'd they let this get so out of hand?

Eventually, Duck thought about the money. It was less than five feet from where he was standing. And Mr. Levy would expect a hired guard to protect it. That was all the reason he needed. Besides that, Levy was busy, still on one knee, firing shots at the Lincoln as well as at the second oncoming vehicle, the Grand Am. Already the man was reloading. Damn!

"There's a car over there!" Levy shouted. "I know this is probably unusual for you, but you must fire your weapon. What the hell are you waiting for?!"

As Duck began firing his own weapon, deliberately missing targets and adding to all the noise, Chico was standing over Mr. Levy. The supermarket manager had his back to Chico, not even aware that the nose of a .45-caliber automatic was leveled at the back of his head. Duck saw it before it happened, with Chico's history planted firmly in his mind—that spur-of-the-moment execution of his wife.

Jesus, he's gonna . . .

Duck never completed the thought.

Chico did it for him.

The bullet tore a chunk of Levy's skull away, dropping him facedown on the walkway. Duck found himself staring at the fallen man, while the Lincoln's backlights disappeared down the way, toward the far end of the loading dock. Primo brought the Grand Am to a screeching halt and Skin jumped out with the AK.

Duck had done it all with L.T.K. The ski-mask robberies, the Kingpin scores down in Chinatown, even kidnapping the reporter. But nothing was so wicked as Chico blasting a man's brains away, not more than ten feet from him. He couldn't help wondering how this guy slept at night with so many bloody memories burdening him.

CHAPTER ELEVEN

"**FRED, I'VE BEEN** thinking," Asondra said, as her husband clasped the diamond necklace at the back of her neck.

Their meeting with the adoption agency had been a success. They were now considered "qualified" to adopt, and they'd met a number of toddlers, one of whom they hoped to call their daughter within the next month. It was time for a celebration: Part 1.

"What's that, sugar-pie. Whatcha been thinkin'?" he asked, kissing her neck right where the clasp laid.

"About all the violence in the city."

"Now, butterscotch, you know you don't ever have to worry about that. I'll protect you and our children with my last dying breath."

"Okay, and I believe you, Fred. Except . . . what I was thinking was that this might not be the best place in the world for a family. I was thinking about Trevor . . ."

"Asondra! Trevor will be heading to college soon. And besides, I thought you said that this was your fairy-tale dream—that you wanted to spend the rest of your life here in Harlem. Don't I give you everything you want?"

Asondra looked at Fred's reflection in the mirror before her and touched her hand to his, there on her shoulder. "Fred, I said I wanted to live here, not die here. All of the jewelry, the clothes and money in the world won't make me happy if I'm dead . . . if my child is . . ." Asondra cut her own thought short and turned to face Fred. Her hand rested against his cheek.

"There's no doubt that I'm living my dream, baby, that big cruise you told me life is. But I can't help thinking that the ship is gonna sink one day. There's all this killing, terror threats, and they were even talking about gangster cops on TV today . . ." Asondra's voice trembled and her eyes watered some. She went on to say, "Freddie, you should know. Your own assistant was killed out on your doorstep a couple years ago. Doesn't that mean anything to you? Hunh? When does it end, when do we do something about it? When it's too late?"

Fred pulled Asondra into his arms and cupped her head to his chest. "Wow, baby. I didn't know you felt so strongly about these things. And all the while I thought you were so happy."

Asondra sighed, "I am. Stuff has been on my mind, that's all."

"I see that. A whole lot of stuff, apparently . . . I remember you being the one to convince me that Harlem was good, that New York was the place to be. You told me all about your big dreams—hell, we've even made a lot of those dreams into reality with Glam, and now we've got another child on the way. But you've even changed my whole outlook on life. I've become a changed man. Made the whole enterprise legit. All the money in the Caymans is applied to good causes, we've got a lot of businesses up and going—saved some mom-and-pop outfits. Philanthropy, jeez, who would've guessed it."

Asondra's determination soured some under Fred's reality check. He was right about those things. She'd turned his whole world around, just as he did for her.

"But I'm afraid, Fred. It's just the visions I've been havin'."

Fred sucked his teeth lightly. "You probably need a vacation, baby. How 'bout we go to Martha's Vineyard? Or maybe to Atlanta."

In a winded voice, Asondra said, "Been there, done that."

"Well, maybe you'd like to leave the country . . . go to

Asia, South America, whatever. Just say the word, sweet-ness."

"You think a vacation would change things?"

"I'm sure of it. You have to change your focus, hon. In a world of dark images, there's still plenty of bright colors to see. It's all a matter of how you look at things. So what if the cops are turning rotten and the terrorists are blowing themselves up. People are gonna be people. Crazy, insane, twisted . . . people."

"And if they hijack the plane we take to Asia?" Asondra's eyes twinkled with girlish glee.

"It'll never happen. The odds are a million to one."

"I hope you're right, Freddie. God, I hope you're right."

From down the hall in the Allen town house, Trevor called out, wondering if his mother and stepfather were ready yet. "Dad," he yelled. "Shanté has been waiting for twenty min-utes already."

Fred pulled his lips from Asondra's. "Can't keep Shanté waiting," he said with his clever smile.

"It's not what you think, Fred. They're just friends," said Asondra, reading her husband's mind.

Fred responded, "Like I've said before . . . you really have to be in our shoes to understand how we think. Try and men-tion leaving Harlem to him and see his reaction."

"A wise man once told me to watch what you ask for, 'cause you just might get it." Naturally, Asondra was refer-ring to Fred.

FOLLOWING THE EVENTS at the Wallace home, Push took the cop's suggestion and moved Judge Pullman to another residence.

Francine Oliver, the record company executive, had two floors leased below the Wallaces. The first floor, where she lived with her teenage son, and the second floor, which was leased by OCG, the record company she worked for. It was set up to accommodate a guest for a night, a weekend or even a month, depending on the *who* and the *what* involved.

Evelyn was there when Push addressed Ms. Oliver.

"The problem I have with that is later this week a group is coming in to record," said Ms. Oliver. "And the sessions will probably continue for a month or longer . . ." She seemed willing to compromise and added, "But, hey . . . if it can help, you're welcome to use the place till then," she offered.

Evelyn was quick to say, "That's fine. And I'll be glad to compensate you for—"

"Don't be silly. I'm glad to help my landlord. And any friend of theirs is a friend of mine," Ms. Oliver said with a generous smile. It was easy to see why the woman made such leaps and bounds in her line of work.

Judge Pullman moved one floor down. It wasn't such a big move, considering his few possessions, but he had Push and Evelyn to help out anyhow.

More important than the luxuries that came with the second-floor dwelling was that nobody knew he was there.

When the move was complete, Evelyn almost had to beg the Judge to take a break from the hideaway. And besides, she, the Judge and Push had business to discuss.

In the Volvo, Evelyn testified, "I got lost up here once. Just kept driving up 95. Didn't even know I crossed the state line till I used the next exit. I eventually found out I was in Connecticut. I was tired of driving, and hungry too. So I just canceled with the probationer, a white-collar offender . . ." She was talking too much; how folks get lost in what is of interest to them, trying to keep it impressive. "I figured I could always follow up on her later."

Push made a face: *I don't doubt it.* From the driver's seat, Evelyn caught his expression in the rearview mirror. "Anyway," she continued, "I found this cute little restaurant in Cos Cob. The best salmon dish you'll ever wanna brag about."

Pullman was thinking that this would be fine, that he was being paranoid about things. *Maybe they backed off*, he thought. *How long can I stay locked in a box before I go out of my mind?*

How long indeed.

He settled into the discreet seating there at the Water's

Edge restaurant and enjoyed the ambiance of an intimate, yet spacious, dining room.

The tastes were a special kind of familiar, including barbecued shrimp, smock rock-shrimp potato salad with corn salsa, and barbecued salmon dressed with papaya applesauce over a bed of white rice. It was the kind of sweet-spicy meal that made eating something to look forward to . . . something an older man could appreciate but not over-indulge in.

When the meal was mostly done with, they got down to business.

"I called this meeting to hopefully put everything on the table in detail. No beating around the bush and no double-talk . . ." Evelyn took the driver's seat in the conversation since it was she who'd brought it all together. "Only the three of us know about this meeting—about this conversation." She stopped to scan the Judge's eyes for a confirmation, and once she saw that in his eyes, she continued. "We want to hire a pro. We're willing to pay well. Whatever it takes."

"I'm listening," said Push, using discretion.

"First off, whether you agree with our proposal or not, I want to let you know you're off of your paper. From this second, your probation is considered satisfied. There's some doctoring I'll need to do with forms and records, but it's no big deal. I'll handle my end."

"No more monthly visits? No more prying into my personal life? My financial situation?"

"You say that like I was going above and beyond the call of my duties, Push."

Push shrugged. "Maybe a little rough in the beginning."

"And you weren't rough?" Evelyn said, hoping he wouldn't make her get into details. "But . . . I was hoping that you would continue to stop by now and then. Ya know, just to say hi."

Push ignored the small stuff. He said, "So, you need a plumber. And I do plumbing. But I charge for what I do . . . for my time. Business is business," said Push.

"We agree," said Evelyn. "As long as your rates are reasonable."

"Any rate is reasonable for this kind of work."

"Agreed," Evelyn said.

"How bad is the plumbing you need done?"

"Very bad. Just one job is all. A one-man job," mentioned Pullman. "Could be dangerous."

"I like it already. Where is the work?"

"Right in your backyard. Harlem. Only, we don't have an exact location yet. We were hoping for your help on that."

And now Push was more comfortable, since the Judge joined in on the conversation. It was the sort of confirmation he needed to know for sure that this was not a setup. If it was, and if, say, one of them had some kind of recording device, then they would be just as culpable.

This thing about gangsta cops intrigued Push. In being honest with himself, he didn't feel like any servant of the people. He wasn't a superhero. But he was being asked by people in powerful positions, with clout, to take down a cop. And finally, it was his pleasure to be open about it. No more hints or suggestions. The real deal.

Evelyn explained some things that she had found out about L.T.K.; that members of the group were probably washed up, burnt out, injured or some variation thereof. "We think this is one of them," said Evelyn. She passed a photo across the table.

Pullman said, "His name is Donald. Donald Cortez. He was once an agent with the FBI's SWAT unit. One of their best."

Evelyn and Push stared at Pullman, both of them wondering how he knew so much.

"Okay," Evelyn said melodramatically. "But you should know that this guy might've shot and killed his wife the night they came for you, Charles. The neighbors couldn't be absolutely sure since it was so early in the morning. But they said it looked like him. In and out. Bang-bang, and off he drove."

"Just like that," suggested Push.

"Yes. Just like that," said Evelyn, and she produced a second photo. With her eyes alone, she dared Charles to know this one. "Push, we have a videotape that a reporter recorded . . . her own little undercover mission."

And Pullman added, "Only this group found out about the tape. They killed her—"

"We *think* they killed her," Evelyn interjected. "But we know for certain that there have been at least two other deaths in relation to this tape. A brother of a police officer and a U.S. attorney. We think—let me rephrase that. We know that they're coming after the Judge for the same reasons."

"Okay. I got that much. I can put two and two together. I'm just wondering what's on this videotape—a confession for the JFK killing? Or O.J. Simpson's confession? Or maybe who shot Biggie Smalls and Tupac?"

"Who's that? Biggie Smalls?" asked Pullman.

Evelyn rolled her eyes and said, "Never mind." Then, to Push she said, "The tape shows what looks like a headquarters of some kind. A hideout, or whatever you wanna call it. Whatever it is, I know it's where they congregate. The video shows a mess of lopsided shots. Some quick flashes of a few faces. But it looks too dark to make a positive ID."

"So, they killin' people over a tape they don't even know about . . . they haven't seen it?"

"Not sure. But it's the thought, I guess. I'd feel threatened if I were them. The voices are clear. And I was able to get two still photos of these two knuckleheads."

"Oh, that's where these came from?"

"A little technology goes a long way," said Evelyn. "And I'm sure they know that."

"You keep saying 'they.' How many is 'they'?"

Pullman took a stab at it, estimating, "Maybe two or three dozen."

"And these two? What roles do they play?"

"This looks to be an enforcer of some kind. That's the best I could some up with, since the details about his wife unfolded. Two huge holes in her face, Push."

"And the other?"

"This sounds like the"—Evelyn noticed how Charles

eyeballed the photo and turned his head away—"the leader."
Evelyn knew she and Charles really needed to talk. There
was more he wasn't telling her.

"Don't tell me. He's with the DEA, or FBI or something?"

"You got half of it right," she said. "He was NYPD, 7th
Precinct, 44th Precinct, 23rd Precinct. Then he went to the
FBI, special operations," Evelyn explained.

"Looks old," said Push.

"Don't underestimate him," said the Judge.

"Dessert?" The waitress appeared out of nowhere, startling them.

"Could you bring us a fresh pot of coffee?" said Evelyn.

"Certainly. Anything else?"

"Yes. Bring the coffee back in twenty minutes," was the
closing statement.

"Oh. Uhm . . . okay."

Back to the business at hand, Evelyn opened a folder and
handed it to Push. "It's classified information, Push. All the
vital stuff, down to his place of birth and blood type."

Push smirked as he said, "Something like the information
you keep on me, isn't it?"

She was expressionless, hoping that Push would keep
with the program and get past the slick comments.

"Smokes a cigar, too. My, my, aren't we detailed. I notice
he has a daughter. Can we find out where she lives?" asked
Push. A second or two later he asked, "What're you both
lookin' all crazy at me for? It's just in case. I thought you
wanted me to get this guy at all costs?"

"We do. But not at the expense of innocent people."

"Huh. All's fair in the game of war," said Push. But he
saw how Evelyn looked at him, like maybe she misjudged
him. "Relax, Ms. W. I'm not goin' after his daughter. I just
wondered where she lays her head at night." Evelyn and the
Judge both breathed easier.

"Can you give us a price?"

"Eventually. Can I hold this?"

"Of course. We're staking our reputations on you, Push."

"And I'm putting my life on the line for you two," replied Push, gazing deeply into Evelyn's eyes.

Another voice interrupted the moment of silence. "Evelyn! Charles! What a coincidence seeing you up here."

Evelyn had the most surprised expression.

"Fred? Hey! How are you?" Judge Pullman spoke up first, as if this was a most normal occasion to see one another outside of their hometown, Harlem.

"Hello, Fred," Evelyn finally said.

"I can't imagine what brings you all up here. I thought the Water's Edge was my own little dining secret. Oh—excuse me. You haven't met my wife, have you? Asondra, meet the Honorable Judge Charles Pullman, our ace man in the federal courts. And Ms. Evelyn Watson, United States probation officer—you're still considered Ms., no?"

"Ahh . . . yes, Fred. I'm still single. Still a Ms."

Fred smiled and said to his wife, "Baby, between these two, I don't know who's more responsible for keeping our neighborhoods safe, for keeping the vermin off of the streets. I'm sorry, I don't mean to ignore you, sir . . . ehh . . . you look somewhat familiar to me." Fred the politician. His brain was slow these days, probably political burnout, and Asondra straightened him out. Fred soon came around, and his eyes darted toward Evelyn. What a freak coincidence! He wished he could disappear all at once.

While he hunted for the right words, Asondra butted in. "Fred! Don't you remember? This is one of the partners with Melrah. We just spoke about you the other day," she said, navigating her comments between both men.

"Sure. Sure," added Fred, dizzied inside of the recollection.

Asondra said "How are you, Mr. Jackson. By the way, we got your call about the funding and I've been trying to get back in touch with your wife, Ms. Gardner—"

Push didn't bother correcting the woman about his marital status. He simply nodded.

"Maybe you can mention that I called," she suggested.

Fred could've been standing on a land mine, as nervous as he was.

"No problem," said Push, who was even quicker with the recollection.

There was so much recent history here:

Fred and Evelyn. Fred and Push.

And all of them were familiar with murder.

EVELYN AND FRED said so much without speaking, the conversations in their eyes being the tale of their souls.

Judge Pullman, on the other hand, thought this was all more fanfare than he experienced during a normal week on the bench. First the meet-and-greet at the Wallace residence, and now here as well, in another state! He didn't think things could be any more coincidental than this.

His usual gesture, Fred Allen ordered a bottle of the restaurant's "finest champagne" for Evelyn's table and suggested, "We should talk someday soon, Evelyn." He might as well have said politely, We need to end this chitchat. At least, that's how Push saw things.

The two tables engaged in separate toasts that night. At the Allen table, Fred led the toast. "Here's to the new and improved Allen family . . . and to the daughter on the way . . . oh, and to Trevor's special friend, Shanté." Fred flashed his practiced smile for the young couple, but it was with good intention.

Judge Pullman led the toast at his table. "To the new business relationship . . . to loyalty among friends . . . and to a job well done," he said.

And as the three tapped glasses, Evelyn couldn't help but sense the strange vapors in the air. Again, she was a party to the decision of taking another person's life, and again, it was Push who was being employed to do the job.

CHAPTER TWELVE

EVELYN WATSON AND Fred Allen decided two years ago that they should stay out of touch. It was a matter of common sense, since things had become way too hot . . . things had spun way out of hand.

Back-to-back murders. FBI and NYPD surveillance, and the two had actually succeeded. They did what they set out to do, and because of that, they got just what they expected.

Who in this lifetime could claim access to $400 million? Enough money to operate a highly industrialized nation for quite some time. Not that they could just take that money and go buck-wild on a shopping spree, because at least there had to be a record of expenditures, in the event of an audit.

But Fred had the scheme figured from soup to nuts. With his dummy committees and dummy corporations and dummy foundations, using any amount of money could always be accounted for. It was as though he had a key to the largest vault in the biggest bank.

It was all about access.

And chemistry.

The strictly business relationship between Fred and Evelyn was born the moment she overheard that discussion in the courthouse cafeteria. She just happened to be in the right place at the right time.

The U.S. attorney and certain FBI agents were plotting to crash Fred's party. And the way Evelyn felt at the time, she decided to speak to Fred—the underdog in the scenario—an old friend from high school and an acquaintance whom she acknowledged from time to time in various Harlem circles.

"I have some inside information," Evelyn wrote on a business card. And she stuck the card in his hand at one of those political fund-raisers he arranged.

Evelyn awaited Fred's call, all the while knowing in her heart that this was the ticket that would change her life. It was a resource that might bring her the good life, financial freedom; she could buy her mother the house, the car and whatever her heart desired. She could work because she chose to, not because she had to.

Most of all, she'd know that sense of security, one that wouldn't leave her as another statistic, another woman who lived an average life with an average outcome, a woman who wouldn't quite realize her dreams.

Fred called just two days later, and so began the "chemistry" between the two. They became committed, as if by a traditional marriage. They agreed that the endeavor would be bigger than the both of them, bigger than Harlem and anyone who lived there.

It was that first serious meeting when Evelyn asked, "So, Fred—enlighten me. If you pulled this off before with the last election, with the Democrats and their Harlem Renaissance Fund, then why would you need to go for it again? Why not just take the money and run? And another thing: Why in the world do you need me?"

"For one thing, Evelyn, just because it was a three-hundred-million-dollar pot doesn't mean I kept it all. Hell, we still did much of what we promised with the money . . . granted, Harlem still has a ways to go, but at least we fixed some streets, some classrooms and installed some community programs. At best, between you and me, I got to keep a little more than five for myself—"

"As in, million?"

Fred nodded. He further said, "But look at my lifestyle . . . the town house on Striver's Row, the two luxury cars, the vacations and a few dozen investments . . . I'm not doing bad—don't get me wrong. It's just that I could be doing a lot better. And then you have to figure in—"

"You don't have to dig deep. I understand. You're strapped for cash because of living large. You had big money, so you spent big money . . . happens all the time. We don't know what we've got till it's gone. Just answer my other question. Why can't you just take the information I've given you, slap a few bills in my hands and call it a day? Why do you say you need my help?"

"Here's where things get ugly," said Fred. The two were at a corner table at the Coconut Sugar Hill Bistro. She was having the coconut-crusted escolar, a fatty fish flown in from Hawaii and served in a refreshing carrot-and-guava sauce. He had the rack of lamb brushed with roasted garlic and Dijon mustard, served with a flaming sprig of rosemary herb. "You know I'm living with a woman named Sara. Sara Godfrey. She went from being my personal assistant to my . . . well . . . my lover."

"Fred! I had no idea. I mean, I had heard . . . people speculate, but it's true? The interracial bit? I didn't take you to be that type."

Fred shrugged. "It was the novelty of it all, at first. My curiosity. And the girl was just so damned convenient to look at, Evelyn. So I had her working at the house—"

Evelyn made that murmur under her breath. *Likely story.*

"But before I even made any moves, I'm talkin' any moves whatsoever, the girl made a move on me. A goddamned intern extorted me!"

"Whadda you mean? Extorted??"

"I made a real big mistake bringing her in my house, Evelyn. She overheard a conversation I had regarding the fund. I was speaking with an old associate—a guy named Julius Anderson. He's doing time now, by the way—"

"Stick with Sara," said Evelyn.

"Well, she stepped to me, talkin' about how . . . and she put it so creatively, Evelyn. She says, 'You need me.' "

Fred recalled the conversation with Sara. He told her adamantly that she was to address him as "Mr. Allen."

But Sara said, "I'll call you Fred . . . as long as you're set-ting up dummy companies, phony committees and stealing money from the fund . . . oh yes indeedy . . ."

"She finessed it, Evelyn. Played me like a fiddle. Said I was the man who's gonna give her everything she'd ever want in this lifetime."

"Meaning?"

"Sex and money."

"And you want me to believe that she extorted and se-duced you—you, the politician whose game is to manipu-late. So, what? The manipulator got manipulated?"

"Not that easily, Evelyn. You wouldn't believe that this—this demon is a Yale graduate, from a good family . . . at least, she's supposed to be, anyway. See, her father molested her at age fifteen. She actually had to have an abortion . . ."

"Oh, shit. That is ugly."

Fred wagged his forefinger. "You ain't heard nothin' yet. See, there were complications. The doctor told her she could never have children. And from there on, I think, she became the devil. She burned her father's belongings in some kind of strange ritual. She did this in the backyard of the family home, with no arguments from anyone. And then one day she snuck in his bedroom and she cut off his thing."

"His thing, Fred?" Evelyn twisted her face.

"His thing, Evelyn. And she used a pair of hedge cutters to do it."

"Jesus."

"But before that, she rigged her college professor's brakes to fail. And there was some incident with some col-lege boy. And here's the whopper with fries and a shake: the doctor—the one who did the abortion—when they found him, he had been given an abortion—now you tell me who you think did it?"

"Fred? An abortion? A man doesn't have a—"

"Oh, trust me. She made one. Used his ass. And he bled to death."

Evelyn had to throw down some water to keep her food from coming up. The images were sickening.

"Evelyn, I'm stuck with the devil."

"And you made this woman the chairperson of the new fund, Fred? How could you? What was on your mind?"

"Jail. Hedge cutters. A bunch of stuff. And I especially didn't wanna have an abortion myself, if you catch my drift. I guess I figured if I couldn't beat her, I'd bring her aboard. Plus, the sex was regular. I needed a, well, you know—a companion. So I went for it. I dove in."

"This sounds like a nightmare, and you're the victim."

"Exactly. Now do you see what I'm saying?"

"Yeah, I see all right, Mr. Mandingo Warrior with the curiosity. So, what does Sara have to do with you needing me?"

"I admit it. I made a mistake. A big one. And I have to bail out now, before Chambers wins the election . . . or before I get whacked."

"Whacked."

"Yes, whacked. This woman is one vicious bitch, if you'll excuse my French. My big mistake was to attach myself to her, Evelyn. We're practically married."

"And you say this to say what?"

"Evelyn, your hook is in with all the bad boys. More of them than I could ever come to know in maybe five lifetimes. And you may think this is crazy, but . . . I need a killer. Whatever the cost . . . I need a real-life, cold-blooded killer."

"You're right, Fred."

"About needing a killer?"

"About being crazy. This woman has made you lose your mind."

"Okay, I agree with you. But let me tell you what's at stake here. I have a way to up the amount of money I can pull down. Ready for this?"

Evelyn already wasn't impressed with taking a life in exchange for five million dollars. But she was at least curious about his idea. "Go ahead."

"I can pull down a hundred."

Evelyn froze. She was almost afraid to confirm what he'd said. "As . . . in . . . one hundred million?"

"You heard me right. But if I don't go through with this—if I can't hire one of your guys—then guess who's gonna get sixty percent of that." Evelyn's eyeballs shifted, thinking. "Sara. She's controlling the whole scheme now. She's appointed the treasurer, the secretary, the vice chair and basically anyone else who saw her point of view. She has control, Evelyn."

"And all because you were thinking with your dick. Hmm. Imagine that."

Evelyn thought about her Sugar Hill Bistro meeting for weeks. She took into account all that she learned about Fred. Like Evelyn, Fred grew up in Harlem. And when they matured, they both happened to take jobs as public servants of one sort or another. Evelyn tried to remain a teacher, but the money wasn't right. A stroke of luck (if spotting a newspaper ad can be called that) got her the position of probation officer, first with the state, and then with the almighty federal government. Better pay. Better benefits.

Fred, on the other hand, wanted to be a lawyer, but he couldn't pass the bar exams. As an alternative, Fred chose storefront politics—he didn't need to be the man running for office, but he could sure sell the product as that behind-the-scenes dynamo, the campaign manager. From one politician to another, Fred Allen developed his skills on the electoral playing field, learning how to manipulate the opinions and whims of the average Joe as well as any spinmeister in Washington.

Evelyn thought about these things, but the butter and honey on the toast was the money. Not just any amount of money that a woman could just get by with, but a winning pot. She had just one life to live, and it wouldn't be fanciful or intangible like a TV soap opera.

It was about that time when Reginald "Push" Jackson came out of the pen. He'd spent fourteen years there, hard time amidst stabbings, suicides and other miserable atmospheres. Stuff that soapbox things couldn't handle. He emerged a hardened criminal. A known killer.

Evelyn's usual routine was to follow ex-cons, repeat offenders and hardened men. Men like Push. The community may not have known it, but she was their protector.

One night she struck gold while tailing Push as he strolled Harlem's cold streets. She was driving a beat-up Dodge—the vehicle she and other probation officers used to snoop undetected. Push ducked into the shadows of a brownstone somewhere on 122nd Street. Evelyn parked quietly, at a distance, yet close enough to see the taxi pull up. A man got out. Push slipped out of hiding and took the man's life at point-blank range, right there on the dark sidewalk.

At the time, Evelyn was so frightened by what she'd seen that she ducked down and waited. Moments later, she drove away, half in shock and half realizing that this was a godsend, the answer to Fred Allen's problems and her ticket to her destiny. It was then, as it was now. Push was still in business. The business of murder.

AFTER DINNER AT the Water's Edge, Push, Evelyn and the Judge headed back across the state line, back to West 128th Street in Harlem.

Push escorted Evelyn and Charles into 440 as though he were a newly appointed bodyguard, carefully examining the stretch of block to be certain, and then the dwelling as well.

"I'm gonna have a talk with Charles for a bit, Push. Thanks a million for your . . . cooperation."

Push made a quick appraisal, gave the briefest wave and closed the door behind him. Surely not Evelyn and the Judge—Push couldn't bear the thought.

"You can't even look me in the eye, can you," said Evelyn with a condescending tone.

Charles made an attempt to stand up to her challenge and looked her dead in the eyes. "And why can't I?"

"Okay. Then look at me and tell me you don't know Sam Foster, the leader of L.T.K."

"And if I do?"

"If you do, then there's a whole lot you're not telling me, Charles. Who is Sam Foster to you?"

"Wow, for a girlfriend of my stepson, you sure do wanna see my whole closet, don't you."

"Just the things that involve me, Charles. And as far as I'm concerned, you have involved me. If I could explain to you how behind I am on my work, you'd call my boss and have me fired. And Charles, not for nothin', but Push is one of many men who I can at least trust is not gonna go buck wild and slaughter a whole mess of innocent people. But the others?" Evelyn exhausted some air. "If I don't do my job, the city won't be safe."

"And," said Pullman, "if we don't take care of this problem with Sam, the city really won't be safe. He's the worst of two evils, trust that."

"Tell me about you and Sam Foster."

Pullman considered it. "I can't, Evelyn."

"Fuck, Charles! You know enough about me to bury me. The least you could do is tell me who this man is. Why, does he scare you so much?"

"Forget the psychology, dear one. You just need to trust me on this. The type of information you're asking me for can get you killed many times over. Things that would open up a can of worms . . . upset a whole lot of people. So, it's best you don't know."

"You make me so sick!"

"Easy, darling. Let me say this . . . Remember long ago when they had the scandal with the LAPD? Because of one or two dozen cops, a school of people were wrongly convicted." Pullman easily overlooked Evelyn's emotions.

"What's the cop's name?" Evelyn's mind wandered. She came up with "Mark something."

"Yes. Mark Furman. His whole 'nigger' campaign was exposed during the O.J. trial. But then, they found so many other Mark Furmans. Add to that the CIA and DEA involvement with some informant. Ricky something or other . . ."

"I recall. Go on."

"Well, I say that to say this: Sam Foster is ten times bigger. At least."

Evelyn seemed to come back down to earth with a clearer perspective now.

"What you should know, Evelyn, is that Sam Foster is a malicious thinker. The type of demon who lives out the most unthinkable violence, with little or no regard for human life."

Hands on her hips, Evelyn said, "Great. That's just great. You haven't said any more than the signs say at the zoo: DANGER! DON'T FEED THE LIONS."

"Sorry, Evelyn."

"I am too. I hope Push gets your man, Charles. For your sake." Evelyn's words were a sharp, stinging reminder of the violence that threatened Charles. Words to spite what she considered his stubbornness.

"For everyone's sake, Evelyn. For everyone's sake."

CLEARLY, JUDGE CHARLES Pullman had a few skeletons in his closet.

He wasn't always that senior court judge with the equal mix of thorough calculation and conscious decisions. There was that long road he walked as a struggling esquire, just like most other young attorneys trying to get some firm footing in the world.

When Charles was a junior partner with the law firm of Fricky, Ellington and Clemons, he sharpened his skills and enhanced his own resume taking on corporate mergers, as well as probate and accident cases. He was the only black attorney with the firm, and as such, Charles wasn't privileged to negotiate the big-money contracts like his white colleagues. So Charles considered alternatives.

It was around then that Charles met Ernestine Griffin. She was a widow and a single mom at the age of twenty-eight, who the lawyer loved and then married. Peter Griffin, her son, grew close to Charles, accepting him as his father figure, and eventually following his lead to become a civil rights lawyer himself.

Although the two loved one another, Charles and Ernestine

experienced tough times together. He was the sole breadwinner, and for a time, he was making just enough money to pay the bills, but never the bonuses that might make his profession an enjoyable one. He couldn't indulge in the fancy dinner engagements and charge such outings to a company expense account. He couldn't keep on top of automobile trends, owning the newest, flashiest cars like his comrades could. And no, he didn't own a Rolex watch.

Furthermore, the types of clients who Charles came to represent were small-time businessmen who could barely afford the fees and who were most often on the ugly end of a lawsuit. That meant, no "juice" when it came to various courtroom proceedings, motions and decisions.

One morning, a court case that was scheduled just before his went into overtime, dragging on well past lunch. It was a civil suit claiming that a competitor was using unfair practices in advertising—the claimant's company name was used excessively and with the intention to defame their brand name. During the proceedings, Pullman had the opportunity to see the work of a private investigator, Sam Foster.

When court recessed, Pullman, who was thinking about gathering the best possible resources for his own practice (the one he anticipated having) passed Sam his business card. He also suggested, "Perhaps I could use your services in the future. I like your presence on the stand. A class act. Truly authentic."

"Thanks," said Foster in more or less a brush-off. "I'll keep you in mind."

And then came Pullman's ground-breaking case. It was an accident case that involved a big name trucking company and a woman in her mid-forties, Doris White. Mrs. White was Pullman's client, and her claim was that the driver of an 18-wheeler fell asleep and his rig swerved, eventually sideswiping her, forcing her vehicle off the road and into a ditch. Mrs. White was trapped there until someone rescued her the next morning.

Since this was a hit-and-run claim, he had only his client's side of the story to go on. Pullman needed more weight to prove the truck driver's negligence and win the case. After all, there was no plate number recorded (Mrs. White was too traumatized to think at the time) and there were at least two thousand 18-wheelers on the road with "G.O.D." printed on the sides. For assistance in this matter, Charles called upon Sam Foster.

Sam had already been with the New York Police Department, and was doing his case-by-case private-eye work until his application to the FBI was processed and his job secured.

"Sam, this is Charles Pullman. You may not remember me, but I passed you my card one day in the courthouse. I mentioned that I might need your services one day."

"Pullman. Oh. I, ahh . . . I probably misplaced your card."

"That's okay," said Charles. "At least you remember me. I'm sure you get a lot of lawyers approaching you."

"I, uhh . . ." Sam was at a loss for words.

"It's fine, really. I'm glad I could find you. Listen, I have this case I'm working on, where my client was sideswiped on the New England Thruway. She lived to tell about it and has since been going through great pain and suffering. Anyway . . . the truck, she said, was one of those with 'G.O.D.' printed on its side. So we're going after them."

"Big company," said Sam.

"Perhaps the biggest, with the company name being anointed and all."

"Who's fault?"

"Oh, I'm sure it's the truck driver's fault. My client says he swerved side to side, like he was sleeping, just before he hit her."

"The rig made contact?"

"Apparently."

"How's the car? Is there physical evidence?"

"About five hundred little pieces. The car was almost totaled. They found the woman in a ditch nearly six hours later."

"I can investigate the driver if you want."

"That's exactly what I want. The trucking company

claims it never happened, and the driver who we believe is the culprit has a squeaky-clean record according to the DMV."

"Wait a minute. I'm missing something here . . . if nobody got a plate number, how do you know what driver—"

"The logs. The state thruway logs luckily detail everything."

"Okay."

"There are four drivers who were in that vicinity at that time. But get this: there's a particular driver whose record shows his license was issued a year ago. His regular driver's license was also issued on the same day."

"Okay, so what? New driver? That's your proof?"

"Too new. Sam, the man is thirty-nine years old. His bank account is a year old. His residence is a year old. Everything is a year old. He's got a bill of health that's cleaner than Snow White's ass."

After a laugh, Sam said, "So the driver dropped in out of the sky, huh?"

"I guess," replied Charles on his end of the phone call. "Either that, or this is fraud at its best."

"Tell you what, I'll look into it, no charge. Fax me the details. Cover my expenses, and when you win the case, toss me a few bones. I'm not greedy, just trying to eat, ya know?"

"Sounds like a winner. Lemme have the fax number . . ."

TWO DAYS AFTER the call and the fax, without the luxury of his own receptionist, Charles answered the phone himself. "Charles Pullman."

"Hey. It's Sam Foster. I need to see you."

"You find out something?"

"We need to talk. Nothing over the phone."

"Sounds important. So, you wanna come by the office?"

"Check your e-mail. I left instructions," said Sam. And he hung up just like that.

THREE HOURS LATER, Charles met Sam at a fast-food restaurant on Broadway and 57th Street. It had a busy atmosphere; however, there was some semblance of peace and quiet at a window seat up on the second level.

They gobbled down french fries and burgers like two men always on the go, and finally wiped their hands in order to get down to business. Sam took out a notepad and ripped off a leaf of paper on which was a list of names.

"All right. I'm puzzled. Who are these guys?"

Before Sam responded, he grew a crooked grin. "Those are your drivers who all dropped out of the sky within the past eighteen months. They work for the same trucking company."

"You're saying they all have fresh identities and squeaky-clean driving records?"

"The works," said Sam. "Like Snow White's ass."

"I knew it. I just knew it!"

"But there's more. Save the excitement till you hear this . . . Your driver is Hector Martin. I did a Web search on him. I couldn't find a thing. But, then I made a mistake and put Hector's last name first. And, oh boy."

"What'd you get?"

"Number one, Hector is an ex-con. He did an eighteen-year stretch in Colorado for armed robbery. And guess when he got out of prison?"

"A year ago?"

"Nope. Three years ago. Only, he's had seven or eight new identities since then. All of those have been responsible for traffic accidents of one kind or another."

"So what's up with these other cats?"

"All of 'em are Hector. He's Alex Snow, the driver that hit a hitchhiker on the New York State Thruway earlier this year. He's Frank Williams, the driver who caused a ten-car pile-up on the New Jersey Turnpike. There's Steven Barns, Ralph Martinez, Horace Stafford, George McKinley and Leslie James. All of those names were responsible for some sort of accident, some of them fatal, a few hit-and-runs, and all of them have bench warrants for no-shows in court."

"Whoa—just one second here! If this guy changed his name, what, seven times in that short amount of a time, somebody at the trucking company has to know about it."

Sam Foster, private eye, made a clicking sound, pointing his finger at Charles. "Bingo. Maybe you should be the private eye and me the lawyer."

"Don't put yourself out there. The job isn't all it's made out to be. At least not for—" Pullman suddenly had a thought. "Hey, I just had a thought . . . if the company is found liable . . . Wow! How many other drivers do you think they're hooking up with phony papers?"

"Charlie, hold on to your seat because this"—Sam looked through his notepad for more details—"this situation with Hector is just one out of eighty accidents that involved G.O.D.'s eighteen-wheelers these past couple of years."

"And?" Charles held his eyes closed, praying as he asked, "How many are unresolved because of missing drivers?"

"Fifty-four."

"Yes!" Charles slammed his fist into the opposite palm. The only prop he was missing was a football to spike. Touchdown! "They have to be aware! I can see it now: a class-action suit . . . G.O.D. on trial . . . this could be a national issue!"

"Shhh!" Sam urged.

"Sam, are you kidding? This is great news! The world should know."

Sam gestured again. "Yes, but if you owned such a monster trucking company and you found out that a person had information that could blow their whole operation, wouldn't you wanna put a stop to it before things got out of hand? I'm talking a permanent stop? I would. I'd probably go to all extremes to cut a guy's throat if he was out to shut down my livelihood—"

"Jeez, Sam. I never thought about that."

"Well, you've got to, Charles. The slightest word gets out about this and lives could be at stake, namely yours. What I suggest is that you safeguard things . . . maybe line up your law firm with your intentions, and then just take it to court. Make sure you do your necessary publicity so that the case is made even before the verdict is read, then you won't have some hit man after you. The word would be out already, and

G.O.D. would just have to cut its losses and try 'n survive the fallout."

Foster showed the attorney some other things he printed from the Internet and wished him luck.

"You're a gem, Sam. Look out for a check in the mail. A nice one."

And Charles sat alone, scanning the many newspaper accounts of accidents, all of them somehow related to the G.O.D. trucking company. As far as he could see, this would be his first big winning case.

Per Sam's advice, Charles went back to his law firm and addressed the senior partners. And luckily, all three of them were available at once.

"I'm bringing a multimillion-dollar case to the firm, Fricky. It's a no-brainer . . . a sure-win."

"How so?"

"There's a pile of incriminating evidence; that would be these—"

Charles laid the documents out on the table, including the matching logs: those of the State Thruway Authority—records compiled at various weigh-stations along the truck route—and those of the trucking company. They were all in folders, neatly organized.

"I figured to bring the case against the company itself for negligence, attempted negligent homicide and fraud . . . not to mention malice aforethought. The way I look at it, the potential award is in the tens of millions. The company is worth five hundred and thirty million, so it is in their best interest to settle out of court before the state attorney decides to bring criminal action."

Ellington and Clemons picked through the folders, one quicker than the other.

"So, what makes you think this is an open and shut case?" asked Ellington.

Clemons added, "That's every attorney's dream, Charles, to catch a multimillion-dollar accident claim. I'd hate to see you get your hopes too high over a pipe dream."

"Fellas, this is no pipe dream, I assure you. There are

probably a hundred or more people out there who are just like my client. Maybe there are worst-case scenarios, as in fatalities. Or others who have been railroaded on account of the malicious practices of this—"

"One thing, Charles. How in the world did you obtain the company's records? I mean, this hasn't even gone to trial yet. No judge had decided on any preliminary motions or handed down orders for discovery material . . ."

"Mr. Fricky, let me answer that the best way I know. We . . . we have an insider's help. Someone at the company who—"

"Did you pay for this information?" asked Clemons.

"No. Not at all. But naturally, once the suit is settled, a small reward might be in order."

The partners all exchanged dubious expressions. Ellington suggested, "Did you ever think that it might be an employee, like your inside man, who might be to blame? And that, maybe, this firm . . . our firm, could be liable for malpractice issues?"

"Lonny is right," said Clemons. "We can't go soliciting inside information on multimillion-dollar corporations without first receiving court approvals and judgement orders."

Charles started to speak, but Fricky said, "Tell you what, Charles. I'm sure you had every good intention here, but allow us to look into this a little further. We'll get Daniel Bromowitz to pick it apart . . . find out what the strengths and weaknesses are . . . see if we have some cohesive issues—"

"Bromowitz?! But he started here a year after I did. He has no seniority. This is my case. My client."

"Mr. Pullman, I'm afraid you're mistaken about that. If you review the terms of our contract with you, you'll recall the clause that clearly states the firm's position as the principal counsel for every case that comes through our doors—regardless of its origination."

Charles wasn't swayed. He said, "That's understood. But, surely you'll allow me to try this case once it come to fruition." Pullman's comment was more of a plea than a confirmation.

"Let Bromowitz check it out first. Don't beat yourself over the head on this, Charles."

And with that pat on the back, the meeting came to an end.

CHARLES WAS LEFT wondering for an entire week, and then he received word. It was a letter sent from the senior partners, all of whom were on vacation as Charles opened his mail.

"We are sorry to inform you that as of your receipt of this letter . . ." It was a pink slip. The firm was kicking him out. The letter was short and sweet, citing "conflicts of interest" as their reason for termination.

"Good," Charles said as he stood in his terry-cloth robe, not yet having had his breakfast. "It's your loss. With the money I make from the *White vs. G.O.D.* case, I'll be able to start my own law firm. Pullman, Pullman & Pullman will be my senior partners!"

But things weren't quite that simple. After breakfast, and a newly thought-out strategy, Charles called his client.

"Mrs. White? Hi, this is Charles Pullman, the attorney representing you—" Charles was interrupted in mid-sentence. "What was that? But Mrs. White, I was the original attorney on your case. You and I have an agreement . . . I'm the one who did all of the work, planning . . . well, I . . . but why can't you talk to me? They have no say-so—"

The phone line went dead with Charles still holding the phone in hand. There was no "good-bye." Charles just sat the phone in its cradle, and he prayed for tolerance. Maybe it was too early in the morning and he was still dreaming.

The phone rang just seconds later.

Thank God! She's changed her mind!

Without so much as a "hello," Charles picked up the phone and immediately began speaking his mind. "Don't worry, Mrs. White. You don't owe me any apologies. Those creeps underestimated your integrity. I can get you out of that contract you signed, I'm just glad you decided—" Charles was interrupted.

"What's that? Oh, I'm sorry. I thought this was—hunh? Oh my God! Where? When??"

Not a minute later, Charles was in his car, flying across Yonkers to the hospital. Ernestine had been in a terrible car accident.

TWO MONTHS HAD passed since the termination, since the takeover of the *White vs. G.O.D.* case and since the death of Ernestine Griffin-Pullman. There was so much that Charles was burdened with, including the funeral, the bills and all those loose ends of Ernestine's life.

Bigger still was the issue of Peter, her only son. His stepson. Charles had two children as well from his first marriage. But they lived with their mom in Staten Island. That meant just two things: child support payments and visits every few weeks. Now that Ernestine was gone, there was an opportunity for Charles to step up and take a more personal involvement in the boy's upbringing. Sure there was his past and the void he had felt since the divorce—being a long-distance father and all. But also, the grief, the loss and the memories that went with Ernestine's death haunted Charles and Peter in a powerful way, and it also brought them closer together.

Sam Foster's phone call was a wake-up and a reminder that he still had a life to live, a profession to carry on.

"Hey, buddy. I saw the papers. Sorry to hear about the mess with the law firm . . . and, uhh . . . my condolences about your wife."

"Thanks."

"I thought I'd let you handle your personal issues before I called you with some good news."

Charles sighed, unable to imagine, for the life of him, what good news Sam could have that would help ease so much pain and misery that impacted his life so suddenly. "Sure. Go ahead. Give me your good news."

"Well, ever since the termination—"

"Not to interrupt, Sam, but how did you hear about that, anyway?"

"The papers. The story about the trucking company took

up three entire pages in the *Post*. They also mentioned the change in attorneys. Some tight named Bromowitz has the case now."

"Don't remind me."

"Well, you know those other victims from the different accidents? I've contacted about three dozen of them. I even have calls coming in from a lot of others who I haven't gotten back to yet. Are you ready for this?"

"I'm holding my breath," Charles lied.

"The law firm you used to work for must be slow, because they haven't gotten agreements from any of those who I called. But I did."

"You did what?"

"I got agreements . . . typed up a letter, made a bunch of copies, and we now have more than twenty-six signatures. We have oral agreements from at least fourteen others. I figure if we can get ten or twenty more signatures . . . we'll use the weight of those I already have, and—"

"I'll be running the suit again," Charles concluded.

"Bingo. That is, if I decide to give it to you."

There was a silence—a pounding in Charles chest. Then Sam said, "Kidding! You're in, buddy! And I'll put everything I own on a bet that G.O.D. will settle with you faster than you can say heavens to Betsy."

"Thanks, Sam. I owe you."

"Big-time."

WHEN WORD GOT out about Charles circumventing Fricky, Ellington and Clemons, how he snatched the victims' claims from under the firm's reach, they called him. And the deal-making began.

"Charles, you know you're not equipped to take that company to trial. Not like we are. Be reasonable."

"Reasonable? Reasonable?? Is this the same man who told me about some damned clause in my employee contract? The same man that sent me a pink slip?? Now who's having pipe dreams?"

Charles let that marinate. Then he continued on. "I can take what I have to any large law firm in the country—maybe your competition would like to have it."

"Competition?"

"Yeah, com-pe-ti-tion. Does Cooper, Cooper & Wadsworth ring a bell?" Charles dropped that name as he dropped the phone in its cradle.

He barely counted to three, grinning when the phone rang again. "Charles Pullman, independent attorney-at-law speaking. Who may I ask is calling—"

"Charles, don't do this. Let's work something out, shall we?"

"I'm sorry, did you want to speak to Mr. Pullman? I'll have to take a message and have him get back to you. He's quite busy, y'know."

There was a sigh on the other end of the line. "All right, Mr. Pullman. You've made your point loud and clear. When can we get together?"

The rest of the settlement was a breeze.

Charles wanted nothing to do with Fricky, Ellington and Clemons; he didn't want his job back. Hell no. He only cared that Mrs. White and the other victims would be taken care of. There was also the small matter of the $2 million Charles wanted as his commission for putting all of the pieces together.

The firm argued, but it wasn't a strong stance. Charles made it clear that he was aware of the $50 million potential settlement from the trucking company, one of the nation's biggest.

"Okay, you win," Charles said. "I'll be happy with eight hundred thousand."

A check was drafted on the following day. Charles paid Sam $50,000 for his help. He put a more expensive tombstone on Ernestine's grave and he fronted another $85,000 to pay for Peter's schooling. He also set up trust funds of $50,000 for each of his grown children by his first wife. Except for the new town house he purchased on the west end of Yonkers, complete with a view of the Hudson River, Charles invested the balance of his money into an interest-bearing money-market account, some mutual funds and a handful of healthy stocks.

When word spread that it was Charles Pullman who had initiated the lawsuit "against G.O.D.," he began to receive calls from top law firms and corporations in and around the New York region, offering him the world if he would only come and work for them. But Pullman never took any of those deals. He wasn't forced to work, under pressure from anyone else. He didn't need any of those big-name reputations to juice up his politics or the hidden racism that often went with such positions.

More a free agent now than ever before, Pullman began representing individual clients on a case-by-case basis.

He won a few settlements, but also negotiated corporate mergers, acquisitions, and real-estate purchases. However, none of his accomplishments or successes could compare to that triumph against the trucking company. His independent practice lost its luster. He just wasn't inspired any longer.

Life's next step for Pullman was to put his energy into criminal defense. It wasn't a foreign field of law for him, since he had studied criminal law in college. Defending individuals was such an intriguing endeavor for Pullman, with such unique characters on both sides of the scales.

"Are you sure that's something you wanna do?" asked Sam when the two got together for their one of their frequent french fry luncheons.

Charles said, "Everything else is a big bore to me, Sam. I'm tired of the suit 'n tie game . . . all of the tight-assed executives you run into could make a man sick. Sometimes I feel weighted down, like I'm living in a pool of mud and every step is accompanied by reams and reams of paperwork and data. I'm drowning in it, Sam, and I know there's more to life . . . Something I can feel lust and passion for."

"Humph . . . lust and passion, hunh? Sounds like you need to open yourself a whorehouse, Charles. You would not be disappointed. The pay is good too."

Charles suppressed a laugh and said, "Something in the

field of law, thank you. Besides, I've spoken with a few criminal defense attorneys and it doesn't sound like a bad experience—"

"Not if you don't mind getting involved with the riffraff of the world."

"Nope. In fact, I look forward to it. Maybe it's as close as I'll ever get to the dangerous side of life. Those people need lawyers too."

"You don't have to tell me that, Charlie. Remember my background—NYPD—nothing but blood and gore every minute. Been there, done that, y'know? That's why I'm stepping up. The FBI is where it's at."

"To each his own," said Charles.

"I'm just letting you know firsthand . . . these cronies, crooks and cons aren't all they're made out to be. Headaches? Yes. But wealth and fame? No way," said Sam.

"But you never know, Sam. I see lawyers on the six o'clock news more than I see commercials for dishwashing liquid. I figure, with the name I've made for myself already and a few serial killers for clients, I could be the next Perry Mason. Even Mayor Giuliani started out as a lawyer before he became a U.S. attorney with the Justice Department. Get it? Lawyer . . . mayor . . . hero to the world. All because I passed the bar exam."

"I've created a monster."

"Just stick by me, Sam. Do what you do best, and I'll never lose a case."

Sam couldn't argue with that.

CHAPTER THIRTEEN

THEY ALWAYS HAD to answer to Uncle Sam. That's just the way it was. One chief over his tribe of Indians; or, in this case, a band of bandits. When it came to the scores that L.T.K. executed in and around New York, it was with Sam's approval. Uncle Sam also took responsibility in dishing out the penalties, discipline and punishment. Being late or not returning with positive outcomes might result in a pay cut. Sam might even yell and scream his disapproval. But incidents like the fuck-up with Judge Pullman were uncalled-for. And now this . . .

These weren't amateur cops, and Sam didn't expect amateur performance.

So far Jesse "Mims" Wallace had escaped Sam's wrath. But now Skin and Primo had to face the music. And with the fear of Uncle Sam in them, they were doing their best to talk their way out of the mess.

"And that's the way it went down, Sam. It was just coincidence that some lovebirds were back there—actually, they weren't back there to begin with, or else we would've spotted 'em and made 'em scram," explained Skin.

Primo kept a straight face, but what he wanted to do was to tell Skin that he wasn't confident enough. Confidence, Primo had explained earlier, is what would keep their asses from getting shot. But despite his suggestions, and just in case Uncle Sam lost his cool, the two had on vests under their sweatshirts. Just a precaution.

"So, two—what'd you call em? Lovebirds—dropped in out of the sky to poop on our party . . ." Sam had on dingy denim coveralls, having just come in from the lot where he was doing light maintenance on his red big rig. His one arm was in a sling, with the sleeve of the injured side hanging unused across his midsection. However, that didn't prevent Sam from working. If he wasn't on the phone calling shots regarding L.T.K.; if he wasn't keeping his ugly (as all hell) niece sexually active; if he wasn't putting his foot down (such as he was now), as that too-cruel-to-be-kind leader of this lawless organization, then that's where Sam would be, spending his leisure time with Big Red, his 13,000-pound truck.

Skin and Primo gave each other the eye, wondering if this was one of Sam's trick questions, as he threw down a half glass of vodka. Hell yeah they dropped in out of the sky!

But then, there was no sense in barking up that tree— might as well push all of Sam's buttons.

Yes, it was their fault for allowing the Town Car to pass by, plowing into Mule like it did. A horrific sight it was. But what could be done now? Or did Sam want to just rehash the episode to death? They could breathe again. It seemed that the man hadn't wanted an answer after all.

"Where's Chico, anyway? Where's Duck? Shit, is there any good news?" asked Sam. And that was another problem. Chico. More answers they wished to avoid.

"Chico, he—I s'pose he figured it was all Duck's fault," said Skin, who probably knew more about Chico and could read the man better than anyone else in L.T.K. "Since he was the one who said it was so easy. It happened right after the manager—"

Sam rolled his eyes. What now?

"After Chico shot him . . . Duck had grabbed the money. We weren't paying too much attention on account of all that happened—Mule's body all torn to pieces . . . the store manager with his brains all over the place . . . All of a sudden we hear another gunshot, and we dove for cover 'cause it scared the shit out of us," said Skin.

Primo added, "Scared ain't the word. I dove and hurt my leg again," still making faces in response to the pain.

"When we looked to see what was up, Chico was standing over Duck's body. He said, 'Everything ain't as easy as it seems.' Then he picked up the money. He took it with him."

"And then what? Took the money where?"

"Sam, we couldn't argue with Chico. He had the smoking gun and that crazy look in his eyes. He said the money was his since he had the most to lose. Then he just cut out. Took the Grand Am too," said Skin, his eyes red and blinking excessively.

The realization of losing another man—two men, really, since it seemed that Chico disappeared with the money—was hard to swallow. Sam had obvious frustration there behind his eyes, and it had nothing to do with the shoulder wound.

"I need to be alone," Sam barked. "*Alone!*" His voice carried throughout the office and down the hallway, the vodka taking its toll.

Primo and Skin didn't hang around to argue. Those were the most relieving words they'd heard in hours. And, in case this was a setup, they backed out of Sam's presence.

Sam made a call, slammed the phone down when there was no answer and swept the desk with his good arm, sending the cell phones, the paperwork and his ashtray to the floor.

There was a poster up on his office wall. "Charles Pullman for District Court Judge," the poster read, just one of the mementos that Sam still had from years past. There was a pistol in Sam's hand now, directed at the poster. Sam closed his eyes for a short time, as if to address some harbored memory. The moment he opened them, he fired three shots at Pullman, hitting one eye, a cheek and the forehead. Now the picture was complete.

Sam stuck the gun back in his holster, there underneath the coveralls and the shoulder wound. The warmth of the weapon somehow soothed his temper, and he lost track of space and time, wandering out of his office and down the hallway. His mind felt warped and so far away from his body's limitations.

Down the hall he could see Reesy and her twin charging toward him, both women with 12-gauge shotguns in their hands, both women ugly as two-legged hound dogs.

"Uncle! I heard shots!" Reesy was excited and breathing heavy. She was close to him now, with the split images finally returning to normal. It was just the two of them in the building. The shotgun fell to Reesy's side as Sam hastily pulled her into his embrace. It was a move to hide how pitiful he felt.

"I'm good, Reesy. Just went a little crazy . . ." Sam put an arm around her shoulder and they strolled like two lovers in a park. "This ol' dusty church . . . you ever ask yourself why we're here, puddin'? Why we call this place home?"

"No, Uncle. You always tell me never ask questions. So I just do as I'm told."

And just like that, the subject was forgotten, though Sam still grinned at Reesy's obedience, amused at how some people got excited for one thing alone: to do as they are told.

Sam led Reesy downstairs to the main chapel, amidst the obstacle course of trash piles, litter on the floor and cobwebs here and there, to the front of the church. Finally, sitting at the pulpit, likely the same spot where the pedophile pastor sat between sermons, Sam deliberated while Reesy leaned on the altar. The butt of the 12-gauge was propped on her hip and the barrel extended up at an angle like a stiff-but-deadly dick.

Reesy, the armed guard, attempted to read her uncle's thoughts. She wasn't the sharpest knife in the drawer, and so probably couldn't decipher all of the mental baggage that had accumulated in Sam's head over the years. It could be turbulent, whipping around in there, threatening to blow his roof off, and Reesy would never know it. Sam's past was simply a dark, intimidating shadow that, although intangible, threatened his own mortality.

Reesy said something but her uncle didn't seem to register sounds at the moment. "Are you listening to me, uncle?"

Sam was in a daze . . . he was out of a daze. In. Out again.

"Come over here," he said, and he took a cigar from his breast pocket, unwrapped it, then stuck it between his lips. Reesy's reflex was automatic. She produced the lighter that was in her back pocket, kept there specifically for these occasions, and she lit the tip of the cigar while Sam puff-puffed to get it going. The bandages dressing Reesy's nose were close enough for him to get a whiff.

"How's your nose?" he asked. It was the first inkling of concern that he'd shown for Reesy's injury since Mims whacked her with the Magnum the week before. It had been just as long since they were sexually active.

"My nose's okay. What about your shoulder?"

"Just another day."

"I kinda like you with one arm," Reesy said. "It makes you look a little helpless . . . and I feel like I'm helping you, like I'm really doin' something around here 'sides doing laundry, cleaning and making your food." Reesy had a nasty nasal tone.

"I don't keep you busy enough?"

"Busy, yes . . . I guess. But accomplished?" Reesy winced. "Counting money and taking messages isn't what I call accomplishments."

"Aw—I'm not neglecting my darling niece, am I?" Sam slapped his thigh and Reesy melted from her grief to sit there as he intended, putting up with the cigar smoke wafting up her nose.

"Do you have to call me that? You know that depresses me . . . makes me feel guilty."

"Oh, on the contrary, my little rosebud. It turns me on, the fuck what you feel . . . now say 'Uncle Sam.' "

"Uncle Sam," Reesy repeated with a guilt-ridden edge.

"Your niece is ready to service you as you please."

Reesy did as he asked, word for word.

"You think you can still handle business with those bandages on your face?" Sam's inquiry—"handle business"—was another way of requesting a blow job.

Reesy answered, "I can still eat with no problem, so I guess tonight I could—"

"Not tonight. Now," Sam replied. Then he gave his niece's ass a smack as he might do with a mule. Reesy rose to her feet only so that she could kneel again.

"Do you think I'm crazy?" asked Sam.

"Hunh?" Reesy asked in light of the awkward moment.

"Answer me," Sam said, pulling at his cigar and blowing out a stream of smoke so that it engulfed her face and down to where her cleavage was visible. Reesy had learned to accept this.

"No," she responded in an unsure high-low pitch. "How could you ask a question like that?"

"I just wanted to know . . . go on. Take care of business," Sam said, switching gears in mid-air. "Blow me."

As Reesy busied herself, Sam sat back and looked way up at the dome ceiling of the chapel. It was darker up there, out of reach from the glow of 40-watt lamps situated haphazardly through the building. The space up there was also suddenly a place where Sam could dwell . . . where he could project his mental strife.

"How is your family, Sammy?" neighbors would ask, feeding that embarrassment that lived with little Sammy as a child. The disputes between his mom and pops were the talk of the neighborhood; the way they fought and argued already influencing the boy's social environment. Sure, the neighbors asked how the family was doing, but what they really wanted to know was the nitty-gritty. What they really wanted to know was, "Why do your parents fight all the time?" "Who started it this time?" Or, "Who threw what at who?" They were merely asking Sammy the question to find themselves an inside source to dish them details to fuel further gossip.

Everyone soon got the answers they needed when Sammy's father, also a police officer, shot and killed Mrs. Foster, then shot himself. Sammy was just a teenager at the time of the terrible tragedy, but the memories never left him, even now, more than forty years later.

Fortunately, Sammy was able to pull himself up by his own bootstraps, attending community college and then applying for the police academy. Despite all of the steps it took Sam to become a police officer, nobody ever knew how much he needed the power of the badge and gun to make up for so much doubt and insecurity in his life. Becoming a cop was a way to justify his life. It confirmed his very existence, and he took it to the extreme, figuring he could be big and strong and powerful enough to outrun pain and misery . . . to escape his past and become untouchable. Almighty.

There were many more men like Sam Foster, men who joined the force and who wanted to be cowboys all of their lives . . . men who felt inferior and who never quite measured up to the boys on the block. This was a complex that was easily concealed under the guise of "protecting" and "serving." It was a way to prove something to everybody else in the hood, in effect saying to the rest of the community: I am somebody! And if you don't believe it, look at my gun!

And that was just what Reesy did now—she saluted Sam's pistol. His gun. His dick. She praised and worshiped it as the only God she ever knew, or thought she knew.

"Stand," Sam told her. And when she did, he unzipped the front of her tight shorts so that she'd get the message. She did, and soon enough Reesy was wiggling out of the shorts. Naked from the waist down, Reesy expected the next instruction, maybe to turn around and bend over, or maybe to come and rub her pie against his face. There were a few possibilities here, most of which the two had exercised in past encounters.

"Put your foot up here," said Sam, slapping that thigh again. Reesy started to bend down and untie her hiking boot, until her uncle stopped her. "No. Just like that. Boot 'n all," he said.

"What you doin'?" Reesy asked with that silly giggle.

Sam was already fitting the mouth of the cigar between her lips—right there inside her vagina.

"I want you to smoke this . . . with your pussy," said Sam, smiling at how idiotic this looked, the cigar forming this unnatural extension from her furry foxhole.

"How I do that? I never—"

"Quiet," Sam ordered as the cigar smoke trickled upward. "Just try 'n make it talk. Do it." Her uncle sat back and watched, a bit unsure himself of how she'd get this done. This was just another of his impulsive, freaky urges that she'd perform, for better or for worse. Reesy closed her eyes and concentrated as best she could. She concentrated so much that she farted. The odor was two feet from his face.

"Sorry," Reesy said.

But Sam hadn't budged, slouched there like a king on a throne, enjoying his jester's foolery and laughing at it all.

Now Reesy took the cigar from down there—

"What're you doin?"

—and she held it in her mouth for a moment. It wiggled when she spoke. "I got an idea," Reesy replied. She used both hands to part her pussy's lips, replaced the cigar down there and concentrated again. "Okay, Uncle. Here goes," she said, wincing like she had before.

The end of the cigar sizzled finally from the air she pushed out, and the smoke crawled out from her folds as it would from a person's mouth . . . as if she was on fire down there. "Hey! It's workin'!"

"That's fun—my . . . oh—my God!" Sam could hardly speak, he laughed so hard. "Okay, okay, enough already! Oh—" He let out a sigh and took the cigar from her. He wedged it back in its rightful spot, there in the corner of his mouth. "Now you think I'm crazy," asked Sam.

"Crazy? Yes! You are crazy," Reesy said as she put her leg down.

"I knew you'd see things my way . . . now take the rest of it off. The T-shirt, the boots. Let's do this right," said Sam.

Reesy smarted her eyes and brandished a devilish grin. She went the extra mile, and tugged the velvet elastic from her hair so that it fell to her shoulders. This was as sexy as it got, although it was still difficult to determine who was the beauty and who was the beast.

Sam turned the cigar in his mouth, sucking at it like a pro and studying his sister's daughter, squinting as the smoke fogged his view. He opened his legs, unzipped his coveralls enough to free his stiff prick. "Have a seat," Sam told her, a sparkle shooting from his silver and blue pupils as he got comfortable on the preacher's bench.

Reesy turned around and lowered herself until she was filled and moaning from the pleasure of it. She rode him slow before building up to a wild frenzy. Reesy, the cowgirl.

These days, Sam was able to control himself as he desired—and, at his age, maybe it was a blessing—and not a moment sooner. So Reesy was the one who climaxed again and again, as long as she could keep bucking up and down like this. Soaked around his groin from Reesy's juices, Sam chuckled under his breath. The messy wench was running like an open valve down there.

When Reesy slowed to a grind, Sam asked, "Are you done?"

"I could keep goin'," she said.

"No, I'm gonna drown if you do. This isn't a marathon here, so let's finish up. Get back on the floor," ordered Sam.

This was how it was—no love, very little affection except for a peck in the cheek, or he'd run his fingers through her horse hair. But nothing more. There wasn't a whole lot to say . . . no I love you's or other such pillow talk to soften things up. It was just relief. Cut 'n dry. Short 'n sweet.

Just as it was with sex, so too was life: cold, unfeeling. Nothing and no one to love. Sam had gone through the phases that most of his comrades experienced. There was a time when he had every good intention. But that lasted as long as his period of probation, when he was a rookie on the police force.

There was enough behind the scenes that was unbecoming of a cop that the atmosphere helped to mold a subconscious state of mind. The code that all cops kept—the wall of silence that permitted everything short of cold-blooded murder—secured every officer's sense of security. This was a college fraternity, a society, a cult. It was a place where you felt you belonged and that welcomed you and all of your issues. From a rookie coming of age, Sam progressed (or digressed) into the macho-cop phase where he worked to etch his own name in the world which he lived. There was a point that he went home to study videotapes of cop shows and movies that portrayed villainous lawmen. It possessed Sam so much that he began to see every day as a challenge, a step down into a holy hell, in a quest to slay or detain all of the vermin who might one day rob and cheat and kill their way into the middle- or upper-class neighborhoods—neighborhoods in which people were supposed to be safe and sound from the worst. Achieving these objectives also felt like Sam's redemption for all the pains of his past.

Inevitably, Sam sunk into the world of deceit and larceny. He'd crossed the line from good cop to bad cop. And why not, since so many others led the way?

Before Sam met Charles Pullman, attorney-at-law, he had developed a routine of shakedowns, extorting various local businesses until he had a lucrative enterprise going for himself. He had learned well the ins and outs of doctoring police reports, raiding evidence rooms and assaulting prisoners. He knew how to wield his authority in order to acquire resources of this type and that. He'd already manipulated his way through at least three Internal Affairs inquiries—one involving the shooting of a suspect—and was on his way to becoming a veteran of bad cops.

As the years progressed, Sam's eyes grew deeper into dark wells that were familiar with blood and gore, and insensitive to life's cries. He developed this wicked leer that promised death and that delivered it as well. The cigar had indeed become a habit, but it was his anger as well, adding a sort of authenticity to his being, a confidence that was automatic with the rich smell, however harmful. There was a presence that Uncle Sam lived with where, regardless of what was going haywire around him, he was always at peace. Either that, or this was an undiscovered symptom of lunacy.

Meeting Pullman seemed to be a blessing in disguise, at a time when Sam had even contemplated suicide. The lawyer needed help. He wanted to win his case and Sam was already a pro at manipulation. The puzzle was to figure out how to satisfy the attorney without letting on about his own grimy tactics. And then there was the $50,000 bonus for Sam's part in uncovering the trucking company scandal. What more was there to say, except let's go with this partnership.

Case by case, the Pullman-Foster partnership flourished. They made a lot of money and they never lost at trial or settlement. Regardless of the defendant's history, or if the government felt they had a "winner" on their hands . . . Whether it was an armed robbery pulled off by the notorious Murder Squad, or a teenager who was seen giving birth and then leaving the newborn in the ladies' room at the West Side Multiplex Theater . . . even the Catholic priest who was alleged to have molested five young boys in his past. Pullman saw no limits. Every defendant deserved protection under the law.

These were Sam's memories as he sat there dazed, inebriated, and erect inside of Reesy's mouth. These were the images that haunted him, as though they were elements of blood being drawn, rendering him weaker by the minute and somewhat semiconscious despite his rising tide of anxiety. He'd visited this state of dementia before, with so many complex ideas surfacing, all of them simultaneously chipping away at his sanity. And as always, the spell ended with the same unnerving sea of guilt. A menagerie of twisted lies and seedy pools of unresolved realities.

The relationship came to an abrupt halt. And it happened, of all places, in the courtroom. Pullman had been defending Billy Bob Shaffer, who the press nicknamed "Billy Bob the Tornado," since he ran through a numerous amount of single Jewish women in a murderous spree of ruthless rapes.

"Billy Bob erred," the prosecuting attorney claimed before a packed courtroom. Plus, the rest of the world was watching the opening arguments on Court-TV. "He left this one alive . . ."

And the DA was absolutely correct. Everybody was, in their assumptions.

The woman had been left for dead, but was saved in time to undergo emergency surgery—a bullet had to be removed from her head—and she had healed nicely.

The district attorney went on a publicity campaign of his own, before and during trial proceedings. "She's an important witness that will inevitably help us put this murderer down . . ." explained the DA.

But once the trial started, there was a problem.

Pullman had done his best to plan for this trial, to defend Billy Bob. And yet he was also prepared to accept his first big loss, knowing the publicity would eat him alive: loser. There was just no way he could win this. Billy Bob didn't qualify for an insanity defense, and even Pullman had to admit his client was a malicious vulture who preyed upon and destroyed the lives of innocent women. The woman who survived was determined to testify and to point Billy Bob out as the man who forced his way into her apartment, raped her and then shot her. As extremely confident as the DA was, and as much as Pullman knew about the case, it looked like the defense was all wrong. The cards were stacked against him. Pullman wished he could remove himself as the attorney of record. He wished he could remove himself from the courtroom.

"We have no further witnesses, Your Honor." It was the announcement from the prosecutor that shook Pullman's world. Rattled him. Everyone from the media, from a number of women's rights organizations and victims' rights groups, packed the courtroom, and the announcement provoked a wave of disorder amongst them.

"Quiet in the courtroom!" demanded the judge, slamming his gavel down in a futile effort to maintain order. It looked like he might break the thing. Sam Foster was there as well, buried in the thick of the riotous crowd. It was as if a balloon busted—one filled with anticipation and yearning for justice.

"I said order in my courtroom!" shouted the judge. And when there was eventually order, when court officers hustled the worst of the crowd out of the venue, the judge said, "I need to see both of you in my chambers." There was an instant when Pullman looked back over his shoulder at Sam— at that smug look in Sam's eye, as though he'd expected this outcome and secretly rejoiced. Sam looked down and away. He was guilty, and there was no way to hide it, at least not from Pullman.

Once the lawyer was behind closed doors with the judge and the DA, there was already the forgone conclusion: without the star witness, a conviction couldn't be achieved.

"I don't understand it myself, Judge. We had round-the-clock protection at the hospital. I was with the woman myself just forty-eight hours ago . . ."

"This court, this jury and probably the city at large was looking forward to your promise," the judge argued. "And now, you can't deliver? We could've pressed on in a different direction. We could've put on the insanity show! Anything, but to let this . . . this . . . abomination loose to roam our streets again . . ."

Pullman stood quietly by as the two argued. In the meantime, he wondered how he'd address Sam Foster about this.

"YOU KILLED HER, didn't you? Somehow, someway you did it. I know you did. And now Billy Bob is back on the loose."

"Relax, Charlie. You won the case, didn't you? Isn't that what we've been doing all along? Winning?? You and me—the dynamic duo. Unstoppable."

"All along? Sure I wanted to win, Sam, but at what cost? Is justice best served this way?"

"Depends on who's serving it, I s'pose. But that's not my job. I'm not the lawyer here—"

"No. You're the—"

"Hey! Watch your mouth. This ain't no telephone conversation here where I can't get my hands on you. Watch what you say to me."

"All this time . . ."

"Right. All this time, you were a winner . . . on top. All this time you've been celebratin' the victories. What—you think there wasn't any hard work behind the scenes? You think what we did—"

"What *you* did!"

"Whatever. You think it was easy? And who cares if

defendants get away scot-free. The damage was done, dude.
Let God punish them," Sam said.

There was a dead silence in which Pullman finally saw
the light. Everything was fixed.

"How did you . . . no, no, forget it. I don't wanna know,"
said Pullman. But then, he thought back and remembered—
"Oh my God. The case with the Praised—all of those boys
refused to testify except . . . one . . . they said he ran away
from home . . . Sam!"

Sam approached the lawyer and put a hand on his shoulder. "Charlie, trust me. It's best we end this discussion. It's
best you don't know certain things."

Pullman trembled. Sam was right. He didn't want to
know what happened to the witnesses or the evidence. *Oh
God . . . the boy.*

The thoughts and the guesswork that Sam relived were
the sick visions, a backdrop to drive him while Reesy made
a project out of this blow job. She wasn't merely lapping at
him or sucking on him, awaiting completion. No, Reesy had
her own undiscovered talent going. The breathing and other
slippery sounds that she made with her tongue in that sloppy,
yet determined way . . . like a thirsty bitch, snaking up and
down and around his erection. Of course, Reesy uttered the
appropriate words: "Oh, Uncle Sam . . . you taste so good."
And that's just how he liked it.

And now that she was so into it, maybe a little frustrated
from how uncomfortable this was, with her nose bandaged
and all, Reesy ran with those sea-otter noises, losing control
as she jerked her uncle hard and fast. Mixing in with guttural
snorts were the whimpers and cries . . . begging him to fill
her throat. Sam shuddered, finally shooting his semen in
wild spurts while she continued a methodic pull and push at
his foreskin. Meanwhile, he had that firm grip of her head,
possessing her with his strength, until he eventually let her
go and flopped back against the bench. It was a dizzy relief
he felt; the lust and pleasure replaced by sin and guilt and
pain. He got what he wanted, a twisted sense of balance between his brain and his hormone count.

And to think that Reesy wanted to feel accomplished . . . like she was (as she said) really doing something around here.

In the world according to Sam, she certainly was. She certainly was.

CHAPTER FOURTEEN

THERE WAS A phone call for Yvette, except she was out with the children, buying them clothes and entering them into the Harlem school.

Stacy hadn't been to school in weeks, and Sharissa hadn't been to preschool, ever. It was painful to see them idle, watching *Blues Clues* on the Cartoon Network all day without having to answer to teachers; and besides, who knew if school administrators were in on the effort to displace these kids. After the power-move that Judge Pullman pulled—that little chat with the DCW lady.

So, Harambe was the best alternative.

"She's not in," said Push. "Is there something I can help you with?" Push, the businessman.

"This is concerning an ongoing discussion she and I were having, business. I'm Mr. Augusta, from R.E.F."

"R.E.F.? What's that?"

"Real Estate Financial. I'm a mortgage broker."

"Oh. Well, I'm Reginald Jackson, her partner. Is this a Melrah issue?"

"Yes. As a matter of fact, it is . . . if you would kindly tell Ms. Gardner that the mortgage papers are ready to be signed and that the closing is set for Monday, I'd appreciate it."

"Mortgage? For the properties on 128th Street?"

"Yes, sir."

"There must be some mistake—" Push could only guess

what a mortgage had to do with his property. "Never mind. I'll give her the message. Thanks."

"Thank you," the banker replied.

The short phone call grabbed at Push and compelled him to sit at the desk where Yvette generally handled the paperwork for Melrah. A mortgage . . . a loan . . . those subjects were a stretch from the things Push expected, what he and Yvette had spoken about. He immediately wondered what she was doing behind his back. There was no need for any mortgage or loan, unless it was coming from the Harlem Empowerment Fund. And even then, there was enough equity accumulated between the two brownstones for very little money to be needed to close the deal.

What's a mortgage for? A closing next Monday? Push also recalled the woman at the Water's Edge that night, "By the way," the woman had said. "We've been trying to reach your wife."

That's all he needed right now, more confusion to clutter his thinking. The paperwork piled neatly about Yvette's desk was mostly familiar: rent receipts, invoices from the various utilities, the tax bills and permits for pending renovations. Yvette would never expect Push to be reviewing these things since it was she who handled the business end, and he the hard labor. Yvette apparently wrote to herself: "Did the appraisal come in yet?" Beyond that, there was a name: Rooney. There was his phone number, then a series of figures both small and large.

The small figures seemed to address fees and payments, while the large numbers appeared to be overall values of Melrah properties. There was that word again: "appraisal," then, "H.E. Fund—no good." H.E. Fund? H.E. . . . . Push took a few seconds to decipher things. Fund . . . of course. H.E. meant Harlem Empowerment. But why was it no good? Push studied some other figures and tried to put two and two together.

The phone rang.

"Good day, sir. Is Ms. Gardner in?"

"No. Can I take a message?" Push didn't mean to be so

short and dry about it, but it was the way he was feeling, especially now with so many foreign ideas hanging unexplained in the air.

"This is Rooney. Ahh . . . could you just tell her that I called?"

"Sure, sure. Any word on the appraisal yet?"

There was a silence.

"Oh. You must be her fiancé. She told me about you, but I didn't know you—I mean, she discussed the appraisal with you? Okay then, good. Could you let her know there might be a bit of a problem?"

"A problem? What's that?"

"Well, I was gonna be there at the closing with her, but my mother became sick . . . down in Jackson."

"Jackson."

"Yes. Jackson, Mississippi. And I'm leaving tonight. I believe I'll be away for a week or two."

"I see. And what about the appraisal?"

"Oh. That's all straight. The guy we got you is good. His stuff stands up to about two hundred for each property."

"Even without seeing the place? Nobody came by here."

"Hey, that's the whole idea here. You're payin' for a service—the written appraisal is all you need. Sight unseen. But really . . . we shouldn't be discussing this over the phone."

"Oh. I . . . I see," Push lied as he continued looking through the papers, feeling lava move through his veins with the caller's every word.

"Okay. I guess that's it," said Rooney.

Oh no you don't, thought Push. "Just a minute, Mr. Rooney. Yvette and I were discussing the mortgage payments, and the terms of the loan. Actually, Mr. Augusta just called from the bank and we talked about a couple things."

"Oh. Alrighty then, without getting too deep into the details—gotta be careful, ya know—it's a basic arrangement. Two hundred is the number, to be paid out over twenty years at current interest rates. I'm sure you're already familiar with the appraisal situation and the reasons why Yvette decided on this route—it's that damned slumlord you guys are dealing with. Scandalous bastard that he is. If he pulled that stuff on me, I'd . . . well, never mind. I think you guys will make out fine. Just be cost-conscious, ya know?"

"Uh . . . yeah, I know. Listen, Rooney?"

"Sir?"

"Thanks for callin'. And I'll be sure to talk this over with Yvette. I'll tell her just what you said."

"Thank you."

"Blessings to your mother."

"Hunh? What—oh . . . right. Thank you. I'm sure she'll get better. Gotta go." The line went dead.

Push put down the phone. With his elbows planted on the desk, his hands clasped, he shut his eyes and prayed for tolerance. He'd heard of this grimy trade, where the value of the property was inflated for the purpose of acquiring a larger loan from an unknowing bank. *But that's illegal!* Push realized. *It involves fraud and deception.*

More important, why did Yvette even reach equity earned and enough cash flow from rent payments to handle the balance? What happened to the Harlem Empowerment Fund? What happened to the deal they had with George Murphy?

And dammit! Why hadn't she spoken to him about all of this?!

There were so many questions Push had, questions that only Yvette could answer. He had to speak with her right away, if not sooner.

JESSE WALLACE NEVER imagined that he'd be on the other side of the game, the side where a loved one had been locked up. Someone so close to you that it felt like your heart was displaced, snatched up out of your body so that blood couldn't pump . . . so that you couldn't breathe, and you certainly couldn't live.

Since Jesse had played a part in so many arrests—most of them legitimate police business—and convictions, with so many of the city's "bad guys" removed from the streets, he considered his contribution to be a resource, especially now. At least he was due some sensitivity. But how wrong he was.

If he was "blue" when he wore his uniform, part of that cop culture with so many comrades to depend upon, then he was jaded now . . . not just a black man in trouble, but a stained man. Maybe even a marked man, so far as anyone could tell, now that a close relative—his wife, for God's sake—was sucked into the penal system.

It didn't matter that Tuesday wasn't yet convicted of a crime, because once you were caught in the web, that was it. You were just like the rest of the scum—bagged and numbered, and left to cope with whatever survival skills you happened to have. You don't have any? Then that's your problem. For good reason. The judge and jury would come in time, but that was after the fact . . . after you were arrested, stripped of any dignity . . . after your orifices were checked thoroughly and your body examined . . . after you were needled like a pin cushion and branded like a side of beef. After all of that, then maybe, just maybe you could look forward to seeing the judge. Whether or not the judge was in a good mood was another story. The point is that you were no more and no less an average Joe (or, in Tuesday's case, a Josephine) who was inducted into the seedy bowels of the crime world, a place known as "the bottom of the well."

Jesse knew this. Hell, he basically lived it.

As an officer, he too assumed that an arrestee or defendant was a problematic, troubled and potentially dangerous malcontent. A desperate animal in chains, forced to bump elbows, to share space, to coexist amongst known convicts, experts at the almighty con, and others who made a living at one thing, and one thing alone: crime. It was only a matter of time before you were accepted, or swallowed by it. Jesse had one mission right now, and he had to hurry before . . .

Damn, if anything happens to Tuesday, I swear! I'll fuck somebody up, big-time.

Tuesday Walllace was twenty-nine years old and could've graced the cover of *Essence*, only the cards didn't deal that to her. Up until now she had been a stay-home mom, taking care of Stacy and Sharissa, putting up with being a cop's wife, putting on excessive weight. Only now, for the first time in her life, she had to face this harsh and impersonal prison welcome just like everyone around her.

There were whites, blacks, Latinos, Asians . . . there were businesswomen, hookers, gangbangers and even college students. So much of it, the faces, the chatter and the vibes were attacking her all at once, like some multicultural hurricane. And being a cop's wife (she soon realized) was of no assistance whatsoever. She wasn't treated any differently than the others. She was merely another woman thrown into the lion's den. Just another sad statistic.

Once upon a time, the idea of a woman locked behind bars was as unheard of as a housecat living amongst wild dogs. Not that women didn't commit crimes; just that the bigger picture was a domestic woman with domestic issues and concerns. Raising children. Cooking. Needles and thread. Barefoot and pregnant, so went the myth. But while that was Tuesday's reality just three weeks earlier, today she was grouped with women who were likely as scandalous as men—if not worse.

She sucked it up, the disgrace of the strip searches, the rubber-gloved cavity checks and the cold attitudes of prison guards as she was poked with needles, checked for tuberculosis and her blood was tested. It all made her feel like a lab mouse. And worse than all of that was this bitch they called Big Momma. She was tall, big-boned, big-breasted and burdened with tattoos. She also couldn't shut the fuck up.

"If I was you, I'd just keep my mouth shut and bide my time." A stocky woman named Yellow was sitting closest to Tuesday, on one of four benches that lined the wall of this room they called "the pen."

"How am I supposed to get a call around here if the guards don't help?"

"Call collect," Yellow said. "Shit, what, you ain't got no ends on the street? I know you got kids. Plus I seen that ring on yo' finger." Tuesday turned her head down, thinking of how stupid things had become and how she got herself in this mess.

"I can't call collect, Yellow. I disconnected my number at home. Me and my husband had a—"

Yellow put her hand up. "Hold it, ma. I ain't tryin to hear your story no more—already heard it. Everybody already heard it. I'm tryin' to tell you some good shit, 'cuz for real, you starting to sound like a punk in here. And they love 'em some punks . . ."

Tuesday scanned the room. Four cement walls. A pay-phone. A skylight and a scorched-up Plexiglas window in the door. A toilet with no partition. The place was crowded with women—maybe two dozen of them who were carted to court earlier. And now they were back, all of them about to undergo another strip search before they were rounded up and shuffled back to their respective dorms.

It was now that there was the greatest mix of prisoners, since the dorms had assigned bunks for varying degrees of women. Tuesday was assigned to dorm 33, where most first-timers resided. It was only here that Tuesday had to hear Big Momma's big mouth . . . and where cigarette smoke was driving her crazy.

"Look here, bitch. We gittin' tired a you cryin' like a baby. Daddy can't help you now—" Momma said this to Tuesday, but Tuesday pretended not to hear. Maybe she'd go away. Yellow got up and moved from Tuesday's side, and so did the hooker to her left. Oh, great. Fair-weather friends.

"Did you hear me? I'm talkin' to you, bitch."

Tuesday's heart was doing the five-yard dash there in her chest. She could feel Big Momma approaching, asking for trouble.

During the past twenty-three days, Tuesday had seen a lot. There was a fight between two rival gang members that resulted in a marathon hair-pulling bout. Another altercation ended much quicker, when one of Big Momma's girls stepped up behind another girl and pulled a pillowcase over her head. Two others joined in until the prisoner was beaten unconscious.

Tuesday trembled at the thought of being in that same predicament. Momma's next target.

"My name is Tuesday, and I'm not a bitch." The room hushed the instant Tuesday rose to her feet. She stood almost a foot and a half shorter than Big Momma, obviously smaller by all accounts. From the brief hush, the room was immediately consumed by catcalls. Momma's girls were making the most noise, instigating this to the next level.

Momma turned to see the crowd urging her on. She gestured to one of her girls and turned back to Tuesday.

Tuesday didn't wait for Big Momma to act, she made the first move. She swung her right fist as hard as she could, catching the troublemaker on the jaw. Big Momma wobbled backward until she fell on her ass. The two dozen women hushed, then roared again, laughing at Big Momma until the fallen woman's eyes burned with rage.

Tuesday knew there was a camera up in the corner and looked to find that one of Momma's girls had applied wet toilet paper there. Shit. Nobody would be coming to Tuesday's aid, not right away. Momma was back on her feet now, rolling back the sleeves of her orange jumpsuit—the popular outfit around these parts.

"Oh—so you wanna rumble, hunh?"

"Big Momma, I don't wanna do nothin'. All I want is for you to leave me alone. I got issues I need to—" Tuesday was grabbed from behind by two of Momma's co-defendants. Just when she turned to see who grabbed her there was a ball of pain that struck her midsection. Momma had punched her. Tuesday buckled and cried in agony. She was too hurt to make sense of anything about now, but Momma was focused enough for both of them. Momma's forefinger was fitted in one of Tuesday's nostrils, used to jerk her back to an upright position. Momma wiped her finger across Tuesday's orange suit, but she did it slow and deliberately, circling the nipples and working the buttons loose.

"I kinda like bold bitches like you—what'd ya say yo' name was? Tuesday? Well, Miz Tuesday, it sounds like today's your birthday . . ." Momma had opened every button, and she reviewed Tuesday's entire body, touching her as she pleased about the breasts and pubis. "You're gonna get a present that's gonna blow your mind."

Tuesday sucked in air and made a hoarse sound once Big

Momma got her middle finger where she wanted, cupping her private like she would a bowling ball. The crowd began to chant, "Go Momma! Go Momma! Go Momma!"

"You like that, bitch? Hunh? So you broke off with you man—you might like this a little too much. How 'bout this, then!" Tuesday squealed from the torture. She was sure Momma just placed her thumb where her finger had been while her middle finger—fingernail and all—now probed her asshole. The fingering went on for a long minute, with Momma making faces like she was getting off on this, like she was in her glory. "Tonight you'll be eatin' pussy pie, you fuckin' ho. So make sure you keeps an appetite!" And Momma licked Tuesday from the tip of her breasts, straight up her neck and cheek and forehead. "Let 'er go."

Tuesday slumped to the floor, still in pain from the punch, with no idea how wet her face was with tears and Big Momma's saliva. "Tonight you'll be eatin' . . ." Tuesday just wanted to die, as nasty and hurt as she felt. If she could help it, there wouldn't be any pussy-pie party tonight, not for her anyway. Not unless Big Momma used her corpse.

JESSE WAS SO frustrated right now. It took him a half day to find out where his wife was.

He first drove out to Riker's Island, thinking that all prisoners went there after their arraignment, but no luck.

"She's still at the Tombs," a record keeper told him. To add to his dilemma, Jesse got caught up in a traffic jam getting back to Manhattan.

"Shit! Shit! Shit!"

It was as if he could feel his wife's misery. His watch said 2 P.M., and he was more than certain that he wouldn't make it by three o'clock, when visiting ended for the day. But Jesse soon turned hyper, pulling a strobe light out from under his car seat, popping it up on the dashboard and plugging it into the cigarette lighter. Then he flipped a switch below the steering wheel. Abracadabra. Instant unmarked police car. With the siren and strobe light to guide the way, Jesse forced his car through every narrow space, over curbs and through construction cones in order to make it to the FDR Drive and downtown to Central Booking, better known as "The Tombs."

It was 2:38 when he reached the visiting area of the jail. Ten minutes later he was processed and seated on an armless stool in one of the many cubicles, facing a thick window through which visitors could see and talk to the prisoners.

Before Tuesday appeared, Jesse had no choice but to absorb all of this—the well-used countertop, Plexiglas window and intercom phone, coated with hair grease, some kind of fruity fragrance (mixed with cheap cologne) and Lord knows what other germs and grime. The odors were conflicting, like a well-perfumed funk that hung in the air . . . like one of those places Jesse and his NYPD comrades raided up on 42nd and Eighth. And yet, this all went well with the way Jesse felt right now. Foul.

Some pimp was two stools over, shouting at one of his workers, as a guard escorted Tuesday to her space.

"Baby—" Jesse was breathless as the guard removed the handcuffs from his wife's wrists. This picture, however it came to life, was worth a thousand words, even if there were a million questions. Meanwhile, this whole thing was the worst feeling—two live rats fighting for a piece of Jesse's intestines.

The guards hadn't informed Tuesday who was about to visit her, so she was just as surprised as August in a snowstorm. And then she saw Jesse's face. For an instant, she choked on air . . . then she exhaled . . . then she felt relief, but that was still restricted. She was overwhelmed and also angry—so many emotions all at once, all jumping over one another for a front seat to her consciousness. Eventually, she shuddered and began to— *No! I will not cry! I will not cry!!!*

"Hello, Jesse," she said into the telephone. And now it was he who struggled with the many emotions. Tuesday knew how Jesse ticked. What made him laugh or cry . . . even if crying was only expressed through temper tantrums or the silent treatment. But then, this was her husband. Maybe he heard about her and came to the rescue—and how on time he was! *My Prince came to rescue me.*

"God. You look . . . it's . . . it's so good to see you. How? Oh, Tuesday—this is all my fault. It is. If we didn't—if I didn't—I'm so sorry, baby." The way he spoke and the look on his face erased the stress and the tension—if only for the time being. Tuesday forgot why they had been fighting in the first place. The fear that Jesse once imposed on her was hidden or pushed away by her sudden exhilaration. Even if they couldn't touch one another, the affection was as rich as when they first dated, as stimulating as their first kiss.

Tuesday shivered with delight and thought she'd fall apart . . . that she'd explode, releasing all of those pent-up emotions in one outburst. The only way to stop herself from crying like a baby was to say something. She had to be strong. "I'm sorry too, Jesse. I only wanted us to get help. I wanted for things to go back to how they used to be. How are my babies? Do you have them?"

Jesse's eyes closed, and Tuesday wondered if she had said and done the right things . . . if she was as much music to his ears as he was to hers.

"They're fine. Baby, we only have a few minutes, so we'd better make the most of it. We'll do the makin' up once I get you back home. But right now . . . I gotta ask you—"

Tuesday interruped Jesse. "Honey, you know me. I never had anything to do with drugs. Never. This is the biggest setup."

"What happened? Try and tell me from the start," said Jesse. "And the kids . . . alone at home?"

"It's my fault. I thought it was okay to slip out of the house for an hour. I just wanted a drink . . . just some time away."

"Tuesday," Jesse said, pulling his palm across his face. "You know better."

"It's not like we didn't do it before, Jesse. Remember when Stacy was younger? Before Sharissa was born?"

Tuesday was sure her husband was thinking the same things as she was recalling how the two of them slipped out of the house for a quick drink at Nikki's. It didn't seem like much of a risk at the time—the baby was sleeping so well every night without waking. And both parents had long hours away from each other, she with the housekeeping and he with the job. It seemed like they deserved a late-night drink . . . just a small toast to mark their unity . . . the beginning of their dream: The Wallace Family.

Tuesday supported her flashback, reminding Jesse, "We were too busy for socializing . . . no vacations, and we hardly had time for us."

"Yeah, yeah," said Jesse with a guilty tone. "But we were so naive back then. We should've never left our child alone. Not for a second. If you could only see with my eyes . . . on the job I've seen so many crib deaths, fires and even electrocutions . . . all because a parent stepped out for a minute. What we did was inexcusable."

Tuesday could read between the lines. She could feel her husband's undertone: what he really meant was that *she* was wrong, that it was *her* actions that were inexcusable.

"I'm sorry. I . . . I was so stressed. You left me alone. I was running out of money. Just a whole lotta shit." But Tuesday was hoping he wouldn't think—

"Money? Is that what this is about? The E-pills they said you had in your possession?"

Tuesday wagged her head with that determined look in her eye. It was that same determination that inspired her left hook earlier that day. "Don't believe that, Jess. I met a guy. It was nothing, do you hear me? You have to believe me. You have to . . . me and a friend—Janice, you know her, from the Sugar Shack Comedy Club . . . She was the cashier, remember? Well, we went down to the Savoy on a Friday . . . it was a . . ." Tuesday hesitated. "Exotic male review."

"Okay. I got that much through the grapevine. I'm not trippin' off of that. You went to a strip show. Big deal. Tell me about this dude."

"His name is Slide."

"A nickname?"

"I guess. He was one of the . . . dancers."

"And what. You met him at the club?"

Tuesday was ashamed and nodded that way.

"Go on."

"Janice and I . . . well, we agreed to have a drink with him. In his truck." Tuesday could see her husband bite his lip, like he was about to blow . . . like he was disgusted with her. She had to get the story out so he'd have the full picture, so that he wouldn't jump to conclusions. "But it was all in fun, Jesse. I was just being naughty, just a sip of Moët."

"Get to the part about the drugs," Jesse snapped.

" 'I need a couple girls like you,' the guy told us—"

"This Slide said that."

"Yes. He said he wanted us to help him run his business. He said he was into supply and demand. But I had no idea he meant drugs."

"Then what?"

"I was in the backseat while Slide and Janice were messin' around. They were kissin' 'n stuff, then she—well, y'know . . . went downtown . . . he turns around while she's doin' him, askin' if I wanna join in. I'm like, fuck no, you nasty nigga. I told Janice I was goin' home. She acted like she didn't hear me. I said y'all are whack and Slide told me to get the fuck out of his truck. I was like psssh, fuck you too . . . but that's when, like, three cars rolled up. They had guns out, Jesse—"

"NYPD?"

"I think. But the cars were those unmarked ones—tinted windows, radio antennas all over. Like yours. But I figured it was okay. I didn't do anything. Unless they were gonna charge me for sipping some Moët."

"One minute!" The announcement came over the loud-speaker and the stretch of visitors began their farewells; some putting their hands and lips to the glass, others copping attitudes like the pimp flipping this fuck-you finger.

"Oh, baby . . . you have to get me out of here."

"I will. So help me God, I will. I just need a little time to—"

"Jesse!" Tuesday pounded her fist on the glass. "You have to get me out of here today!"

"What's going on? Are you okay in there? Is anybody threatening you?"

"Today, Jesse. Today!"

"Let's go, lady. In the back!"

Jesse was up against the glass, his palm slapping it desperately. The door was shut between them and Tuesday's visit was over. The escape from reality was nice while it lasted. But now Tuesday had to return to dorm 33 and Big Momma.

CHAPTER FIFTEEN

"AND THAT'S WHEN they were arrested," Jesse explained to both the Judge, Pullman, and to the landlord, Push.

The three were inside one of the second-floor residences now, the Judge's second relocation. And even the Judge had to admit what a strange environment this was—so much different from the last, with plush carpeting, the avant-garde furnishings and platinum plaques hung throughout. If he wasn't so taken by the details of Jesse's story, it might be difficult to concentrate with so many fascinating things to look at—to bask in.

"I wouldn't be coming to you, Judge, if my wife was wrong. But she's not. She never dealt with or used drugs a day in her life. It's just . . . she got herself caught in a situation . . . just stupid choices, I guess."

Judge Pullman felt like a lawyer again; a defense attorney people turned to when all else failed. There was Push's nephew at the 28th Precinct, then the talk he had with Grace Shamm, the social worker, and now this.

Where is Evelyn when I need her?

"Listen. I don't mind helping you, but you've got to realize that I'm a Senior Court Judge. There are certain things that I can and cannot do. There are procedures that I am required to observe, and only certain shortcuts and red tape I can get around. Do you understand? There's just so much I can do before my integrity is questioned or revoked. There's such a thing as censure . . ."

Jesse was part of the plot to kill this man. But that was then and this was now and Pullman never asked. Jesse would just have to maintain a superior attitude about the coincidences, for Tuesday's sake.

"But," the Judge went on to say, "I'm gonna need a little more than just stupid choices as a reason to get involved here. Was it twenty E-pills they say she had?" Pullman didn't mean to, but his disbelief showed in the dramatic expression masking his face.

"That was the allegation, Judge. Only, she never touched them. She didn't even *know* about them. It was some guy she and her friend met. A stripper named Slide . . ." Pullman and Push looked at one another, provoking Jesse to say, "That's a *male* stripper, Judge."

He didn't intend to be offensive, but Judge Pullman had no clear understanding of what the circumstances were—damned peculiar, they were. And he settled with whatever the issues were. To each his own. It wasn't important either way.

"Does Slide have a record? Is there anything to show that he's a drug pusher? Perhaps he's dragged other women into past encounters with the law."

Jesse didn't seem to have answers, since he was brooding.

"I mean, anything to help me believe this was a setup," said Pullman.

"Let me do some checking on the guy. Can you keep an open mind for a couple of hours till I get what you need? I really need to get Tuesday out—tonight if possible."

"Hey, I'm not going anywhere. But . . ." Pullman checked the Michael Jackson clock on the wall. It was a quarter of the superstar's actual size, but the arms and legs were contorted to read 4:30. "You'll need to hurry if you're thinking about getting her out today. Certain offices will be closed, and . . ."

"I know, I know. Lemme make a couple of calls." Jesse lunged toward the nearest phone, aware that his determination opened the eyes of his company. The Judge and the landlord were having a private conversation on the orange art-deco couch as Jesse waited for someone to pick up the other end of the phone. "Hey, Greg. It's Jesse, what can we find out about a drug pusher who goes by the name of Slide?" Jesse expected a wait, maybe he'd even have to call back for answers.

But Greg replied in short order. "Slide, yeah, he was part of a drug bust up at the Savoy on Jerome. You heard of 'im?"

Jesse blinked a few times and pressed his thumb and middle finger to both temples. Now he shook his head. "Say that again, Greg. I wanna be sure I heard right."

A moment later, after the call to Greg, the Judge spoke for both himself and Push. "What is it?"

"That was a buddy of mine who works in Homicide. He says he knows of only one person named Slide—and he's a cop . . . one of the arresting officers in Tuesday's case."

Once Jesse laid out more details, things that Tuesday mentioned, Judge Pullman said, "See if you can get a hold of the girl. Was it Janice? If she wasn't detained like you say, then where is she? If she'll confirm the things your wife says, then you've got an advocate, buddy. I'll get your wife sprung so fast that light speed will be too slow to keep up with her."

"Thank you, sir," said Jesse as though using his last breath. "Thank you."

A good sob story and a friend in the records department was all Jesse needed more than six weeks ago, when he requested his leave of absence—ever since that dispute with his wife. Most other officers would've called in by now, maybe even been subjected to a pink slip. But being L.T.K. had its benefits. And now that time was of the essence, Jesse had to get back to work, quick.

"GOOD TO HAVE you back, Jesse."

"Thanks, Greg. But my problems aren't over. I need to see about a few things. Get life in order."

"Smart thinking," said Greg. "Anything I can help you with? I've been working my ass off with paperwork today— already I've had a fire that caused the evacuation of an office building up on Broadway, then there was an armed robbery at First Union around noon, two car-jacks and a playground shooting."

"Your plate's full, Greg. I'll make do on my own."

Greg pulled Jesse aside, out of earshot from others in the squad room. "You look strung out, Jesse. Just say the word and I'll put it all aside, man. Just say the word."

Jesse looked across the office and saw how some of the activity stopped in mid-motion. They must know about Tuesday, he assumed. "Don't let me disturb you!" Jesse shouted, addressing some fifteen or so officers who were watching. "I mean it! Unless anybody has any answers to my problems! Johnny? Celia? How 'bout you, Dominic?? Nobody has answers?? Okay, then mind your goddamned business!!"

"Whoa, whoa, whoa! Jesse, come on, come on . . . Let's have a talk," urged Greg. And Greg physically guided Jesse to the windowless interrogation room for a one-on-one.

"Here. It's on me," said Greg as he pressed a cold Dr. Pepper into Jesse's hand. As much as Jesse denied it, the cold one was much appreciated. But in the big picture it was but an ice cube tossed in a bed of hot coals.

"I've been wanting to talk to you since you took off. You know IAD called me in."

"You? For what?"

"Because that's what they do when distressed wives call to report abuse. They come to your sidekick first."

Jesse wanted to curse.

"Don't sweat it. I covered you. You're not the first cop to go off at home. And the blockheads down there at Internal Affairs don't know their ass from their elbows. So, what's the deal? Tell me I didn't make a mistake getting the bloodhounds off your back."

Greg Schwartz was one of the coolest white cops that Jesse ever met. Unlike a lot of others who came packaged with their own belief about blacks—uniform or no uniform—Greg easily crossed the color barrier by his open-minded desire for understanding, and because he had grown up in a neighborhood on the Lower East Side. Greg also kept himself in good shape and despite tiny pockmarks about his face he was a considerably good-looking man. A *Monday Night Football* type of guy.

"You didn't have to go out of your way for me," said Jesse, already overcome with guilt.

"I didn't. Trust me. You'd be down in their office right now if I wasn't bangin' Ginger the OIC."

Jesse managed his first smile in so long he thought he'd forgotten how. "You crazy, Greg."

"My mother used to say that. So, what's up with Tuesday?"

"She's locked up in the Tombs."

"No shit. Only the whole precinct knows, Jesse."

"But it's bullshit, Greg. She was caught in some random sweep with a friend. They found twenty E-pills and they're trying to pin 'em on her."

"That's why you asked about Slide?"

"Slide. What's his real name, Greg?"

"Whew, beats me. But we can easily find out. He's with one of the street teams, one of their roughnecks."

"Yeah, well . . . that roughneck will soon see me, sooner than he'd like to."

Jesse gave a brief explanation of Tuesday's side of the story. Slide the stripper/cop was in the truck that was raided, he was not one of the arresting officers. Not only that, Janice wasn't locked up with Tuesday, and she was the one who dragged her into this mess. Jesse also mentioned his new friend, the Judge.

"Then we have to find the girl," said Greg.

"Exactly. And we have to find her fast. I can't figure it out, but Tuesday can't handle the Tombs for one more second."

"Then there's nothing left to talk about," said Greg. And he grabbed the phone.

CHANTEL PALMER, OTHERWISE known as Star, was a Jamerican who wore her hair in dreadlocks and who had the most captivating exotic eyes set apart—but not too far—in her oval face. She had one of the NYPD's most resourceful positions, assistant to the Police Commissioner. Her follow-up phone call to Uncle Sam's interest in Judge Pullman was unhelpful. Sammy (she called him that when nobody was around) was barking up the wrong tree, and was probably better off checking with Vegas German, since they were still active agents with the Secret Service.

"That's federal stuff, Sam. Why don't you try that route," she had told him.

"Just look into it," Sam replied. And he put down the phone.

And now Star was getting back to Sam in person, at The Abyss, and looking rather elegant in her formfitting leather skirt, a yellow V-neck blouse and pumps. Her shoulder-length dreadlocks were tied up and looking like a porcupine's needles or an Indian's headdress. Whatever she did with her hair, it was always creative, how a tendril was left to drape down here and there . . . how it all blended so fabulously with her dark mocha complexion and her sunny attitude.

". . . and one more makes a total of four thousand. Now gimme your John Hancock right here, Star." Reesy watched nearby, arms folded. Uncle Sam was issuing Star her monthly dividends for her contribution to L.T.K.

Star sucked her teeth, thinking that Sam was being so silly with the whole John Hancock bit. As if he would forget he'd paid her already. She picked up the money.

"Um, Sam. Aren't you forgetting something?"

"Am I?"

"I have a few loose ends to cover this month, like the coroner's office. Does the name Hitler or El ring a bell? How 'bout Mule? And Mr. Duck? That's, uhh, a whole lotta cops whose records we've had to shuffle around, mister."

"Reesy? Could you excuse us?"

Reesy said, "I'll be just down the hall if you need me." And she raised an eyebrow to warn Star, before closing the door behind her.

"You got a problem with the way I pay you? Didn't I tell

you that bonuses were only paid out quarterly?" Sam came from behind his desk and was using his finger as a weapon, poking Star lightly about the chest, right above her cleavage, to the point that she backstepped against the wall.

Star's eyes had that "how dare you" look in them and her head was cocked, appraising Sam with her round-the-way attitude.

"What? Am I being hard on you?" asked Sam. And yet he didn't wait for an answer. Sam pressed himself up against Star and attacked her with his tongue full in her mouth and his hands groping her firm breasts.

There was nothing but snorkeling sounds for a time, until the suction sound—their lips parting from the wrestle.

"And another thing, asshole. I didn't appreciate you hanging up the phone on me!" Star would've growled had her voice not been so high, so undoubtedly feminine.

Sam's response was swift.

He slapped Star across the cheek so that her face hooked away, with her loose tendrils flinging.

Star gradually faced Sam again, letting off a steamy rumble that could've come from deep down in her stomach.

"You . . . bastard," Star said in a guttural tone. And then she attacked Sam, her left hand clutching his testicles while shoving him up against the wall where she had been.

Sam grunted from the pain in his shoulder, realizing he was at a disadvantage here with his arm in a sling and the bullet wound still stinging.

Star's maneuver was so abrupt it evidenced the defense training that she'd participated in—one of those job requirements.

And now that it was Sam who was at her mercy, Star reached up to grab hold of his ponytail, turning his face down in a rough manner to meet her own. This kissing continued, only now it was Star with her tongue deep in Sam's mouth. Meanwhile, her other hand changed from a power grip to a frenzied rubbing of Sam's bulge—something familiar to her.

Between the tongue jostling and the heated hand-to-body

contact, the grappling and fighting for supreme passion, the two still carried on with business concerns.

Sam said, "For your information, those were . . . Oh shit, the arm, the arm . . . Ohhh . . . Those were ex-cops we buried."

Star was licking the older man's neck, hungry for the taste of his flesh, eating at his Adam's apple, trying to get the best of him.

She sighed. "It's still . . . uhmm . . . my work that saves your ass . . . every time . . . you fucker . . . Ohhh."

"Right there—right there—oh Jesus, that's so good," said Sam, responding to her hands as they wandered inside of his coveralls. He said, "They were washed up anyway, and . . ." Sam was breathing heavy, trying to keep up with Star. She was opening his coveralls still kissing his hairy chest. "Hitler was a nut . . . What are you doing?"

"I don't care, Sam—I get paid for my services!" Star pressed up against Sam's body, the coveralls half off and his bare chest exposed. Her face now in the crook of his neck. Star said, "I want a quickie, Sam."

"I told you: I pay bonuses at the end—"

"I don't care . . . I wanna get paid—*now*!"

Sam managed to free Star of her blouse and now they were both bare-breasted.

"Will a couple of grand . . . ? Oh, that's good, baby!" Star was eating at Sam's nipple and his testicles were being fondled simultaneously.

"Three thousand . . . and not a penny less." They couldn't talk anymore, at least not about business.

Eventually Sam had Star bent over his desk, with the money spread out under her face while the one-armed freak plowed her fertile soil with his shovel.

Reesy was in the next room watching every bit of this through a hole drilled in the wall months ago. At one time she only suspected this was going on behind her back—these sexual encounters that her uncle was having with Star, with Pinkie and Fonda too—so she made the hole. When she learned the truth that she wasn't the only one he made love to, it upset her and she considered killing herself. But the more Reesy saw, the more she began to change her perspective on things. And soon she began to make this a routine—as much as he had his private encounters. She even enjoyed it, and while she watched she played with herself. Reesy masturbated often, watching her lover take this woman and that . . . learning so that she could do things better when it came her turn.

When they were done, Star rolled her beautiful eyes at Sam, saying so much with her sigh—how she liked his rough ways, no matter how rough.

"I feel like I'm a basement sale," said Star as she gathered up her money from the desk and floor.

Sam shrugged one shoulder. "Well, you are the cheapest fuck I've ever had."

Star cackled and said, "Fuck you, asshole." Star fixed her blouse and skirt, pulled out a mirror from her handbag to check her hair and makeup. "Oh, by the way. I heard something about that Judge you asked me to—"

Sam threw up his good hand. Hold it. And he went over to the wall, lifting a framed picture of Hitler from one place and putting it conveniently over the hole in the wall. "Okay," Sam said, lowering his voice and pulling Star further from Hitler. "What about the Judge?"

Star made a curious expression, first looking at Sam, then Hitler, then Sam again.

"Come on, come on . . . the Judge," Sam insisted.

"Yeah, right . . ." Star became absentminded all of a sudden. "It's not anything I'd consider Class A information, since it's grapevine-shit—"

"So what's the grapevine say?"

"It's a little gray, but . . . A cop and his wife had some kind of beef, and for some reason she was locked up. They got kids, so DCW was called in."

"Okay. What's child welfare got to do with—"

"I'm not done. Would you shut up and let me tell it?"

Sam pursed his lips.

"The woman visits the cop's house to see about the kids and guess who she finds there?"

"Pullman?"

"There you go."

"When was this?" Sam had an impulsive interest.

"A day ago. Maybe."

"Any idea what cop? What address?"

Star smiled. "I though you might want that. That's why I didn't argue about the money."

"Huhn?"

"I just knew this would be worth another two thousand." Star had her hand out ready to receive the money. "Cough it up."

Sam inhaled and exhaled. He took two steps so that his stone-cold stare was close enough to stab Star in the face. "If you don't gimme that information right here, right now, I swear to God I'll tie your black ass up like a steer and set you on the nose of my truck and drive across town until you piss yourself."

Star twisted her lips. "Would I be naked too, Sam? Because it wouldn't be worth me pissing myself if I wasn't naked." Her nostrils flared, accepting defeat. And she passed the slip of paper to Sam. "Stingy mothafucka."

"Thank you very much," Sam said. He slapped Star's ass affectionately and told her to take her ass home.

Sam contacted his uptown squad at once. Cali. Ape. Turk. Skin. All of them were expected for a midnight meeting at The Abyss. It was time to get the Judge.

"Son of a bitch. Chico would've been just right for this," Sam said to no one in particular.

Reesy happened to walk in. "Who are you talkin' to?" she asked.

"Ahh, don't mind me. What's the new member's number?"

"Which one?" asked Reesy. "There's four altogether"

"Okay, he's got a slick name. And he strips for a living, if I'm not mistaken."

"Oh yeah," said Reesy, a special interest in her tone. "I remember his last name is Canasta. I can check if you want."

"Doesn't he have an alias?"

"A nickname? Slide, of course," Reesy said with an appreciative smile.

"Mmm-hmm. How 'bout we get him down here by midnight?"

Reesy saluted. "Yes, sir, Uncle Sam."

Sam turned to take up one of his cell phones from his desk while his niece went about her orders. "Hey, D.C. Glad I could get you. Can you and Sanchez make it down here by midnight?"

"Jeez, Sam. I don't know about Sanchez but we've got an early morning raid over here."

"Well, get at me as soon as you can, hunh?"

"You got it," said D.C.

Sam dialed another number for Sanchez. More bad news. He was caught up at Kennedy Airport where another of those bomb scares had shut down everything and required as much manpower as possible.

"Okay," said Sam. "Handle your business." And he hung up the phone. "Hold down the fort."

Reesy shook her head, busy on the phone and jotting down a phone number. Slide's, no doubt. And as Uncle Sam left the office, he noticed Hitler had been moved again.

CHAPTER SIXTEEN

IT WAS TIME to clear the air. There were some unanswered questions and other loose ends that Push needed to address. They'd been hanging over his head for far too long . . . so many concerns that he'd rather nip in the bud than have them sit on his conscience.

"You gonna be okay, Judge?"

"Oh sure. I'm just as cozy as could be, living like a rock star," he replied with his nose turned up and his eyes closed.

Push was amused, if only briefly. "Good. I need to step away . . . to take care of some personal business."

"Oh please. Go right ahead, young man. And thanks for the company. I feel like we're related, as much as we've talked."

Push smirked as he went for the door. He thought about the gun he gave Pullman. *I hope he never has to use that.*

NEXT DOOR, YVETTE was with Stacy and Sharissa in an all-girl powwow. Crystal had been with them as well, but had to leave for work.

"So, my little princesses, the moral to the story is nothing can dim the light that shines from within . . ."

Both girls sat on the Melrah office floor with wonder in their eyes. Yvette had just read one of Maya Angelou's passages, which followed a home-cooked meal, which followed a day of shopping.

"Miss Yvette, can I be a fa-mom-al woman too?"

Stacy, the older of the two, rolled her eyes and assisted Sharissa. "Fe-nom-i-nal, Sharissa; right, Miss Yvette?"

Miss Yvette. Yvette held a laugh to a simple affectionate smile. She had finally gotten the message across to Stacy—always help your sister.

"That's right, Stace. Now let's glue the pieces together. Phe-nom-inal. Say it."

They did. Stacy was on point and Sharissa wasn't far off.

"The only thing you must remember, young ladies, is to say it often enough so that you will soon be it."

"Yay! Famomamal!"

And Stacy rolled her eyes again before all three in night-gowns, slippers and pigtails laughed it up together.

Yvette sensed that someone was in the hallway and turned to see Push. "Well, look who the wind blew in!"

Push presented the phoniest smile and checked his watch. The watch had become a necessity; however, it was one of those conveniences that he found it hard to get accustomed to. Seven P.M.

"Hi, Push!" the girls chirped together.

"Hi, girls . . ." and to Yvette, "I need to see you," he said in a partially hushed tone.

Yvette made a face reminding her boo that she had company.

"How long?" Push asked, again with the secret-agent lip synching.

Yvette put up a forefinger. One hour until bedtime.

Push was immediately frustrated and wanted to go vent—442 was just next door. A hop, skip and jump to the heavy bag, chained up in the basement of his next renovation project—a project that he feared might be in limbo if what he concluded about the real estate negotiations was correct.

And now that he thought about it, anything related to real estate sparked off some nausea deep within him. The idea of something shady going on led him to make all kinds of presumptions, with all kinds of angry, hateful images corrupting his mind.

Normally, it might take a lot more than this to make Push snap. But this was his woman, whom he trusted with his heart and soul. Why was she deceiving him?

One hour.

Thanks to Yvette, Push would use that hour to take care of unfinished business; something that would give him relief so that maybe he wouldn't go off on someone he felt strong feelings for.

Better to finish off someone he hated with a passion.

NATHAN AND ALONZO Nixon weren't that much different from one another, except that Nathan was a few years older and (he figured) wiser than his brother.

It had been quite awhile since the two had ventured out on their own to share this apartment they rented above Sammy's Crab Legs on 125th Street. Their parents still lived on Manhattan Avenue in a two-story brownstone walkup that the sons outgrew by their early twenties.

For better or for worse, they were stuck with each other now. Alonzo needed his brother's half of the rent (as much as Nathan needed Alonzo's) to make do. And this wasn't the most desirable rental in Harlem either, since the stench of crabs penetrated every fiber of these two, all day long and late into the night.

Crab legs. They were boiled, baked and buttered for a customer base that loved seafood and didn't mind paying the price.

Unfortunately for the Nixons, the taste had everything but nothing to do with the foul aroma that hung in the air. The smell was an instant reminder: there's pussy and there's crab legs. One was for fucking and the other for consumption. However, both had that same oceanic, salt-water odor so pungent that you could even taste it in the air. Even if you tried, you'd never forget the smell.

Tolerating the odor was easier since it was reason of a recent rent adjustment, making it a cinch for the Nixons to cover the monthly payment of $400—dirt cheap by today's market standards.

For income, Nathan was an usher at the Apollo Theatre on the weekends and a busboy at Sylvia's Restaurant on weeknights. He also had a side hustle going—he helped sneak a few people in here and there to catch the more popular entertainers who came through the Apollo.

Alonzo was a sweep-up man (although he'd call it "maintenance") at The Magic Johnson Theater from 4 to 8 P.M, and he also hustled on the side. The drug pushing could've been a full-time occupation—he'd have to increase his clientele by at least ten more buyers per week—but jail frightened him. The amounts he sold might buy him a fly pair of kicks once a month, but in the big picture, as far as five-o was concerned, he might pay a fine or serve some probation. And that was only if they could catch him. But no prison.

No way he would ever wind up like his old friend, Block, who died when a weight bar crushed his neck . . . in prison.

That situation still had a fishy taste to it since Alonzo never knew Block to be any weightlifter. But then he also heard that prison changed men, at least one way or another.

"I'm taking the night off, Lon." Lon was Nathan's nickname for Alonzo. No more stupid a practice than playing the name game as a twenty-something—Lonnie, Lonnie, fo-fonnie . . . "There's a hottie I'm trying to holla at."

"Who?"

"Her name is Apple. And you better not laugh."

Alonzo choked on the laugh instead.

Nathan said, "Whatever . . . I'm gonna need the crib tonight."

Alonzo cursed. Then he said, "I know she ain't givin' you no cha-cha."

"Nigga, suck the cha-cha. I'm goin' for the apple juice tonight! So have your ass over on Manhattan Avenue—or better yet, you ain't gotta go back home, as long as you get the fuck outta of here."

He wouldn't mind that he and his brother looked so much alike if it weren't for Alonzo being so dumb. They both had the same corn-bread complexion, the captivating silver eyes, the conked rust-colored hair and the objectives of sticking their carrot sticks in somebody's Jell-O-pudding, so long as that somebody had tits and ass.

"You got that," said Alonzo. "Just know that it's me and Donna tomorrow night."

"Tomorrow? Shit, Lon! I'm with Karen tomorrow night. And that's sho-nuff cha-cha."

"Well, you better choose, 'cuz we share this spot equal. I need my piece of ass just like you."

Nathan was flustered. He didn't want to choose. He wanted both girls. Apple was a virgin—she had to be—or at least, as close as he'd ever come. And Karen gave him "knowledge"— another name he used besides "getting brain," a "Lewinsky" or a blow job—that made him wanna cry during the encounter.

"There's gotta be a way we can work this, Lon."

"You're right. There is."

"Hunh?"

"See, I don't think Apple is givin' up the cha-cha. To be honest, bro, I think you're makin' an excuse to get me out of the apartment so you can keep beggin' her—or whatever you're doin'."

"You trippin', nigga. That ass is mine."

"Okay, okay. Cool out. If you say you can get the ass . . ." Alonzo had to think about it. ". . . then let me watch."

"What!"

"I'm serious. Let me watch you and Apple . . . and if you tellin' the truth and she gives up the ass, then you win. I ain't no pussy-blocker or no playa-hater. You can even have the spot to yourself tomorrow with Karen and I'll just take Donna to a movie—a boring one if you know what I mean."

"I don't know, Lon. That shit sounds freaky as a mothafucka."

"Exactly. But it beats stayin' with the parents. Come on, Nate, lemme see your work—the work you *say* you're doin'."

Nathan thought about it, grunting until he worked up a chuckle, then a laugh. Eventually both of them laughed, followed by an argument and a high-five.

"You better not be checkin' me too close."

"Come on, man. You my brotha. We used to be in the bathtub together."

"Damn!! Did you have to bring that shit up??"

"Get your mind out the gutter, Nate. Well . . . at least about that. I just wanna see pretty-assed Apple's cha-cha. Is she really a virgin?"

IT WAS NATHAN who was getting the biggest kick out of this; the whole idea of busting Apple's cherry first while his brother watched. *I'll show him how a pro does it,* Nathan told himself in the house prior to his date with Apple. And it wasn't really a date at that, since Nathan knew from experience that it didn't cost much, and he wouldn't need to do much to impress a teenager. Even if Apple was eighteen, she was still naive to the ways of a mack—such that Nathan felt he was—and his mack maneuvers. Spend as little money as possible and take as much physical pleasure as possible. Once she feels like she's invested something she'll wanna do everything under the sun to be your main girl.

The deflowering of Apple began with orchestra seats at the Apollo. It was Amateur Night. And, naturally, the tickets were free, despite Nathan boasting how he paid top dollar for them. Some girls fell for anything.

And now the two were out eating at a place where Nate was expecting to spend no more than an out-of-state phone call might cost. A burger and fries, he figured, should do the trick. Apple would feel like a queen for the night. More important than Mickey D's value menu was the geography involved. It was just across the street from Sammy's Crab Legs and, of course, the Nixon brother's apartment.

"Hey! Isn't that your brother?" Apple pointed out of the large picture window.

And Nathan did see Alonzo, but pretended not to. "Where??" Nathan asked, swinging his head, looking beyond. "You must be mistaken. Lon is at the movies with some girl named Donna." *What the fuck is wrong with that nigga?*

"Oh. I guess . . . whatever," said Apple, and she went

back to her Quarter Pounder with Cheese. Nathan wanted to keep the momentum here and went back to the seduction: He stared deep into her brown, wide eyes, imagining how deep he'd get into her tight cha-cha.

Alonzo was hoping to get his brother's attention, not Apple's. *Shit!* He thought he could get Nate to step away from Apple for a minute so that he could tell him about his little change in plans.

Originally, Alonzo was supposed to lie in wait outside the apartment, maybe downstairs in Sammy's or on the first floor under the stairway, until Nathan got the girl in the bed. Then, assuming Nathan followed his end of the plan to leave the door open just a bit, Alonzo wouldn't have to be all noisy with keys and whatnot. He'd simply creep in while Nathan was busy with the foreplay. The brothers also forecasted that there'd be enough activity—heavy breathing and moaning included—to help cover any clue of a third person's presence.

However, that was the old plan. Not that Alonzo changed his mind about the voyeurism—hell, no, he wouldn't miss that for the world. It was just . . . he didn't feel comfortable with the walk-in. *What if Nate doesn't get into the foreplay in time? What if Apple sees me?*

A minor adjustment in the plans shouldn't be a big deal.

And now that Nathan didn't catch on to Alonzo's signal that he wanted a quick powwow, Alonzo figured what the hell. It would still be the same in the end, the down-low, taking in every possible morsel of the Apple-pie.

There was something else.

Alonzo was supposed to light up candles and incense so that the intimate atmosphere would be mysteriously ready and waiting for Nathan and his fresh fruit. He was supposed to have an answer in the event Apple questioned him: I did it by remote control. But Alonzo also had second thoughts about that part of the plan. *What if the candles start a fire before he gets home? Then he won't have a place to peel his Apple . . . I won't have a place to get with Donna. Naw—bad idea. Shit . . . well, maybe just one candle wouldn't hurt.*

Alonzo waited a good fifteen minutes until he was sure
Nate and Apple were heavy into their burgers. Then he shot
over to the crib and lit up one candle and one incense. Finally, he sat in the window and kept an eye on the golden
arches. (Where the BILLIONS SERVED had been changed to
TRILLIONS SERVED.)

IT WAS A matter of timing. Something that Push knew well.

From the thrust he gave to a man up on the rooftop, to the
weight bar he crushed into a man's throat, to the men (and
one woman) he had shot on any number of Harlem's dark
streets—for each individual who Push executed, the event
involved timing.

It could be well planned, or it could be short notice, but
there was always pacing, or careful study, or even instinct
that he had to observe. He could look back over the course
of fifteen years and see what mattered: Timing.

Push was on 125th Street now, a strip that he had visited
so many times he had lost count. This was once his stomping
ground, before the stretch in the pen. He once sharpened his
hustle skills here as a teenager, graduating from a "hook"—
one of those expendable dozens who loitered along the
strips, soliciting the impulsive buyers—to a lieutenant who
managed the hooks, to a block captain. With just a few years
experience under his belt, Push lucked into the leadership
role when Goat, the crack lord and H.N.I.C. of the 125th
Street Crew, was gunned down.

Push took the steering wheel, driving that organization
from a mere enterprise to an empire that often ran out of
places to store its cash. And here he was today, more than
fifteen years later, in those same boutiques, beauty salons
and small bars—businesses in which Push invested venture
capital, never expecting a dime in return. There were so
many who owed their jumpstarts to Push, who didn't have to
do what he did. He didn't have to instruct his boys to "drop
off" those unmarked gift boxes of cash to the doorsteps of
his proprietors . . . he didn't have to forgo agreements or
contracts, or notices regarding the who, the how, or the why

behind the "gift." As wild as he was back in the day, he could've just as well burned cash for the hell of it—just because he could.

But Push, being of that desperately generous mind, chose to give, not knowing that it would ultimately lead to the raid, the trial . . .

More recently, Push passed this way to keep an eye on the apartment over Sammy's Crab Legs. Plotting for the very moment. Alonzo Nixon. There was a time when taking a person's life was routine for Push, since things got to a point where he averaged a body every few weeks. Just three killings occurred, but it was so rapid, so back-to-back, that it didn't feel any different than daily hygiene; nothing to it but to do it. The very last shooting was too close to call; the news reported that the FBI was in the immediate area, conducting an ongoing investigation on that very block—Striver's Row. It behooved Push to lay low for a long time—immersed in his real-estate construction.

But now that seemed so long ago. Long enough for him to assume, though not necessarily conclude, that he'd gotten away with murder. Again.

The trail was ice cold, Push realized. Yet, that was before Evelyn—Ms. W—his probation officer, made it clear that she watched a lot, if not most, of his work. That thought was beyond comprehension, a puzzle that was bizarre enough to put away and try to forget about. And that's one of the things that Push wondered about now, as he sat in a booth against the wall toying with an order of french fries. He couldn't help but look over his shoulder two or three times. *Is she watching me now?*

But then there was a strange sense of security that Push felt as well . . . like Evelyn was his guardian angel . . . that she wouldn't allow him to fuck up. And now come to think of it, he wished she was watching this, him finishing off the last one on his hit list.

From what Evelyn said, she knew about the three punks—Block, Miguel and Alonzo—who murdered Push's parents almost twenty years ago. And now that Block and

Miguel were history, crossed off on Push's hit list, there was just Alonzo left.

Push decided that his would be the most painful, the most violent finish—just because he needed to vent, and because he had an hour to do it. Finding out Alonzo's last name had been simple. But Push went so much further to plan this. He knew that Alonzo had a job sweeping at the Magic Johnson Movie Theater and that he peddled weed on the side. He had a baby momma, some young joint who was taking him to court for child support. His brother also lived with him. *And if he gets in the way he can catch it too.*

The building with the crab joint also had three apartments. Push realized that there were many customers traipsing in and out of Sammy's, but that they'd be too hungry to pay him any mind once he made his move.

The vestibule to the right of Sammy's was the entryway to the apartments upstairs. It was isolated from the traffic and had no lighting. They still hadn't replaced the bulb that Push broke three weeks earlier.

The weather was mild, and the street sounds of cars passing, doors opening and closing, a ditty-bopper and his boom box, were the evidence of constant activity, even as many of the area's businesses were closing for the evening.

Push left Mickey D's and went to stand in the doorway of Harlem Office Supply where the gate was already down. McDonald's, the Apollo and Mart 125 were all within a stone's throw . . . all helping to illuminate the streets and sidewalks. Especially brilliant tonight was Heavenly Glam, the full-body salon where Push had escorted Yvette on occasion. The place was still open with its neon lighting and busybodies inside.

For the moment, Push visualized his actions. The door where he'd be entering was badly damaged from either a police raid or a break-in, he couldn't care less which. It would be past eight when Alonzo would likely come home from work.

Push knew that Nathan worked at Sylvia's during the weeknights, so he didn't have the brother to concern him.

He'd force his way through the door at the street level. If not, if the door fought him, he might wait for someone to go in or come out. Whatever.

Before Push took another step, he noticed a couple hugging up one another, approaching the building. He immediately knew that it was Alonzo from his 100-foot perspective, and he had some girl, a young joint, with him. It didn't appear to be the girl who Push saw with him with weeks earlier—this one was wheat bread, the last was oatmeal.

Push was quick to shrug it off as Alonzo, the mack in action, came closer, and ideas began to fly at him. *(Run up on him. Toss the girl aside. Take him in the foyer. Bing-bing-bang and it's over.)* But that would be messy. And the girl would be screaming besides. He acted on another idea, getting close enough so that once they stepped in, he would wedge his foot in the door so that it didn't quite close all the way.

There were a few passersby at this time of night, and they were apparently on their grind, too busy, trying to get somewhere soon. If anyone was interested in some black dude in a leather coat, a Red Sox cap, with his foot in a threshold, it would be to offer him help since he seemed to have lost something, with his head down and face turned from any full view.

No such bad luck.

Push waited a short time before he too stepped through the door and took the steps quietly, two and three at a time. Push huffed when he realized someone was coming down the steps. Instinctively he shot back down and found cover, the underside of the stairway. He shifted a bicycle over some and ducked down so as not to be noticed. The very shock he felt was odor. Someone had been where he was and used the spot for a toilet, compliments of a broken entrance. Wincing, Push listened, wondering if this was Alonzo and company.

The footfalls stopped midway on the steps. Voices. One deeper than the other. A woman, Push guessed.

"So, are we clear about tonight?' asked the deeper voice. "You will never walk beside me or in the front, always a step behind. And you will answer to the name Peachfuzz. Do you understand me?"

Push was thrown for a time, listening to how one person—*it definitely ain't Alonzo,* he realized—was so condescending towards the other.

The talking had ceased, but Push knew they hadn't left the steps. He could almost feel their weight above him, bearing down on the wood so that it creaked. *(Do they know I'm down here?)* There was grunting and moaning now. They were carnal sounds, as if sex was ongoing. *(On the steps?)*

Venturing for a peek with his Ruger .45 in hand, Push eased around, carefully leaned past the bike and eventually faced the railing—that illusion of jail bars—to find two women with their mouths connected like hungry beasts. Push stepped back into the fecal fumes and sighed inaudibly. He flipped the safety on the gun. *(Lipstick lesbians. Great.)*

He prayed that these two would cut the shit, especially the slave master with the ranting, and go on their way. He'd come this far, no sense in going crazy now. So Push marinated there like a vegetable while the steps creaked on with heavy breathing.

"Maybe we should go back up," said the high-pitched voice.

"Bitch, I though I told you not to speak unless spoken to?"

"Sorry."

"Disobey me again and you get the belt . . ."

Push looked to the sky, even if he couldn't see it, and he pressed a palm to his face wondering if this wasn't some kind of test or maybe a way to punish him for the sin that he was set to commit. Again he prayed for this to end.

"Now follow me, Peachfuzz."

Push looked to see the two women leaving, one with a leash and dog collar pulling her along.

"**WOW! WHEN DID** you have time to light this?" Apple asked. "Do you have more? It's kinda dark in here, and I'm a good girl, y'know?"

Apple's mention of being a good girl caught Nathan off guard, causing him to forget what his response would be for that question. Then he recalled the remote control bit and trashed it. It suddenly sounded like a silly idea amidst such a serious occasion—one he intended on making a serious occasion.

Nathan sidestepped the question altogether, smiling at Apple in a way that challenged her to figure it out.

(When is Alonzo gonna come in? He better have good timing.)

"Maybe now isn't a good time for questions and answers, Apple. I'm glad you agreed to be alone with me . . ." Nathan took her hand and led her to a couch, expecting it to become a bed very soon. "I'd rather spend some quiet time with you. No McDonald's employees, no kids running around like they lost their minds . . ." Nathan clasped her hand with his. "I want to inhale your scent, breathe your used oxygen . . ."

Nathan found the remote control and pressed the necessary buttons. The CD was preselected, and so was the song. Within seconds, the crooner/sex addict let loose.

"Temperature risin'

"Your body's yearnin' . . . hold me . . ."

While the song asked the big question, Nathan eased back on the couch, intending to lay down his smoothest delivery ever. He wanted it more than anything else in the world—like a ten-year-long drought. And he'd say or do anything to make it happen.

"What're you doing?" asked Apple, removing Nathan's hand from her thigh.

"Easy, babe. I'm just tryin' to make you feel good. Like a princess should feel. Now you're not gonna tell me you're not just a little attracted to me, are you?"

Nathan was trying to warm Apple into some direct eye contact. It wasn't only his words that usually did the trick, but it was also how he buried his expressions into a girl's soul. The words were to penetrate her mind; while the deep gaze was to stimulate her just as his touch would along her thigh, between her legs; he was using every bit of his imagination to make this happen. Touching her physically probably startled her, but—*trust me.*

He'd get there eventually.

Plan B.

"I'll be right back," Nathan said, as if to keep the fire warm—even if it was his alone. He bounced to the kitchenette for a glass—some Hawaiian Punch, one of those pills.

Push couldn't have been a luckier predator. The apartment door was open some. He had no idea what this punk was thinking: it being dark outside, this being Harlem, crime being at an all-time high.

Whatever.

This job was getting easier, finally.

But then . . . *Is the open door a setup?*

Push took this opportunity, his moment of contemplation, to slip two aspirins from his pocket. And just as quickly, he popped them in his mouth and began chewing. It was his way of bringing back all of his past challenges: all of the bouts he'd had with death, and this way of life was so cold and uncaring. Tart, bitter and unagreeable. And now Push recited his first rule this criminal persona lives by: Never underestimate your target.

A lot was going on in here.

This was an atmosphere suited for lovers, Push determined as he light-footed his way into the dark apartment:

The candlelight flickering against the far wall.

The music and jasmine in the air.

And as Push moved further, there was the panting and smothered cries, consuming enough to be sex. Exciting, maybe for someone else.

Push was not deterred.

His second rule: Stay focused, no matter what.

So far, this was a best case scenario for him; the shadows grinding on the wall and then . . . there they were. The two bodies casting the shadows.

Damn.

Alonzo was half-naked, there on the foldout couch with the girl. Both of them in the his 'n her position of a doggiestyle performance. It was obvious, at least by the look of things, that the girl—whoever she was—was a willing participant, how she was carrying on. Her face was planted in the pillows, her body was available, on all fours . . . no, sinking from that position as she received his wild thrusts again and again. Her cries escaped the pillow pile now and then, with a sense of desperation to them. But even Push had been here with his lover, occasions that he'd rather not think about right now. Thank God the two bodies were too busy to realize what was about to happen. Push may as well be a ghost.

Sorry to mess up your evening.

Now for the approach. The task itself.

Rule number three: Use the element of surprise whenever possible.

He already had the automatic by his side, fully loaded, including the round in the chamber. A silencer was snapped in place and now the barrel of the weapon was hooked on his target. Alonzo.

Even as the punk was in motion—beating up his partner's love pot, fucking her brains out—Push reached over the guy's sweaty body and grabbed a handful of his locks. He didn't need to see his face to know that this was his man—Alonzo. The last one on his list. Everything added up: Alonzo's apartment, Alonzo's being home alone at this time each night—he was the one, as far as Push knew.

But as precise as Push strived to be, even he could make a mistake.

Confidence stirred inside of him, and he was ready to get it over with. No time to think. Push pressed the nose of the weapon to the man's temple.

It was done.

The report was abrupt. A cough was all.

Although dark, the blood and guts were obvious, splattered about the sheets, the pillows and the girl's back. The girl hadn't even realized she had a dead fuck with her. Push released his grip and the dead body slumped lifelessly on top of the living one.

It was a fast exit. He pulled a rag out of his pocket, wiped his hands and his tool and peddled his way out of the apartment.

Minutes later he's strolling down 125th Street, across the promenade in front of the Harlem State Office building. He dipped over to 126th and slowed some for the remaining two blocks. And then, home.

Suddenly the problems and issues of an hour ago were less important (or less threatening) than those he left behind above Sammy's. And with each step forward, Push began to feel the fulfillment, the satisfaction and power.

He couldn't wait to tell his sister the news.

CHAPTER SEVENTEEN

IT HAD BEEN a long five minutes that Alonzo Nixon kept his scared ass hidden. And it was a good thing he didn't tuck himself under the foldout, his initial intention. That, he had quickly realized, was a stupid idea, right after the one about unprotected sex, one of his own self-righteous hang-ups. So Alonzo hid in the apartment's only closet, close enough to watch the intercourse . . . and his brother's murder.

Paranoid and shocked, Alonzo eased out of the closet, immediately engulfed by the conflicting fumes of blood, of flesh, of sulfur and of sex.

Apple was shivering like she'd been left naked in the cold. She'd broadcasted some haunting shrieks minutes ago, grabbing herself up in a ball, frozen and electrocuted from the revelations. Now Apple's shrieks digressed into those of a dying opera singer. The blood and gore was smudged, sprayed and streaked about her body.

And all the while R. Kelly was repeating: *Do you want it, babe? Do you need it, babe? Do you want it, babe? Do you need it, babe?* The CD was stuck and R. Kelly had been asking the same question ever since the killer left.

"Nate? Nate??" Alonzo tried his best to revive his brother. The odor in the air, together with the look of things, made him want to vomit.

He had no idea why his vision was blurred, or why his eyes were burning. If he hadn't been beating his dick in the closet, his eyes opening and closing with his rhythm, with his sensation, he might've noticed that he, his brother and Apple weren't the only ones in the apartment. He might've interrupted the killer . . . maybe even attacked the dude. But that was a thought after the fact.

Right now Nathan wasn't moving. And Alonzo was sick to his stomach, with the awful feeling that Nate was—

"Oh God, no! Nooooo!"

Alonzo's shouting caused Apple to scream again, louder than before. And she kept screaming, thinking that this guy Alonzo was the one. He was Nathan's killer. "It was you!" she cried.

He was the only other person she'd seen in the room, and not a minute after Nathan fell dead on top of her. Apple's state of mind was warped, influenced by the pill that Nathan slipped into her Hawaiian Punch. However, she had some sense of things. Her limbs might've felt like bricks and her sex like processed beef, but she could still put two and two together.

Who else could've done this?

"Apple, no! No! It's me, Alonzo! I'm Nate's brother."

"And you killed him! You killed him!" And Apple screamed some more.

It wasn't even the issue of Nathan being dead, just that the impact of this was right in her lap . . . all over her body.

"No! No! No! It was . . ." Alonzo's voice fell to a whisper. "You?"

But then he recalled the images he saw while he whacked his Johnson. There was a third person. Of course. Nate couldn't be two people—one doing the fucking and the other doing the standing.

"It was somebody else," Alonzo muttered, coming to his own conclusions. "I was in the—oh my God! Nate's dead! He's . . ."

This all turned to mush before Apple's eyes. The sights and sounds were just too plain confusing to comprehend. All she could manage for now was the rocking back and forth, the self-talk and the tears. She wanted this to all go away so she curled up on the bed, pulling some of the bloodstained sheets and pillows to her breasts, keeping the greatest distance from the corpse, and from Alonzo.

She didn't believe any of this. But most of all, she didn't believe Alonzo. No one could ever convince her Alonzo didn't kill the man who raped her.

CHAPTER EIGHTEEN

PUSH WASN'T HIMSELF right now. He couldn't think like a common man, or confront these other concerns with his best state of mind. But he had to straighten things out with Yvette. It couldn't wait another minute.

He wanted to hear the truth and he wanted it *now*.

"So that's why you're going after a mortgage? Because of this fool, Murphy?" The instant Push saw Yvette alone in the front office, he jumped on the issue as if this was an ongoing conversation. He went about it this way so that she wouldn't be able to weasel away from the truth. He didn't want her to have that opportunity to fuck things up more than they already were.

Yvette got up from the desk and calmly went for her handbag. It made Push wonder what she'd come up with, maybe some documents or other evidence of her innocence.

Not even close.

Of all things to do. Yvette went and took out a pack of Newports and shook one loose with an amateur's unease. The cigarette couldn't stay still between her lips and she made numerous failed attempts with the lighter.

"No you didn't just pull out a cigarette and ignore me," he barked. Before Yvette could respond, Push snatched the cigarette away; it was the closest he'd ever come to hitting her. The cigarette crushed and tossed aside, Push took Yvette with both hands. His strong grip on her arms was like a harness, and he shook her like a malfunctioning vending machine.

"What is wrong with you?" Push growled. "Why you ignoring me? And when did you start smoking?"

"You're scaring me," said Yvette, finally breaking her silence. "Lemme go."

"Haven't I given up enough of my life for the both of us? You have to go and do something illegal?? Something that could put us both in jail?" Push was too furious, wanting to know the heat that Yvette produced, the way she was sweating buckets under her nightgown.

Now he let her go.

Still with a frightened expression, Yvette was feeling all the way exposed, her guilt no less evident than the tears falling down her cheek.

"All of my—"

"Uncle Push, please don't hit Miss Yvette," said a tiny voice.

Both Push and Yvette turned to see Stacy, her arm around Sharissa's shoulder, as if to protect her from potential harm. The plea for mercy sucked all of the anger and distress from the air.

Push turned his head away and went for the door.

"Push," Yvette was breathless. "Please—"

"I need some air."

Yvette was already with the girls, hugging them with promise and unloading her own grief.

"We're just arguing, ladies. He's not gonna hit me."

"My daddy did. He hit Mommy all the time when they argued."

"Lord help me," Yvette prayed at a volume too obscure for little girls to decode.

"You mean Jesus? Mommy always says that: Help me, Jesus," said Sharissa.

"Shut up, Sharissa. Dang."

"Oh, boy. Looks like I've got a couple of college girls for company. Come on, bedtime."

"Miss Yvette, you could sleep with us if you're still scared. We'll protect you."

Push was ill at ease. And thank God the Wallace girls were around because this was crazy. He devoted himself to this woman—a woman whom he wasn't ashamed to feel love for, the mother of his—

Awww, shit. How could I forget she's pregnant?

Push wanted to kick himself in the ass for the way he'd acted. He needed to control himself from getting hyper at a time when he needed to be calm. Especially now.

THE SUN WENT from bright yellow, to a fiery orange, and then it disappeared altogether under the horizon until it was dark. But with each phase of this loss of light, Jesse Wallace's hopes were melting away. And now that the evening had fallen over New York City, there was no telling what hope was left.

At the police station during his records searching, and now as he and Greg Schwartz climbed the steps toward the woman's front door, Jesse kept repeating Judge Pullman's words: "See if you can get a hold of the girl . . . I'll get your wife sprung so fast that . . ." The Judge's promise was Jesse's fuel, even now, after so many difficulties.

First off, there was no "Janice." The name of the cashier, the woman whom Tuesday befriended at Club Savoy, was actually Janet. Janet Burrows. But finding Janet wasn't quite so easy. Jesse had to find the promoter of the specific function—those male stripper reviews that were staged once in a while at the venue.

The promoter, the events, the cashier had nothing to do with the Savoy proprietors, therefore things weren't so cut-and-dried where Jesse and Greg could stop by the Savoy to look over the employee records, or pick through a Rolodex. Instead, they went on a pain-in-the-ass cat-and-mouse chase.

They had to hunt down the promoter once the girl was identified because there was no criminal record for Ms. Burrows. Which meant that the NYPD data bank was of no help. Once they finally got hold of some guy named Lex Dot

Com—the name he went by—there was another hurdle: Lex didn't want to give up the information. "I need to protect my staff," he told Jesse.

"I'll tell you what, Lex Dot Com. This is a life-or-death issue here. And if you don't come up off the number and address I'll be sure to bring half of the police force down to your next event for a nice little party of our own. If the information I need sounds like too much of a problem for you, then maybe I'll try reaching through this goddamned telephone for a piece of your ass!" Jesse had become loud and abrasive, with very little doubt in the air that he would do just what he threatened to do.

"Are you threatening me, Officer?" Lex Dot Com asked, like maybe he'd call Jesse's boss or something.

"Better than that. You can either help me now, or lose a whole lot of sleep—"

"All right, all right. Slow up with the tough guy shit . . ."

And now Jesse and Greg were at the front door of this woman's Chelsea town house.

"I guess this means she's got dough," said Greg.

"Mmm . . ." was Jesse's reply as he rapped at the front door. "But at whose expense. To me, this already stinks—the girl's using the name Janice and she's supposed to be Tuesday's friend? You don't give friends fake names. Plus, I never saw a cashier livin' so swanky . . ."

Jesse's eyes swept the area, all of these pre-war Victorian walk-ups and redbrick buildings—nothing like the grubby city streets that he policed for years.

"You read my mind. This spot's still gotta be worth seven, eight hundred grand—easy."

"And if you add the woman's immunity from arrest—"

"And your wife taking the rap for it all? Hunh, I'd say there are some peculiarities here."

"Who is it?" A woman peeked out of the pane-glass window over the gated-in garden. Both Jesse and Greg flashed their badges, disinterested in talking through windows or doors. Open up.

When the door opened, Jesse recognized the pretty face,

the braided hair, and only today did he realize her eyes to be shifty, instead of how he saw them in the cashier's window a year or so before.

"Yes?"

"We need to have a word with you . . . Ms. Burrows."

She seemed stunned that they knew her name and became immediately defensive. She wouldn't let them in. "What is this about?"

"It's about you, the arrest at the Savoy over a month ago—Tuesday Wallace."

"I'm sorry; you'll need to speak with my lawyer unless you have a warrant. Good night." The woman started to close the door, but Jesse put his weight against it. He went a lot further, however, thrusting the door and the woman so that he was inside with nothing to get in his way.

"Jess—" Greg started to say something but couldn't stop Jesse. He was already manhandling the woman, with her arm in his firm grip.

"Lemme go! You don't have any—"

"Shut up and sit," barked Jesse, unimpressed with the costly surroundings. The woman was living like a princess.

Greg stood behind Jesse, more or less endorsing this by his presence alone. Maybe he'd stop Jesse if he went too far. Maybe. Already they'd broken like fifty rules and at least three or four laws.

"You and Slide escaped arrest and Tuesday didn't. Why! Why was she set up?!"

"Do you have a warrant?" Janet said, her arms folded, her lips turned up in a snooty attitude.

Jesse pulled his hand back and was about to let go against the side of her face, but Greg jumped in to stop him.

"No, Jess . . . don't beat up another witness. Please!"

"Greg, if she doesn't talk, I'll make her talk!"

"Yeah, but you put that last one in the hospital. Please, I can't stand to see blood again."

The Burrows woman flinched and pulled her legs up to her chest in a nasty fetal position. Her mouth was open and her eyes bulging.

"If you don't want to see blood, then turn your back, because"—Jesse took the pistol out of his side holster—"it's about to get messy!"

"No! No! Nonononooooo! Please! Whatever you want, whatever! Just don't—" The Burrows woman hid under her lanky arms, squealing with one last cry.

Greg tapped Jesse on the shoulder. "Put it away, Jess. Please put the gun away . . . Take a walk because you're hot right now. Go on—" Greg gently pushed Jesse away and turned back to the woman. "You okay?"

She was still suspended in time. "No, he wasn't gonna shoot me."

Greg made a face, not wanting to tell the woman the truth. "Easy, ma'am. He gets out of hand now and then—good thing I stopped him this time."

"This . . . time? You mean he has shot people?"

Greg pretended to grieve, with his hand rubbing his forehead, as if to banish the gory memories. "I don't want to go into details . . . if you know what I mean. Let's just say that the lawyer you asked for? He wouldn't be able to help you, once that man finished with you. It wouldn't be pretty at all." Greg took a brief look at things. "Nice place you have here. You live alone?"

"Sometimes—or, what I mean to say is, I have friends who stay with me now and then."

"Oh . . . you must have a nice job, all this top of the line furniture. And this . . . what?"

"Please don't touch that, it's . . . it's very fragile."

"Oh."

"It's a Max Ernst."

"I should've known. Stupid me. I almost took it to be a plain ol' sculpture. Listen . . . mind if I have a seat?"

"Go ahead."

"This is a real simple problem to work out. It is. We don't need to get all into your personal business. It's not my business how you make your money, but see my friend?"

"The one with the short temper?"

"Yeah, that one. See, the woman who was arrested?

Tuesday? Well, that was his wife. And right now there's nothing that he wants more in the world than to get her out of jail. Now, I know you have some information to help us, so why don't you start with your relationship to Slide?"

Janet took a deep breath and went into it.

The good-cop-bad-cop routine worked like magic.

Eventually, Jesse came out, having spent some time eavesdropping and some time snooping around the Burrows home. Greg made the gesture of officiating a more civil introduction before the three got heavy into the what, the how and the why.

"So you're telling me that Slide, this sometimes-boyfriend of yours is a dope dealer on the side."

"Just the E-pills, as far as I know."

"And you help him with some of the sales?"

"I didn't say that."

"Yes, but I did. Now, how or why did you drag Tuesday into this?"

"It was Slide's idea. He said he wanted to have me and a perfect stranger . . . together."

"Uh-hunh," said Jesse. "And she agrees to this ménage?"

"Well, I think maybe she would have if Slide had gave her a pill. They usually go for it after—"

"Hold up . . . you said usually. You mean you and Slide have done this before?"

"Lots a times."

"With E-pills?"

"Sometimes. And sometimes without."

"So this was all about the stripper getting his freak on."

"Well . . . yeah. Except nobody expected five-o."

"I'm glad you mentioned that. Let's talk about the part about the police. How many cops were there?"

"A bunch."

"What's a bunch?"

"Maybe four . . . five . . . It all happened so fast."

"So you, Tuesday and Slide are in the truck doing what?"

"Just talkin'."

"Is that right. Okay . . ." Jesse and Greg looked at each other, reading between the lines.

"What happened next?"

"They yell and shout, 'Police, hands up,' plus they point their guns 'n all."

"And Slide? They pulled guns on Slide?"

"At first. But then he was talking to them by the left side of the truck, like some private ish."

"What's private ish?"

Shwartz leaned in to hear Jesse explain. "Ish is slang for shit. I though you were from the hood?"

"Oh . . . my bad," said Greg.

"You both are too funny."

Jesse wasn't laughing.

"After Slide spoke with the cops—they took his hand-cuffs off."

"Is that so?"

"And mine too. But they had Tuesday in another car already. Separated 'n stuff. I never saw her after that."

Jesse and Greg tried to imagine the bigger picture.

Greg asked, "And what about Slide?"

"They just disappeared and left me and Slide in the back of Savoy. We lucked out, I thought."

"And didn't you think about Tuesday?"

"I did, but Slide said she had an outstanding warrant. So what could I do?"

"Oh—I dunno . . . maybe try to bail her out with your Max Ernst or something! I thought you two were friends enough for you to at least give a damn . . ."

"Easy, Jesse."

"Fuck easy. You're tellin' us here and now that you didn't know Slide was a cop?"

"A cop? Slide's a cop? But I'm selling—"

"What happened? Cat got your tongue? Lemme guess . . . you're selling Max Ernst sculptures for him?"

The two cops stepped away from Janet.

"Think she's telling the truth?"

"Some of it. At least about the bust," said Jesse.

"What do you make of the cops letting her and Slide go free?"

Jesse said, "I'll tell you what I think, Greg. But there's not enough time right now. We need to get the girl to Judge Pullman."

"I agree. But we can't force her."

"You mean, we're not supposed to force her," Jesse said and he went back over to Janet. "I'm gonna need your help."

"Don't tell me you want me to come down to the police station—that you're gonna make me testify against Slide. I won't—"

"No. No police station."

"Then where?"

Jesse would've chuckled, but got right to the point. "To my house."

"Oh really?"

"Oh really. And right now . . . really."

YVETTE HAD AN olive silk robe on, something she just threw on to go outside and speak to Push, finally wanting to clear the air about things—how she had been willing to do whatever it took, whatever risk, just to help see his dream come true.

Yes, she knew there were issues of legality; issues about how she paid $1,000 to have a property appraisal inflated. Yes, she realized that if someone found out that a mortgage or bank loan was acquired using such fraudulent information . . .

Yvette would just have to tell like it is, hoping that Push would understand, and that she could undo things.

How they would follow through with the plans for 128th Street, she couldn't fathom. But, at least she could be 100 percent honest with the man she loved and that was all that mattered now. It was all she cared about in the world, next to her unborn child.

Push was out on the stoop, thinking with hands clasped. And he felt Yvette's presence behind him. "All my hard work . . . our hard work . . . the money we sank into the project . . . How could you jeopardize everything, Yvette? What were you thinkin'?"

"Push, I . . . I was afraid to tell you. I didn't want you to—"

"To what?"

"To get angry at Murphy. Angry, like you were in there with me. God only knows what you'd do to Murphy."

As Push listened, the thought of the slumlord—his face and his actions—began to gnaw at him. He pressed his eyelids shut and drew in some air.

Yvette was still rambling. "I didn't want you to go back to prison, Push, I'd do anything to see our dreams come true. I'd take any risk because I have so much faith in you . . . in us. Don't you know you mean the world to me? That you are my world? You, this baby, our properties . . . it's all worth the risk. I've already withdrawn most of my money to help—"

"What? Your money?"

"The expenses, Push. I couldn't get help from the Harlem Empowerment people. They helped us with the original guarantees, yes. But it's been two years and a lot of things have changed there. They have some kind of new process now—a bunch of red tape, if you ask me."

"Yvette, I just ran into a lady the other night—the one we met at Percy Chambers' offices. She said she's been trying to reach you. I think they wanna help. But how would you know if you don't return calls?"

"I was so busy with the girls . . . and, well . . . I've been going to the doctor for these nauseous feelings I get sometimes. Plus my job and the meetings about this mortgage."

"Fuck that mortgage," said Push. "It ain't happening."

"But . . . the closing for the brownstones. The other projects—"

"Did you hear what I said? I'll talk to Murphy. I'll straighten this out."

Just then, Yvette wobbled. She put her hand to her forehead and appeared weak all of a sudden.

"Yvette!" Push jumped up, catching her in his arms and sweeping her off her feet. The weight of her felt so good in his arms, a sense of possession that he so missed.

"Push," she breathed his name as she melted into his strong arms. He rushed her into the front office and set her on one of two couches. The moment Push knelt beside

Yvette, there was a distant *bang!* It was a month and a half before Independence Day, so Push figured it wouldn't be fireworks.

A car backfiring?

There was another *bang!* And now, Push was certain it was a gunshot, loud enough to come from the next property over, 441.

The Judge!

His mind racing, Push sprinted to the bathroom, grabbed up a washcloth with cold water and hurried back to put it over Yvette's forehead. "Stay put."

"W-what's wrong? Why are you—"

Push didn't want to appear excited, but right now his mind and body were ready for blastoff. "I—I gotta run. It's probably nothing, but just to be sure. Maybe a lightbulb exploded or something."

"A lightbulb? Push, I'm a little dizzy, not out of my mind."

Push kissed her cheek and went into a closet. "Just relax. Let me look into it," Push said. He spoke loud enough for Yvette to hear, but also hoped he disguised the sound of metal as he worked clips into his two Ruger pistols. He wedged both of the weapons behind his belt and pulled his shirt out from his waist to let it hang over to conceal them.

"Stay here," he said, leaving Yvette in a state of wonder and worry. He was gone seconds later.

CHAPTER NINETEEN

GUNSHOTS WENT OFF. Two of them. And Push was sure they were from next door.

If he thought they were from anywhere else other than on his property, it wouldn't be an issue. Just another night in Harlem.

But Push felt that proprietary interest. And besides, he had given Evelyn his word. *Don't worry . . . he's safe with me.*

More gunshots.

This was more than serious. It had to be L.T.K. Sam Foster. And that one Evelyn had mentioned, the bastard who shot his wife.

Push felt feverish. The hype was stirring inside of him again.

Judge Pullman had become more than a mere acquaintance since the two met. And for the life of him, Push couldn't figure out how this had happened, how the universe brought together such irony: a man whose job is to uphold the law, protected by a man who had obviously broken the greatest law, even by God's standards: Thou shalt not kill.

And now that they knew so much more about one another, Judge Pullman was a friend. A mentor. It was the strangest feeling, when the two sat and talked, how the Judge filled a part of that void . . . that missing force of reason in his life. Push couldn't admit this to anyone, but the man seemed like the perfect father figure. And that further fueled his adrenaline rush. Alonzo. Yvette. And now this . . .

Push was the most alert ally a man in danger could have right now, someone who was more than capable and willing to go to war.

"COME IN AND GET ME!"

Pop . . . Pop-pop-pop . . . The gunshots were deafening from Judge Pullman's perspective, there inside of the second floor residence of 441.

"What are you waiting for?! Come on, you pussies!!"

Pop. Pop-pop.

"You weren't scared to try me before! So what's the problem?!"

The shouting and threats and tough talk made Pullman feel weird; they were actions that were so uncharacteristic of him. And firing a gun at the door!?

It seemed that Charles had died and come back as an action hero, the way he squeezed off these gunshots so easily. He wasn't counting the rounds he fired, but he was sure that the clip would empty soon.

Push had left him three additional clips of ammunition to accompany the weapon, as well as shown him how to release the empty clip and how to replace the new one. Of course, Charles had to ask Push to do it a second time. The young man had so effortlessly dropped a magazine from the handle of the gun and then smacked in a new one to refill the cavity. It took two seconds, if that. Too tricky a maneuver for an amateur. Eventually, Charles had a try during their rooftop tutorial, and it turned out to be not so difficult after all.

And yet, he never, *ever* imagined that he'd actually be put to the test!

How in God's name did they find me?

Pop, pop, click.

Jesus.

Pullman bluffed his way through the downtime. Then: "A bunch of chickenshits! All of you!"

The inside of the door was a mess, bullets having ruined its wood surface with splinters and bites. Small thing, though. Charles would compensate Push for the damage. Charles Pullman, a.k.a. Mister Do-Right.

It was a good thing that he couldn't sleep. No thanks to the limited entertainment available. He had plenty of newspapers and magazines to breeze through. There was a book called *The Last Kingpin* that Evelyn brought him, raving about it so much that Charles felt the need to jump right in it. "It's over seven hundred pages, Charles. It should keep you busy for at least a week," she told him. Sure. Except the book was so full of action and drama and humanity that he couldn't put it down. It turned out to be the fastest novel he'd ever read. Three days.

When the book was done with, he found himself thinking about Michelle, and wound up watching cable TV. Infomercials. Reruns of *Sex and the City*. The shows kept him awake, more awake than he thought himself capable. Especially at his age. It was the killjoy of not being able to relive those exciting thoughts that sent him to the window for some of that fresh night air—which was when he saw them. It was a highly unusual sight: those three vehicles pulling up to a stop outside of the house. The block had been the same barren, gray construction site for the few days he had been here, with large Dumpsters parked where cars would otherwise be. The moon's glow helped to illuminate things for his dreamy eyes, enough to recognize danger coming. But, this was enough activity to be an announcement. *Visitors!* Five or six of them so far as he could tell.

Quick thinking brought him to run for the gun Push left him, and he had time to snatch up a wireless telephone. Only Charles was too nervous to recall Push's phone number. And there was no sense in dialing 911, the way things were going. No point in adding to his problems.

And now he was shooting at those visitors. *The Gunslinger*, starring Charles Pullman. He found himself tossing the phone, and he resorted to blasting at the door, warding off those persons, however unknown, on the other side. He only hoped his shouting and gunshots would be the battle cry that would signal Push (or anyone, for that matter) to come to his aid. And if Charles did say so himself, he was doing one helluva job holding Sam's cronies at bay.

CHAPTER TWENTY

PRIMO WANTED IN the very moment he heard about this latest attempt on Judge Pullman.

"He's staying at Jesse's house," Uncle Sam had explained. Primo rolled back his head, as if he didn't believe what he'd heard.

"Jesse who?" asked Primo

"Jesse Wallace—as in, Mims, the fucker that shot us."

That's when Primo's eyes had turned to flames. Bad knee or not, he was going. And the group of them left: Skin, Cali, Turk, Primo, Ape, and the new man on board, Slide.

Once they arrived on 128th Street, it was agreed that there should be a lookout, and that Primo (with his injured ass) should be the one. Primo was slumped there in the passenger's seat of the silver GMC truck when he noticed someone running from one brownstone to the next, right there where his L.T.K. partners broke in.

And the fucker had a gun!

"Ohhh, no you don't," Primo growled with his voice filling the cabin of the truck. And once the stranger disappeared inside the doorway of four hundred and forty-one, Primo made his move.

He could feel a weird sensation in his leg where the pain would otherwise be killing him right now, except that he was high as a kite. The painkillers made it so that he didn't feel shit!

His only struggle was to walk (or wobble) fast enough to catch up with this guy, whoever he was. Probably one of those U.S. marshals to protect the Judge. But Primo knew better, from that most recent experience, how marshals were not immune to bullets, pain or death. They were human too.

Alert and hyper, Primo was now the one with his back up against the door outside of 441. Through a glass window in the door, Primo could see the hero-gunman on the steps, climbing aggressively toward the second floor.

Then he heard shots being fired.

Shit!

As Primo eased through the door, he realized he'd left the shotgun shells in the trunk.

Shit! Shit! Shit!

But he couldn't stop now. Maybe the guy would be frightened enough to drop his weapon, and Primo could—

More shots. Maybe they shot him down.

Empty shotgun in hand, Primo scaled the steps. The stranger had his back turned and—

Oh, man.

—his buddies were spread about the floor. There was also plenty of blood. And now the guy was standing over the bodies, about to finish them off.

That's when Primo's beeper sounded. And the quick-thinker that he was, the bum-kneed goon swung the butt of the shotgun at the man's head, dropping him to the floor, where he lay unconscious.

A single shotgun suddenly sounded from inside the door where Skin was down with bullet wounds to his thigh, shoulder and hand. Slide was close by, struggling to peel away the Velcro straps of his Kevlar vest before the still-hot lead burned any further into his chest. Cali had caught the worst of the attack, with his face oozing blood in a stream that snaked alongside of his nose, cheek and neck.

"Fuck!" exclaimed Slide, at a loss for solutions. "What the—"

The door opened and Turk stepped out, having apparently lost his glasses. The age-old gaping wound was displayed where his eye once was. It was an ugly reality.

"Damn!"

"This fucker . . . he came in after you . . . I came in after him."

Turk looked down at the stranger with his one eye. And then he realized Cali was . . .

"Aw, shit!"

Slide hollered, "Could somebody help me out of this fucking vest? This shit is burning right through my skin!"

UNCLE SAM WAS feeling good enough to shoot pool, still with one arm in a sling. "That one was luck," said Pistol. "But there's no way you can win this with one hand."

"Humph . . . just watch me," said Sam, buckling down and aiming behind his pool cue. He squinted an eye behind his lit cigar, concentrating on the cue ball, the one ball and the corner pocket.

Vegas was standing by, announcing the balls that were sunk and others that weren't. "And the big uncle sinks the one ball in the corner!"

Pistol pursed his lips and pitched a hard look at Vegas.

"Don't you have to get back to Washington or something, Secret Agent Man?"

"Oh, don't be a sore loser, chum. The man's about to whup you with one arm in a sling."

"Right. Well, the fat lady hasn't sung yet!"

German was getting a kick out of this, how Uncle Sam was working the one good arm he had. It made him wonder what he'd do to Pistol if he used both hands to shoot.

All of them were in one of the smaller chapels that had been converted to a lounge, with a giant-screen TV, assorted furnishings and some coin-operated arcade games.

Reesy stepped in on the tail-end of the fat lady comment with a pitcher of chocolate milk in hand.

"What was that, Squirt?"

"Now, see that? There you go again, jumping to conclusions. I said fat lady . . . not the big, ugly seven-foot goon with the watermelon tits."

Even Sam had to laugh at that one.

"I'm tellin' you, Squirt, I'll crush your puny behind if you keep it up."

"Would you two stop it before I die laughing? Reesy, how 'bout some of those liverwurst sandwiches . . . Lettuce and tomato, all right?"

Reesy sucked her teeth and pulled her salty gaze from Pistol.

"I'll be sure to bring some Puppy Chow for your pet poodle, Uncle."

"That line is played out," said Pistol, as Reesy left the room.

She missed his next shot and Pistol licked his lips.

"So, where were we . . ." asked Sam.

"The Bureau," said German from the couch.

"Oh, yeah . . . If the Bureau expects to devote additional manpower for the holidays, we'll just have to step up our game plan. I'm not gonna call off the state park scores just because a few agents are on standby. Those parks bring in close to sixty grand in a single day. That's worth the effort."

"Sam's right, Vegas. We'll just have to be . . . *creative* about it."

"I just think we should be wise about this, Sam. I know they're putting agents on every landmark where crowds gather. The Empire State Building, Central Park . . . even the Brooklyn Bridge. It's all part of the show, to deter potential terrorists," said German.

"Cross-side," said Pistol. "But it's hard to tell if it's all just smoke and mirrors, or if they're honestly receiving threats. A lot of this shit is a show for the media . . . part of puppeteering public opinion."

"Either way—casualties, threats—we're goin' for it. Those attractions we're planning to hit will gross us nearly a quarter million for one day's work. Maybe more," said Sam.

Pistol missed the bank shot.

Sam toked at his cigar and then washed it down with chocolate milk—just another contradiction in Sam's life; the good health habit by morning with things digressing through the course of the day.

"It wouldn't be the first tough job," Sam said, exhaling cigar smoke with his comment. "Any other tips from the Fed, German?"

"Just a heap of shit to do with the president. Where he's gonna be and when. Nothing much beyond that. No big money moves," said German.

"Corner pocket . . . two ball," warned Sam. But before he could bear down on the shot, there was noise down the hall.

Primo and Ape dragged a body into the lounge while Turk was a crutch for Skin behind them. Slide brought up the rear with Cali slung over his shoulder like roadkill. The atmosphere in the lounge turned into a mesh of startled expressions and gasps.

"Jesus!" exclaimed Sam, his cigar dropped to the floor. "What the fuck—tell me you all screwed up again."

Skin buckled from the pain of his bullet wounds but Turk was quick enough to help him. Vegas hurried over as well, and Skin was set on the couch. With all the activity, nobody answered Sam.

"Can somebody tell me what happened here?" Sam's eyes turned to mean dark pockets.

"Some guy came and started playing hero. He shot up the place . . . but I caught him sleepin'," answered Primo.

Sam turned to Slide. "Is he alive?"

Slide dropped Cali's body on the pool table for all to see, blood and all. Pistol shared a disturbed look with German, his emotions mixed between concern for Cali and grief for his interrupted pool game.

"We couldn't just leave him behind," said Skin.

"What about the hero you talked about? Where's he?"

"He's out in the trunk of the car. So is the Judge."

Sam lit up. "You got the Judge?!" And now there were smiles. "Is he alive?"

"Both of 'em are, unless they suffocated to death on the way over." Primo laughed.

Ape and Primo started to speak at once. Ape made it through and said, "We wanted you to have them for yourself . . . like you did the girl."

Sam was bouncing in place, rubbing his hands together. This was too good to be true. "That was a *damn* good idea," he said. "Bring them in here. I wanna see the dead meat that did this to Cali."

Ape and Primo couldn't wait to get crackin'. Sam made a gross snorting sound as he looked at Cali again.

"Pistol . . . Slide . . . maybe this is a good time to get this man's body off my table."

Reesy showed up with her mouth agape and about to scream. Sam knew that the woman was afraid of mice and could hardly stand this, a bullet wound in a man's face. He stepped over, turned her away and whispered a direct order. Reesy hurried away. Things hadn't yet begun to get messy.

"You think you can carry the Judge alone?"

"I'm already one leg short, and my high is starting to thin. We better carry 'em in together, one at a time, before I'm the next one layin' on my back," said Primo.

But once the two reached the rear lot, they found another surprise. The BMW had been broken into and a green Porsche was speeding away.

CHAPTER TWENTY-ONE

REGGIE HAD HIS own little hustle going, unbeknownst to his Uncle Push or his mother. It wasn't like he was selling drugs, just that it wasn't something his uncle would respect since there was no hard work involved.

And Ma-duke would frown on it too, to know that Reggie was getting paid good money to housesit for Francine Oliver. Not only that; as protective as Crystal was, she'd have a hissy fit to know that Reggie was working for someone like Ms. Oliver.

Ms. Oliver wasn't just any woman. She was a woman whom others envied . . . whom others were jealous of.

Reggie remembered when his uncle pointed her out in an issue of *Ebony* magazine, where the woman was showcased as one of the nation's thirty most eligible bachelorettes. And, according to the article, Francine had mad juice money. The luxury at the office and at home. Her car was dope. Her audio-video unit at home was *bananas*. And her bedroom! Folks just couldn't deny that the woman had it goin' on.

Reggie could imagine his mother's shock. *You're house-sitting? For her?! I bet that's not all you're doing.*

The scrutiny would persist and somehow Ma-duke would use something somehow to force Reggie to quit. Even if it was extra love and devotion, Reggie wouldn't have a choice. Blood was thicker than all else. So Reggie kept this his little secret. And sure, he thought about sex too. Only it never got to that point. Not yet. But why shouldn't he take a shot at it? He *was* of legal age. Plus, Kibby Jordan wasn't givin' up the cha-cha, even after so many costly dates.

Why should I wait around for Kibby to do me when this woman has experience? She could do me, and stud me.

Of course those were merely thoughts that had crossed Reggie's mind . . . had his "man" standing now and then. Ms. Oliver was also calling on him more and more these days, and it made Reggie wonder if she knew of his subtle interest.

"Could you come and watch the house for me, Reg? The keys to the Porsche are on the wall if you have to move it for some reason . . ."

Reggie was too fascinated to consider whether or not she was manipulating him with her all-access atmosphere, calling him on his pager when he least expected it, and even pulling him away from the so-so adventures with Ronnie and Logic, his ace boon coons.

Even if she *was* manipulating him, the money was worth the energy—enough to squirrel away so that he could one day have a car that was *off the hook* and a crib that was *bananas*. Add those buttery expressions that the woman always threw his way. One moment she'd be all business, giving him instructions like some commander, and another, she'd turn into a mother figure, having dinner waiting and making every sort of accommodation available and it was a wrap. She could count on Reggie anytime.

"You should see her *bathroom*, dog . . . all pinked out and plush, like a big ol' rabbit foot. I almost didn't want to sit on her toilet, as soft as the seat was, like I might fall in or some-thin'."

Ronnie sucked his teeth and said, "Get the fuck out."

"I'm tellin' you, the woman is livin' phat. And I'm the man of the house when she goes away."

Now Logic rolled *his* eyes. He'd heard it all. "Tell me more about this hi-fi hook up . . . You said she got a theater in her crib?

"Might as well be. And a rack full of DVD movies, too."

Reggie's friends looked at one another, and in their own mini chorus, they said, "We don't believe you."

That's just how the three of them ended up inside of Francine Oliver's crib on the night of the shootout. None of them heard the break-in of the front door, the volume on her surround system was up too high. They didn't even hear the footfalls when the group of gunmen charged up the steps to the third floor or when they broke down the door of the Wallace residence and searched through it. There was one loud noise that caused Reggie to lower the volume for a heartbeat. But he just as soon shrugged it off once he looked to see that the Porsche was okay.

Then came the gunshots.

Now, quickly, Reggie got the message. The sound was like someone hammering upstairs. Ms. Oliver had mentioned a guest staying up there but didn't say who. So Reggie was left wondering. That is until he heard the yelling.

"I better go see whassup," he said to his present company.

Ronnie grabbed the remote control to get the sound back up to snuff. "Man, you gonna miss the good part of the flick," he warned.

More hammering noises.

"Yo, I'm checkin' this out," said Reggie with his lips tightened some.

A moment later, he stuck his head out to see his Uncle Push moving up the steps with two guns, one of them pointed at *him*.

Go back inside, Push had instructed without so much as a peep from his mouth. But Reggie comprehended just fine.

"*Shit*," Reggie muttered after he quietly shut the door.

"Whassup?" asked Logic.

"My uncle . . . that's whassup. There's some shit goin' on upstairs. *I know it*."

The hammering noise again. And now Reggie's heart jumped in his chest. It was the guns his uncle had.

"The hell! Some wild shit is poppin' off up there."

Now all three bucks had their heads and eyes turned toward the ceiling; toward some divine revelation.

"Somebody's bustin' shots?"

After the last set of gunshots, the three heard what might've been sacks of potatoes thrown on the floor.

Then another bunch of footfalls, like a stampede heading back down the steps. Reggie suddenly felt a knot in his stomach.

"Look," said Logic, with his face practically pressed up to the window. "Ain't that your uncle they carryin'?"

"Yo, look at this shit *here*. Bodies movin' out of here like used rugs, dog."

"Oh, no, man," Reggie's voice trembled. His face was a toss-up between fear and pain and he was shaking like a vibrating motor.

"Uncle Push," he cried, and he wanted to bust through the window to help. Ronnie and Logic held him.

"They got guns, yo. Slow ya roll."

"I don't give a fuck! We gotta help him!" And Reggie broke free. He sprinted through the Oliver home and out onto the sidewalk, no weapons to bear. But he was too late. The GMC truck, the white Maxima and the blue BMW were way down the block and moving west.

There was no other choice. They went for Ms. Oliver's keys and as quick as they could (so as not to lose sight of the posse who had Reggies's uncle), they fired up the Porsche and raced off.

From a block-long distance, they followed the vehicles across 128th Street until they crossed Lenox and turned north on Adam Clayton Powell Boulevard.

The trail led them for another turn down 132nd where the vehicles eased into an open-fenced driveway, the rear parking lot off the old Abyssinian Church.

"Yo, that church been closed forever," said Logic. And they got out of the Porsche for a better look.

"Why they takin' your uncle in there?"

"That's not my uncle. That's one of them other bodies— the one they dragged."

Logic had his cell phone out. "We gotta call 911 . . . the cops, something."

"Put that away, man. Ain't no time. Come on."

Logic and Ronnie both looked at Reggie like he had three eyeballs. "Yo, they got guns! We *need* five-o."

"Man, fuck five-o," said Reggie as he kept an eye on the three goons in the lot. They were carrying a body into the back of the church. Another was helping an injured man.

"Don't you remember what the fuck them pigs did to us at PJ's? We ain't had shit to do with no fake Gucci argument."

"He's right, Logic. His uncle might be in some trouble in there. But five-o?"

"My uncle hates them niggas," said Reggie. "Especially down at the 28th."

"So, if we can't call for help, what *can* we do? We ain't got no guns. All them dudes are big enough to kick our asses."

"Not if we move fast. If they only takin' a couple inside, that means my uncle could still be in the trunk." Reggie was full of snap decisions. "Let's see if there's a crowbar in the Porsche."

The rescuers could see most of the parking lot, except for where the big red truck and other vehicles blocked their view.

The rear gate had been left unlocked. But the gate wasn't the issue, getting into the trunk of that BMW and/or Maxima was the issue. And they had to act quickly, before any of those gunmen showed their faces again.

There was no crowbar in the Porsche. However, they found a jack—a small one that folded like an accordion.

"What're we gonna do with this?"

"Watch and see," Reggie announced as they scurried like rats in the moonlight, through the open fence, toward the BMW.

There was no stop-and-wait at this stage. Reggie was sure of himself, taking the jack and smashing the back window of the Beamer.

Reggie climbed into the back of the car. "I seen this before, where a dude pulled the backseat out to get in the trunk."

"Oh, yeah," said Logic. "*Uptown Saturday Night*, with Cosby and Poitier."

"Naw," Ronnie responded, "that was *Let's Do It Again*."

"Would y'all cut the shit? Help me!" Reggie whispered harshly.

And all three were at once were pulling at the backseat of the BMW until Reggie saw him.

"Uncle Push! Come on, y'all! Pull harder!"

There was a metal frame there to separate the seat from the trunk, but it was no challenge for the three young men combined.

"It *is* him," Reggie confirmed once a better view became available. And he tugged at his uncle, hoping to get a response. They didn't even have him tied well, just somebody's leather belt binding his wrists.

Again Reggie tugged at Push, but there was no response.

"Help me get him out of here. Hurry," ordered Reggie. And that's what they did, moving, pulling and manipulating his body until it was free from the trunk of the car.

Serving as three human crutches, Reggie, Ronnie and Logic moved Push across the lot, clearing the sidewalk and then stuffing themselves into the Porsche.

"What about the other body?" asked Ronnie. Logic pointed out the two men at the rear of the church and Reggie gunned the accelerator and the car shot off from zero to 60, perhaps faster than it had since leaving the showroom floor.

JESSE AND GREG raced back toward Harlem, hoping that there was enough time left, enough hope left. Janet was in the back of the car holding on tight.

"Man, it's almost nine-thirty. You think it's too late for Pullman to make this happen?"

"We'll have to see. I do know that this is the wildest non-sense in the history of the NYPD since . . . since, hell, since *I don't know when*. We've got cops executing phony busts, cops dealing dope, cops doing the striptease. And you know that where there's drugs, there's sex and all other kinds of crap. Nothing but trouble . . ."

Jesse didn't respond to Greg and he didn't fill him in on all the rest.

"A bunch of bad cops we got in New York, Jesse, and the Blue Wall's gonna maintain their secrecy unless something's done. If something isn't done, we'll get to a point where the regular folks won't be able to tell us from the bad guys. Then what?"

"I agree," said Jesse, trying to cross sides from being the problem to being the solution.

"I gotta tell you, Jesse, your wife is pretty important right now. Let's see if we can get her out of there. But there's a sour taste in my mouth about these cops who pulled the raid off at the Savoy. Dirty sons of bitches."

Jesse cared for Greg, especially now, with how much help he was in the quest for Tuesday's freedom.

"Excuse me, but that was a red light you ran," harped Janet.

"Don't worry, doll. We're pros at this. Just shut your eyes and imagine you're floating on a cloud."

"On a cloud. That's what the hell I'm afraid of."

"My hunch is that there's more than just the NYPD involved, Greg. Like, maybe some Feds are mixed up in this mess as well."

"So? A bad cop is a bad cop, Jesse. What do I care?" Greg got to thinking. "If there were Feds involved, wouldn't this be a federal case? Wouldn't Tuesday be down at MCC and not in that pigpen lockup she's at?"

"Maybe so, but don't you see? If this group is *that* organized, it could be dangerous for any of us to take this personal. And that means you, Greg." Jesse, the psychic. So much talk about bad cops had Jesse thinking about Uncle Sam and L.T.K. "Thanks for all your help, Greg. It's good to have a man I can trust by my side."

"Don't sweat it. Let's just get Tuesday free."

DORM 33 WAS much worse than a slum. Even wild or stray animals received better treatment in zoos and shelters.

Bolted to a hard concrete floor were a dozen steel-framed

bunk beds, all of them busy with a flapjack-thin mattress, a sheet and toiletries.

The women here had no choice but to make do with what was issued them and to scramble for extras in a twenty-four-hour quest for available resources.

If a woman received bail, there might be an additional pair of panties, socks or a nightgown left on her bunk. If there was a fight and the guards happened to find out, then there might be twice as many resources to cop since two women would be sent to deep-lock for breaking the rules.

In the meantime, this environment was where the strong survived and the weak did not. Anybody in between merely existed, much like squatters do in homeless shantytowns.

Tuesday had grown to cope with the climbing up and down from a top bunk for the month-plus that she lived here. But just days earlier her bunkie was "shipped" to a designated prison upstate where she'd serve her four-year sentence. That meant Tuesday could move down to the lower bunk. No more climbing up and down for her food trays, to use the toilet stall or to line up for the "counts" that took place every two or three hours.

But now that Big Momma had threatened Tuesday with her infamous pussy pie party, the lower bunk didn't feel like the most desirable spot to be in. Even if most threats were never carried out, there was still Big Momma's track record to consider. Plus, the threat was only six hours old. So, Tuesday didn't sleep.

As a gift, her old bunkie left a Walkman, so there was music to listen to. She flipped the stations from the wag on WBLS to Ladies Night on Hot 97 to KISSFM for some old school, but the Stylistics were putting her to sleep so she switched to Power 105.

Lights went out at 11 P.M. and a tear quietly slid down Tuesday's cheek. Jesse was probably out laughing, drinking and having a good time, unconcerned with a wife who was overweight, locked up and more trouble than not.

He's probably leaving me here to roast, thought Tuesday. And then she thought about her children. No photos to pon-

der at, only memories. No letters to read over and over. Suicide didn't seem like such a distant thought.

Tuesday looked down the way toward the rear of the
dorm where Momma slept. Usually there were cigarettes
glowing and chatter, about what this or that nigga did to this
or that woman. But it looked dead over there tonight.

Close to Tuesday's bunk, maybe ten or so feet away, was
the guard's desk. Carol was working tonight, one of the cool
guards. And Tuesday's new bunkie from up top was over
there talking with her about favorite authors. That's all Tuesday needed; a bunkie to talk her to death about Walter
Mosley, Terry McMillan or E. Lynn Harris. Oh, brother.

Feeling safe and drowsy, Tuesday drifted off to sleep, into
another chase. This time, she was running from four overweight track stars. This time, they were the ones who were
naked, and not her. This time, they were slick with sweat and
panting like overworked horses, not her. This time, she let
them catch her and one at a time she was entered forcibly.
They were so rough with the grip on her love handles, the
hair pulling and the doggie style thrusts that Tuesday cried.
She cried because of the abuse, but also because she liked it.

Eventually, the track stars laid Tuesday on her back and
pressed their nasty feet into her face, her hair and her stomach. They were so heavy, standing on her body, and she
thought she'd break, or that she was already broken. Finally,
they entered her all at once, each one in a different hole.

"Ouch," Tuesday moaned, still enjoying the penetration.
Her hair was being pulled from behind and there was a hand
cupping her mouth. And now her limbs were taut. There was
a loss of air and a pressure about Tuesday's neck that caused
her eyes to open wide. When did she stop dreaming? She
gasped desperately but couldn't get a scream or a whimper
out. They were nearly suffocating her.

A sheet was swapped around her mouth and she was
dragged across the floor. Tuesday could see that her bunkie
was no longer with Carol, the guard. *Where did Carol go?*
Her heels burned against the rough concrete. Tuesday was
pulled along the floor to the back of the dorm.

Big Momma. Oh, God.

The large woman was afforded a special bunk, longer for women her height. Tuesday felt a series of hands holding her limbs and neck down. She couldn't breathe, held captive on Big Momma's bed.

"Make a fuckin' peep and you die, bitch." It was Momma's voice. It was Momma's hand. And now the pressure eased on Tuesday's neck. Oxygen. Tuesday hadn't even noticed her nightgown was ripped open with her slightly glistening body exposed.

"Pussy pie party time, Wallace. You're about to become one of my girls."

Big Momma was all up in Tuesday's face. Her breath was awful and stank of Black Mild cigarettes. She had a towel tied around her head, not in post-shower style but in a pirate's style, ready for battle. "I'ma give you the rules so this can go smooth . . ."

Tuesday whispered, "Big Momma, I don't want no trouble. Please . . ."

Big Momma's hand fell against Tuesday's cheek. "I said not a fucking peep!"

Her girls laughed in low undertones, holding Tuesday's limbs tight enough to stop her blood flow.

"Now, like I said, you's about to be *made*. Like all my girls. See, if I didn't see quality in ya, I'da had yo' ass stabbed already. Feel me?"

And only now did Tuesday *feel her*, with some sharp plastic utensil against her throat.

"Number one, you're about to eat my pussy. That means you use your tongue and not your teeth. You get that?" Momma's voice was hushed, yet her words were determined as she breathed that ugly taste into Tuesday's face. "Number two, first timers have to eat the ass. *I said not a peep!*" Momma's hand grabbed Tuesday's cheeks, squeezing her mouth shut. There was no way to argue. No way to rebel. Tuesday was defenseless, ready to surrender, ready to stop breathing, even if by her *own* doing.

"Number three, if you do a good job, you get to live. But

if not, they'll be trying to donate your lungs and heart by to-morrow. You got me?"

Big Momma pulled up her gown and positioned herself on the bunk. Tuesday could see nothing but a bush there, not two feet from her face.

"Be a good girl," Momma said, and she bent her face to Tuesday's. She took Tuesday's head in her hands and kissed her full on the lips. "Don't take this the wrong way, but I like you. I want you down with me. Just do right by me and you can get whatever you want in this place. I can even arrange a contact visit."

Tuesday had been wondering where the guard was but it was now all too clear. Big Momma arranged something. The *what* or *how* wasn't clear but what was clear was that there was no help around. And no other prisoner would dare go up against Momma and her girls.

"Now be nice . . . Start lickin'."

Tuesday was trapped somewhere between a past life of motherhood, of a marriage and an unhappy home, and this, some beastly woman's unwashed pussy closing down over her mouth.

The plastic shank was lying against Tuesday's neck with less pressure now since she began doing what Momma ordered. The smell was somewhere between urine and insecticide. The taste was that of sour grapes and rotten flounder.

Big Momma began to get comfortable, easing her musty snatch up and down along Tuesday's mouth. "More tongue, butch. Do it," Momma panted. "Lick that pussy good."

Tuesday thought about Sharissa and how cute she'd look for her first day of school. She'd have raspberry bows in her hair, a pretty dress and matching shoes. Maybe a tube of ChapStick. Tuesday would snap photos for the family album. Something to look back on. Joy, joy, joy.

"Smile, Sharissa!"

"Cheese!"

Big Momma turned around now.

Oh, God.

Her ass was near Tuesday's nose. Unclean. Her moist,

hairy pussy was back over her mouth, rubbing back and forth. The beast was grunting.

Stacy in grade school . . . In high school . . . At the prom. Stacy on her first date. A steady boyfriend . . . Tuesday could see it all.

"In my ass, Wallace. Put your tongue in my goddamn ass," Momma ordered, now with the whole crack of her ass over Tuesday's face . . . painting her nose and mouth with such horrid revelations. Tuesday did her best to let Momma have only the surface. Her lips providing most of the pleasure. Her tongue going for the least amount of work. Tuesday could maybe get over this . . . eating another woman's pussy. Shit, her dignity (as far as she was concerned) was already stripped when her body cavities were probed. When she was strip searched, arrested, even when she was home, a battered wife.

She'd lost so much . . . given up every last ounce of her body and soul for this life. But this thing about eating this woman's dirty ass was too much to bear. *No.*

Tuesday opened wide and sucked up a mouthful of Big Momma's pussy. Then she took a meat-cutting bite out of Big Momma. The scream interrupted the deepest dreams and the loudest snoring prisoners in the dorm. Some merely rose to upright positions, wiping their eyes, while others were frightened out of their nappy weaves.

Big Momma grabbed her bleeding crotch and fell forward over Tuesday's legs.

Big Momma's girls removed their hold on Tuesday's limbs, too shaken by their leader's grief to launch any retaliation.

With a wound that wouldn't let her keep still, Momma rolled off Tuesday and onto the hard floor, hocking and choking on air.

"Aughhh! You bit me, you bitch!" Momma's voice peaked and fell as she went on with her tantrum. When she saw her own blood, she screamed even louder. "My pussy! My pussy won't stop bleeding!" And she pulled on the nearest sheet, pressing it to her bleeding folds.

While Big Momma cried for help, and while Tuesday coughed and spit and eventually vomited, there on the bed, the lights came on. Carol, the guard, was fixing her gray uniform, fastening her pants as she emerged from a shower stall. Tuesday noticed that her bunkie, the bookworm, emerged just after Carol.

Tuesday was too sick to her stomach to give any second thoughts or to draw conclusions about the guard. All she knew was that she went to sleep with nightmares only to wake up in her own living hell.

Someone was laughing nearby. Another joined in. And when word spread, the entire dorm was buzzing. Guards rushed into the dorm with nightsticks and flashlights, trying to make sense of things.

"Oh, man," said one guard. "Looks like Big Momma met her match." And a few guards laughed. Tuesday lowered her head, holding her stomach full of rocks. A roaring applause filled the dorm and some of the women came to Tuesday's aid. Within minutes, Tuesday attacked a bottle of mouthwash, a toothbrush and face soap, doing her best to erase the memories of Big Momma.

THREE CONCERNED WOMEN occupied the couch in Melrah's office as Henry Perkins, Crystal's boss, paced back and forth with the telephone to his ear. His deep authoritative voice had Crystal, Yvette and Francine glued to every word.

"Okay, then do me a favor, Gordy, stay on this until you can get me something, anything. Wait . . . instead of paging me, take this number . . ." Mr. Perkins looked over at Crystal and Yvette for a confirmation. Could he give the number printed on the phone? Yvette nodded to let him know that it was cool. "Got a pen?" Perkins asked. Then he recited the number and ended the call. "I've got connections all over the place, so hopefully we'll hear something shortly."

Francine Oliver was quietly concerned, afraid that it was a big mistake to leave Reggie to house and car sit. She didn't even care if the Porsche was lost, stolen or whatever. She only worried for Reggie's safety.

Yvette's legs were crossed, with her arms folded and resting on her knees. Her foot wouldn't stop shaking.

Crystal was near mortification by all that transpired. She didn't know whose fault this was. Why was Reggie in the Oliver woman's home with his friends? Why was he even with those friends after all they'd been through with the recent arrest? If Yvette heard shots, if Push ran to see what it was, if the boys raced away in the Porsche. If, if, if . . .

Crystal was at a loss for answers. And if she was left in the dark too much longer, she'd lose her sanity as well. *Don't lose it, Crystal. Stay calm. Everything's gonna be all right.*

"We can't just sit here!" Yvette finally blew her top, her nostrils flaring and her suspended hands rattled.

Perk responded with his rational consoling voice.

"If you ladies don't mind some words of wisdom, I suggest you put some water on. Maybe have some tea to calm your nerves."

Francine volunteered, wanting to do anything to redeem herself, anything to feel better about this mess.

"Now, from what you've told me about your brother, he's a strong man with sharp survival skills. The type of fella I'd trust my life to. The man paid his dues. He's doing something good for the community. I don't think you should jump to any sudden conclusions. He can handle himself, I'm sure. And whatever he can't handle, trust me, I'm here to help. We all are."

Perk was pushing sixty years old and he had the heart of a racehorse. The heart, along with the wise conscience, made anybody wanna listen (and listen good) to what he had to say.

"The last thing these cowards want is for Perk to step back in the game, 'cause if I get to shootin', Harlem'd end up lookin' like Hiroshima. We'll rake the whole neighborhood until we find——"

Partway into Perk's declarations, there was the sound of tires screeching outside.

Yvette was the first one to the window. "Oh, God! It's them!" And she peeled away from the window, almost taking the curtains with her.

Shortly thereafter, as many hands as could manage were

helping to get Push back indoors. Reggie, Logic and Ronnie had relieved expressions, as though they'd been through wash, rinse and spin cycles at the laundry. And soon they were explaining away while Yvette and Crystal took care of Push with a compress held to the contusion at the back of his head, and a cup of hot tea to get him to feel alert again.

"I'm okay. Really. Reggie, bring me a phone, would you."

Reggie did and the office was hushed as Push made his call.

"Evelyn, it's Push. I got a big problem. Meet me at 128th. *Immediately.*" And Push hung up. No love for answering machines.

Yvette's eyes bugged, as though she'd just swallowed some sour milk. *Did he just call that woman Evelyn? His probation officer?*

"Son, if you need anything at all, I'm in your corner, ya hear?" Perkins said.

"Hey, thanks, Mr. Perkins. I'll keep that in mind."

"Crystal, you keep me informed, okay? If you need to take tomorrow off, lemme know."

Perkins left and Push wondered what help the elderman could be for such extreme circumstances. That man had no idea what Push was up against. There wasn't a lot of time for what he needed to do. And regardless of whether Judge Pullman was alive or not, regardless of whether or not his fee was available, Push was ready to do this job *on the house*.

Within a matter of hours, what Push agreed to do had become very, *very* personal. And the lump on the back of his head was *nothing* compared to the blow he intended on returning. He didn't yet know how, but he did know that the war had begun.

The telephone rang. Evelyn was in the car and would be on 128th in less than twenty minutes.

"I'll tell you when you get here," said Push. "Yes, it's about the Judge." And Push left her in suspense.

In the meantime, while Reggie smoothed things over between his mom and Francine Oliver, Push had a word with Logic.

"Any idea how many there were at the church?"

"Maybe five who were with you, but I think you took one down. I couldn't tell how many were inside the church but did you say you left a *judge* behind?" Logic had only picked up pieces of specifics from his friend's uncle.

"Yes. That's why the information you give me is very important. Now, how many vehicles were there? Any idea?"

"A half dozen. A big red truck, a Jimmy, a BMW and a couple others. I can't remember all—"

"And this church is on ACP and 132nd?"

"Yeah. But they only use the back 'cuz the church is shut down. For years now."

Push turned to his wall map of Harlem. It wasn't that he didn't know the directions or the location, just that he was envisioning this like a general would. He was zooming in with his own radar on the target.

More tire skids outside.

"Someone else just pulled up," said Ronnie from the window. "A spankin' new Volvo."

Push sprang up, immediately feeling the pangs of a monster headache.

"Push?" Yvette had hurried behind her man, into the bedroom at the rear of his home office. She was just in time to see Push choosing from a suitcase full of firearms. "Push, don't ignore me." Yvette was closer now, fearful that her pit bull—Push—might snap at her without conscience. "Oh, my God," she gasped.

"Baby, this is not the time to get in my way. No time at all."

"Push, did you forget I'm pregnant?"

"Why are you bringing that up now? Huh? Can't you see the problems we got here?"

"Yes, and that's why I need to talk to you. I need you to hear me." Yvette, the barrier.

Push stopped everything to stare Yvette deep in the eyes, then he returned to the arsenal, sticking a .45 automatic in his waistband, another in a holster he strapped to his upper left thigh and a palm-size 9mm pistol for the holster on his lower calf. He also attached a strap to both ends of a sawed-off shotgun and wore it across his back like an archer's bow.

Now for the ammo.

"Lawd, have mercy on my soul," said Yvette. Her eyes crawled up and down Push, how he was all soldiered-up for a battle. "Push, I don't want my child to be fatherless. Do you hear me? Can you *understand* that?"

Push was insensitive at present, unmoved by the images Yvette put out there. And he was all ready to step off, except that she grabbed hold of his arm. He could feel her shaking, a reality that fought his cold, bitter heart; that merciless attitude necessary for the job ahead.

He said so much to Yvette in that instant, how he squinted and placed his hand over hers. "I got this. Now *move* and let me do what I gotta do." He sidestepped Yvette and pressed on, trying to revive that adrenaline.

CHAPTER TWENTY-TWO

IF 128TH STREET was only a little busy earlier, then it was a virtual rush hour now. Ronnie only observed the small picture. Yes, there was the new Volvo, which was Evelyn Watson's car.

But just before she pulled up, Jesse Wallace, his partner, Greg, and Janet Burrows had stepped out of a black Jeep Cherokee.

Not only that, three additional vehicles arrived behind Evelyn and the others. Just as Ms. Oliver warned, her record label's rock-soul group known as Special, four men and two women, were just getting into town, straight off of a string of live performances out West.

The group had tried calling Ms. Oliver during the past hour but couldn't get an answer. And since Joko, the group's lead singer and manager, had the address to where they'd be staying, it made sense to come straight to Harlem.

Evelyn was at once dumbfounded by all of these people that more or less flooded the sidewalk of this residential area.

With her hands on her hips, standing there in her white Juicy sweatsuit, some of her off-duty gear, Evelyn found herself counting heads and looking for, maybe, someone she knew.

There was the tall guy with the buzz cut and the goatee. He was stepping out of one of the cars with a cell phone glued to his ear. Behind him was a chick with golden brown skin, a blinding 70's blow-out Afro and some psychedelic red-framed sunglasses.

There were a few others, but according to how they were dressed, with one outfit clashing against another, it dawned on Evelyn that this was them: the music group that the OCG Records lady talked about.

Evelyn's attention was drawn to three more who emerged from 441, looking as though they'd lost something. She was somewhat nervous about these three, since 441 was where Charles was staying.

Jesus Christ!

It was Push, shooting out from his office, skipping steps and flying toward the three strangers. Evelyn had no idea what was happening until he attacked one of the three, charging at the guy until he had him pinned to the hood of the money-green Porsche.

And every one of a dozen or so people, including others who were spilling out of 440, seemed just as surprised as Evelyn was.

Crystal shouted her brother's name, then Yvette and Evelyn. But he heard no one, too busy yelling himself.

"It was you! You let 'em know where we hid him!" Push had Jesse Wallace, the father of those two little girls, within his grip, thrusting his weight and power into the man as if his hands were paddles sending unlimited volts of electricity into Jesse's body. And now Jesse's partner was tugging at Push, trying to get him off.

Push whipped around with a left hook that popped Greg hard enough to knock him back to the sidewalk where he struggled for consciousness and lost. Within seconds a melee began.

The tall singer with the buzz cut thought he was doing a good deed and went to restrain Push. At the same time, Jesse went for his gun. Young Reggie shouted, "He's pullin' a gun!"

But it was Evelyn Watson who seemed to be the only one thinking straight. She already had her Ladysmith in hand

and pointed to the sky. She fired three times and everyone stopped moving or dived for cover.

"The next shot is for the person who makes a move. Anybody!"

Evelyn could've been the cover girl for a book called *Gangsta Boo*, how she posed with both hands on her weapon, smoke snaking skyward from the barrel. "I don't know what the hell is going on around here, but I'm not gonna stand by and watch you all kill yourselves. Not while I have anything to say about it." With her pistol still in one hand, Evelyn reached down to help a woman, one of the members of Special, from the sidewalk where she ducked for cover. "Now, if you all don't mind, even if I have to play cop, let's have some order around here . . ."

Evelyn was especially looking at Push, since he appeared to be the one who jump-started this mess. Not that she intended on shooting him—hoping he'd at least stop and explain what in the world was happening.

"And who are you?" Evelyn asked the man as he backed off the Porsche and kept his hand away from the Porsche.

"Jesse Wallace. That's *Officer* Jesse Wallace."

Evelyn didn't shrug, but by her facial expression, she might as well have.

"And that's my partner, Officer Greg Schwartz. And you are interfering with police business."

Huh, that's a laugh.

And Evelyn became more interested, still with her weapon leveled and ready.

"Do you mind not pointing that at me?"

"Yes, I do mind, Officer Wallace. Cops seem to be at the root of my headaches these days, and I'm not talking speeding tickets."

"Can I at least check on my friend?"

"Fine. But I'll take this." Evelyn reached for his weapon. "Hands on the car, please," she uttered with a snide smile and executed a pat-down. "My, my. Packin' heavy, aren't we?" She motioned to Yvette and had her hold the guns.

"Ma'am, you're making a big mistake. If you check my wallet, you'll—"

"Find your badge? Or your license to kill? Which is it?" Evelyn was only speculating at the moment, but until she was clear about the who, what, where and when of things, this Jesse Wallace was the bad guy.

"Says here that you've been on the force since . . . Wow, eight years."

She stuffed the wallet back in his pocket then went to see about his partner.

"Well, Jesse Wallace, unfortunately your badge only makes you a suspect for all I know. Better come check on Greg. Hmmm, Greg Schwartz . . . That's Greg Schwartz minus one .38 special."

Jesse went to kneel beside Greg while Evelyn discussed things with Push, Yvette and Crystal.

"That one there—he's one of 'em. He let your L.T.K. cops know where we had the Judge."

"Charles? Attacked? Where is he?! Is he . . ."

While Push did his best to explain, it was Evelyn who turned toward the two cops with malice intent. Her head could've spun off of her shoulders.

"Man, what are you talkin' about? I said nothing to no one about his whereabouts. I told you where I was going."

"Then how did they find him? Why were we attacked?"

"Attacked? When?" asked Jesse.

"Attacked?" asked Evelyn.

"Aw, don't gimme that shit . . ." Push looked around at those standing by. "You know damned well we were attacked. You set it up! How else would they know where Pullman was?"

"Man, I don't know. Who is *they?*" asked Jesse. But just as he did, just as Push cast that doubtful expression, he realized what had happened while he was away. L.T.K. Jesse wondered if they finally did it. If they finally got Judge Pullman. And if they did . . . *Oh no. Tuesday.*

Now, more than ever, Jesse was enraged. Putting the

pieces together, he could see that it was an L.T.K. activity that got his wife wrongfully imprisoned, and it was L.T.K. that was helping to keep her there.

Jesse, you have to get me out of here today! Today, Jesse, today!

Tuesday's voice pounded in his head like a metal drum.

Evelyn, Push and all the others were staring at Jesse. Something so close to guilt was written all over him. Something he couldn't hide.

"Can you believe this dude?" Push said, mostly speaking to Evelyn. "Lyin' right in our faces with that stupid look. If it wasn't for your two girls, I'da slumped you by now."

Evelyn finally got around to asking about Charles. With all that was going on, all of the revelations, this was all a bit much to swallow and digest at once. She was afraid to ask and all of the energy appeared to sink her eyes and face into a depression. "Charles?"

"That's why I got you here. They came in a posse. Guns and all. Just ran right in, broke the door."

Push pointed to the door. "There was a shootout. I almost got shot. Then one of 'em clubbed me from behind." He did his best to explain, filling in with details that he'd learned just minutes earlier.

Crystal was urging her son and his friends to move inside. Better late than never. And Francine Oliver grabbed up her group, escorting them to safety as well.

If there was ever a time for explanations, it was now.

CHESTER GALANTE, OTHERWISE known as Ape, was at a crossroads.

"What now?" he asked, once he and Primo found the BMW with its backseat ripped away from its frame. The frame itself had also been broken away. "How's the guy just gonna bust out like this? Is he Superman?"

"No, man, the dude had help! Can't you see that?" barked Primo. "And you know what else? We'd better catch him too. 'Cuz I'd hate to know what Sam might do when he hears about this."

"Hey, it's not my fault the gate was left open."

"Right, man. It's not your fault. It's not my fault. It's no-body's fault, is it?"

Ape shook his head slow and doubtful.

"Sam ain't gonna take this well, is he?" Primo thought about that.

"Ah, don't worry about it. At least we got the Judge. Help me get 'im inside."

"Then what?" Ape asked as they went to the Maxima.

"Then we play it by ear."

The two carried Judge Pullman's half-conscious body in through the back of the church and set him on the couch.

The gleam in Sam's eyes was both evil and satisfied. "Go ahead and untie him. He's harmless."

They did as Sam asked and Pullman gradually came back to life.

"Welcome to the Abyss, Your Honor. Nice of you to visit."

Sam was rolling up his sleeves as though preparing for some intense labor. "I'm getting a kick out of this already. And what're you two waitin' for? Get that other lunchmeat in here. I wanna get some target practice in. Some payback for what he did to Cali."

Sam had to clap his hands to get Ape and Primo to snap out of their stupor. As they turned away, Ape said, "See that?" And once they were out of range, he went on to say, "Shit, Primo, I'm not tryin' to be the next one that man drops. You think you have an itchy trigger finger? Well, it's not even close to what that man'll do when he finds out this dude is missing."

Primo rubbed his face, searching for answers.

"Why don't we head back to 128th? It's only a few blocks away. We know the address."

"And what is on your mind? There's probably Feds all over that spot. Don't you get it? We just kidnapped a judge, man. Listen."

"Where you goin'?"

"Hangin' around here is like playin' Russian roulette with my life. I'm cuttin' my losses. This is where I bow out."

"Don't do that, Ape. You and me been through too much for you to just up and leave."

"Primo, are you even listening to what I'm sayin'? We're droppin' like flies around here. Have you forgotten already? El and Hitler. Mule. And what about Duck? Chico just creamed his ass when that Shoprite deal went bad. Pow! And now it's Cali in there turning all of the pool balls red. We're either dyin' off or . . . Damn, Primo! Don't you get it? You yourself watched that man trying to execute Mims."

"Okay, so he got a little out of hand. What about the money we're makin'? Sometimes you gotta take the good with the bad. Roll with the punches."

"Oh, you are out of your mind. There's no question about that. Sam's got you. But he doesn't have me. Not anymore."

Ape had his hand close to his gun, ready for any sudden move. He realized now that he was no better than a traitor and traitors were but enemies, even in *his* book.

"Don't try and stop me, Primo. Don't."

Ape made it to the BMW and found his keys.

"Fuck Uncle Sam, fuck L.T.K., fuck the money. I saved enough to make certain moves. I can get a rent-a-cop job. A top salary. Maybe hold down a night watchman post somewhere. Whatever. But I'm outta here," Ape announced from the driver's seat.

"Jumpin' ship just like that?"

"No, resigning, Primo. Just like that. And you'd be smart to do the same."

The Beamer buzzed off with its taillights fading into the night. In a way, his exit symbolized yet another dent in Uncle Sam's organization.

"Suit yourself," mumbled Primo and he turned to go back inside.

"So where is he?" asked Sam, somewhat anxiously. "Ape bringing him in?"

"Not quite, Sam." Primo had a sudden craving for more painkillers and he looked down to see that the bandage was soaked again. Sam noticed the blood as well.

"You'd better listen to Doc's orders and lay off of that leg some."

"I guess," said Primo. And he also explained some things. The BMW, the back gate, the Porsche and Ape's resignation.

"Resigned? What's going on around here? Is there something in the air that's turning our people into pussies?" Sam threw the pool cue like a spear and it broke the face of a pinball machine, sounding off zings and bells.

Sam took a pause to regain his composure, something a pull on his cigar helped to accomplish. "In other words, our headquarters is threatened and we should be expecting visitors."

"If I had to take a guess, if that guy was a marshal or something, then you could be right. An army could be on the way."

Uncle Sam panned around to scrutinize his subordinates. Then he took out a fresh cigar and executed all of those ceremonious procedures before wedging it between his teeth. While he did the honors of lighting the cigar, he brandished a confident grin. It was as if an idea had been born.

"Ya know, there's no point in avoiding the inevitable. If it's gonna be a fight, then it's gonna be everybody's fight. I'm ready to get my hands dirty; ready to give 'em the fight of their lives. What I need to know is . . ."

Sam looked everyone in the eyes. There were only seven members present but it was enough for Sam to get a feel of things to come.

"Who's with me and who isn't? Because in the next hour or so we could be in for life's next big challenge. Now, who's in?"

"Shit, Sam. I came this far and I lived. What the fuck. If Doc can wrap me up and dope me up like he did Primo . . ."

"Easy, Skin. You need a *head* doctor if you think I'm gonna put you on the front line in your condition. But shit, if that ain't some true soldier there! Now who else? Speak up."

"Hey, I'm with ya, Sam. You never turned your back on me. Plus, any law enforcement team I've been with, whether it's NYPD, ATF or military, is always the same. One for all and all for one. L.T.K. is the baddest, meanest, most together group I've been with in my life. Even if we're crossing back and forth, that whole good and evil bit . . ."

"Pistol! Sheeze! It's gonna be Christmas soon. Are you in or out?"

"In, Sam. I'm in to stay."

"That goes for me, too, Sam," said Turk.

Vegas said, "In."

Sam turned to Primo.

"Now you know better than to ask me, Sam. I've put my life on the line for L.T.K. L.T.K. till I die, baby!"

The group all looked toward German, who was quiet, leaning against the pool table.

"I'm afraid you'll have to count me out of this one, gents. Heck, I still can't believe I'm standing here with a dead cop on the floor. This isn't right, Sam. It's just not right."

"Gee, that's too bad, German. We could really use a man like you."

"Are you kidding? I'm not built for all of this rah-rah crap. Don't get me wrong; I want to see you succeed. But not like this. And besides, I haven't been to the firing range in a month of Sundays."

"Oh well, what about you, Slide? I know you're new to L.T.K."

"Don't say another word. I'm the hungry rookie right now. Goin' for heads and as many notches as I can get on my belt."

"A soldier, huh?"

"You got it."

"Okay, soldier. Could you do me a favor?" Sam circled around behind German, slowly, so that nothing seemed peculiar.

"Anything, Sam. You name it."

"Could you escort Mr. German out of the building?" And now Sam had his 9mm Beretta out, pointed at the back of German's head. The sneak move stunned everyone watching.

The blast was final; to the point. And now there was more blood. More guts on the pool table. Sulfur fogged the air.

"But," Sam went on to say, "you might need a body bag," in a very matter-of-fact tone.

More than ever before, Uncle Sam was on a demolition course. And it wasn't so much about salvaging the L.T.K. headquarters; he could set that up most anywhere, in or out of Harlem.

No, what Sam needed was respect. All the work he did, organizing, planning and executing L.T.K. activities: diamonds, armed robberies and other big-ticket heists. They even hit the bank where the mob laundered their money.

All of those major scores. And what did the newspapers report?

A rise in the city's crime rate . . .

The announcement was a slap in the face. As if this wasn't the ultimate crime spree. As if this wasn't a mastermind plan. The work of a genius! The person who could devise such an intricate scheme to strip the bad guys of their wealth was worth at least a crown.

Anything less, according to Sam, was damned disrespectful.

"SO, I CONTACTED your girlfriend, Charlie. Yup. I figured a little publicity would do the trick. We could've left people mystified, you see. Picture the headlines: The Phantom Avengers! I had it all played out in my head. A little media attention could've gotten our city's crime dogs all riled up. That's when the fun would really begin."

"I always knew there were a few cards missing in your deck, Sam. I just never spoke on it."

Pullman was himself again, but for the pain and swelling around his neck and collarbone where someone struck him from behind. He grunted now and then, especially when the throbbing peaked or when he moved his shoulder even a little.

Still, Sam's overtures were hard to ignore with the man pacing back and forth there in front of Pullman as though this was the time for testimonials. It was also evident that, set aside the arm in a sling, Sam was in good shape for his age. It was his brain that was questionable.

"So I'm senile now, Charlie? Is that it? I've lost my mind? Well, if that's the case, since we're about the same age these days, what have you lost, Charlie? Don't tell me you've got all your marbles."

"I don't kill people to get my way, Sam. And what's more is, I'm not gonna burn in hell for it either."

"Stop it, Charlie. Just stop it. Who the fuck made you the judge? Oops, excuse me. It was me!" Sam blew on his knuckles and rubbed them on his chest.

"Don't toot your horn so fast, you maniac. It was hard work and diligence that made me a judge, not your malicious deeds."

Sam made a loud buzzing sound. "Wrong!"

He gestured so that he and Charles would be alone. Turk expressed concern, tilting his head and grunting. Shaking his head, Sam said, "I've got this, Turk. The day this man can kick my ass is the day the sky turns green."

"Real sure of yourself, aren't you, Sam?"

"Call it being sure. Confident. Use whatever term you want. But I suggest you watch what you say in my house, Charlie. You're not a judge 'round these parts; you're just a man. A captive man at that." Sam strolled over to a table with various liquors. "A drink?"

"Yeah, later. After they bury your ass."

"I don't blame you for being salty with me, Charlie. I don't. After all, I've chased you out of house and home. The U.S. marshals couldn't even protect you, God bless 'em."

"You're a cold-blooded killer, Sam. You were never on the right side of life. You don't deserve the air you breathe."

Sam appeared to give that some consideration, however cynical an expression. "Hmmm, you know, come to think of it, has there been a great leader in all of history who prevailed without flexing a little muscle? Without a few dead bodies to help maintain a little influence?"

"You killed Michelle," said Charles with tight lips and clenched teeth.

"Kill . . . Such an overused word. Like the word 'love,' don't ya think? Plus, kill is such an understatement in Michelle's case, since we made Swiss cheese out of that whore. Hung her up like the waif she was and—"

"Bastard!" Charlie attempted to get up from his seat but the pain held him back like a steel gate.

"No need to get excited, Charlie. What's past is past. Besides, you didn't—*wait a minute!* Charlie, you were stickin' your pickle in her jar, weren't you! Well, I'll be damned. I used the girlfriend term loosely but she really was your . . . *Wow!* Imagine the newspapers running with that. *Senior judge courts Times reporter almost 40 years his junior!* Get it, Charlie? Courts? Junior?" Sam laughed. Pullman looked up at Sam through half-opened lids, hard enough to punch holes in him.

"Tell me, Your Honor, how's it feel to be a dirty old man? She made you feel young, didn't she? Like you put Viagra on the map, right? Man, if we could only issue a young piece of ass to every man over fifty."

"You son of a . . ." Charles made a greater effort to get at Sam, this time rising up from the couch.

But Sam was quick. He had a pool cue in his grasp and swung it around as if it were a sword. The tip of the cue was but an inch or so from Pullman's eye.

"Use your head, esquire. Do you honestly believe you can beat me to the punch? I'm a Thoroughbred compared to you. Been takin' care of these two hundred and twenty pounds for decades. Now, sit down before I break you like cheap crystal."

The blue-tipped cue stick poked Charles in the face and could've easily taken his eye out by now. And yet Charles still deliberated on his possibilities of going up against Sam.

"This is my courthouse, Charlie. I call the shots here; not you. Now, sit down."

Sam used the tip to prod Charles, a reminder of the pain awaiting him.

"Thank you. Now I'm sorry about your Lolita, Charlie. I'm sure she was taking good care of you. Problem is your girlfriend got a little too adventurous. She had to go and be extra with sneaking some hidden video device in here. *All I agreed to was a simple interview.*"

Charles felt Sam's appeal, as though he were attempting to justify Michelle's murder.

"She should've been glad. I contacted a number of reporters at the *News*, the *Post* . . . But no, I gave her a shot. An exclusive, man. And now look at things. Extremely messy."

"Messy enough to get you the death penalty."

"See, that's where you're wrong. It's Michelle that received the death penalty. It's that U.S. attorney, Dudley, the cop's brother, and, tsk, tsk, tsk, those poor marshals. It's you, Charlie, who's receiving the death penalty."

Sam tossed the pool stick and in the same smooth motion slid his Beretta out of his waistband.

"You can kill me if you want, Sam, but it's not me who's on the tape, it's you. I'll be dead but you'll be hiding for the rest of your life. And besides that, it would only be a matter of time before all of your personal business is public."

Charlie did his best to play it cool; even if underneath it all he was sweating like a desert camel. But he carried on, using the details of Sam's life as his only weapon. "Your history will be all over the six o'clock news, buddy, just like I suspect you want. Only they won't call you Robin Hood or an avenger. No. They'll talk greasy about you, Sam. They'll call you a psychopath."

Sam aimed the pistol at Pullman's forehead.

"They'll talk about your parents . . ."

Charles could see Sam tickling the trigger with his forefinger. He could feel his life coming within a hair of its mortal ending. But still he went on punching with words.

". . . how your father shot your mother before he killed himself . . ."

There was a click, a sound that made Charles close his eyes. A split second wherein his life flashed before him and where he could imagine death even in its absence. Then something made Charles open his eyes. He was still alive. Winded, but alive. He realized that Sam had his eyes closed as well, maybe from all the memories that were bottled up; memories that he couldn't escape, no matter how distant.

When Sam opened his eyes, they were bloodshot with rage or with pain. Charles couldn't tell but surely something was keeping him alive. He wondered if it was the videotape.

"Killing you, old friend, will be my pleasure," Sam said.

PISTOL AND THE others went downstairs to a choir room that served as a virtual armory. Weapons of every sort were stockpiled here since the inception of L.T.K. There were all types of rifles, shotguns, assault weapons and handguns. There were grenades. Primo expressed specific interest in the antiaircraft artillery while Turk geared up with holsters and a vest. He took a vest for Sam.

"Just what should I expect?" Slide asked. "Not that I'm scared or anything." He was wide-eyed, with his attention fixed on the cannon on Primo's shoulder. "That thing looks like it could sink a battleship."

Pistol ignored the question and swung a vest into Slide's arms.

"I doubt Sam's gonna want a vest," Pistol told Turk. "He swears against 'em."

Primo had his eye up to the scope of the missile launcher.

"I hope I get to use this thing," he said.

CHAPTER TWENTY-THREE

EVELYN WAS ABLE to inject some order amidst so much confusion.

There was a bottom line here, no matter how it happened: Judge Pullman had been kidnapped and he could be experiencing any manner of torture right now.

"I swear on my children that I didn't say anything to anyone about the Judge or his whereabouts. I was with Greg all day."

And Jesse detailed the day's activities to all present. Greg was conscious again and confirmed Jesse's information, despite the bruises. The difficult position for Evelyn was how Jesse was so utterly believable. And yet, she also had to agree with Push. *How else would anyone know where Pullman was being kept?*

But then there was the matter of this woman, Janet Burrows, who reiterated her involvement with Slide and all she knew about Tuesday's arrest. Her story struck everyone's soul; how it was now obvious that Tuesday had been wrongfully accused and how maybe they had misjudged Jesse all along.

"Now, if I need Judge Pullman to help free my wife, why in the world would I want to see him hurt?" Jesse asked. At least that made some sense, if nothing else did.

Jesse divulged things that he (somehow) knew about L.T.K. without telling everything. There was a mountain of burden on his shoulders; however, he looked at the past as just that—what's done is done.

The greater priority was Tuesday. Every hour that she was in jail was another piece of his heart being eaten away and in order to help her, he had to help the Judge. He had to help Push and Evelyn. He had no choice in the matter. Jesse's only hope was that Uncle Sam hadn't. *Perish the thought.*

"I say call in the troops," said Greg. "Since we already know they're at this church."

"And don't you think that might put his life at risk?" asked Evelyn, already with the answer in mind.

"Sure, but what other option is there?"

"We could go in and get him ourselves," Push suggested, his mind all wired for battle.

"Not a good idea," Jesse said.

And they looked toward him, the somehow know-it-all, for further explanation.

Jesse merely meant, "Look at how prepared these guys are. The manpower they've shown. We're gonna need an army to do what you're suggesting."

"That's why I say we call for help," said Greg. "A SWAT team is gonna be much more capable of handling a hostage negotiation than we are. Just running in there with good intentions will not only get the Judge killed, but a few of us as well. On the other hand, one phone call and I'd bet my life that every Federal agent and local flatfoot will come to the rescue."

Jesse didn't say it but he knew that any threat would flip Sam's switch, turning a crazy man into a space case.

"I know we're pressed for time here," said Greg, "but do you all mind if I have a word with Jesse?"

There were gripes but the two stepped out into the hall alone.

"What are you holding back, Jesse? You said *trust me*, as if you know more than you're telling. Why not the troops? Is there something you wanna tell me?"

Jesse shrugged. "Just an educated guess from an experienced police officer."

"No, fuck that. What's the deal here, Jesse?"

Jesse looked away but he eventually looked Greg in the eye. "Call me a mind reader. Did you ever do something you regretted? Something you weren't too proud of?"

"Plenty of times. What's that gotta do with this dilemma?"

"But did you ever do something so off the wall? Something that, maybe, got out of hand?"

Greg thought about it and tried to make a connection. "Can you spare me the ninety-nine questions?"

"Greg, I haven't just been a controversial husband; I've also been a controversial cop."

"Controversial? What's that mean?"

"It means, I crossed the line, Greg. I got tired of all these other cops pretending to be Goody Two-shoes, when the truth is, everybody and their momma is on the take. Corruption is so deep-rooted in the force that you couldn't detect it if you tried. It takes the idea of *resources* to a whole 'nother level . . ."

Greg made a strange face, more or less disagreeing with Jesse.

Jesse sucked his teeth, saying, "Oh, come on, Greg. Don't act like you don't know what I'm talkin' about. From the rookie to the top brass, all of us use our positions for one benefit or another. I don't care if it's squashing a parking ticket or using your influence to get your kid on the high school football team." Jesse had his arms folded.

Greg took the mention of football personally, since Jesse was referring to him.

"Oh, you didn't think I knew about that? Don't get me wrong, Greg, I'm not pointing fingers. I'm saying that there are some situations more extreme than others. Every time I turn around, I'm seeing our co-workers with expensive cars, second homes . . . I know at least three of us who have mistresses on the side, holed up in fancy high-rise apartments.

"These activities have been swirling around me for years,

Greg. Only I got it hard. No good fortune has come along my way. And I feel like I'm missing out on life. Fuck, Greg. *We only live once.* And the life you and I do live . . . we live a high-risk life every goddamned day. Who's to say we don't go out on a call and get ambushed like Peters and Grillhard did. Or what about Cox and Prentice? Remember them? Even off-duty, those two caught it bad. Cox shot up at the Elks Lodge. Prentice trying to stop an armed robbery. Shit, man, ninety percent of the force doesn't even live here in Harlem. And they don't give a fuck about those who do; at least not like they do their own families in the apple-pie suburbs. Yet they don't have a problem shooting my neighbors in the back. They don't have a problem with arresting teenagers who they *suspect* are doing dirt. Greg, you know I'm not referring to you. You're one of the few tried and true. One of the few I'd put my life on the line for. But you and I both know about the beat-downs—before the arrests, after the arrests, down at the stationhouse . . ."

"Where you goin' with this, Jesse?"

"Where am I going? I've already gone there. Where I'm goin' is, that we're no better than the average street mob. Only we have more rules to follow. More red tape and policies; people we gotta answer to. So I was introduced to this guy they call Uncle Sam."

"Uncle Sam?"

"It's these nicknames we went with. Like masks. My name was Mims. Greg, you might as well know now: I was part of L.T.K. Licensed to Kill. The same group that does the robberies we talked about—the three Shoprite markets said to belong to the Generossi crime family; the hit on the Triads, down at King Chow."

"L.T.K. did that? Whoa. And all the time the talk was about some rival faction."

"Nope, it was us. And this thing with the Judge. Uncle Sam wants him something bad. He's got a videotape of some kind. A reporter interviewed Sam—some stupid publicity stunt he planned. Only it backfired and things haven't

been the same since. I mean, it was all square business before the girl. We were comin' down on crime lords, drug
dealers and even legit businesses owned by crooks. About
the only thing we *didn't* do was killing. We were like a bunch
of bandits with a conscience.

"But then the bodies started dropping. The reporter was
just one of them."

Greg put a hand on Jesse's shoulder. "Jesse, you killed for
this guy?"

"No, no, I didn't."

Greg studied Jesse for a time. "How long have you been
with these guys?"

"A few months. I was fuckin' up at home. Me and Tuesday had it out and I just said, *fuck it*. And I went with Sam."

"A big group?"

"Phew . . . at least three dozen. They've been scoring for
two years. Growin' stronger and stronger. Everybody from
Secret Service agents to the FBI to the NYPD is involved.
There's Customs agents that allow drug shipments in at the
airport. There's girls who work in different records departments, fixing anything you can imagine, from moving viola-
tions to bench warrants. Even coroner's records. It's big,
Greg. Big and getting too out of hand."

Greg couldn't look Jesse in the face at this point. He
seemed to be at a sudden loss for words.

"Greg, I left L.T.K. I was hoping to get my life back in
order. That'll never happen if you . . . turn me in."

"Turn you in? Man, I need you to tell me more about this
church. We need to get—"

"Are you two quite through?"

It was Evelyn who stuck her head out into the hallway, her
voice startling them. "You two are spending precious time
while my friend is probably being tortured somewhere."

"Ms. Watson, is it?"

"Yes."

"I have an idea and you can help me if you're game."

"Tell me about it."

Now it was Greg with his hand on Evelyn's shoulder. "Can I give you my theory?"

She was waiting.

"Jesse's not the enemy. That's the first thing. And your friend, the Judge, is gonna be fine for the time being. Here's why. I understand that the man responsible for grabbing the Judge is looking for a videotape."

"You're sure about that?"

"Let's say I'm ninety-nine percent sure. And I don't think this guy will have much to bargain with if he kills his only hostage."

"So what if you're right? What do we do, set up a switch? The videotape for the Judge?"

"*You* have the tape?" asked Greg, entirely surprised.

"And I've watched it fifty times."

"So what's so special about it? Why does this Sam character want it so bad?" asked Greg.

"Oh, I thought you were the one with the answers," said Evelyn with a pinch of sarcasm. Then she said, "It exposes him. A few people could be identified as being part of this mob. L.T.K. they call it."

"I've heard," said Greg. "Do you happen to know anybody on the tape?"

Evelyn had a crazy hunch here, and she was so close to acting on it. *Jesse. I've seen Jesse on the tape.*

"Not that I know of," she said. "Not so far anyhow." And Evelyn saved the expression she wanted to cast at Jesse. For now, she wanted to get on with this idea of Greg's.

"I can tell you this, the letters stand for Licensed to Kill. The group is made up of cops. But I suspect you both know something about that."

Both men hung on to Evelyn's words.

"Judge Pullman knew all about them. Plus, he had the only other tape, which is why they came after him. He warned me about this some time ago. And the tape is under lock and key."

Greg said, "And the marshals couldn't protect him?"

"Yeah, go figger," said Evelyn. "That's why I can't trust a cop right now. And I hate to say it, but I barely trust you two. If it wasn't for this man's wife being locked up . . ."

Again, Greg assured Evelyn. "Well, I suppose we'll just have to wait and see, won't we? Life's full of risks, right?"

Evelyn wanted to get more into this "idea" they had but she had to say one more thing. "If I find out that you two are some-how a part of this L.T.K., that you're trying to protect this Sam Foster, believe you me, you're gonna have one bitter woman on your hands. A woman with menopause and a Magnum."

"**WHAT HAPPENED TO** your friends, Charlie? Did you lose your influence all of a sudden? Did you piss somebody off besides me?" Sam didn't expect Charles to come up with an educated answer, so it was okay to have him sitting here, his prisoner, with that sorry look on his face. Sam pulled the palm-size two-way pager system from his belt—one of those elite communications systems compliments of Joe Schmo, the taxpayer.

"Do we have anything at all? I mean, this is getting bor-ing," announced Sam into the device. Primo was the first to respond, not before brief static interference.

"All clear from up here," said Primo. "And if it's any help to you, I'm as much afraid of heights as you are bored." It was a joke.

"Try hopping on one leg. I hear that's a fix-all."

Primo laughed. "I'm already hopping on one leg. I have no choice."

Sam got his first big laugh of the day.

"Skin here. Nothing out back."

"How's Big Red?" asked Sam, with nothing better to do but make small talk.

"Shinin' like a candy apple," replied Skin.

"Good God, what about you, Pistol?"

"Yo, I have Slide with me, walking the perimeter. Noth-ing yet, sir." The voice squawked over the open mike.

"Walk it three more times. I know somethin's cookin'. I can feel it. Over."

Uncle Sam took a moment to reflect and Reesy returned with a tray and two cranberry juices.

"For you, Uncle." And Reesy approached the Judge with his glass but not before she made a nasty snorting noise, something like a hog, and spit a glob of phlegm into the cranberry juice.

"And for you, Your Honor."

Pullman looked at the glass, then at the Amazon woman again. "Your hospitality is despicable," said Pullman.

"Ohhh, so sorry," said Reesy. And she laughed as she turned to place the glass on a side table. "Just in case you get thirsty," she added, and laughed some more.

Sam witnessed this, wagged his head and gave that quick head jerking gesture for Reesy to get lost.

"You should excuse my niece, Charles. She was born with hate in her blood." Sam went to give Pullman his own glass of cranberry juice. "If she likes you, she loves you. If she doesn't, God bless. Come on. Take it. Compliments of the host."

"Why are you prolonging this, Sam? Why don't you just kill me and get it over with. Put me out of my misery."

Sam put down the juice and backed up to the blood-stained pool table. He sucked at his Cuban cigar, wishing he could read Pullman's mind. "Too easy. Much too easy. If you knew what we went through to get you here, you'd ask yourself the same questions I'm asking. Like, who was the one who tried to stop us this go 'round. This one who some-how escaped."

Pullman laughed and said, "If I told you, you wouldn't believe me."

Sam flashed a smile, as if he got the joke, but he switched to a frown just as quickly, to show that he didn't. "Humor me," he said. "I'm in the mood for a good joke."

"He's a local thug who was hired."

"Hired?" He chuckled. "Pray tell. What would *you* hire a local thug for? To sweep your front porch?"

"No, funny man, we hired him to kill you. Now, stick that in your cigar and smoke it."

Uncle Sam laughed hard, as if we were being tickled over and over. Between the tickles, he said, "A, a thug . . . You hired . . . a thug. For a hit man . . ." The roaring laughter filled the room until Sam choked. And now he did need to drink to refresh himself. In one sweeping breath, he said, "Sorry to be an Indian giver" before throwing down some juice.

"I hope you're enjoying yourself," said Pullman, "because when he does get ahold of you, I feel sorry for you."

Sam wasn't laughing anymore. "Sorry for me? Charlie, the day a thug can finish me off is the day they'll be squeezing pickle juice from apples."

The Judge had an unamused look about him.

"Come to think of it, that son of a bitch was the one to come crash our party. He killed one of our men, Charlie. So maybe I should take him seriously." Sam stepped up close to Pullman and planted his boot heel on the couch between his legs. "But then, Cali and me are two different beasts."

"I suppose. Maybe I misjudged you. Maybe you're bulletproof." Pullman flashed a cynical smile.

The statement moved Sam to action. With his foot, he pushed Pullman back against the couch and fixed a one-handed grip to his head, palming it as he might a basketball, with his fingertips hooked right there at his eyebrows. With Pullman's eyelids forced wide open, Sam leaned in with the cigar so that the glowing end was within an inch of an eyeball. "How funny is it now," Sam growled, still with the cigar wedged between his teeth. "Huh? Huh?" Sam pushed himself away.

The Judge lost sight of Sam as he circled the couch. But he could feel him watching from behind. "You're not human, Sam. And your pseudo-ethical front together with all the rationale in the world will never fix what pain you've caused. Pain you've caused me as well."

From behind Pullman, Sam said, "Hmph. If I didn't need you alive, I'd drop you right here and now." Sam had the nose of his Beretta pressed against Pullman's head, right there by his ear, and he was close enough to have his prisoner feel the heat from his nostrils. Before Pullman could anticipate it, Sam executed a swift motion, gun in hand, delivering certain dizziness and pain and inevitable darkness with a blow to the head.

"Bad host," said Sam as he stood over Pullman's unconscious body.

CHAPTER TWENTY-FOUR

Kennedy International Airport—mid-morning

IT TURNED OUT that this was but another routine drill for Port Authority officers, U.S. Customs agents, as well as just about every other employee throughout the terminal.

Another bomb scare. Another double shift.

Ever since the various terrorist plots, the suicide bombings and anthrax scares, ever since that tragic day in September 2001, these evacuation procedures have been the bane of major airports throughout the nation and abroad.

There were full alerts that shut down the entire airport, and there were partial closings, when a certain wing was sealed off until the "all clear" was given and the threat was inevitably considered a hoax or a false alarm.

On this particular morning, as in the past, there were dozens of emergency vehicles securing the perimeter of Kennedy International Airport while at the same time the National Guard was alerted, the area hospital on standby, the departure terminal evacuated and numerous flights rerouted. What frequently triggered this paranoia could've been misinformation, someone's idea of a joke or even the real thing. But this morning, as usual, it was *not* the real thing.

Despite what it may have looked like, or what some hyper, anal-retentive shot-caller may have thought, the bottom line was, as usual, chaos. And the atmosphere during these times always included the sirens, the barking dogs, plenty of whistles and the echo of announcements over the public address system.

There, in the meat of the mess, was Sean "D.C." Wilkerson and Jose "Sanchez" Martinez, both of them on their respective jobs as police officers.

Sanchez was a senior Customs agent in charge at Kennedy. However, the position served as a perfect front to see that major drug shipments made it through, right into the hands of key L.T.K. members.

He was standing off from the baggage area with a two-way in hand when he spotted his comrade in crime, D.C. He waved him over and they shook hands.

"What brings you here? I thought you had a raid happening."

"Are you kidding? They called off the raid. They pulled a group off of desk duty and there's a shitload of meter maids, all of us out here for this exercise since last night."

"Right. That new zero tolerance policy: all passengers are asked to follow the guidance of officials. We are sorry for the inconvenience . . ."

"This gets messier and messier every go-round."

"Dig it," said D.C., his eyes canvassing a cattle call of passengers as they were ushered to safety. "Another false alarm, I'm sure."

"Things are slowing up now. This shouldn't last more than another hour or so," said Sanchez. "Then, I don't know about you, but I'm ready for some R and R."

"Then you'd better not answer your pager, 'cuz the man has been trying to get a hold of us. He didn't explain, he just said it was important."

"Unless it's a bonus, how important can it be?" said Sanchez, and the two agreed by giving each other the soul brother pound.

"Hey, you didn't speak a minute too soon. They're letting the gates open," said D.C., who was out of uniform except for the badge hanging around his neck.

"Mmmm, this is the part where we stand here and look as

official as possible. Come on, fold your arms and fix your face. You know the drill," said Sanchez, half joking and half serious in full uniform, weapon on his hip.

In the meantime, passengers scurried across the atrium floor, destined for airline counters and luggage handlers, all of the activity stretching across the length of the terminal.

"Man, I'd hate to be one of those baggage guys right about now," said D.C.

"Don't I know it."

And the two trained their eyes, almost naturally, looking for red flags that might indicate illicit activity.

"Look at this one; the chesty woman."

"Yellow sundress and black purse?"

"Exactly," said Sanchez.

"Cute but I wouldn't give her more than a seven."

"No, no. I don't mean looks. Don't you notice anything?"

"Lips . . . Tits . . ." D.C. was headed south with his guessing.

"Come on, D.C., the woman's traveling without luggage. And her shifty eyes; like she's afraid."

D.C. considered that and said, "Maybe a skycap has it."

"I doubt it. I can usually spot a mule from a mile away."

"Get out."

"Twenty bucks says I'm right."

"You're on," said D.C., and less than a minute later, they approached the woman. She was waiting in line to pass through the metal detector; the inactive side.

"Pardon me, miss."

"Yes?"

"We were wondering if you might need help with your luggage."

"I, well, I don't have any. I'm traveling light."

"Is that so?" said Sanchez, his eyes blinking once before he looked at D.C.

Just then a skycap spotted the woman and signaled her with a wave.

"Aren't you gonna acknowledge him?"

"Who?" the suspect asked, looking far and wide.

"The skycap over by the luggage rack."

The woman raised her hand, pretending to wave, but both Sanchez and D.C. could see she was actually motioning for him to stop.

"I believe he's trying to get your attention."

"Oh, no, that's just an old friend I met here once . . . in the terminal. Small world."

"Mmm. It sure is. Would you excuse us for a second, miss?"

"You see that?"

"Do I?! The woman is a fish out of water," said D.C.

"And my money says that yellow suitcase on the skycap's cart belongs to her."

"That's a no-brainer," said D.C. "So she was lying. What now? It's your world."

"Smells too funny to let it go," said Sanchez. "Follow my lead."

The cops reapproached the woman.

"Ma'am, there's no sense in you waiting on this long line. Why don't you allow us to escort you through a shortcut. We'll help you avoid some of this traffic."

"I, well, okay. That's . . . nice of you.," she said, and she went along, escorted toward the door where a sign read NO ADMITTANCE.

Without notice, D.C. broke away to see the skycap on his own.

EVELYN WAS UNEASY about Greg's plan to infiltrate the L.T.K., especially since it involved her possession of drugs, or what might've appeared to be drugs.

"But if you think about it," said Greg, "you'll be in the right frame of mind to carry this out. You've got to act nervous. That's the only way to get his attention."

"I don't know," said Evelyn. "What if some *other* hard-on stops me instead?"

"Easy. You don't put on the scared suspect act until you're sure this guy is watching."

"Plus," said Jesse, "we'll be there to see that it goes down the way we planned. If anything goes wrong . . ."

"I know, I know. You'll step in. You just have no idea how secure that makes me feel."

"Ms. Watson, we're sure of this. Sure enough to line up a trustworthy district attorney so that it's controlled; so that it doesn't get out of hand. We're simply setting you up for the phony arrest. At least we *think* they're gonna keep it phony," said Greg.

Jesse added, "We know this guy is one of them, Ms. Watson."

Evelyn was too consumed with other concerns to ask how they knew.

"And the instant they find out you're an officer, they're gonna wanna know who you're workin' with. They're gonna want you to join up with them."

Is that how it happened with you? Evelyn wanted to ask, but kept her mouth shut.

"They'll cut you in," said Greg.

"We hope," she said.

"You're a bad cop, or at least you'll *appear* to be a bad cop in their eyes. They'll go out of their way to protect you. They need people like you—a risk taker. Someone who's not afraid to act above the law."

"Can you guarantee these things you're saying?"

"I can do better than that. I can have you speak with the DA yourself. This way, everything will be out in the open. No misunderstandings."

Evelyn pursed her lips and weighed the pros and cons. But in the end, she could only think of her friend Charles. And those thoughts carried her through. They gave her that extra push.

"WE'RE GONNA NEED to see some identification, ma'am," said the Customs officer.

Evelyn could have smiled at how well this had gone; exactly according to plan. The willies in her belly were going away, too. So far, so good.

"Sure, I—what is this about?"

"Maybe nothing . . . Miss Watson, is it?"

"Yes, that's right."

"Oh. Okay, and this other ID? Is this *legit*? You're a United States probation officer?"

Evelyn examined the name tag: J. Martinez. It didn't ring a bell at first, but then she considered the J. *Okay, it must stand for Jose.*

And Jose was the name that Jesse mentioned. One of those he suspected to be with L.T.K.

"Probation, parole, it's all the same. I watch the criminals after you all lock them up. After they've done their time."

"I see," he said, still examining the identification.

The second man, the one in plain clothes, came in the room just then. He said something to J. Martinez in secret. Some headshaking occurred before they looked at Evelyn and then again at the identification. Martinez seemed confused.

He said, "Can you explain to me why . . ." His words were cut short by a call on the two-way.

"Martinez, this is Stewart, over."

Martinez cut a look at the second officer. "Get the skycap." Then, into the two-way, he said, "Stewart, what's your twenty?"

"Ticket center. Second floor."

"Give me that extension."

"Ahh . . . Three, four, seven."

"Stand by," said Martinez. "Excuse me, ma'am; I need to make this call. But in the meantime, I want you to work on an answer for me. I want to know why you lied to us when we asked about your luggage."

"I . . . Well . . ."

"No need to rush. Just think before you speak because what you say will have serious consequences if it's not the right thing."

"The right thing? Consequences?"

Evelyn's inquiry went unanswered as the officer stepped away to pick up the telephone on the far wall.

Sacrifices, Charles; I'm making serious sacrifices.

The second officer returned with the skycap and Evelyn was nothing but relieved to see the man's face. Greg Schwartz, the skycap.

"You said that this man is an old friend of yours?" asked the second officer while Martinez was still on the phone.

Evelyn had been doing as best she could to ear-hustle. All she heard was Martinez downplaying this incident. Apparently, the two-way call from Stewart had been an offer of support; support that Martinez explained was unnecessary.

"Well, yeeah, how's it goin', ahh . . ." Evelyn pretended to read the skycap's name tag. "Beals."

"Oh, so she knows you?"

"I've never met this woman before today. She hired me to carry her suitcase here; that's all."

"Is that so? And what do you have to say to that, miss?"

Evelyn feigned a sigh and rolled her eyes. And now Martinez came back. He cut to the chase.

"This her suitcase?"

"Yes, sir," answered Schwartz, the great pretender.

"Lay it here."

And the yellow suitcase was set on the desk with all three parties focused.

"Tell us again why you lied."

"I honestly didn't think it was any of your business," Evelyn said.

Schwartz's smile cast blame.

"Ma'am, I urge you to hold off on the attitude, for your own sake."

"Okay, well, I'm sorry. Now, why do you have me in this room? Am I being arrested?"

"This is our investigation room. And no, you're not under arrest. Not yet. You may leave, Beals. We'll call you if we need you."

"Yes, sir," said Schwartz, even shooting what was supposed to be a cynical wink of his eye, and he left.

"Please turn around and face the wall, ma'am."

"I want my lawyer."

"You'll have plenty of time for that. Now turn around and face the wall. I'm sure you know the procedure."

Evelyn bit down on her lips and squeezed her eyes closed as she turned around. Before she could guess what was next, her arm was pulled up to the small of her back and her body was pressed up to the wall. Handcuffs were clipped to her wrists.

"Ouch! You're hurting me!" Evelyn was loud, hoping Schwartz would hear. She never anticipated this. Not *handcuffs*.

"Then cooperate," said one of them. "Don't resist and you'll be fine."

"But I thought you said I wasn't under arrest." Evelyn did her best to sound desperate. However, she couldn't help the confidence that carried her. She couldn't help knowing that a district attorney and two police officers were nearby.

"You aren't. I'm detaining you. Watch her. I'm gonna check the suitcase."

"But—"

"But? But what? What is it you want to say, Miss USPO?"

Evelyn made herself fume. Through clenched teeth, she said, "I swear, if you don't take these handcuffs off!"

The second officer forced her up against the wall. She grunted.

"You're not making this easy," he warned.

With her cheek against the wall, Evelyn said, "Get me your supervisor." Only now did she wish she had worn the wire that Schwartz had suggested. At the time it sounded dangerous. However, now . . .

"I've got all the supervision you need." His hands were on her.

Oh, God. No he didn't!

Martinez had just unleashed the last strap on the suitcase. Evelyn could see him opening it as a hand slid up her thigh, raising her dress with it.

"You freak!" Evelyn said, feeling cruddy sensations.

And now his other hand was around front, groping her breasts. When she resisted, he wedged his large body, pinning her. "Just a pat search, Miss. Nothing personal. It won't take . . . Ugh!"

Evelyn raised the heel of her shoe so that it made a clean connect with the man's sac of marbles. When he buckled, Evelyn turned around. She shot a swift kick to his midsection and another to his calf. He howled. Within seconds, both men were pouncing on Evelyn, one with a bear hug, the other grabbing her unruly legs.

Eventually, they wrestled Evelyn to the floor and held her there until she agreed to calm down.

It took all of three minutes. Once they helped her to her feet with her frazzled hair and sore wrists, a chair was pulled over.

"You're a feisty one," said Martinez, almost laughing at how his partner was wincing, hunched over and holding his nuts. "And I like it."

"Fuck you."

And now Martinez did laugh. "A lot of nerve, too. Say, how much dope is in that suitcase anyway? About three keys?"

Evelyn was quiet.

"And I'm almost sure that if we x-ray you, we'll find more. But listen, relax, will you? We're all on the same side here. So chill."

Evelyn's nostrils were ventilating so much heat right now that the man's words didn't register. There was still that indignity; the impression of that man's hands were still on her skin.

The officer put his hand to Evelyn's knee.

"Don't *touch* me!"

"Miss, I apologize. Really. If we offended you here . . . Lemme take the cuffs off. I just want your confidence right now."

"I want my fuckin' lawyer," Evelyn uttered in a breathy voice. And it caused him to hold back his handcuff key.

"Maybe you don't understand how serious this is. Do you know there's enough junk in that suitcase to put you away for a long time?"

Evelyn was too upset to give a damn; busy with a series of deep breaths, countin' to five each time, letting out the heat and tension with her exhales. *What for? Carrying six pounds of baking soda? I can't believe what just happened here!* The suitcase and its contents meant nothing at this point. Only she, Greg, Jesse and about six other officials knew the truth. The threat of an arrest or prison was the furthest thing from her mind right now. Right now, the only thing she wanted, the thing that drove her, was her Ladysmith. Either the .45 caliber or the .357 would do. The idea of putting the barrel to that cop's head and shooting him between the eyes was causing her high anxiety.

"I can't imagine what you were thinking, with all that the world is going through, to try and make it past airport security with three kilos . . ."

The door swung open. *Schwartz.*

"Is everything okay in here?"

"Excuse us, cappy. We're conducting an investi—"

"Hey! Call a supervisor in here! They're trying to rape me! Please!"

"Easy, lady. These are cops. They'll do right by you. Just relax."

"Out! And close the door before I arrest you!"

"Jeez. You don't have to be so—"

"He said out!" The perverted plainclothes cop stepped forward and escorted him.

All the while, Evelyn was saying things with her eyes, trying to broadcast her outrage and distress. She was a heartbeat away from calling this whole thing off.

"Easy, buddy," said Schwartz, rebelling and unwilling to be a pushover. "You take it easy, ma'am." And just as the door was closed in his face, the cops looked at one another with their own sense of distress.

Seeing Schwartz settled Evelyn's nerves some, although she still felt nasty and craved a shower and an hour-long bath. *The cuffs. I thought you were gonna remove the handcuffs.*

"Is this the first time you've tried this?"

"Tried what?"

"Miss, you're not making this easy. I'm trying to cut you a break here. If you'd just work with me. Just lighten up, would ya?"

Evelyn forced her eyes to water, and quietly rejoiced as the cuffs were removed. She tried to rub away the sore red rings around her wrists.

"What're you doing, Sanch—Martinez?"

Evelyn caught the slipup. Sanchez.

The uniformed cop shot a scolding expression toward him. Then he excused himself to pull him aside. Evelyn could still hear them.

"Cool it. Do you know what the street value is? Over a quarter of a million. Just let me handle this."

Even in pieces, Evelyn could hear the two compromise. *It's working.* Closing her eyes, and pretending to be thankful, Evelyn began to see right through these creeps. They were trying the good cop, bad cop routine on her, despite them both being bad. Their charade was exposed, however.

"Don't make any deals with that . . . one call will get her twenty to life."

"Let's see where it goes. Do you mind?"

And the two eventually turned toward Evelyn. It took a lot but she squeezed the words out of her system.

"Okay, I fucked up," she said in her best defeated voice. Her eyelids were only half open and she wore a sorry frown. "So what now, you said you're trying to work with me. I don't wanna lose my job. It's the best positioning in the world for me to make my moves. I know it's a lot but I figured with my badge, I'd get away with it, like I usually do."

"Relax. I know we can do something for you and you can do something for us."

"If this is some kind of perverted sex bit, you can forget it. Go ahead and lock me up. I'll take my chances and ride the wave."

"Evelyn—mind if I call you that?"

She wagged her head. No, she didn't mind. *Just keep*

talking, asshole. Then she shrugged. Whatever they wanted, it was okay by her.

"Hey, no hard feelings, huh?" The pervert cop had his grubby hand extended for reconciliation. "Didn't mean anything by it, really."

Evelyn bit down on the inside of her cheeks before she replied. "No problem," she said. But instead of shaking his hand, she reached up . . .

I should slap the shit outta you, you idiot.

And she smoothed her hand along his cheek. "I understand. Part of the investigation, wasn't it?" She forced a promising smile.

In a bit of a spell, he replied, "Yeah, that's right."

"Hmmm, then maybe we can continue later where we left off."

He couldn't hold himself together. There was a blush. Evelyn was performing for two; the uniformed cop was watching from a distance and salivating, so she maintained the act, winking at them both.

Oh boy, are we gonna continue later.

There was a bathroom to the rear behind a closed door where Evelyn strutted and where she inevitably exhaled.

The plan was working. She was scared as shit, but the plan was actually working. Now, for the hard part.

CHAPTER TWENTY-FIVE

OATMEAL WITH RAISINS and a Cinnabun was the breakfast that tussled around down inside of Evelyn's intestines. It wasn't usually this way, so she realized that the willies were coming back. And the conversation that she was having with D.C. only made matters worse.

"It's a very complex setup, but simple from our individual point of view. Think about it." He was painting the big and small picture while Evelyn drove, sometimes peeking in the rearview mirror at the car behind them. Jose. The toll booth for the Triboro Bridge was approaching.

"A score here and there . . . all of us contributing to the same pot . . . every two weeks—bang, a nice piece of change for everyone, no matter how big or small your score is."

"Does everyone deal in drugs? Is that the only—"

"Oh, no way. Especially not our women."

"Why is that, D.C.?"

"Well . . . y'know . . . women usually have the cushy jobs, like records or secretarial positions. Basically, the way it would be in the corporate world. You don't think we'd have you doing the grunt work, do you?"

"Oh, of course not." *Asshole.*

"You're not really built for that."

Evelyn nodded, totally agreeing with him.

"But maybe you're one in a million—"

You got that right, jerk-off.

"—because I am even surprised you're a P.O."

"Umm . . . somebody's gotta do it," Evelyn said.

"But, don't you deal with the dangerous types? Like killers? Or maybe you deal with the white-collar boys."

"Oh—never the killers. Whew, can you imagine? The worst criminal I deal with"—Evelyn had to think fast—"maybe got caught in some type of fraud."

"Of course, of course."

"And then there's the child-porn people and the bank fraud."

"What—like robberies?"

"Oh, dear—no. Never anything to do with guns or violence. My supervisor sends those types to the big boys . . . you know, the macho-man P.O.s who can handle those types of situations."

"Right."

"'Cuz God forbid they give a woman such cases."

"Yeah, God forbid."

"Not that I'm afraid or anything. I mean, I'll fight for a cause . . . for some goal or objective."

"Ooo-wee, you don't have to tell *me* that," he said smiling with a hint of the painful memory.

"Sorry I went off like that. I shoulda known better. Really. It's not like that was the first time it happened—"

Evelyn was beginning to enjoy this. So much so that she was losing herself in talk . . . talking away the jitters. Better that than biting her cuticles or something worse.

"—they're much worse in Florida."

"You're shittin' me," said the pervert.

"Oh no, just last month I made a run and there were three Customs boys, and a fourth, a *woman*."

"No shit." D.C.'s voice trembled.

"Mmm, mmm, mmm . . . they worked me over something *awful*." She dragged the word *awful* as if it were pleasurable.

"H-h-how's that? Worked you over?"

"Did they ever. The handcuffs, the leg irons . . . they gagged me . . . two of the men took turns with—and the others—"

Evelyn wagged her head and leaned against the driver's side window as if this were a memory that was too much to bear.

"The others *what?*"

"They violated me, D.C., that's all I can tell you. In the end, I lost the shipment. Six kilos. But the people I did the job for were understanding since I'd already made them a bunch of money . . ." She felt herself rambling, but got a big kick out of the web she weaved so easily. It reminded her of some of the classic liars who'd come on her caseload throughout her years with the probation department. "In the end, it wasn't so bad. You see, I bounced back."

"Did they . . . did they hurt you?" D.C. asked.

Evelyn made it seem as though she had to think about an answer. "At first, I can't lie, it was a pain in the ass—literally, if you know what I'm sayin'. But when I got home, the boss I was working for called me a soldier. And it kinda made things better—"

"What happened with that? With you and your boss?"

"He cut me loose. Said it was a matter of principal, but he also said he'd keep me if it was up to him; said I was one of his biggest resources."

"Wow. Wait'll Uncle Sam meets you."

"That's the only reason you stopped me today?" asked Evelyn. "I was trying my own score. Desperate, I guess. A single woman's expenses can be unmanageable without a consistent cash flow. My mortgage is beyond what my government salary can handle. Then there's this car . . ."

"And a helluva car it is," declared D.C. "These Volvos are supposed to be the safest."

"Yeah. Safe luxury."

"But you don't have to feel desperate anymore, I'm tellin' ya. When Sam meets you he'll be so impressed. He'll put you on some juicy assignment—you'll show 'em your stuff, and you're in like Flynn."

"Ya think?"

"I know."

She expressed her sense of security with a soft smile and easy shrug; Evelyn, the lovable cat. "Well, here's the church.

I can't see *why* anyone would want to meet here . . . it's closed down . . . isn't it?"

"Wait'll you get a load of this," said D.C.

Just before Evelyn, Sanchez and D.C. stepped through the rear entrance of the old church, she turned to activate her car alarm. A quick press of the remote control on her key chain and—*blip blip*—it was done. Only, she didn't press it once. She pressed it twice. That is, she turned her car alarm on, then off again. Unbeknownst to the clowns who were escorting her and her yellow suitcase inside, the trunk of the Volvo was open.

For the entire thirty-minute ride from Kennedy Airport, Push, Jesse and Greg were curled and piled in the back, awaiting this very moment.

It was daylight out. A clear sky, with no records set either way. And yet, what was probably taken for granted by most folks was a relief for these three fatigued souls. Fresh air! Push opened the trunk just a sliver, to get a look. More relief; Evelyn had parked as he had suggested, in an area where there were few vehicles—diversions really—so the three could keep with their surprise party.

"Before we climb out, let's be clear," said Push. "I want this Sam dude for myself."

"We're not gonna *execute* the man," said Greg, "that is, unless he threatens you."

"I'm considering myself threatened. Got a problem with that?"

Jesse said, "Let's get out of this damn trunk, then we'll see who has the problem."

"Hey—shh! Look across the way, near the fence. Two of 'em, armed."

"Okay," said Jesse. "See the short one? Looks like a bookworm."

"Right," said Greg.

"Well, that's the dangerous one. Vicious with a gun."

"So am I," said Push.

"But," added Greg, "we can't afford noise so soon . . . not till we locate the Judge."

"Small as that punk is, I could choke him with one hand," said Push.

"Well, we might need that done—what about the big guy?" Greg asked Jesse.

"That's Turk. He usually wears two guns—"

"So do I," said Push, just plain hungry to get it on with these L.T.K. goons.

"—and, as I was saying, the reason he wears those sunglasses is not because of the sun. He's got one eye. He was shot in the other."

"What a shame. Anything else we should know that's *life threatening*?" asked Push with a mouth full of sarcasm.

"Just don't underestimate these guys," said Jesse.

"Nah, I won't. Let's *do this*," said Push. "I'll take the twerp."

INSIDE THE ABYSS, Vegas was listening to the sports scores on a clock radio when Sanchez and D.C. showed up with their guest.

"Say hi to Eve," said D.C., as if he'd known the woman by his side for decades. "Eve, meet Vegas, one of our main men in Washington. Eve is new . . . she's one of the Feds too."

"Oh?"

Sanchez asked, "Where's the big man?"

"Somewhere in the basement. Want me to catch him on the two-way?"

Sanchez shook his head. "Never mind. We'll surprise him instead."

The way Sanchez and D.C. were looking, this could be something special, so Vegas decided to go along.

"What's the AK for?" D.C. asked.

Vegas held up the assault weapon, inspecting it with a sense of pride. "Some new developments while you were on the job. Ape cut out, and Cali—well—he had an accident." Vegas wasn't sure if he should divulge every detail with this stranger present.

"Is everything all right?"

Vegas saved the expression he wanted to make. "I'll let Sam do the explaining. You know me . . . just visiting."

"With that in your hands?" asked Sanchez. "Looks like more than just a visit to me."

PISTOL AND TURK were parked with their backs against the perimeter fence, passing a pint bottle of Jack Daniels. This sentry position had been an all-night affair, and they were glad to contribute to Sam's objectives. But—

"He's out of his mind if he thinks we're gonna post out here all damn day too," said Turk.

"Of course not . . . that's why D.C. and Sanchez came in. They're here to relieve us."

"I wish they'd come on, then. Who's the woman who went in with them?"

"Beats me. The more the merrier," said Pistol. "Especially since we just lost some members."

"Man . . . don't remind me. Did you see the look on Cali's face? And they say dead men tell no tales."

"After this thing with the Judge is over, I'm gonna propose that we regroup, Pistol. 'Cuz there's no way we should lose four men within the space of weeks. We have to be better organized."

"I don't think better organization would have helped German—and by the way, the count is six, not four. You're forgetting Duck and German. But I don't think they count as losses. More like liabilities that we got rid of."

"Well, how about Mims and Ape and Chico? Count them, and we're missing about ten."

"Don't worry, we're adding too. Don't forget Slide . . . and this woman they brought in. Say, whaddaya think about going in and checking her out?"

"We'd be leaving the post."

"Look around you, Turk. It's broad daylight. Who's gonna try anything? This place is like a fortress."

"I'm holding post. You can go in if you want."

Pistol sucked his teeth, rolled his eyes, and gulped down the rest of the Jack Daniels. He tossed the empty bottle up and over the fence so that it broke in the alley on the other side. Then he took a cocky walk toward the rear entrance of The Abyss.

Jesse had five quarters in his hand and he was lying underneath the GMC truck. When the twerp walked past, he tossed the coins so that it might seem as though they'd been dropped. As expected, the man froze in his tracks and back-stepped to pick up the quarters. Push was circling the truck by now, and he was very ready to put a slug in the back of the small man's head, but it was unnecessary. He was bent over and vulnerable. More important the fool slung the weapon he had over his shoulder, unready for the attack in progress.

Without warning, Push grabbed the belt at the small of his victim's back, while he swept his right foot around, causing the man to fall facefirst to the pavement. There was a cry of pain, but Push wasn't trying to induce cries. He grabbed a handful of the man's hair at the back of his head and pumped his face into the concrete one more time, hard, so he'd be unconscious.

"Heard you were nice with the gun," said Push, only humoring himself.

"Pistol? You say something?" the voice called out from the distance.

"Shit." Push grunted, and with a strong hold of his victim's collar, he dragged him around the truck, out of sight.

A short time later, Greg came running. "The other one is down."

"G'damn. What happened?" asked Jesse.

"No contest," Greg said. "Easy tackle."

"Whatever. As long as they're down," said Push. "What now?"

"Like we talked about," said Jesse. "You and Greg go in. Expect a loud crash in . . . five minutes." Jesse turned his attention toward Big Red, Uncle Sam's truck.

"How about three minutes," said Push.

Greg intervened. "You think we'll be ready in time?"

Push couldn't answer. He'd already taken off for the double

doors of the church. Greg expressed a measure of disbelief and charged after him.

SLIDE KNEW IT would only be a matter of time before it went down, because Reesy had been checking him out from the moment he'd been introduced to Uncle Sam, as much as a month earlier.

He wondered what part she played in all of this, and if all she did was hang out and clean up around the church all day. *What a boring life*, Slide determined. But he also told himself that this was probably the ugliest woman he'd been accosted by. A full foot taller too.

First, there were the subtle passes she made, once winking at him, and another time brushing up against him. *Maybe she's just the friendly type*, thought Slide. But then, when he'd returned from the kidnapping of Judge Pullman, Reesy caught Slide off guard. He'd gone to the kitchen for some sandwiches. "Reesy will show you where they are," Uncle Sam had said. But once they were alone, this Amazon bitch put her weight up against him.

"I'm so sorry, but . . . I can't help myself. You're so *fine*. And I think you're so brave after a gunfight, and—" She craned her head down to his cheek with saliva.

"Look . . . Ree—" Slide could hardly say her name. Reesy breathed heavy in his presence, and appeared as though she had to use the bathroom. "—Reesy, or whatever you name is . . . I cannot mix business with pleasure," Slide lied as best he could.

Reesy, however, was persistent. She backed up some and put her hands on her stacked hips. "What? You don't like me?"

Say the right thing here, playboy. You don't want to hurt her feelings. The boss's niece. "You're fine. But that has nothing to do with it."

Reesy was on him again, her double Ds pressed against his collarbone. "Look at these . . . I know you like 'em."

"I . . . uhh . . . Reesy, we can't—"

The she-man lifted Slide off of his feet.

"Oh shit," muttered Slide.

"Now, you wouldn't be rejectin' a girl, would ya?"

Slide was suddenly a party to a sick dream. This broad with thick eyeliner, a heavy jaw and too many teeth inside of those fish lips, was all in his face. Her hands felt like a lumberjack's and the perfume she wore was overdone, tainted by underarm deodorant.

"No—I . . . of course not."

"Then fuck me."

"Oh no. I . . . no . . . no. No, I can't."

"Why? Are you homo?"

"Hell, no. Listen—put me down."

"Ask nice," she ordered with a frown. *"Please."*

"Please, Reesy, put me down."

"Only if you fuck me." She brandished that so gruesome smile again.

"Reesy. Your uncle would kill me."

"He'll kill you *anyway*," she said, and let him go.

"What are you talking about?"

"When I tell him you raped me, he'll do you like he did German."

"Reesy, no. Now why would you tell him something like that? That's *crazy!*"

"Well, I'm crazy about you . . . I heard about you, Mr. Strip-Tease Dancer. I know you probably fuck every woman who wants it."

"It's not like that, Reesy."

"So you *are* homo."

"Well . . ." *That's it! That's the solution!* "Okay. I . . . I admit it. I'm gay." Slide felt so much relief saying that. For sure, she would lay off of him now.

"You're lying!"

Slide looked around, hoping nobody heard her yell. "No . . . I am. I . . . take it in the ass."

"Then that's even better."

Slide sighed. "Now, why in the world is *that*, Reesy."

"Because . . ." She got all smitten now, and close enough to whisper. "I have a strap-on."

Slide nearly choked, and he could feel his rectum tightening till it hurt.

He'd eventually told her he'd lied, and now it was near midday. He'd had a three-hour nap. The nightmare that haunted him was *insane*; how he'd stuck his dick in Reesy's ass, and how she'd somehow sucked him in until there was just his head sticking out between her butt cheeks. There was his shortness of breath, and he thought he might die, but then he saw her—and it wasn't a dream anymore. It was Reesy, in the flesh, standing over him.

"Get enough sleep?" she asked as she woke him.

Shit. She is real. Slide told himself.

Before he could reply, she said, "I found a room for us. I put a mattress in there while you were asleep. Plus—*look* . . . I got the mask you asked me for."

Jesus.

"Where in the *hell* did you find that?"

"I know, right," Reesy agreed with that sunny look on her. "It's a little gift someone bought me."

Slide wondered which L.T.K. member had already been through this with her, who had the same disgust for her, unable to perform such a beastly duty. He wondered these things while being at a loss for words, shocked at how she so excitedly addressed these stipulations that he threw in her face—things he assumed would discourage her.

"Okay, Reesy. You win. I'll gladly give you what you want," Slide had told her earlier. "But I'll only do this on one . . . er, two conditions."

"Yes, yes, yes. Whatever . . . you name it!"

And Slide came up with (what he was so sure were) a couple of doozies. With a determined look in his eye, Slide said, "First, I really respect your uncle, Reesy. And I'm afraid that . . . well . . . seeing your face—your pretty face—I'd never be able to, well, get it up . . . if you know what I mean."

"Oh," Reesy said, with that shadow of discouragement to suffocate her big dream.

Then to spill more salt on her fire. "And the other thing, Reesy. I couldn't live with the thought of him walking in on

us. I know you barely leave this place, but he'd kill me if he
were to . . . *stumble* on our . . . *fun.*"

"You're right," said Reesy. And for the most part, it
seemed that her flame had been put out. "Do you mind if I
try and think of something?"

Reesy's pout was so telling that Slide felt sorry for her. So
there was that compassionate response he gave her. "Sure,
Reesy. But don't go out of your way . . . it probably wasn't
meant to be."

And that was the discussion *before* the nap.

Now she was holding that black leather mask on her middle finger. "Look at the zipper. The way it works is—"

"No, I understand how a *zipper* works, Reesy. No need to
explain *that.* But what about the other thing we spoke on?
What room are you talking about, that your uncle *doesn't*
have access to? 'Cuz, I'm tellin' you—"

"Come on!" Reesy pulled Slide up from his comfortable
spot in the lounge.

"Won't he see us?"

"My uncle is down in the basement somewhere. Trust
me." Reesy said.

With no more excuses to prevent this madwoman, Slide
went along without argument. There was a third-floor sanctuary that was messy with used or broken furniture, donations
of toys and canned food that were never distributed to the
needy and signs of one sort or another. ABYSSINIAN CHURCH
FAIR TODAY . . . ABYSSINIAN FLEA MARKET TODAY . . .
ABYSSINIAN FUNDRAISER/BAKE SALE TODAY.

Bright daylight struck the room, since the stained glass
had been removed—replaced by wood or pane glass. There
were still cobwebs in places where Reesy hadn't swept, and
the mattress she mentioned was on the floor by the rear window. Slide had a resolve in mind that, since he had come this
far, he may as well go through with it. Maybe it wouldn't be
so bad after all—to fuck another admirer behind someone's
back. They didn't call him Slide for nothin'. It wasn't like
this would be the first time, or the last. Lord only knew how
many women had seen his act, or how many of them—

housewives, professional women and celebrities too—had offered up incredible money for "just one fuck." Indeed, how many of them had stood in this very position?

Reesy took it all off, except for the Lady Timberland boots and her tube socks. She was bent over, bracing herself, with her hands on a waist-high iron radiator; a fixture sturdy enough to withstand the pressure. In the meantime, Slide was punishing her, ignoring L.T.K.'s security, with his two-way idle on the floor near his trousers and his monster dick—his claim to fame—driving one hole or the other. And the way Slide instructed her was just as crazy as Reesy was, but it all served the purpose.

He worked himself in and out of her ass, while he had her beg him to tap the alternate hole. "Put it—in my—cunt—please—put it—in my—cunt—please . . ."

Gasps and breathless monkey noises came from her, but she still kept with his rhythm . . . as though the words and raspy cries took the place of her inhales and exhales.

When Slide eventually switched entrances, he worked it for a short time. "Fuck me—in the—ass—please—fuck me—in the—ass—please," she was instructed to beg. And Reesy would whimper with distress and dissatisfaction.

Back and forth, Slide plunged his log, despite his midday nightmare . . . despite how unsanitary it was or how god-awful it smelled. She wanted it rough, and so he delivered. As she had on that leather mask over her head, it was enough to balance this. Even then, he had his eyes squeezed shut, while smacking her cow ass and imagining this was someone else—that music video chick he saw shaking her thing on MTV just the other day . . . the soap opera chick who millions adored . . . that movie star . . . the model in the swimsuit issue . . . The mask and his wandering mind were all he needed to make this Amazon bitch a worthwhile fuck.

Somewhere between Reesy's cries—"Yes, yes—ohh, Slide! Give—me the umm, umm, umm . . . monster . . . umm, umm, umm . . . yes, yes, yes . . . aw Gawwwd!"—and the foul stench that rose from between their wet bodies, Slide's eyelids fluttered open.

"Slide! Come on, Slide!"

He saw daylight . . . the skyline over Harlem's east side. He turned his gaze down toward her back . . . her spine rippling under her sweaty skin; all of her bucking under his strokes. There was that final switch when Slide figured on using Reesy's ass as his receptacle. In less than ten seconds, he'd be wasted inside her back door.

Five seconds.

"Slide! Come on, Slide! It's Primo!!"

Three seconds.

"Slide! The parking lot. Goddammit! Where are you?!"

One second.

"Fuck!"

And now Reesy screamed like a fire engine. Slide came in spasms; a shock therapy patient. A much bigger ending for a simple sympathy fuck. Slide had never come like this before. Shivering and slumped over Reesy's back, his watery eyes unconsciously glanced toward the parking lot . . . someone was knocked to the ground. Even if he tried, he couldn't make out the faces, too limp at the moment to do much of anything.

"I'm goin' down there, Slide! I *knew* it was a mistake bringin' you on!" barked Primo.

CHAPTER TWENTY-SIX

CALL HIM CRAZY, but Sam wasn't in a trusting mood.

"So, that's it, lady. If you say you want in, if this is your cup of tea, and you're willing to do whatever it takes to prove yourself, then there's a test you must pass . . ."

He led his men and their new L.T.K. candidate to the firing range. It was carpeted in navy blue and the sofas and chairs were blood-red. One of the walls was actually a curtain, also blue and presently closed.

"So what's it gonna be?"

"Aren't you gonna give me a hint as to"—Evelyn let off a slight laugh as she asked this—"what I have to do?" She pulled her jacket lapels together as though sex might be involved. "I thought the three kilos was enough to show my dedication."

Sam wagged his head—short wags with his face scrunched up. "Nope. Not for nothin', but you're a cop, just like all of us are, or were. What's to say you're not here as a setup?"

"But, Sam," D.C. started to say.

Sam threw his hand up. A stop sign. "How'd you get in this? If I ask for your input, you'll know. Meantime, shut up." He turned back to Evelyn and softened from his tough-guy attitude. "Now, what's it gonna be? Right here, right now. You agree to the test, or not?"

Arms folded, Evelyn looked at the men. D.C., the pervert; Sanchez, the black Cuban; some barrel-chested man they called Vegas . . . and . . . *So this is Uncle Sam*, she thought, adding up all that she'd seen and heard during these past minutes. All the while, she envisioned what her comrades might be up to. Had they overcome the two men outside? Were they even inside the building yet? She at least sensed the security of having Push on the premises, *somewhere*, considering how quick and deadly he was . . . characteristics that she'd witnessed and now felt empowered by.

"Sure," Evelyn said flippantly. "Why not, I've got everything to gain, don't I?" She had no idea what was in store, but her intuition said to keep these guys busy until her backup came.

"Good choice," said Sam. " 'Cuz I'd hate to show you the last one who said no to me . . . in fact his body's still warm. Here . . ." Uncle Sam stepped over toward the curtain. "Let me show him to you." He pulled the drawstring a few times, revealing a huge glass wall. On the other side was the firing range. A man's body hung there, naked, with his bound wrists draped over a meat hook. A black hood was over his head. Evelyn gasped at the grim scene.

"Sorry to frighten you, but it's all to the good. See, this here fella is what's known as a rat-bastard . . . the type of guy that knows nothing about honor, or allegiance. The type of guy"—Sam had his arm around Evelyn's shoulders, and she wondered if he could feel her shaking . . . if he knew how disturbed she was at this instant. *Oh my . . . God . . . Charles*. She could've fainted at the sight of her friend in there. Even though he was more than twenty-five feet away, even though he had the hood on, this was unmistakably him. And now she noticed blood and bruises and—"who deserves no mercy, so . . ." Sam startled Evelyn by shaking her, the way a father might do to his son (*you can do it, young man*), pulling her into his side as they looked beyond the glass. "This couldn't be a better opportunity for you to . . . *hmm*, prove yourself."

"What could I do that you haven't already done?" asked Evelyn. "He's dead, isn't he?"

"Oh, no. No . . . you've come just in time to witness that part. Come with me."

The oatmeal and Cinnabun were acting up again.

The five left the gallery and soon stood at the counter—one of a half dozen that were accessorized with earmuffs, eyewear and intercom phones. Evelyn felt the presence of the three men behind her, and that they were probably just as stumped as she was. What was Sam about to do?

"So here we are. Me, the boss . . . the soldier . . . the delegate. My job"—Uncle Sam put his hand on Evelyn's shoulder again—"is to give the orders. Your job, my dear, is to follow orders." Sam turned toward the others as he said, "Now, how's that for democracy?" He had a broad, evil smile across his face, and his voice carried all throughout the firing range.

Sam pointed his free hand at the target. "Now I want you to finish the job for me, Miss Eve. I want you to earn your place with L.T.K., because—as of this moment—we are about to change history. The real L.T.K., you know what I'm saying? Licensed—to—kill." As though this were a ceremony he needed to prepare for, Sam took out a fresh cigar and went through the motions.

In the meantime it was quiet, except for the motor of a fan in the ceiling.

Evelyn noticed bloodstains on the floor where Charles hung motionless. A tear welled up in her eye and she ran her fingers through her hair as a diversion—a way to wipe that tear away.

Oh no . . . you've come just in time to witness that part.

It was the only thing to give her hope . . . the only thing to keep her from surrendering to the weakness pulling at her body.

"Okay. Let's do it," said Sam. "Where's your gun?"

"Oh . . . I . . ." Evelyn looked back at D.C. and Sanchez as though they were her sponsors. She needed an endorsement right away. "I explained that I leave my weapon at home. I'm not one for violence," she lied. "My caseload is—"

"Fuck your caseload, lady. You're holding me up." Sam reached down and pulled up the pant leg of his jumpsuit. He ripped away the Velcro strap of his ankle holster and smacked it and the .38 special it held on the counter. "I'm sure you parole people have to practice firing your weapons every now and then, so I don't need to explain things. There's your weapon, soldier. Prepare to fire." Uncle Sam stepped back to be with his disciples, leaving Evelyn to follow directions. Or not.

"What seems to be the problem, Miss Eve?"

"I'm sorry, I just—" Evelyn was thinking up a good excuse on one hand. On the other, she thought about turning this gun on the four of them. Or at least she could threaten to fire, that could be more effective. "I don't know if I can do this. I mean . . . what I meant to say was, I'm out of practice."

"Well, do the best you can, missy. And please . . . don't piss yourself in that pretty dress of yours."

There was some mumbling, D.C. with some sexist remark. Loud laughter followed. Sam said, "Then go get the Polaroid." More loud laughter. And this time it triggered something bitter inside of her. She turned her back to them and slipped the .38 from its nylon holster.

The moment felt so now-or-never, to hold this weight in her hands, and her eyes watered until, finally, tears rolled down. She whispered, "It's me, Charles . . . can you hear me? We're here, old friend. We're here to get you. Just hold on a little longer. I won't let—"

"Ahem!" The throat-clearing took place inches away, jolting her.

Evelyn turned to see Uncle Sam standing within arm's reach. He had a pistol in hand, the nose leveled with her face. For a time, Sam said nothing. He used the end of the gun to caress Evelyn's cheek, following the tearstains—one or the other—before eventually sticking it up under her chin. He seemed to be enjoying this, how death was in his total control.

"Lookie here, gents . . . our new friend is crying. Now why is that? And *why* are you stalling?" Sam turned to his audience again, studying something. "You say you met her at Kennedy?"

"Y-yes, Sam. She was walking through the terminal. We stopped her."

"Really . . . hmmm. Where were you going?"

Evelyn swallowed before she replied. "Home—"

"Coming from where?" Sam snapped so as not to give her time to think.

"Florida."

"What airport in Florida? What flight number? What was your seat? Answer!"

"Miami International . . . flight three-five-eight . . . I had a window seat."

"Seat number."

"I don't remember. Somewhere in the middle."

"Seat number!"

More demanding, with the gun pressed to her cheek, Evelyn said it louder. "I told you, *I don't remember*!"

"Don't raise your voice at me," said Sam. Eventually he stepped back to get a full-on view of this stranger. "Didn't mean to scare you, lady . . . ever since I got shot in the shoulder, I've been kinda crazy—you understand?" Sam took the weapon down so that he could manage with two hands, and he slammed it, sleeve back, readying a round. There was that *shhk-shhk* sound. "Which, if you think about it, makes me sharper . . . and more alert . . ." The nose of his weapon raised up once more and he pressed it against her forehead.

"Let's just say that I don't believe you . . . nothin' personal, but you could've set it up so that my men spotted you— *whatever*. From right now, you're a liar to me. Now . . . if you do as I instructed, then you'll prove me wrong, won't you?"

Evelyn did her best not to fall apart, however she was uncontrollably trembling inside.

"Turn around and prepare to fire," said Sam, the gun still threatening Evelyn. "I'll give you until three to pull the trigger . . . and you better not miss the target. I sure won't miss mine. One!"

Evelyn closed her eyes and asked the Lord for guidance.

There was no more stalling. She raised the .38 with both hands.

"Two!"

She felt the nose of the gun move from her head, but she was sure it was still pointed. Evelyn Watson, the bull's-eye.

I love you, Charles. Lord, forgive me . . .

She aimed the .38 at Charles.

She fired.

CHAPTER TWENTY-SEVEN

JESSE'S PART IN this was to use Big Red, Sam's pride and joy, as a tank, a distraction. He wouldn't bring the stone church down, but he would damn sure put a big-ass hole in it. He laid his weapon on the passenger seat and reached up to the visor where he knew Sam kept the spare set of keys.

It was something ironic . . . something to laugh at now, those recollections of Uncle Sam showing off his truck to Jesse and a few others. Sam, the braggart. "Lemme show you how quiet this monster is! You'd never know she was running!"

Jesse laughed out loud now that he'd started the super-cruiser himself—not just because of the memories, or because it was such a cinch to do this with the spare keys. No, Jesse was laughing away his fear, because what he was about to do was fucking *insane*, driving this 28,000-pound rig through the back wall of the church. He figured the advantage was on his end, with a six-cylinder diesel engine that served up the power of 300 horses and 860-some-odd foot-per-pound of torque. "This zinger can haul twelve 18-wheelers down the highway . . . Ford ain't never made a more powerful toy. This mother would scare the lizard shit outta Godzilla!" All of Uncle Sam's praises were coming back to Jesse now, and it made him all the more secure. However, he couldn't let go of that punch of doubt . . . that *what if*.

"Fuck it!" Jesse yelled. And he blasted the megawatt

sound system, threw the stick into first gear and pressed down on the accelerator. He started singing aloud with *whatever* was on the radio, and had no idea what was coming from his mouth—he merely sang the words he heard, or *thought* he heard . . . anything to direct his attention as the building came closer . . . and closer. "Do-do-dooo-do, da doo-doo-dooo

"I said shot-gun!

". . . Do the boogie-bay-bee

"Shoot the motha right now . . .

"Shoot it for me, baybee

"Doo-doo, d-doo doo doo . . ."

Jesse carried on as though he were part of Junior Walker's band—both the drums and the horn section.

Twenty-five feet till impact, and Jesse envisioned Tuesday on their wedding day—so elegant in her flowing white gown . . . an angel, floating . . . awaiting him.

Ten feet till impact, and Jesse remembered Tuesday in the orange jumpsuit, behind the glass during their visit . . . tears in her eyes.

Get me out of here, Jesse. Today, Jesse. Today!

Jesse gunned it . . .

Five feet till impact . . .

He closed his eyes to the thought of Stacy and Sharissa. Then he braced himself. *God help me.*

PRIMO HUFFED AS he endured the agony, the pain in his knee. The bandage was soaked again.

He had the missile launcher strapped over his back with one shell lodged in its chamber and was taking the steps like an athlete, skipping as many as three or four at a time, sliding down the railing here and there. He stumbled, cracked his knee and screamed like a bitch. No way Motrin was gonna stop *that* shock of pain. And it was only *after* he sucked it up and pressed on that he realized the danger.

What if the launcher went off right there in the stairwell? What if—?

There was just no time to think. L.T.K. was at risk right

now—men were attacking down at ground level. *Mims?* The thought of the man who shot him further motivated Primo, and he soldiered on.

One more flight to the main chapel.

Somewhere along the way, maybe during the fall, Primo dropped his two-way. But he thought past that, dragging his leg along, into the great domed chapel, pulling out his .45 automatic. There was a crash that sounded . . . a vibration that shook Primo like a bomb was dropped on the building.

Straight ahead, the wall, the balcony, glass and every manner of debris imploded. A red cannon, it seemed, was at the center of it all, barreling until it showed itself fully.

Primo took cover, more or less falling behind a pile of broken pews—by no means a sufficient barrier. When he looked again there was Big Red, Uncle Sam's truck, covered in the destruction it caused, slowing to a stop there at the point where a wedding march might begin; where a bride and her father might start that long walk down the aisle towards the groom. And that's just where Primo was holding fast—near where a groom might be waiting for the love of his life . . . for his bride-to-be.

As loud as the collision was, it set off a sonic whistle in Primo's ear. A ringing that, together with his own pain and torment, caused a state of madness. Madness!

Primo couldn't believe his eyes.

Mims was in the driver's seat of the cruiser. The windshield was broken away and rubble had fallen into the cabin, apparently holding him in place. The fog of the crash had cleared and there was a mist hanging in the atmosphere. But Primo was sure it was him.

And he was alive! That was him yelling . . . rejoicing?!

Nostrils flaring, Primo hopped up to a half-assed standing position and began firing his pistol. But so disillusioned was he that none of his shots made their mark. They ricocheted off of Big Red's hood; they created sparks along the front grill—shots were fired at him now from somewhere else in the church.

Primo took cover and returned fire. With the mist in the

air he couldn't see where the shots came from or who the shooter might be. Primo merely improvised, doing the best he could to ward off the attackers. Turning back to Mims stirred that rage again. The muthafucka was alive! He tossed his .45 down and whipped the missile launcher onto his shoulder. Seconds later he was aiming the tube . . .

"Aahhh!" Primo cried. Something struck him. A bullet. He wasn't sure where, but it brought him down to his injured knee. The trauma ultimately toppled him like a wounded soldier. He was able to pull himself together, lying broken on the floor, positioning the tube and bringing the projectile of the weapon to his reddened eye. It didn't matter that he was hurt and dying on his back; all he cared about was his target Mims, and one capable trigger finger.

Primo let out a howling laugh before he gurgled blood . . . before that moment of peace and that wicked smile . . . before he pulled the trigger.

The missile hissed when it discharged, taking on a life of its own as it traveled, creating a streak of white exhaust across the church aisle, until finally it made contact with Big Red.

GREG SCHWARTZ WAS the shooter who hit Primo, unsure of the results. He was careful as he approached, all too aware of the damage Jesse had caused with the truck. And thank God *he* seemed to live through it, by the outcry of joy.

A perfect diversion!

Was the shooter Uncle Sam? And was that a—

Oh shit!

Greg's reaction would have been to shoot the man where he lay laughing, except the weapon had been fired. There was no time to act.

HISSSSSS—

Greg sprinted in the opposite direction. Only God could help Jesse now. The explosion was blinding, even if it was behind him. Greg didn't have time to pray, not an official one anyway. All he knew was his body hit the dusty floor, and that he had perhaps lost his hearing. He too was in God's hands.

JESSE HAD SAID something about the basement; something about a firing range. And this was on Push's mind as he made his way through the church, a hallway, and then a wide staircase.

All the while, his ears were tuned in, sensitive to any sounds. His eyes were alert for any sudden movement, and his two Rugers were loaded, swinging around sharp corners inches before he did, directing this way and that as if they were his seeing-eye dogs, waging a greater threat than God— that is, the God who ruled in *this* corrupted church.

Further into the basement were a pair of double doors; beyond them a gymnasium where events and banquets might have taken place. Push was absorbed in his surroundings; his body was relaxed, blending in with the room temperature. He could've had his eyes closed and still he'd know if danger lurked in this dreary atmosphere.

A humming sounded constantly overhead. The wood flooring gave some, as it would where there had been flooding and water damage.

A gunshot went off, and there was laughter. Then a large crash upstairs, which caused a rumbling—the beginnings of a quake. Push walked toward the gunshot, faced with the decision of whether or not to charge through the door in front of him. He wondered how a firing range might look and what obstacles, if any, there might be. He wondered what danger Evelyn was in, and Judge Pullman, if he was indeed still alive.

EVELYN'S SHOT WAS intentionally directed toward the wooden beam around which the rope was affixed—the rope which secured the large meat hook holding the Judge in mid-air.

Not that she was an expert markswoman to be able to hit the rope, but she'd at least make an attempt. And even if she didn't hit her target, the sound of the gunshot was all she needed. She was sure that the men behind her, Uncle Sam included, would watch to see the bullet's impact. That would be a natural occurrence, their hunger to witness death—the blood and gore of it all. Evelyn counted on human nature to help her, and she got more than she bargained for. The shot caused Pullman's body to jerk. Not only that, he urinated as well. It had to be a sensational sight to make her sparse audience laugh like they did. But it was just a part of the diversion Evelyn wanted. The other part was the loud crash and how the building seemed to shake.

"What the—" Uncle Sam turned toward his goons as if they had answers.

Meanwhile, Evelyn went to work with her back still to the others; she brought the .38 special down, sliding the barrel up under her opposite arm, and with mere estimation she began blasting away.

The next shot was the one to result in a deep cry. The next two or three she was uncertain of, but she brought enough action to put herself in a better position.

When Evelyn turned to fire some more, D.C., Sanchez and Vegas had scattered. She was sure they were still alive, hiding behind the table, the couch or in the doorway that led to the gallery.

Evelyn looked down and saw Uncle Sam was wounded, but not dead. He lay on the floor holding his side, writhing. It seemed as if he had lost all of his power, and it almost made Evelyn smile.

Almost.

She went to grab his weapon, but more gunfire erupted, the bullet clipping the counter and partition where Evelyn stood. She immediately turned and fired in the direction she thought the gunshots came from. It was Sanchez who she chased with her assault. As he ran to her right, she opened fire, shattering the glass window of the gallery, creating a floor full of glistening shards.

More gunshots behind her.

Evelyn's weapon was empty.

"Get down!" someone yelled.

When she did, she noticed an adjacent door was wide open. A gun was pointing through the doorway, firing in one direction, then another. It was all happening so fast that Evelyn didn't realize it was Push behind the gun, doing battle with Vegas and DC.

"Get the Judge!" Push shouted between exchanges. And he went back to his attack. Evelyn had one of Sam's pistols in hand now and she scrambled to back away from his limp body until she felt a soft wall behind her. But then that soft wall moved.

"It's *me*," were the tender words in her ear. And she was startled. "Don't worry, I'll protect you."

Evelyn looked and saw it was D.C. whose lap she was in. She closed her eyes thinking . . . wondering what the hell he was talking about.

D.C. put his arms around Evelyn—it was an affectionate embrace, with his cheek to hers.

"I'm sorry about that. He's lost his mind," said D.C., looking over Evelyn's shoulder at Uncle Sam.

Evelyn opened her eyes one at a time, and it occurred to her that she somehow had a new friend in D.C.—the pervert.

She turned with her nose coincidentally nestled in his neck and earlobe, a position in which lovebirds might find themselves.

"D.C.?"

"Yeah," he replied, probably more frightened than she.

"Pop quiz . . . if you're gonna protect me from *him*, then who will protect *me* from *you*?" Evelyn was amused by the strange expression on his face, but she didn't give him a chance to respond. Uncle Sam's gun was under her arm again this time, pointed conveniently at the pervert's groin.

When she pulled the trigger, the blast was swallowed inside of D.C.'s massive body and he lurched away from her, carrying on like an excited ape onto the floor.

"You shot me! My balls!!" he cried. "My balls! My balls!! Aaahhhh!!!"

Evelyn was already going for Charles. She climbed over

the counter, ignoring the gun battle behind her, and she aimed at the rope. She fired once, then twice, but only now did she realize that it had been some time since her last visit to the range.

Snatching the hood off of her friend's head, Evelyn asked, "Are you okay, Charles?"

Charles was weary as he said, "My arms feel . . . like they're ripping from their sockets . . . and I've just pissed myself, but . . . I'm breathing."

Evelyn ignored all of that, stepping into the puddle, hugging the naked body—

"Hold on, Charles."

—and she struggled to lift him up enough to get his tied wrists off the meat hook. It took three tries, and his testicles were almost in her face, but she did it. When she got him down, the Judge flopped back over Evelyn's shoulder and she carried him as far as she could out of harm's way until she could set him on the floor. Only now did she wince at his facial wounds.

"Here," Evelyn said, and she took off her probation department jacket to cover Charles. Next, she lifted his wrists and put the nose of Sam's pistol against the knot that kept them bound.

"Turn your head if you can't handle this," said Evelyn, the sharpshooter. With all the other gunfire in the room, Evelyn's single shot seemed to get lost, but it worked, and she unraveled the rope and hugged Pullman.

PUSH RELOADED CLIPS into the wells of both weapons and considered the state of things. He could see Evelyn and the Judge in the distance, in a corner, and he had a good idea where his adversaries were—one to the left, and the other to his right. As usual, it was him alone against the world.

The exchanges of gunfire seemed to stop while he reloaded, and he wondered if the opposition was as prepared as he. Push considered the rules—first and foremost: Never underestimate your target. However, it was his third rule that would help him most right now.

Push aimed for one of three light fixtures in his view. He fired his weapon twice before it popped and immediately turned his weapon on the second, then the third. He also shot the exit sign. Now, although he didn't know much about his surroundings, at least there was the darkness to help him execute his "element of surprise."

Even with the lights blown out, somehow there was a dim glow. Push was already wearing black—his favorite color, for many reasons—so he was certain he'd be a difficult target. However, he did get an eyeful of his targets—the one to the left, with the sky-blue U.S. Customs shirt and the other with a dark jersey with bold red embroidery that read F.D.N.Y. Besides that, both men had light complexions.

He eased around the doorjamb and duck-walked towards the left, keeping an eye out for the sky-blue Customs shirt.

By the looks of things, these sectional couches were part of a lounge area—maybe where these cops sat to watch TV, or their buddies when they fired weapons.

Push had one of the empty clips on hand and tossed it toward the far end of the lounge area. It clattered about the floor. Until now, things had been quiet.

"Sanchez?" The shout came from the other side, and Push could see FDNY on his mental radar.

"Yo!"

"You okay?"

"Yup—you?"

"We got company, can you see 'em?"

Push wished he were on the other side, near the talkative one. He'd have shot him down already as an easy target. For now he zeroed in on the one with the short answers. *Sanchez.*

"Might be near you."

"Nah. I heard somethin' your way."

Push tossed another empty clip. It made a louder noise.

"See that?" said the FDNY guy, and he began firing random shots. The Customs guy fired in the same direction, and Push was sure, now more than before, that he was sandwiched between two cops who were afraid for their lives and shooting at ghosts with their eyes closed. Push raised his torso up, enough to see the flash fire of both weapons.

The one closest to him was his first target, and he fired both his Rugers until he heard cries from his assault, until he heard the body hit the floor.

"Sanchez? You get 'im?"

"Yup. Think so." But it was Push who answered, doing his best to imitate the voice he'd heard. "He hit me . . . the leg."

"Hold tight, partner. I'm comin'."

Push crawled to the foot of the couch and waited, guns pointed up and across, unsure of where this other one would show his face. As quiet as the guy was, Push realized his battle wasn't over.

Never underestimate . . .

The FDNY guy had to be the biggest fool, using a cigarette lighter to see his way. All he actually did was create a moving target for Push. The letters were clearer now, practically adding reflection to the lighter's glow. A few more approaching steps gave Push that additional assurance and he squeezed his trigger repeatedly until the FDNY letters were tossed backward, out of sight. *Thump.*

"HOW IS HE?" Push asked Evelyn. Once he was sure he'd scooped up the guns from his victims—and made certain the dudes were dead—he'd headed straight for her and the Judge.

"He's all right, Push. He's all right." Her voice broke into small grateful sobs.

The three of them managed to leave the basement, for the most part, healthy and free of vital wounds.

ALL OF THE gunfire made things easy for Greg, and he did his best to get there (wherever *there* was) in time to assist. But the noise ceased when he reached the church gymnasium. There were voices that he was sure included Push and Evelyn, except it was too dark to see.

He was about to speak up when he heard another voice.

"Now who's surprising who?! I oughtta break your fuckin' neck, you two-bit punk!"

There was some kind of struggle, and then a gunshot, its flash directed downward. A hell-raising cry followed. Someone was hopping around. Even in the absence of light, Greg could see Push swinging around with his pistols aimed at the ready.

Greg's reflexes called for self-defense, but he kept his weapon concealed. "Push—don't shoot. It's me, Greg."

And he took two steps, sweeping his right foot around, bringing the hopping man down with a final thud. "You'd better get those two outta here. No telling who else is roaming around down here."

"What about him?" asked Evelyn.

Greg already had a pair of handcuffs out, and he bent down to secure the wrists. "This is our man, isn't it?"

"And then some," said a weary Judge Pullman.

"Well then . . . maybe they'll make Push a hero for bringing him down," he said, attaching the first cuff.

"Nah, that's okay. You can keep all that nonsense. I'll settle for his ass in general population, somewhere that the big, greasy convicts can have him for dessert." Push grinned with contempt.

Uncle Sam yelled when Greg snatched his wounded arm to apply the second cuff.

"Oops," Greg said with a smile. "Hope I didn't hurt you."

PUSH AND EVELYN assisted the Judge, finding an old choir robe to cover him, then escorting him upstairs where firemen, EMS technicians and uniformed police tried to make sense of the fires and destruction. Pullman was taken to an ambulance and treated while Evelyn did the explaining to the officers on the scene.

"I'm sorry," Push heard one officer ask Evelyn, "did you say the guy's name was Slide? And he's a dancer?" Meanwhile, he watched as Jesse Wallace's corpse was bagged.

"And a cop," said Evelyn.

The officers whispered something amongst themselves,

and they stepped over to another area in the church where
two more policemen were in a discussion with a third man.
Push smirked when the third man was told to put his hands
on the nearest wall. Then he was frisked, cuffed and his
rights were read to him.

Maybe there was justice after all.

CHAPTER TWENTY-EIGHT

PUSH ARRIVED HOME, care of a police escort, and his emotions flared up once more.

"What do you mean, she's not here?" he asked Crystal.

Crystal shrugged her shoulders as if to say, "I'm not Yvette's babysitter."

There was no way for Crystal to understand all that he had been through during the past ten or so hours—the waiting at the airport, the ride in the trunk of Evelyn's car, all the shit at the church—and there was no patience in his grasp to help him explain things. Nothing to calm his inner rage.

"Aren't you gonna tell me what happened?" Crystal asked, speaking both for herself and Janet Burrow, who had been instructed to (in official terms) stay with Crystal and Yvette.

"As soon as I find Yvette . . ." Push suddenly remembered. "Damn. Today's Monday, isn't it?"

"Last I checked," said Crystal.

Push was off toward the front office. He picked through the desk full of papers, mumbling to himself. "There it is," he told himself. Then he picked up the phone and dialed.

"You have reached Mister Rooney's office. We are closed for three weeks of much-needed vacation time . . . Should you have immediate concerns—"

Push pressed down on the auxiliary phone line for a new dial tone. He dialed the second number he found.

"Mr. Augusta's office, may I help you?"

"Great. Is Mr. Augusta in?"

"He's in the middle of a closing right now. May I ask who's calling?"

"This is Reginald Jackson calling. I just . . . well, I wondered if my—" Push had to shift gears; inject some business savvy in his tone. "Is Yvette Gardner with him?"

There was silence.

"She just left."

As the secretary spoke, Push recalled the phone calls he happened to intercept just a day or so earlier.

". . . tell Ms. Gardner that the mortgage papers are ready to be signed and that the closing is set for Monday . . ."

And the second call from Mr. Rooney:

". . . I was gonna be there at the closing with her, but my mother became sick . . . I'll be away for a week or two . . ."

But these thoughts only further infuriated Push, since he came to realize what Yvette was getting herself into, since he thought he'd made himself clear: "Fuck that mortgage . . . it ain't happening . . . I'll talk to Murphy . . . I'll straighten this out."

And now, after all the talking, she was still going through with it.

The secretary really blew his mind with her next statement. "In fact, Mr. Rooney was with her."

Push slammed the phone down and cursed. Then he marched through the home office, past Crystal and Janet Burrows, into his bedroom. Into the closet where he kept additional ammunition clips in a shoe box. He didn't realize his sister was behind him.

"Push, please slow down and tell me what in God's name you're doing." Crystal's eyes brushed over the threatening items and settled on her brother.

"I'm gonna find Yvette."

"With that? Have you lost your mind?"

"Crystal, please let me do what I gotta do. Please!!"

"You need to slow down, Push. Give yourself some time to think."

"I'm past thinking! This is my life here! My world! And I gotta do what I gotta do to protect it! Are you hearing me? Do you comprehend?!"

Crystal was mortified. Her brother never raised his voice at her like this. Never.

Moments later, Push was taking giant steps down 128th Street, headed for the 6 train with the address to Rooney's office tight in his fist.

GREG SCHWARTZ WAS in the passenger seat of a squad car, with Officer Diaz at the steering wheel. There was another squad car out in front, leading the way down to 1 Police Plaza.

Greg yawned and stretched.

"Long night, hunh," asked Diaz.

"Long ain't the word. If I told you all the trouble we went through to catch this creep. Man—nothin' worse than a bad cop."

"You motherfuckers! I'm dying back here! Whatever, ughh, happened to procedure?"

"Well, we don't find your wounds to be life-threatening, creep."

"I'm bleeding to death!" cried Uncle Sam.

"Schwartz, check the glove compartment for a Band-Aid."

The two officers cackled while they waited at the red light.

"Yeah," said Schwartz. "Maybe he can stretch it around his foot."

More laughing.

Greg turned to look at his prisoner through the metal mesh divider. They locked eyes like worst enemies. Only Greg had a message in his eyes that told Sam to look to his left.

The two-car escort was noisy, broadcasting their presence with dual sirens and emergency lights. They were coming off of the FDR Drive, snaking around the off ramp, destined for a number of traffic lights, before the down ramp where most perps were taken.

When Uncle Sam looked over, there was no way he could miss what was waiting. Fate.

Greg turned his head forward again, only briefly acknowledging the view outside of the vehicle. He braced himself and closed his eyes.

THE PHONE CALL came in just twenty minutes earlier. It was the direct line to Bobby Chin, reputed leader of the Triads—the New York branch. He smiled when he got the message and didn't need to respond. He merely turned off the cell phone.

"Ki," Bobby said, and he put down his chopsticks to wipe his mouth. There was a moment of digestion before he spoke again. "Take two men. Use the cycles. Strap up. Our man will be coming off of the FDR in ten minutes," Bobby spoke in their native Cantonese language, but Ki understood perfectly. They'd been waiting for this.

Ki had a wide-ass smile across his face.

"I want to see his obituary on the six o'clock news."

"You got it, boss."

Ki was one of Bobby Chin's missionaries. For the sake of his brother, he would do most anything. However, this was a walk in the park, a piece of cake. There were three Triad soldiers altogether, all of them on Kawasaki motorcycles, with tinted helmets and machine pistols, better known as "baby Uzis."

WHEN THE POLICE escort descended the off ramp of the FDR, a driver happened to be stalled at the foot of the exit.

It wasn't just a convenient obstacle, but a setup. The car eventually got going, in time enough to leave the police escort waiting at the light. Ki and his brothers pulled their motorcycles up to the sides of the escort. The short cement walls separated the service roads from the single-lane off-ramp, but the gunmen could get close enough to get the job done. Still harnessed on their seats, with the motors in neutral, all three Triads fired into the back of the second car door and windows, causing their target an undue violent fit.

They also took out the tires on both police vehicles before their speedy escape.

While Uncle Sam was reduced to bloody chopped meat within the space of seconds, the four police officers were un-harmed.

"**NOW THAT YOU'VE** come this far, I'm sorry that I ever men-tioned the shady route," said Rooney. "And you had everything to lose—"

Yvette's face scrunched some as she responded, "Don't sweat it. Remember, I was the one to push you. Not the other way around."

"I just . . . I apologize. You could've gotten into some se-rious—"

"Please don't bring that up. Don't remind me of what could've been or what might've been. The point is that we got the deal done, and that other stuff is behind us."

Yvette parked in front of 440 and shut off the engine. "Well . . . here we are," said Yvette. "My boyfriend is away last I checked, so don't be so nervous."

Rooney said, "It's not so much that, Ms. Gardner. I was just thinking about my mother. It's one of those things, you know? I never thought about this—how it might feel to go on with business as usual. Knowing how that part of me is gone forever."

"Oh—Rooney . . . don't . . ." Yvette felt compassion for the man and wanted to comfort him. But she had to stop her-self; such things were for family alone. For her man and for her forthcoming child. Yvette opened the compartment that separated the driver's seat from the passenger's side. Tis-sues. "Here, Rooney. I hate to see a grown man cry. Snap out of it, mister. Life happens in cycles, okay?" Rooney busily wiped his eyes and snorted into the tissue—a full blast. "I'm thankful that you decided on a later flight—how thoughtful is that? With your mother just passing and all? Wow . . . if nothing else, she sure bred you with some heavy sense of duty . . ." Yvette was doing her best to uplift the man's spir-its. Trying to make the best of a grim situation.

"Th-thank you." Rooney sniffled. "I wanted to see your deal through to the end."

"Well, you did. And I really want to thank you again. Now, are you gonna be able to finish with this without falling apart on me?"

"I'll be okay. A quick cigarette and I'll be good as new." He took a pack of Kools from the inside pocket of his blazer.

"I thought you said you've become a changed man?"

Rooney frowned and handed the pack to Yvette. "Here, I'm losing my mind. Maybe you can find somewhere for these."

"Can I?" Yvette took the cigarettes, her purse and attaché case. "Come on, sir. We've got business to finish."

PUSH NEVER GOT on the train. Instead, he took a stroll down Fifth Avenue and found a vacant bench at Mount Morris Park. It would be summer soon, and the surroundings already evidenced the welcomed weather.

The park didn't exactly have exotic birds flying about, only pigeons nosing around for crumbs; no couples strolling about, holding each other and sharing their hopes and dreams, but bag ladies searching trash cans for bottles to collect the five-cent deposit. Instead of children making their own fun on the swings, the slide or the jungle gym, there were stray dogs and homeless folks and drug addicts who made this place their home.

Push thought about the life he now lived compared to the way it once was. He'd come a long way from nothing to allow himself to fly off the handle and maybe destroy whatever it was he did have. He had the love of his sister, Crystal, the respect of his nephew, Reggie; and then there was Yvette, who, regardless of her errors, proclaimed her unconditional love for him. All of this grew from a life that was stripped of its value, a life that was abandoned and experienced unfathomable torture, a life that was left for dead.

Push came all the way from rock bottom, where he could hardly breathe, where the light at the end of the tunnel was out of sight, and he climbed the hard way to a level where he could claim a stake in the life, however small. If someone had told him ten years ago—even five years ago—that he'd become a real-estate developer who could transform condemned properties into livable dwellings for families and notable professionals, Push might think that they were out of their mind. But here he was today, a winner. A man who came from the dirt and beat the odds.

He sat in a daze, oblivious now to all that surrounded him. In a sense, he had made a statement by forgoing the streak of rage; by his decision to take a detour from the 6 train, he had (in his own way) shouted at the top of his lungs: Stop the world! I wanna get off!!

He realized that there was so much to lose. The big picture he was painting would wash away unless he made educated or at least streetwise decisions. He also had to admit to himself that he was more than lucky to have survived these latest trials and tribulations. There was also an inner rejoicing concerning his parents and their killers. Despite the shadow of emptiness that remained, he felt a certain closure where there was once bitter pain.

Not that all of his pain was relieved.

Perhaps he'd never be rid of it all, or he was somewhat jaded and beyond the point of correction. Even he couldn't make sense of the burning desire subdued at the core of his being—that hunger of a lion, ready to prey upon any person who dared to interfere with his world. Push needed reminders that life was bigger than him alone. He needed to focus and relax and get back to the foundations that made him the man he'd become.

The challenge, however, was for him to come to this realization on his own, since there was no one to give him that wisdom. And he'd have to do so before it was too late, before he destroyed himself as so many potential leaders had.

He couldn't do battle with half the world, even if half the world was corrupt and unfeeling and selfish. He had to be smart to maintain his stake and commitment, his contribution to the world.

Push considered all of these things, and yet he just

remembered: *Oh damn . . . I'm gonna be a father.* The thought of his son or daughter going through life without a daddy because of his own impulsive actions made his stomach ache. He turned his head down and rested there with his arms stuck to his knees. This was that much-needed thinking time; one of those zones to get lost in, reviewing perhaps zillions of thoughts and images within the space of seconds.

"'Scuse me, mista. You okay?"

It took time for Push to reply. "Just thinkin'," he told the woman in her soiled clothing and haphazard hairdo. "What . . . you lost or something'?"

"Nope. Just wanna make me five bucks to feeds my chirdrin."

"Your chirdrin, hunh? Why don't you get a job?" Push asked with a sense of tough love in mind.

"I *do* got a job . . . lemme take you to da van 'cross the street 'n show ya."

Push looked across the street at the rusted, wheel-less van. There was plywood in place of its windows. "Girl, you betta get somewhere."

She poured on the sensuality, however overused it seemed. "I know you got money. I could tell."

Push felt the weight of the Rugers, holstered under his Windbreaker. "And if I do, *what*? You gonna rob me?"

She said, "No, stupid. I just wanna suck your dick. Five bucks and I'll make you *love* me."

Push couldn't believe how direct she was, and he looked around to see if this was some sort of practical joke. "Woman, you straight foul. For real. Now take this"—he pulled out whatever money was in his pocket. Two $20 bills, one five and a few singles. Almost $50. "—and clean yourself up. They always got jobs down on 125th. Go get yourself one."

The woman stared at the money in her hand and didn't move for some time.

Meanwhile, Push eased off of the bench and made his way back home. Seeing the woman in the park was another reminder that maybe he didn't have it so bad after all. There would always be worst-case scenarios that men and women would survive.

Why am I trippin'?

UNANNOUNCED, PUSH STEPPED into his home and office a new man.

Yvette's car was outside, so he was ready to hear her out, whatever she had to say. He always knew her to be a woman with good sense, so this shouldn't be any different.

The Burrows woman was at the dining room table eating, while Crystal was on the cordless phone. When she saw Push, there was a surprised look and he couldn't tell if it was relief or shock.

The bedroom door was cracked some, and Push immediately went in that direction. Just before the bedroom, in the hallway, was the bathroom. And now that door opened.

A stranger stepped out—a white man, who was fixing his zipper—and nearly bumped into Push.

"Oh—excuse me," the man said.

Push swung his head toward the bedroom, then back at the stranger and his zipper. *Rooney?*

And now Yvette called out to Crystal, sticking her head out of the door. "Baby!"

Push's eyes bugged out at the sight. Yvette had on a dress that wasn't fully covering her. She pushed the door aside and went to dive into his arms.

But Push held her off. "What is this?" he asked in utter disbelief.

Yvette suddenly looked down to see her dress had fallen off of her shoulders. Her brassiere was embroidered with floral prints, and the shadow of her nipples made impressions therein.

Crystal approached now, and she covered her mouth.

Yvette's face twisted with embarrassment and she quickly covered her breasts, excused herself and shut herself back in the bedroom.

"Push, may I speak with you?" asked Crystal.

But he was still dumbfounded by what he'd seen. *Yvette and Rooney?*

"You! Back in the bathroom," Crystal ordered and pointed.

The stranger quickly retreated back behind the closed door. The lock was turned as well.

"Cry-stal," Push said with a low-high inquiry in his voice.

Crystal took her brother by the arm, practically dragging him back into the living room. There was a lot of explaining to do.

CHAPTER TWENTY-NINE

PUSH ONLY BEGAN to laugh once he saw everyone else laughing until their eyes watered.

"Can you believe it! Me and your woman—haha . . . that is hilarious." Rooney was getting out of control, with his eyes doing more than just watering.

"What's up with this?" asked Push.

Yvette had to stop laughing to explain, "That's why he came with me today, honey. His mom *was* sick, but she died suddenly—"

Rooney said, "Yeah. So I figured, what the hell . . . the old lady's already gone, so what's the rush—hahahahahaaaboohoohoo-ooo . . ."

Push turned to his sister and Yvette, his expression saying, "Damn, dude is really fucked up."

The four of them were sitting at the dining room table while Yvette and Rooney explained things. Crystal had already cleared up the slight misunderstanding, how it appeared that this mortgage broker had just finished doing the nasty with his pregnant girlfriend.

"And think about it, Push. What kind of sister would *I* be to let something like that go down behind my brother's back while I am in the next room?"

Push never considered that. "I guess it went to my head."

"But you were right to think that way. Shoot, I'd have done the same—maybe worse," said Crystal.

Rooney was pulling himself together and Janet Burrows was heavy into her meal, watching and listening to this like the insider at a juicy movie screening.

"So the deal's really done? As in, we're gonna renovate the block?"

"You don't know the half, Push. After Fred Allen called . . . after I explained to him my situation with old slumlord Murphy, he called Murphy himself—"

"Fred Allen did?"

"Exactly. I obviously don't know what they talked about, but when they finished talking, that son of a gun called me and apologized a thousand times. He went back to the original deal: one hundred thousand per home—he even said he'd give us options, ahem, *in writing*, on the rest of 128th Street. Baby, we did it!"

Push wanted to feed into the excitement, but there were all sorts of red flags going up in his mind—*everything isn't always what it seems,* he thought. So he had questions.

"Did you ever wonder why Fred Allen put so much effort into making things happen?"

"It occurred to me to ask that, Push, but I felt the sincerity. Yes, I know he's a notorious politician—and, yes, I took into consideration what you told me, how those guys can be no good. So it was simple . . . I just plain came out and asked him if he was trying to screw us over."

"You said that?"

"Did I? Humph . . . if I could've taped that conversation."

"I can vouch for your woman, Mr. Push—"

Push held back his smile, how folks didn't know how to address him: *Mister Push . . . Push Jackson . . . Just call me Push,* he'd tell those people who seemed confused.

"That Allen guy has the bucks. And he's investing in Harlem, *hard.* Half of my clients are begging for his attention . . . his interest money. Plus, the money has a twenty-year payout. How can *anybody* beat that?"

"But what's the catch?"

"Sir . . . honestly, I can't say. For some reason, this Big Willie has an interest in you and your real estate project. The vibe I got was that he *needed* to help you. The bottom line is that paperwork in front of you. The man came down to Mr. Augustas' office in *person* . . . his John Hancock on the dotted line, guaranteeing any money you need."

"Well, if a mortgage company is in business to make money—"

"I know what you're thinking. How can they afford no-interest money?"

"Yes, there's that. But if the mortgage company is putting up money, then where's Mr. Big Willie's dough?"

"Okay. This is what's going down. Maybe we didn't explain things clearly. Murphy wants a hundred grand for his properties—"

"One hundred each," Push clarified.

"I know, I know."

"Let him tell you, baby," Yvette said.

Push sighed.

"The Harlem Empowerment Fund, thanks to your good friend Fred Allen, is laying out the hundred on all seventeen properties you went into contract on. That's one-point-seven mill right there. He brought that check with him this morning. On top of that, any deposits you paid are now back in your Melrah bank account. So you can breathe again. On top of *that*, the HEF covers the interest *and* guarantees the mortgage money."

Yvette said, "The congressman has some kind of tax rebates he gets for assisting with so many housing developments. I'm telling you, baby, they really mean it when they say they're putting Harlem back on the map."

Push was silent. He couldn't think of any more questions. Not now anyway.

"So now . . . there's only one catch to all of this good news," said Rooney.

"I *knew it*. There had to be something."

Even Janet Burrows couldn't wait to hear this.

"It has to do with Yvette's dress . . ."

"Uh-hunh . . ."

"Fred Allen and his wife have requested that you join

them for dinner later this evening. Their home is over on Striver's Row."

Push slammed his palm on the table. "See! I knew— *huhn? Dinner?*"

"Yes, sweetie. They're celebrating a new addition to their family, and they'd like us to celebrate our success as well. That's why I was changing."

"Can I talk to you? Alone?" asked Push. Yvette excused herself and followed Push so they could be alone in the bedroom.

"What's wrong?"

"What do you mean what's wrong? Everything that was wrong *isn't* anymore. And that's my problem. I want some time to digest all of this . . . good news. I don't need some bigwig in his fancy crib to help me celebrate. If there's any celebratin' to do, then you and I know good 'n well how to do it."

"Oooh . . ." Yvette cooed and pressed herself against Push. "I *so* like that idea. When do we start?"

Now that Push had her alone, it seemed okay to ask. "We really did it? We're in business?"

"Not only in business, boo. Our deal today just made you one of the newest real estate developers in Harlem."

"Me? I . . . it just—" Push was speechless, and it brought tears to Yvette's eyes. Happy tears. She bounced up on her toes and smoothly attached her mouth to his. It was a long, welcome kiss.

"I love it when my thug nigga is speechless."

Push made a face, not accustomed to the title she painted him with. But there was that smitten way she had about her that made him mushy . . . made him feel that he was out of place, in some white man's soap opera.

"Yes . . . I said my thug nigga. Now, I'm going out there to chase everyone out of your house . . . I have a friend upstairs who's watching the Wallace girls—"

Push was startled. *Jesse Wallace*.

"And I want you to take these clothes off—"

"Baby?"

"—and get ready for Mommy to—huhn? What's wrong, boo?"

"It's about Jesse Wallace . . ."

Yvette seemed to sense the tragedy before he relayed the details. "Oh my God," said Yvette. And now fresh tears streamed. "Is he—?"

Push took Yvette back in his arms and caressed her however he could. "He's gone, baby. He's gone."

"Oh-h-h-hoo my God . . . those little girls . . . Oh-h-h-hoo, Push!" Yvette cried and snorted and sobbed into the crook of his neck.

He could only hold her tighter. There was nothing much he could say, already familiar with life's tragedies and how they seemed to repeat themselves without reason.

BANDAGED AND BRUISED, Judge Pullman was standing in the foyer of the Manhattan Federal Courthouse, watching as Evelyn Watson stepped off of the elevator. Two U.S. marshals stood by, ready to escort the two down to a waiting car.

"Hey! If it isn't Robert and Hal," chirped Evelyn, catching the two marshals off guard. If they didn't know already, they did now: Evelyn had done some thorough checks on these two between their rescue of the Judge from his Yonkers home and now, the day after the hostage crisis.

Judge Pullman smiled until it hurt, touching his hand to his sour cheek.

"You okay, Charles?"

"Some rest is all I need. I still feel like I'm on a rollercoaster ride, with all the tests at the hospital, the interviews with the FBI and just being here at the job so soon. It's dizzying."

"Aww . . ." Evelyn gave her old friend a peck on the cheek.

"Okay, all better now," Charles joked, but he winced immediately thereafter.

"We've gotta get you back home," said Evelyn. To the marshals she added, "Shall we?"

In a slow stride, the entourage left the courthouse, descended the steps in front and loaded up into the waiting vehicles—a Cadillac limousine with SUVs at the front and back.

"So did you straighten things out with your boss?"

"Stop kidding, Charles. Don't you think I know you called her?"

"Am I that easy to figure out?"

"Easier."

"So, what now, Evelyn? A vacation? You and my boy oughtta get away for a while."

"I was thinking that me *and your boy* might just do that. Right after his leg heals. Then he's gonna *nurse* me for a while."

Pullman laughed some. "We're not going straight to Yonkers, you know."

"Oh?"

"There's some unfinished business I want to go and handle myself."

The three-vehicle transport moved swiftly uptown, through daytime traffic, as if the president was being escorted to his destination. By the time they reached 128th Street in Harlem, they were one passenger heavier.

Outside of 441, Yvette and Crystal stood with their hands comforting the shoulders of Stacy and Sharissa. The little girls seemed frightened . . . that is, until their mother stepped out of the Cadillac.

"Mommy!" the girls cried out in a sweet duet. And Tuesday ran to scoop her daughters up in her arms. She couldn't get enough of them, wetting them with her kisses and tears.

It was a sweet and sour moment for everyone, even for Push, who watched the reunion from inside Melrah's office window. On the desk beside him was a duffel bag—the bag Jesse had when he came home to find his wife and daughters missing. There was more than $200,000 in there; money that Push figured had come from some L.T.K. heist. It crossed his mind to take this as his fee—money that he felt he had earned since he had been dragged into so much hell so quickly. But knowing what the Wallaces had been through weighed in as the heavier justice.

Push considered strolling out there and handing her the bag. Whomp. Right there on the sidewalk. Solution to all of her problems. Funeral. School. Even college money for the girls once they got older.

No, he told himself. He decided instead to put the money elsewhere.

The doorbell rang, and he went to answer.

"Well, well . . . long time, no see. May I?"

"Please. Be my guest, Judge . . . oh, hi. I didn't see you," Push said to Evelyn as she stepped up from behind. She sucked her teeth.

"You didn't"—Evelyn kissed Push's cheek—"see me. Sure."

"I'm really sorry I didn't stop them sooner, Judge Pullman."

"Sorry? Son, you saved my life. Maybe two times."

Push shrugged. "Evelyn deserves the credit, really. She really went through it—sacrificed a lot for you, sir."

"I know. And I'm grateful to her. There is the small matter of our agreement. Your . . . fee?"

"Sir, please. Don't even discuss that. Money is out of the question. What I did was from the bottom of the heart. I'd do it again if I could've saved Jesse's life."

Evelyn and Pullman glanced at each other.

"Push, you didn't know? Jesse was one of them. He was part of L.T.K. And sometimes . . . sometimes we get what we ask for in life."

"Damn. I knew something was funny about him."

"Well," said Pullman. "From what I hear, he had the easy way out."

"How's that?"

"Another one of them goons, the one who I'm told killed his wife, died a horrible death."

Push had the curiosity, and Evelyn the answers.

"He went by the name of Chico," she said. "And without going into too much detail, let's just say that they had a hard time identifying him. But more important, it seems that most of their organization is now either dead, arrested or on the run."

"And I have to say that much, if not all of it wouldn't have been possible without your help. We put you at risk, Push, and it's possible that—God forbid—you may have wound up dead."

"But those are the stakes in war," said Push. "You play for keeps."

"Be that as it may—"

"Judge, I'm telling you, I'm not asking. Put that checkbook away. There's no amount of money—"

"Okay, then, how about an investment?" Judge Pullman didn't stop with the check writing. Push made a face.

"Give it up, Judge. I respect your gesture, but—" Push put his hand over the checkbook.

Pullman looked to Evelyn for assistance. Evelyn said, "Push, you're a good man, indeed. But you don't need to be modest here. It's not just his money that's involved."

Push didn't understand. "Whaddaya mean?"

"Sorry. I can't go into it. But we, as in the Judge and I, want to invest in Melrah, and if you deny us that . . ." Evelyn had a frustrated look on her face. "I'll . . . I'll violate you. Right here and now, I'll lock you up for . . . whatever."

Push snickered at the idea, until he saw Evelyn with her handcuffs. "Okay. What kind of investment?"

Yvette happened to come in on the tail end of the conversation. "Did someone say investment?"

"Oh, hi, Yvette. We were just—or, *I* was just wondering if I could borrow your man," said Evelyn.

"Huhn??" Yvette saw how she was twirling those handcuffs and she immediately copped an attitude. A hand went to her hip. "Excuse me? Did you say 'borrow my man'?"

"Yes," Evelyn said, eventually realizing how freaky things might appear. And she put away the cuffs. "He's gonna need to come down to my office soon for his last visit."

"I'm sorry. Did you say *last* visit?"

"Exactly. *Your man* is officially off of probation."

Yvette's face lit up, knowing how important such freedom was to Push. She rushed to hug him, ignoring the others. "Baby? Are you happy now?"

"Oh . . . there's a couple of things I need to do before I can say that . . ." Push looked over at Judge Pullman. "I'm gonna need this man's help to set up a trust fund for the Wallace family. You *are* still a lawyer, right, Judge?"

"Of course, son. And my services will be on the house."

Yvette said, "Okay . . . and what else?"

"I'm gonna need to get right with my nephew . . ."

"And? What else?"

Push knew Yvette was hinting. "Hmmmm . . . well, there is this certain woman who I wanna marry. That is, if I can get a straight answer out of her."

"Oh, Push!"

Evelyn said, "Shall we give these two a little breathing room?"

Pullman didn't answer; too busy staring at the young lovers. Evelyn hit the Judge playfully.

"Ouch!"

"Well then, *come on*."

"Where? Back to the hospital?"

Evelyn finally got Pullman out of the house, haggling every step of the way.

Yvette asked, "It's customary to celebrate at a time like this, isn't it?"

"As long as we can start off with a shower," said Push. And he swept his woman off her feet, kissing her all the way to the steamy bathroom.

READ ON FOR AN EXCERPT FROM

LADY FIRST

BY RELENTLESS AARON

COMING SOON FROM
ST. MARTIN'S GRIFFIN

I KILLED SOME time by straightening up the guest room where I slept from time to time. These days I was feeling as though I had two homes, two mothers, and two ways of life. Back home it was our distorted color TV with only the antenna to provide us with four or five channels—Public Broadcasting was the clearest of them. Back home it was leftovers from Kentucky Fried Chicken; Troy was managing the store now, so he always brought home the chicken, corn, potatoes, and biscuits that weren't sold. There was a point when I was having chicken for breakfast, lunch, and dinner. And, of course, back home I had to cope with the stench that hung in the air from Mom's home-beauty salon. African braids were the trend now, so there was a lot of that going on. Sometimes the smell got so wicked, I wondered if the women who were her customers even wore any underwear. *Something* was letting those carnal fumes run free.

At the Stern home life was different. Desirable. A world away from stray dogs barking, babies crying (should one of Mom's clients decide to spend the night out), and synthetic horse hair everywhere I sat down. The Stern home had the 54-inch television with a 500-channel satellite. There was the pool, the Jacuzzi, the playroom, a warm fireplace here and there. The livin' was lovely. Tia liked to dine on seafood and salads that I would've never tasted if not for her. She took me on quite a few shopping sprees, and she even made the peo-

ple at the pier allow her to use David's yacht. They were unsure of whether or not to do it, not able to get Mr. Stern on
the phone. But her willpower and how she said, "Dare you
question my authority?" made them comply with her wishes.
Tia and I spent the whole weekend on the yacht—it was Labor Day weekend, too, when boating is in heavy demand during end-of-the-summer flings. I found out later that the yacht
crew and an employee of the pier were fired. I laughed so
hard about that. The life of a personal assistant, what a time I
was having. Tia would act crazy sometimes, directing me to
scrub her kitchen floor or to hand-wash her panties and
brassieres. But I put up with those humiliating tasks and the
perks that I got once in a while. My wardrobe was on blast
now. Tia even had a credit card issued to me, in her name and
mine, so that I could pay for the things she needed and which
I often shopped for. Many times I left my Volvo parked in her
four-car garage and took a hired limo out on the various er-
rands. Other times I drove her Jaguar. Even sported it back in
the 'hood, feelin' like the ultimate pimp.

That day was crazy, too. One moment I felt like the big
fish, like I had it all goin' on. The next I was a slug again. I
came back to tell Tia about the experience and she flipped.
At first she sucked me in, made me think I did good.

"So you got a kick out of that, huh? Did they all stare at
you?" She had her arms folded with a smile.

"I felt like a celebrity or something, Tia! It was bananas. I
even showed off to Jody, an old girlfriend."

"Bananas, huh? Jody . . . the old flame." Tia hummed and
said, "Sounds like you had a good ole' time."

"Yeah," I sighed, success oozing from my smiling lips.

She nodded, a grimace across her grill. "Well . . . now
that the fun is over there's work to be done. When you finish
with putting those groceries away come to the patio. I have a
job for you."

"Something wrong?" I asked.

"Oh . . . now what would make you think that, playboy?"
I shrugged. Tia was already leaving the room. "And don't
drag your feet."

The house had an indoor and outdoor patio. And since it was mid-October, I knew the Mrs. wanted me in the room that sat off of the dining area. It was a glass-enclosed patio, all types of greenery growing like an atrium greenhouse effect.

When I got there Tia was relaxed in a wicker lounge chair. She was wearing one of those T-shirts that exposed her trim midsection and a terrycloth towel-skirt. It was the summer wear that a young sexy, voluptuous woman would have on at a beach. I had to admit, even she looked young, sexy, and voluptuous.

"You wanted me?"

Tia said nothing for a moment. She looked over at me. "I wanted you . . ." There was another pause that seemed like forever. "I sure did. Go get the lotion," she said and laid back on the chair. "Some champagne, too," she called out just before I left the area. *Champagne. Lotion. A glass. Ice and a bucket.*

This was the kind of self-talk that I'd grown accustomed to as I went off on gofer tasks. It was a routine that enabled me to remember things without writing them down. I returned and automatically poured the Mrs. a glass of champagne.

"Did I say I'd be *drinking* champagne, Spencer? Are we assuming again?"

"I, uh . . ."

"I—uh—*nothing,*" she said. "You really think you call the shots around here, don't you?"

My eyes widened. I couldn't imagine why she said that. Or maybe this was another of her tangents. Her games.

"Doing things I haven't asked, like . . ." she reached out and took the glass from me. She tossed it to the ancient stone floor where it shattered in its own tiny puddle, ". . . like pouring champagne. Like parading my car all around your ghetto neighborhood. Like negotiating *my financial affairs!*" Her eyebrows furrowed. I swallowed and told myself, *Oh shit.*

"Boy . . ." Tia gritted her teeth and slightly wagged her

head, "what you really need is a good old-fashioned ass whuppin'."

"But I—"

"What'd I tell you about talking back to me? Give me that bottle," she commanded. I obeyed, passing her the champagne. I figured she was gonna throw it at me. "On your knees," she said.

"*Whoa.*"

"Whoa?"

"No," I protested. Then I explained, "It wasn't a reply . . . more like a-a-a response. A reflex. Not an answer. I . . ." I just did as I was told, ran out of excuses. I also closed my eyes knowing for sure she was about to bash the bottle over my head, or worse. For three grand a month I was every bit of the punk she wanted me to be.

The next thing I knew champagne was dribbling, streaming, pouring over my hair, my face, and my body. She emptied the bottle over my head. Tia was positioned sidesaddle on the lounge chair now, hunkering over me as if she were on a toilet seat. I was still kneeling before her, wet with champagne, with that sorry-ass look on my face.

"For your information, I'm going to accept the deal," said Tia, her eyes changing their meaning from fearsome to proud. "But the next time you do something like that behind my back . . ." Tia had her face inches from mine now. Then she closed in and kissed me open-mouthed on my lips. "I'm gonna break your neck. Got it?"